Putting My Foot in It

Also by René Crevel in English

Babylon
Difficult Death

René Crevel

Putting My Foot in It

translated by Thomas Buckley
with a foreword by Ezra Pound
and an introduction by Edouard Roditi

Dalkey Archive Press

First edition published by Éditions du Sagittaire, 1933; second edition published by Éditions Pauvert, 1974; © 1974, 1979 by Société Nouvelle des Éditions J.-J. Pauvert

Foreword © 1939 by Ezra Pound. First appeared as "René Crevel" in the *Criterion*, vol. 18, January 1939. Used by permission of New Directions Publishing Corporation, and Faber and Faber, Ltd., Agents for the Trustees of the Ezra Pound Literary Property Trust. World rights reserved.

Introduction © 1992 by the Estate of Edouard Roditi.

English translation © 1992 by Thomas Buckley

Library of Congress Cataloging-in-Publication Data
Crevel, René, 1900-1935.
  [Pieds dans le plat. English]
  Putting my foot in it / René Crevel ; translated by Thomas Buckley ; with a foreword by Ezra Pound and an introduction by Edouard Roditi.
  Translation of: Les pieds dans le plat.
PQ2605.R47P513   1992   843'.912—dc20   92-504
ISBN: 1-56478-002-3

First Edition, October 1992

Dalkey Archive Press
Fairchild Hall/ISU
Normal, IL 61761

Printed on permanent/durable acid-free paper and bound in the United States of America.

Contents

Foreword

Ezra Pound

I

A NATION WHICH DOES NOT feed its best writers is a mere barbarian dung heap. The social function of writers is to keep the nation's language living and capable of precise registration. Laws set down in ambiguous phrases are a paradise for shyster attourneys and a boil on the neck of the people. The fester of Dutch banking has been protected by such and the swindle made easy because economists do not understand each other's language. Let alone when translating from one tongue to another. Does, for example, beni commerciabili, render or improve on Dr. Schacht's "Verbrauchsgüter"?

I repeat, and I hope that every line of my criticism will be impregnated with the statement, that men of my time have lived through an epoch of unspeakable intellectual squalour and degradation. Irresponsibility has been canker in every craney of the time from 1890 till the Italian awakening. I agree with Mr. Eliot that criticism may be a bit better at the top, provided we take that top to be little more than the apex of a tapering obelisk. And I think the betterment probably started with our attempt to discuss one thing at a time and keep criticism of art and writing to their separate techniques. That is where Aristotle started his mental analysis, and, as I have elsewhere indicated, the talking bureaucracies do not start theirs.

Nevertheless, once the axes of TEXNE are established, the discussion of incomplete or imperfect, even though highly meritorious work may almost require a discussion of its where and amid what. Provided always that the critic be aware of the danger inherent in such discussion. (And provided the next reader of this note do not leap over the essential words "once the axes" etc.)

Corruptio optimi pessima. I have had very considerable sympathy with the decade of writers who are ten or fifteen years younger than Mr. Eliot and myself. I think they were up against a worse proposition than we were, and worse in France because the sense of intellectual responsibility had been higher and the complete belly-flop and wallow of that country had thereby the greater momentum. Men of Crevel's time had no local elders whom they could respect. Mr. Eliot and I do remember the existence of venerable and venerated precursors.

Calendar dates from one country to another are simply not simultaneous. Crevel died before the new hope had reached France. Rugged individualism had given his time little but foetor. Take the American pseudo-democracy; whatever one may think of Wilson, Harding, Coolidge and Hoover, one would under no circumstances suggest that their lives would make profitable reading for schoolboys. There is nothing whatsoever in them that could serve as model or aid to the forming of desirable character. The American legend had given respectable models which no amount of research destroys, Washington may not have been Parson Wynn's plaster, etc. Jefferson may have been garrulous, but both they and the Adamses and Jackson and Van Buren provide stimuli that one would be glad to have in one's family.

Joyce wrote in the slither of corrupt usuriocracy. Crevel revolted but knew nothing else. I think a sense of this is possibly necessary if one is to understand why certain constructive components are absent from Crevel's writing. His sheer talent *as writer* more than justifies the present effort on my part, even though I think each generation should provide its own critics and announcers. The date of my writing is, let me say it in my own defence, due to the failure of René's own time-group to broadcast him efficiently. I don't take it as my function to review current novels by the young. Some at least of Crevel's were worth it. Apart from Cocteau's productions I think they are the only productions by my French juniors that have given me a first class, as distinct from second or 4th or nth rate literary delight. Though I admit a "high second" for some of the later Romains (not my junior) and even some early pages of Simenon (gone to hell, etc.). And I admit (to the weakening of invective) that I may have missed some meritorious and laborious (emphasis on the laborious) cranks.

On the basis of Mr. Eliot's "plenum of books" formula, I think a man in middle life has the right to read matter of first degree interest *first* even if he does miss something uncertain. The challenge of a new book, or put it the impertinence of a new book, is that it asks attention, quite often, in place of work that would afford considerably more nutriment or soulagement to the qualified or specialist reader.

II

In the six by eight rez de chaussée of the Hours Press, I suppose about 1930, a gust of fresh air (quite immaterial air) youth, gaiety, and the cause of it suddenly peeling off a jersey, five inch cicatrice on the back of his Belvedere torse, and speaking perfectly good English, not frenchman's pigeon.

I have heard two people speak french, Cocteau and an unknown young lady reciting at a wholly ridiculous tea party. (Or rather a meeting without any tea, devoted mainly to argument.) Most of the rest of the denizens wheeze, sniffle, and exude a sort of snozzling whnoff whnoff apparently through a hydrophile sponge, accompanied by the catarrh (naturally of Paris) or they else speak a simpatico Toulouzhain or Normande or some other dialect full of humanity.

Anyhow Crevel was perfectly real, authenticly young, authenticly anything that he was, and apparently perfectly healthy despite the pneumothoratic red line that marked where the rib had been excerpted.

Secondly, a few years later: *Les Pieds dans le plat* also authentic and convincing.

Thirdly, that must have been 1935 (or even '36) news of a suicide . . . And one couldn't help wondering why? It preceded a congress. Not congressista, but having seen authors assembled, and considering the probably (understatment that . . .) the in short faked nature of that congress the utter hoakum wherein any man present would have been at least momentarily drowned, one couldn't help wondering whether rather than face that swamp of hoakum (*toc, fumperpey,* masquerading as conviction, the final disgust), as the only possible gesture of absolute dissociation of himself from any such hokus-pocus Crevel hadn't chosen EXIT.

This is guess work, I know few of his friends and none of 'em has shed any light.

Somewhere about 1920 Louis Aragon sat on my decrepit sofa in the Hôtel de l'Elysée and told me about suicide. He admired it, programatically. Someone HAD etc. and all that is a long time ago. The surrealists were (once?) (programatically) committed to approval of suicide.

Crevel was a writer, born, more born, I should have conjectured, a writer than born to programaticality. And how, and damn it, he is dead.

And I am not to be put off with "You go and discover things after everyone else has forgotten them." A great many people haven't even forgotten it.

As long as Crevel was alive, there was no need of my introducing him . . . any more than there is ever any need of anyone writing in

English introducing any french writer . . . because any french writer whom any of us can read with respect is always known to a great many more people than we are.

The high piled frumpery of the Brit-Am reviewing system has insured the non-circulation in "eighth editions" of every good English book until at least 15 years after it is written (and published).

A few of our good books get into Tauchnitz 15 or 20 years "after" (comprising perhaps 3% of that collection).

The "after everyone has forgotten" examination is necessary to sort out the real from the book-stall flush.

Once or less than once in a decade someone, in, or printed in, London, goes berserk and writes a little about french writers. It is nobody's job to send a steady report of Paris to London or at any rate no one does it.

As they say in Paris "the old beards have the power" . . . England specializes in infants of this species born with whiskers, frumps in the cradle, adolescent constructions of papier mâché. It is not only impossible to print translations from the french, but impossible to accept the facile excuse that there IS an english public which reads the originals and naturally don't want the traductions.

Simenon, yes. Romains' *Hommes de bonne volonté* (also heard of, I suppose) not quite satisfactory but serious digging. Sense of duty, there ought to be a XXth century Comédie Humaine, and J. Romains has shouldered it, with quite sober scenes here and there.

Some day the novelists will admit that the technique of the "tec" is just as serious a part of the total novelist's technique as any other. For 20 years we have looked for the criminal. A small scattering of serious men have looked for the real one. The dilettantes have been oriented by escape mechanism. Something was obviously, if to their minds muzzily, rotten, and they sought relief from the day, in the pursuit of a wooden soldier (that is, burglar, forger, or preferably killer, when it wasn't an accident, stroke, or horse's hind foot or whatever).

And there is very little writing that can be read save from a sense of duty.

I admit Lawrence (D. H.) had a gift of words, H. Miller also etc., the sober patience of a MacAlmon convinces no vendor and that was in another country already a decade behind us, and getting on for 2 decades. America is full of his followers.

Headline stares at me from floor: Commonsense tells us. If so, "us" are the "eelight."

Crevel is of the sons of the Sottisier, that is of the Great Flaubert, going on after *Bouvard,* and *L'Encyclopédie*. In *Les Pieds dans le plat* we had the utterly convincing proof of his, call it, genius, or whatever term you use to define the born writer. The abundance, the sense, general and inclusive, of the utterly blithering frumpery, post-war, of Paris, of the conglomerate of countries that hadn't had the sphincter strength for revolution. The utterly god blithering mess of Madame de Thebes, Roehm, Léon Blum. The world wherein the *faits divers* of the morning paper were possible. Wherein the morning paper itself was manifestly, if incredibly, possible. There the damn things were, are, and logically can be, *à la Descartes* with his little pin wheel, they exist, ergo they have some sort of existence. They jut out. They, as the dogs in Salzberg or Kuffstein station are by notice and sign post affirmed to be, RAUMLICH.

Unlike the dogs, they can NOT be kept off the Bahnsteigs.

Crevel sent me the book and there was (1933) no doubt of its authenticity. Aged war horse registered reception. Waited to see what next. Next, bullet. And so far as I know, the british young haven't put up a monument, sense of responsibility and dislike of leaving it for the decade after the after-next one: friends of C supply no information. Paris bookstores, being Paris bookstores and therefore the most inefficient in all Europe do not connect with the post office. Hence delays, disorder in sequence. If reader don't like it let him get out and reform our damned universe, especially the sow pits of Europe.

By 1929 (teste, *Etes-vous fous?* n.r.f.) Crevel knew how to construct a prose volume. Manifestly an heir, that is one using his cultural heritage, immature in so far as Laforgue and Cocteau are present on bits of surface in the first 50 pages, flotsam. Lazarillo de Tormes, or the picaresque novel revived . . . no reason to suppose as imitation, but from inner necessity. Sane men rediscover everything—Ethics, methods, devices, literary forms in their cycle. The gift of the word was René's.

The "copia," the long bustling sentence, "un-french"?, no, not unfrench, sentences like a bon père de famille carrying 43 parcels, piled to chin, held in both hands, tied with string one to another with the large loaf spiked on his umbrella's point, but OF, imperatively OF the time, the god damned bourgeois, loan-capitalist supernumerary, footling footless, ineffably modified time. Post-Proust, and goodbye to it. Post the damn lot of 'em and good BYE to it, 1929.

Note that even in *Les Pieds dans le plat,* Crevel had not got into the clear. He had not got into the time of Gesell, he is eternal youth, plunged into the tail end of a ten tailed epoch, among all the god damned feather boas, bustles etc. left, damn it, OVER from the bloody Nineteenth century, frousting the start of the twentieth, the first quarter and then some of the twentieth.

BUT not respecting it to the point of cataloguing all the stale cakes, high hats and meringues in the ash can.

Gentle reader about to be of *Etes-vous fous?* you are not, that is to say you will not, during even the opening pages be in a Beckford redivivus. All this fantasy isn't mere fantasy (not by no means).

In one sense, il n'a rien INVENTÉ, save in the basic sense of the latin root. He has not contrived it, he has found it. The stuff was there. The fantastic lie on the surface, being by 1929 the ONLY mode of showing reality.

I admit that it hangs fire, a little, somewhere about page 112 (say 100 to 120 or thereabouts) but passing that danger point it is justified.

The camera, photo method is NO good for reality, urban, metropolitan of the epoch. And by page 180 the inventor of the *simplexe anti-Oedipe* has proved his sobriety. By no lie less extensive could true perspective emerge. His writing is no more un-realism than the two dimensions of the draughtsman's paper are sur-real.

The horse's foot in the fore, does NOT touch the branch of the oak in the background.

Crevel's exterior world held, as we know, and occasionally admit, Freud's epigons, Blum, Madame Tabouis or whatever, Berlin of the post-depression.

All of which we avoid, at least in moments of weariness via the connoisseurship of the tin-soldier-collectors society (disguised as Crime Clubs and whatever). And might well go nuts (I mean worsely) if we didn't.

Yolande and her fakir are the necessary prelude, foreground for estimate of Le Suisse and Frau Dr. Herzog. What Crevel heard from Le Suisse in 1928, I had heard ten years before just off Regent St. This is our (and god damn it) Europe. Crevel n'a rien inventé, save in the sense: Thus he found it. This is the veronika, the true image.

It will not be printed in English. The french have for over a century, and let us say three or four centuries, specialized in printing those natural observations of fact which we utter only in private among those, of both sexes, whom we trust, in the dimension of their refinement, in the confidence that they will not take it amis.

Hence the greater freshness and let us say coolth of frog writings.

Crevel had the freshness of Excideuil, of the Dordoigne country. Heaven knows where he came from, but there is the fresh field inside him. No Paris fugg. Hence the phantom air, the stir of his entrance into the press room of "The Hours."

Les Pieds is a larger work, Comédie Humaine in one volume. Unlaboured, not a *Balzac de nos jours* as by the dutiful Romains . . . and this with no mépris for J. R. Let the "reader" begin on it, if she benevolently wishes to approve of my attempting this essay. Cummings did Russia, and before that a prison. Joyce at no point touches the cosmopolitan life of our time. *Ulysses* is local in scene, reaching universals. To reach universals you do not pass through all specific particulars. I recall Picabia's swiftness in seeing that two witnesses seeing the same externals lead to a belief in reality, "Dieu" or whatever. As a concurrent witness I affirm *Les Pieds dans le plat.* Such was the ambience. And the ambience is, emphaticly, the novelist's subject, he thereby attaining whatever general affirmations or negations he is capable of attaining.

III

It may (doubtless will) be objected by those who have the cult of criticism as such, but have forgotten its (criticism's) scope and original purposes, that I have not much discussed the "art" of R. Crevel. Technically I should have spent more words on his "how," and the condemned reviewer for his weekly rent would furnish MM. les lecteurs with "the faded and stuffy atmosphere of the bourgeois home" etc. etc., my position being that the novel (as such) was carried to its development by Flaubert and H. James (with parenthesis already indicated in other notes by the present expositor) that *since* (underlined) Mr. Joyce carried on from *Bouvard* there has been probably no development. I don't mean no good novels, no particular cases, Rodker's *Adolph* as a delicate variant, Cummings' *Eimi* as a masterwork dealing with a particular subject matter, masterwork because its author recognized that that matter could not adequately be presented in the idiom of James or Flaubert, but outside these specific examples one can only say of a given novel that it is a fine (or other) specimen of a known category. I mean that is all one would say in speaking of the book to one's most intelligent friends.

Crevel was a *born* writer in the best sense of that term, meaning that he didn't just trust to being born but exercised his admirable faculties through a series of novels (*Babylone, Mort difficile,* the better known *Mon corps et moi*), and culminating in *Les Pieds dans le plat.* Reading matter for the readers of novels that emerges from that publicly useful domain into reading matter for whomever is alert to the life of letters.

As the living tongue this work can be compared usefully only with that of Romains of 1911 and 1912 and with Cocteau's, among Crevel's french contemporaries, he being younger than Cocteau and a whole generation younger than Romains.

As to the novel as such, its stature will not be changed by any man who can not put 40 years on the job. That is what I am trying to get at in the paragraph before the last. One can say that such or such young man has seriously tried to extend the category and "might" etc. but beyond recognizing that he has honourably laid out a camp in known territory one is limited to explaining the relation of his work to a time.

As I see it, Crevel died in an era, one reads him in retrospect, but not as dead matter. One will increasingly read him and not the more bloated names of the elder men who acquiesced in the deliquescence. The serious young writer, 1938 onward, must read him, lest he illude himself with the notion that he can do less, be less mentally athletic than Crevel.

Looking still further back to the joys and excitements of the first decade of the century I repeat that the young writers now are up against a worse proposition. They don't have and can't have, for a few weeks, the pleasures that "we" had . . . This is not a life sentence. Once they wake up to the possibilities of the ERA there is a lot doing (for them). But this means that they must first recognize a new orientation. The live brains are not now in la vie littéraire, they are in la vie même, including all those verbal manifestations and processes which went into the codes of Constantine and Justinian, which filled the reading matter of John Adams and Jefferson, and which had for centuries been part of the "clerc's" existence and nutriment. It was only in the grovelling age of usura and usuriocracy that letters were lowered to mean merely "belles lettres" and that the subject matter was gradually reduced to personal titillations. Ending in infantilism (vide Mr. Lewis' (W. L.'s) diatribes) and the "pale and obese young men led by an udder."

A new awakening will mean that even youngish men will no longer read Dante and The Bard for an occasional adjective, that not only will Iago come to life after observance of living Iagos, but that the whole contents of great work will be read with a totally different critical spirit and with a comprehension of why Shxpr drags in the "two Usuries" whereof the lesser was put down and of why Dante included Philippe le Bel. The whole system of Reference in these major works has been annulled by pettifogging verbalists. By rough analogy Ribera and the Seicento looked at dresses and draperies; Simone Memmi at his whole subject.

BIBLIOGRAPHY

Détours. N.R.F., epuisé.
Mon corps et moi. Kra. 1925.
La Mort difficile. Kra. 1926.
Babylone. Kra. 1927.
L'Esprit contre la raison. Cahiers du Sud. 1928.
Etes-vous fous? N.R.F. 1929.
Paul Klee. N.R.F. 1930.
Dali ou l'anti-obscurantisme. Ed. Surréalistes. 1931.
Le Clavecin de Diderot. Ed. Surréalistes. 1932.
Les Pieds dans le plat. Sagittaire. 1933.

Introduction

Edouard Roditi

THE FRENCH SURREALISTS tended, at least in theory, to be suspicious of the novel both as a literary genre and as a legitimate form of literary expression. The writing of a novel, they argued, required too much previous planning, so that the final product, like that of most painting and sculpture too, lacked the spontaneity of automatic writing. André Breton and the more doctrinaire Surrealists nevertheless agreed in the long run to accept that painting and sculpture, if only for strictly technical reasons, could require the kind of previous sketching or planning that precludes the sheer spontaneity of doodling. However much their paths may have ultimately diverged, both Paul Valéry, the most rationalist of all French poets, and André Breton, the most eloquent theoretician of Surrealist irrationalism, happened moreover to have been, in their earliest published poems, equally disciples of Stéphane Mallarmé. Like Valéry, Breton also appears to have never later been able to subject himself to the fictional discipline of simply writing, to quote Valéry's famous parody of all narrative: "The marquise went out at five o'clock."

Breton nevertheless expressed his admiration for such masterpieces of "Gothic" fiction as Horace Walpole's *Castle of Otranto,* Matthew Lewis's *Monk,* and Robert Maturin's *Melmoth the Wanderer* as well as for the wildly romantic tales of Achim von Arnim and Poe. Only in his own *Nadja,* an autobiographical account, based to a great extent on dreams, optical illusions, and hallucinations, of a love relationship with a hauntingly elusive, mysterious, and ultimately psychopathic young woman, did he condescend to display his very considerable talent as a narrator, much as Philippe Soupault did too in *Les Dernières nuits de Paris.* Robert Desnos then followed their example in *Deuil pour deuil* and *L'Amour la liberté,* two books of rhapsodic narrative that perhaps have more in common with Lautréamont's *Chants de Maldoror* than with any more traditional forms of fiction. But can these four Surrealist narratives still be described as novels?

Louis Aragon thus felt free to develop his own very considerable talent as a novelist after abandoning Surrealism and joining the French Communist Party. Only then did he begin to express admiration for such masters of fictional realism as Jules Vallès and Emile Zola, to follow their example in some respects, and even display his skill in historical novels that required a great deal of previous planning and research. His novels indeed became increasingly traditionalist or even academic in nature and style if not in politics too, in fact so typical of a kind of fiction that had been popular in France some fifty or more years earlier that many of his middle-class readers could even ignore his communist political message while enjoying his talents as a narrator.

René Crevel proves to have been the only Surrealist writer who, in spite of Breton's condemnation of the novel, consistently and almost exclusively expressed himself in the form of fiction. His avant-garde novels are of a kind, however, that remains typical of his age and generation rather than of the more restricted French Surrealist group to which he staunchly claimed allegiance while other Surrealists repeatedly expressed disapproval of his fiction and his way of life behind his back. In a discussion that several of them held in his absence and under Breton's leadership, most of those present thus condemned homosexuality in no uncertain terms. Very pointedly, Breton then declared that he could tolerate homosexuality only in the case of the marquis de Sade and of the decadent turn-of-the-century writer Jean Lorrain, thereby refraining somewhat prudishly from mentioning Crevel's name or indeed the names of two other homosexuals, Jacques Vaché and Raymond Roussel, for whose writings and personality Breton never ceased to express great admiration throughout his life. A summary of this discussion was subsequently published in an issue of *Le Surréalisme au service de la révolution* so that Crevel couldn't ignore it. Yet he continued to remain devoted to Breton and to the Surrealist cause.

Breton had never known Raymond Roussel personally and can be suspected of not having been at all aware of this strangely cryptic writer's homosexuality, which isn't suggested by any of his published writings nor by any of the accounts of his various eccentricities that can be found in the writings of contemporaries who knew him. It was thus left to the investigative talents of the Italian writer Leonardo Sciascia to discover, many years later and from the Sicilian police's reticent or bungling reports of Roussel's mysterious death in his hotel room in Palermo, that this ruined former millionaire, who always traveled with a kept mistress in order to conceal the real nature of his love life, had driven to Sicily all the way from Paris in a taxi, with the driver of which, like Proust in the case of Agostinelli, he had apparently become enamored. All the evidence gathered by Sciascia from the confused or embarrassed reports of the Palermo police indicate that Roussel was found dead, lying on a mattress on the floor of his hotel room, where he had spent the night with this chauffeur, who then panicked and fled back to Paris in his cab before the writer's death could be discovered by his mistress or the hotel personnel. In Paris, some time later, the chauffeur tried to blackmail Roussel's brother-in-law with threats of revealing the nature of his real relationship with the dead writer, who had apparently died of an overdose of some drugs to which he was addicted.

One may well wonder what bearing this strange story may have on Breton's apparent reticence in failing to add Crevel's name to those of Sade and Lorrain in the above-mentioned Surrealist discussion in the course of which homosexuality was so violently condemned. Its only bearing consists in its quite remarkable similarity with the circumstances of the death, likewise from an overdose of a drug in the course of a homosexual encounter, in a hotel room in the French city of Nantes, of Breton's handsome and gifted young Dadaist friend Jacques Vaché on January 6, 1919. Until his own death many decades later, Breton never ceased to proclaim his passionate devotion to the memory of Vaché and to affirm again and again that he had committed suicide. Breton even refrained from ever admitting that Vaché had actually been found naked and dead of an overdose, in bed with Paul Bonnet, another young man who was likewise naked and dying of an overdose. Two other companions are known to have survived this orgy of opium, according to newspaper reports, and, as it appears, of sex. One of these, an American soldier, A.-K. Woynow, panicked in time, warned the hotel management that two of his companions were dying in the room from which he had escaped, and was promptly, it appears, shipped back to the United States, where no trace of him was later discovered. The fourth participant in this fatal party, André Caron, was the young son of a local Nantes physician. He too panicked and managed to make his way in time to his father's office, close to the hotel, and was given first aid and saved. For the rest of his life, he continued to be known locally as a homosexual.

From all this it seems that Jacques Vaché exerted on Breton a curiously homoerotic appeal, which survived his own death as well as Breton's three marriages and all his other known relationships with women. But Breton never admitted to himself or to any others the real nature of this physical or emotional appeal. Instead, he repressed his emotions, concealing them at all times beneath his officially expressed homophobia. Handsome and gifted as he was too, Crevel may indeed have exerted on Breton the same kind of appeal as Vaché had a few years earlier, and this may have been why Breton never mentioned

Crevel's name either in his loudly voiced condemnations of homo-sexuality, or in the same breath as the names of Sade and Lorrain, whose homosexuality he was so exceptionally willing to tolerate.

But Crevel proved, in spite of his great loyalty to Breton and the Surrealist cause, to be a rather marginal or different kind of Surrealist in other respects too. Whereas Aragon, as already stated, made his career as a novelist only after abandoning Surrealism, and also became overtly homosexual, much to the surprise of many of his communist friends, only after the death of his wife, the Russian-born novelist Elsa Triolet, Crevel continued for several years to be the only novelist, avowed homosexual, and Paris society playboy of the whole Surrealist group. Among the French Surrealist writers, he was also the only one who could read and speak English and German with any fluency and who displayed a real interest in any contemporary developments in English, American, or German art, literature, or philosophy. Towards the end of his life, in an essay entitled *L'Esprit contre la raison,* he thus contrasted the somewhat obscurantist existentialism of Heidegger with the far more intelligently critical logical positivism of Ludwig von Carnap and the other mathematical logicians of the Viennese School. Over twenty years later, Breton still proved, in conversation with me, to be completely ignorant of the very existence of Ludwig Wittgenstein, nor did he ever display, whether in conversation or in his writings, a serious interest in any modern philosophy.

At least until the publication of his sixth and last novel, *Les Pieds dans le plat,* Crevel was the only writer, among the French Sur-realists, to be at all times a welcome guest in those circles of the high society of Paris that displayed an interest in contemporary art, litera-ture, and music and considered themselves patrons of the avant-garde. A close friend of Marie-Laure de Noailles, one of the wealthiest, most aristocratic, and critically most discriminating of Paris hostesses and patrons, Crevel attended some of the most sumptuous fancy-dress private balls of the extravagant gin age that preceded the 1929 Wall Street Crash. Most of the other French Surrealists refrained con-temptuously from close social contacts with this "capitalist" world, except occasionally in their love lives, for instance with such attractive heiresses as Breton's first wife and her sister, the wife of Raymond Queneau, or Nancy Cunard, in the course of a love affair with whom Louis Aragon translated into French *The Hunting of the Snark,* published by her Hours Press.

Crevel's many friends and occasional associates in the American expatriate community of Paris included Harry and Caresse Crosby, Gertrude Stein, Kay Boyle, the pianist Allen Tanner (who was then living with the Russian émigré painter Pavel Tchelitchew), the composer Virgil Thomson, and the painter Eugene McCown. With the latter, Crevel is known to have had a stormy homosexual relationship from 1924 to 1927; it inspired one of his best and most moving novels, *La Mort difficile,* published in America, in David Rattray's excellent translation, as *Difficult Death,* by North Point Press. Crevel probably also met Hart Crane, who associated closely, during his short stay in Paris, with both the Crosbys and McCown. Oddly enough, he appears to have somehow met Ezra Pound too.

Crevel's closest German friends were the young writer Klaus Mann, who was one of the sons of Thomas Mann, the Berlin sculptor Renée Sintenis, her Berlin dealer Alfred Flechtheim, the daughter, Mopsa, of the expressionist writer Carl Sternheim, and the painter Carl von Repper, actually an Austrian, who married Mopsa when Crevel expected to marry her and known among his friends as "Jack the Ripper." In Berlin, Crevel also associated briefly with the famous sexologist Magnus Hirschfeld and his circle, described in satirical terms in Crevel's fifth novel, *Etes-vous fous?,* which remains in many ways untranslatable.*

Several years before taking his own life in 1935, Crevel had already formulated, in the course of one of the published discussions of the Surrealist group, the proposition that suicide is "probably the most legitimate and definitive of all available solutions" to personal or existential problems. In this general context, it may well be significant that Harry Crosby, Hart Crane, Klaus Mann, and Crevel himself all committed suicide, as did also a few of Crevel's French Surrealist friends and associates.

As a novelist, Crevel never handled, except perhaps in *Etes-vous fous?,* any specifically Surrealist themes, but he remained haunted by a limited number of psychological problems, above all by those of suicide and homosexuality. These remain typical of the era which one of his more cynical contemporaries, the French writer Maurice Sachs, once called, as the title of one of his books of memoirs, *The Decade of Illusion.* It was also the heyday of the Paris community of American expatriates, with many of whom Crevel associated mainly in the bars of Montparnasse, as well as of Jean Cocteau's novels and those of his young friends, Raymond Radiguet and Jean Desbordes. With all three of these Breton and most of the other Surrealists remained at daggers drawn in their literary controversies, but Crevel's earlier novels, *Détours, Mon corps et moi, Babylone,* and *La Mort difficile,* have more in common with those of Cocteau and his younger disciples, than with Breton's *Nadja,* Soupault's *Les Dernières nuits*

Publishers' note: David Rattray is translating this for eventual publication by Dalkey Archive Press as *Are You Crazy?*

de Paris, or the two even more oneiric or rhapsodic narratives of Desnos. Only with *Etes-vous fous?* did Crevel attempt to break away from the psychological preoccupations of his first four novels and undertake a more subversively Surrealist critique of society in a less traditional form of fiction.

The origins of Crevel's peculiar preoccupations with both suicide and homosexuality can probably be attributed to a profound emotional shock experienced in his adolescence, when his father, a music publisher, appears to have been compromised in some homosexual scandal and suddenly hanged himself in their family home. This occurred in one of the more elegant middle-class neighborhoods of Paris, in fact only a few hundred yards from the home of my own very conventional and plutocratic parents. Crevel was then fourteen years old and his mother, an apparently sadistic moralist, insisted on displaying to her children their father's corpse in order to impress on their minds the full extent of the "shame" that the poor man's "sin" and death had brought upon his widow and offspring. Until her own death twelve years later in 1926, she continued to lead an abnormally withdrawn life and, until Crevel's inevitable emancipation at the time of his military service in the French army, to impose on him equally rigid disciplines, thereby tending to deprive him of normally free and friendly relationships with other adolescents of either sex.

Two years before his mother's death, Crevel published *Détours,* his first novel, while he was already living openly with the notoriously narcissistic and promiscuous American painter Eugene McCown, a former satellite of Cocteau's circle of young men and a minor disciple of the same so-called neo-romantic school of painters as Pavel Tchelitchew, Christian Bérard, Eugene Berman, and a few others who are still remembered while McCown remains deservedly forgotten even in his native Kansas City.

Détours offers its readers an almost autobiographical description of Crevel's family background. He avenges himself here on his mother, however, by having his fictional counterpart's mother commit suicide too, while attributing to him the moral responsibility of having discreetly suggested suicide to his own father, a high-ranking French army officer who has been compromised in a homosexual scandal and abandoned his family in order to live more freely his "life of shame."

Far from being at all Surrealist, *Détours* is written in much the same manner as the slightly earlier novels of Raymond Radiguet, *Le Diable au corps* and *Le Bal du Comte d'Orgel,* or of the first novel, *J'adore,* of Jean Cocteau's young friend Jean Desbordes, who quickly replaced Radiguet in Cocteau's affections after Radiguet's early death. In all four novels, one can detect a quality of confessional writing that might perhaps be attributed to the fact that the three young authors had all been recently reading the *Confessions* of Jean-Jacques Rousseau. Both Cocteau and Desbordes are indeed known to have been reading them when Cocteau wrote his anonymous *Le Livre blanc* and Desbordes wrote *J'adore*. Crevel himself is moreover known to have displayed a great interest in the fiction of Diderot, on which he began to compose a dissertation, so that one has good reason to suspect that he was familiar with Rousseau's major writings too.

Within the next few years, Crevel's first novel was followed in rapid succession by *Mon corps et moi* in 1925, *La Mort difficile* in 1926, and *Babylone* in 1927, all three published with some success by Editions Simon Kra, which later became Editions du Sagittaire and was also the publisher of Breton's *Surrealist Manifestos* as well as of Robert Desnos's two novels. In these three new and increasingly mature novels, Crevel developed, with ever more novelistic skill but also more and more satirical or emotional bitterness in his depictions of what had once been his own respectable middle-class family background, very much the same themes of suicide and homosexuality as in *Détours*. While remaining almost obsessed with suicide, he began to stress ever less insistently the homosexuality of his heroes, even allowing them to become sometimes involved concurrently in bisexual relationships with both a female and a male partner. Only in *La Mort difficile*, a fictional account of his painfully disastrous relationship with McCown, did Crevel develop somewhat more insistently the homosexual element of the novel's plot.

In 1929, when Crevel was ready to publish his next novel, *Etes-vous fous?*, Editions du Sagittaire was in financial difficulties, having become involved in an over-ambitious program of publishing limited illustrated editions of classics that suddenly ceased to find a sufficient number of subscribers. Crevel therefore shifted his allegiance to Editions de la Nouvelle Revue Française, which insisted in his contract on reserving an option on his next novel while also commissioning him to write two small art books, one on the Berlin sculptor Renée Sintenis and the other on Paul Klee. These were both published in 1930.

Of all Crevel's novels, *Etes-vous fous?* remains in many ways the most puzzling, in fact perhaps the most overtly Surrealist in both plot and style of writing, no longer at all comparable with the fiction of Cocteau, Radiguet, or Desbordes. Still basically autobiographical, *Etes-vous fous?* offers us a satirical account of a period of profound crisis in its author's life. Thoroughly frustrated in his passion for McCown and embittered by disappointments in more casual relationships with handsome boxers and other young men picked up in bars, Crevel had become deeply involved in an emotional relationship with Mopsa Sternheim and even planned to marry her. Suddenly, she then announced from Germany that she had married Carl von Repper, and this additional disappointment occurred at a time when Crevel was already demoralized by his enforced isolation in repeated cures for tuberculosis in Swiss mountain sanatoria where he was again and again kept for months on end. On one of his returns to Paris, he attempted to solve some of his emotional problems by subjecting himself to a psychoanalytical treatment under Dr. Allendy, a pioneer Paris analyst of the Freudian school. But Allendy proved, both in Crevel's case and in the case of two other famous literary patients, Antonin Artaud and Anaïs Nin, to be quite exceptionally authoritarian and unperceptive. From Nin's *Diaries* and Crevel's satirical account (in *Etes-vous fous?*) of his own analysis, Allendy appears to have been all too prone to expound to his patients his own theories, but almost unwilling to listen to theirs. On the subject of the Oedipus complex, he could be particularly eloquent, like the late Dr. Edmund Bergler in New York, and thereby immediately antagonized Crevel, who had not come there to be reminded again and again of his mother. Allendy also believed, as Anaïs Nin explains in her *Diaries,* that tuberculosis can be brought about by a neurosis, presumably by an Oedipus complex in the case of Crevel, which is, of course, microbiological nonsense.

Be that all as it may, *Etes-vous fous?* consists mainly of a satirical account of Crevel's botched analysis, of his unhappy relationship with Mopsa, and of his subsequent association in Berlin with Dr. Magnus Hirschfeld and the staff and patients of the latter's weird sexological institute. Because so much of this somewhat transitional novel is couched in a more overtly Surrealist style than any of Crevel's earlier novels, it has never been very popular. In order to be fully understood, it requires even today more familiarity with some of the details of Crevel's private life than any of his other novels.

Towards the end of 1932, Crevel then submitted his next and last completed novel, *Les Pieds dans le plat,* to Editions de la Nouvelle Revue Française, which very soon rejected it, so that Crevel returned to Editions du Sagittaire, which accepted it and published it in May 1933. I happened at that time to be working in the offices of Editions du Sagittaire as an assistant to the writer Léon Pierre-Quint, the firm's director and editor in chief.

My personal relationship with Crevel was brief and quite casual. He was ten years older than I and a young writer of considerable promise and repute when I began, in 1928, to publish some of my own work in *transition* and a few other American expatriate or French avant-garde periodicals, such as *Les Cahiers du sud,* which also published some of Crevel's work. I met him for the first time in the company of the poet Georgette Camille, who was the editorial representative in

Paris of *Les Cahiers du sud,* a Marseilles publication. When I was about to travel to Germany in 1930, Crevel suggested that I look up in Berlin the sculptor Sintenis and a couple of his other German friends. I had not yet read enough of his novels to draw any conclusions about his private life, so that it was in Berlin, where such matters were discussed more openly than in Paris, that I first became aware of his reputation as a homosexual.

On my return to Paris in 1932, I became a partner in an unwise attempt to improve the finances of Editions du Sagittaire and revive its activities. I thus happened to be working in the firm's offices when it published *Les Pieds dans le plat* in 1933. I then had occasion to meet Crevel several times, either when he came to our office or when I brought him proofs of his novel to the hotel where he was staying on the Rue de Montevideo. I was shocked to see how far his physical appearance had deteriorated.

Ever since 1926, Crevel had suffered from tuberculosis and, by 1933, had already undergone several strenuous mountain cures, sometimes in the company of the Surrealist poet Paul Eluard, whose lungs were likewise infected. In 1929, Crevel then underwent drastic surgery on one lung and had four badly infected ribs removed. All this, as well as his disappointing involvement with Mopsa Sternheim, depressed him so much that he decided to undergo psychoanalytical treatment under Dr. Allendy, though with no more success than Antonin Artaud or Anaïs Nin. In *Etes-vous fous?* Crevel's auto-biographical hero begins by suspecting that he may well be insane, but is soon led to conclude, like the insane hero in the great German expressionist writer René Schickele's last novel a few years later, that the world in which he lives is far more insane.

When I now saw Crevel again in his hotel room, he had lost most of his almost legendary good looks and much of the playful manner that had long assured him both his social and his homosexual successes. Whether from his illness or from the drugs that he took to relieve his pains, his face was swollen and abnormally flushed. For some time, there had also been something feverish in his restless activity, in his sudden trip to England in 1928 and, in the fall of 1931, to Spain with Dali, then also to Berlin. He had become increasingly involved in political activities, even joining in 1931 the Association of Revolutionary Writers and Artists, probably at Breton's instigation, and signing a number of leftist or outright anti-fascist declarations sponsored by the French Communist Party.

The very title of *Les Pieds dans le plat,* an idiomatic French expression that means "putting one's foot in it," was apparently intended to signify to Crevel's more faithful readers his definite break with those sections of high society and the homosexual world which, attracted by his good looks and his entertainingly playful manner, had hoped to convince him as a gifted and relatively successful young novelist to abandon Surrealism and all its subversive or outright leftist activities in order to come at last to terms with the Establishment. The latter is represented, in *Les Pieds dans le plat,* by a very recognizably satirical portrait of "the Prince of Journalists," that is to say, of Léon Bailby, the notoriously homosexual and politically reactionary owner and editor of *Le Jour,* one of the most powerful and widely read daily newspapers of the French capital. An ardent anti-fascist, especially after Hitler came to power in Germany in 1933, Crevel realized fully that Bailby was attracted to him sexually and sought to seduce him at least as a talented younger contributor to *Le Jour* and to *La Revue de Paris,* edited by Bailby's lifelong lover Albert Flament. As early as 1932, he also knew that Bailby was allowing himself to be used in France as a journalistic puppet by both Italian fascism and German National-Socialism. Soon after the February 1934 Paris riots, Bailby even began to employ, as secretary-general of *Le Jour,* a notorious French fascist, Darquier de Pellepoix, who later became, during the German occupation of France, its Commissioner for Jewish Affairs, directly responsible for the deportation of over a hundred thousand Jewish men, women, and children from France to the extermination camps of eastern Europe.

Crevel's satirical portrait of Bailby in *Les Pieds dans le plat* was so controversially recognizable that Editions de la Nouvelle Revue Française appears to have been very pusillanimously scared of facing the political scandal of publishing such a novel. When we published it a few months later at Editions du Sagittaire, we were not only widely recognized as the publisher of such "subversive" writers as Breton, Crevel, Desnos, and other Surrealists, but also as a Jewish-owned firm that was committed to fighting fascism by publishing more overtly political books, such as those of a few economical theoreticians of the French Popular Front Government of Léon Blum and even some works of communist theory, such as those of the Marxist philosopher Henri Lefebvre.

Practically no French newspaper of any significant readership dared review *Les Pieds dans le plat.* Even the French communist press proved to be too prudish to cope with Crevel's unblushing references to homosexuality, although the novel was also interpreted in some Paris homosexual circles as a statement of its author's farewell to his own homosexual past, now that he was known to be in love with Tota de Cuevas after his more unfortunate experience with Mopsa Sternheim.

But Crevel's critique of homosexuality, as expressed in *Les Pieds dans le plat,* appears to have been of a more social or political than personal or emotional nature. He continued indeed to remain a close friend of Klaus Mann as well as of several other young homosexual German artists and writers, such as the Berlin poet Wolfgang Helmert, who was living in exile in Paris and died there a couple of years later of an overdose. Crevel's critique of homosexuality is limited to those who practice it shamefacedly while defending a socio-political order that condemns it.

In spite of the negative reactions of the communist press, which was in those days as critical of homosexuality as a "bourgeois vice" as Catholicism is of it as a mortal sin, Crevel continued for a while, together with Breton and the few remaining orthodox Surrealists, to be active in the Association of Revolutionary Writers and Artists as well as to participate in other such activities that were more or less directly sponsored by the communists. A few months later, however, Breton and most of the Surrealists were expelled, under pressure from Moscow, from the Association or from the French Communist Party.

After the Paris riots of February 1934, Crevel and a few other Surrealists or former Surrealists became briefly and more seriously committed to anti-fascist political action while Darquier de Pellepoix, who had been slightly wounded in the riots, was managing to impose himself more and more as a political figure of sorts in French fascist splinter groups until, a few months later, he attracted the attention of Léon Bailby and became secretary-general of *Le Jour*.

Early in 1935, after another series of treatments in a Swiss mountain sanatorium, Crevel returned to Paris, at last convinced that he was cured of his tuberculosis. No longer agreeing politically with Breton, who could never tolerate any opposition to his own "papal" opinions nor any policies dictated to him from above, Crevel now opposed Breton's excommunication of Dali from the Surrealist group. In June, he participated actively in the preparation of the communist-dominated Paris Congress of Writers in Defence of Culture, where the Soviet delegation, in spite of Crevel's efforts, refused to allow Breton to take the floor. On the same day, June 17th, Crevel discovered that the excruciating pains he was suffering were caused by tuberculosis, which had now spread from his lungs to his kidneys. That same night, he committed suicide by inhaling the gas from his oven.

Although *Les Pieds dans le plat* continued to be more or less ignored by the French critical press long after its publication in 1933, it was suddenly praised enthusiastically and at great length in London in 1939, four years after Crevel's death, by no less a personage than Ezra Pound and in no less a periodical than T. S. Eliot's *Criterion*. Writing from the provincial depths of Italy, where he was already fully committed to fascist doctrines and policies, Pound had completely misunderstood Crevel's political motivations. Instead of detecting in the novel its author's fairly obvious anti-fascist and even communist sympathies, he even failed to understand Crevel's violent satire of the proto-fascist French forces that were already plotting, in secret alliance with Hitler and Mussolini, to undermine the French Third Republic. In "Uncle Ezra"'s zany opinion, *Les Pieds dans le plat* was actually a critique of the "decadent" French Third Republic's anti-fascist Popular Front government.

Nothing could have been more surprising to poor René Crevel, had he still been alive in 1939, than such a weird misinterpretation of the last novel that he was able to finish and publish before his death. Was Pound remembering here his own chance encounter with Crevel, probably in Paris in 1932 in the expatriate circles of Caresse Crosby and her friends, or perhaps in the company of Richard Thoma, the editor of the *New Review,* in whose circle young Paul Bowles and even I occasionally met Pound in Paris around the same date? Was Pound only remembering the handsome playboy Surrealist lover of Eugene McCown and author of *La Mort difficile?* The mysterious ramifications of Ezra Pound's critical mind remain often quite inexplicable.

Putting My Foot in It

1

One of the Mighty of This Earth
One of the Opinion Makers

SUN AND TRADITION. A dazzling light and the firm intention not to let yourself be blinded, etc., etc.

Symbols need not limit their scope to this pendulum swing of images. But a well-balanced mind won't try and roost on a swing of antithesis that, at the height of its arc, would only look down on treacherous metaphors and promenades strewn with wolf traps that snare innocent beige fawns in flight, rather than large carnivores.

Here, today, the herd of cavorting ideas would hardly seem threatened. Fog-toothed melancholy can only sink its teeth into moonlight. And presently, it is high noon. So much for time. As for place, the Roman Empire passed through. It even stayed, blended with the dirt on this hillside, disciplined it, militarized it, metamorphosing amorphous terrain into terraces.

One of the mighty of this earth, one of the opinion makers whose sense of order takes pleasure in evoking the grand classical past, not for vain regrets but for quite virile resolutions, is jaunting merrily along—although there is nothing merry about the thoroughfare in question—snugly ensconced in a motorcar worthy of the Roman road. This brand-new car is French-made, for if the era of the Caesars, including the subsequent period, was the age of hippic locomotion, it is important, when purchasing motor vehicles, to observe a certain solidarity which, if not specifically French, is Latin or, at the very least, European, but strictly European, for after all of the tricks they have played on us, those sons of Uncle Sam with their Bonus Armies, their gangsters, their crashing and crashed millionaires—they can go hang themselves elsewhere.

With a light breeze tickling the white hairs on his chest and those which serve as a nest for a certain bird and its septuagenarian eggs (fresh as a daisy, moreover, thanks to Voronoff), the man who rejoices in the title of the Prince of Journalists savors the joy of living.

Here, in the hollow of a small valley, is a ruin used to transport water before the birth of Christ. Thus, to the paradoxical and nearly imperceptible accompaniment of an almighty motor, thoughts can let themselves float along. It won't be long before they reach the banks of reverie. They won't, moreover, lose any of their moderation in the process. Mustn't forget that, if Fragonard and Hubert Robert measured up to this landscape, then any French mind worthy of the name can and must, out of the greatest disorder, out of a certain shambles, indeed out of a complete mess, compose a garden, a French garden, to be exact.

And to think that the great redheaded barbarians sung (though not in earnest) by Verlaine dare return to our countryside, to our beaches, to attack our spas, to talk about how old this country is, and even spend their money on the rags that insinuate, with each venture undertaken by the Prince of Journalists, that this time it could be his swan song. A Prince of Journalists' song, if he is aware of his national rights and duties, can only come out as a cock's crow. The Gallic cockerel's. His head is bursting with bugles. He is always ready to sound the charge. Even his dreams are dedicated to his country—only last night, he dreamt he was the Unknown Soldier's widow! Ah, that cadaveric stiffness!

But to be aware of one's rights and duties as a Frenchman is first of all to be liberal. Thus, the Prince of Journalists agreed to have lunch today with an Austrian woman. An archduchess, of course. And if other compatriots of our former enemies should try to slip in behind the grand dame, he will take care of them. And above all, watch out for so-called philosophers, poets, and filmmakers from Central Europe. Each morning, the director of a large daily dutifully reminds the editor of his *Arts and Letters* column that an intellectual invasion never fails to foreshadow the other kind. So guard and watch all frontiers—the frontiers of the mind no less than those in the north and the east. Defend the moral heritage of France, French culture, the culture of French thought, French gardens, French-style gardens, the French-woman's gardens, with boxwood-lined paths, the wood itself being carved into a darning egg; for the owner, the Frenchwoman, the bourgeoise Frenchwoman (any Frenchwoman worthy of the name being a bourgeoise), even athletic or a touch brainy, is and will remain, until the end of time, thrifty enough to keep both the woolen stocking, wherein lies the family nest egg, and her own nylons from unraveling, mending them as soon as they begin to run.

Sitting at her window, with a song on her lips, a flower in her bosom, but never with a fire down below, this guardian of traditions, next to a table adorned with the tastiest fruits of her orchard—isn't it something right out of Chardin?

The Prince of Journalists is moved. He melts. And not only from the midsummer heat but from the warmth, far more touching, of memory. In his mind's eye he sees his father, his mother, the decent people who spent their lives growing old. By the time they procreated him they were in their twilight years, hoping that very solid experience would compensate for certain congenital and perhaps hereditary handicaps. The good souls had no reason to worry. Their son, although he is short and lively tempered, holds himself straight as a ruler and, at bottom, always masters his reflexes. Actually, he turned out well enough, both mentally and physically, to savor, with his utmost gratitude, in the scene before him, the memory of the ruin which had been built, on his father's orders, near a pond whose waters were confined by exquisite little banks. The wise old man, after having asked the valet who never left him for a second to set up his folding stool and cover his shoulders with a Scottish plaid, was ready to sit down, aim, shoot (wasn't this firearmed fisherman an expert on refraction?) one, two, three, four times. He killed the father, the mother, the little boy, the little girl bleak-fish.

Only the most genuinely French virtues had caused this carbine fisherman to become an Olympian statue of warm fabrics at the edge of autumn's waters. Beneath such majesty he was hiding a painful secret. Our firearmed fisherman's mother, in the days when she was carrying him, had been assaulted on a dark night and, before she even had time to catch her breath, got hosed—and, what's worse, from the flip side. How could the unborn child have possibly avoided the repercussions of this heinous violence? Expecting his offspring to bear a double original sin which no amount of baptism would wash away, the husband of the woman sodomized in spite of herself, a great friend of Cambronne, used his connections to get enlisted and heroically killed immediately, at the head of a small troop which had only recently bestowed upon him the proud title of commander.

Every sin, even unintentional, can be forgiven. Of course, the orphan paid for this forgiveness with congenital epilepsy. He was all but deprived of the joys of childhood. He can still remember his mother's mustached nieces sitting in a circle all around her, the woman sodomized in spite of herself. These cousins, if his distant memory serves him well, were neither fish nor fowl, neither hide nor hair, but salt and pepper and more bitter than sweet. They were going to prevent a further accident at all costs, which is why they lived on the plains of Beauce.

On the horizon, there wasn't a single grove that could conceal a satyr. As soon as the wheat reached a certain height, the young widow was confined to the house until the last row had been gleaned.

As a result of her adventure, she had become prone to melancholy. The sweet, desperate automatism of certain gestures which she repeated indefinitely made her guardians conclude that she was eccentric, or even obsessed. For days upon end she would caress her hair, which was naturally wavy, but straightened each morning. She hardly ever opened her mouth. On one exceptional evening, however, she was talking a great deal when, perhaps, she was frightened by a reproving stare from one of the old women? In any event she jumped up and took off running. Since one of the jailers had just made sure that all of the doors and windows were securely locked, none of them bothered to follow her. The young woman didn't get far, of course, no farther than the dining room; but there, out of a Dutch candelabra she pulled a purplish candle (everything was mourning and half-mourning in her charming little interior) and, in a pious kiss, brushed her lips against its wax, which was softer than the softest human skin.

This contact produced a frenzy which spread through the mucous membranes of her virgin palate and, taking advantage of this opportunity, her widow's tongue proffered its route of ecstasy, a route which, instead of stopping at the first foothills of her tonsils, went on and on. Already, night was falling. The cousin who, that very morning, had filled the candelabra with her own hands, came quickly, anxious to see the magic of the dancing flames. To her surprise, one of the candles was missing. This was in fact the same candle which had emigrated into the mouth of the young woman lying motionless on the rug. Every trace of color had already deserted her face. The cylinder of wax appeared blacker, bigger, and more scandalous.

Sixty years of virginity tried in vain to dam the waters of instinct as they burst through the granite of good intentions, the rock of irreproachable conduct.

The spinster yelled words capable of making the cadaver blush. And with that her companions rushed in and saw that the lips of the woman sodomized in spite of herself were no more than a wedding ring slipped onto the finger of some monster of lethal virility.

Reduced to the passive role of epileptic orphan, the Prince of Journalists' father felt admiration for the presence of mind, the family spirit shown by his relatives throughout the funeral ceremonies. Their first move was to restrict entrance to the room where the poor little thing, as they said, slept her last sleep with the candle, which rigor mortis had made impossible to extract, still firmly between her teeth.

Since they couldn't get a word out of the old maids, the onlookers— who were determined to make their trip worthwhile—asked the child insidious questions, but he did exactly as he had been told and answered, regardless of the query: "My mother died of a *transport*" [seizure].

Disappointed, the visitors would become ironic. They wore a malicious smile, shrugged their shoulders with a mere hint of pity, scornfully offered their "sincere condolences," and, on the pretense of patting him on the cheek, pinched the orphan's neck as hard as they could.

When he imagines his father's childhood, the Prince of Journalists can't help comparing him to the young Spartan who, as history tells us, let a fox devour his abdomen rather than confess that he was hiding the animal under his chlamys. But, just as the little Lacedaemonian had paid for his heroic silence with the skin of his stomach and with his insides, the brave little epileptic boy suffered, after this incident and all his life, the ravages of the word *transport.* On the day of the funeral these two syllables, innocuous to the rest of mankind, set to work inside of him like hungry cannibals.

Suddenly the expression got stuck in his throat. Hardened by repetition, the letters bored into his palate, worming their way into a tiny hole which their insistence widened little by little. This was the opening of a triumphal passage to the heavy jaw that served as a head for the word *transport.* The two syllables, one by way of a body, the other a face, had but a meager vowel-skin stuck to their consonant bones. But it was so hot in the orphan's brain that the substantive's skeleton and cranial cavity began to melt and, rather quickly, they coagulated, turning into a gelatin that immediately spilt into two stretches of highway, with the first (which was the last, as in the Gospel) running the other off the road. Transport. Port. Trance. Port. *Port,* turned around like a worm, became *trop* [too many], and this caused too many trances. But *trop,* also reversible, reassumed its initial form and, with the additional remorse of seeing spelling rules violated, the little boy witnessed the toilsome birth, behind his forehead, of a porker [*porc*] named *trans.* Popular wisdom tells us that "little pigs have never eaten big ones." And yet, the pigheadedness which gave birth to his ugly mug, snout and all, caught fire, so that his boiling brain is now ready to melt and turn into the exact same milk [*le lait*] which feeds any so-called milk-fed pig [*cochon de lait*]. And with that the orphan fainted, reviving a few minutes later in the arms of his cousins, to the jolts of a solemn and voluminous hearse, one of several, he is told, that are transporting the family to the cemetery. But, if the consequence of having "transports" is transportation to the cemetery, how can he escape from the enemy word?

Not even ten letters long, this rodent seized every opportunity to assail him through the eye or through the ear. Thus, on the day he came of age, when the notary delivered his small fortune to him, the orphan already had the pleasure of seeing that his inheritance consisted mainly of Transit Authority stocks. All of a sudden he read this subtitle: *Mass transportation.* And so, despite his innate sense of thrift, he threw the whole wad on the fire. Heroic but pointless sacrifice. A two-syllable cannibal can be as ferocious as those measuring two meters. He is always superior to them in flexibility and cunning. The day after his marriage to a delightful little hunchback, at the top of a perron laid out harmoniously in front of the charming little castle that she brought as her dowry, our epileptic, with his thumbs in the arm-holes of his waistcoat and his other fingers fluttering around his jacket lapels like the pigeons on Saint Mark's Square in Venice, stood wait-ing for his furniture and clothes which were to arrive at any moment when, lo and behold, the two Percherons pulling the precious cargo appeared. He was already making poetic comments about the con-trast between the wonderfully raked sand and the tracks left in it by the rough wheels. Didn't the strength of these kind beasts of burden bring out the delicacy of the façade in which the Gothic blended so nicely with Romanesque memories, a few Renaissance observations, an Algerian discovery, and two extremely Oriental hypotheses? Birds were singing around the large mansard roof which had just been com-pleted on the dining room veranda with its vanes made of the glazed tiles used by the Chinese to roof their pagodas. Life was sweet. After the Percherons turned around, using all of the resources of coquetry at the disposal of sturdy, easygoing horses, they began to unload the furniture. Then, deceitfully, fate placed before the very eyes of the young groom an inscription whose gigantic letters covered the entire cart: *Transport and Moving.*

In order to ward off any questions about the authenticity of the delirium, the cousins told the rest of the family that, several months before her death, the woman sodomized in spite of herself had begun to move off her rocker. Transport and moving. . . . A tall fellow goes straight ahead, pushing aside everyone and everything in his way, to cut a far more glorious path to the ill-fated Dutch candelabra which, with its livery of dark candles mysteriously intact, looks like a strange monstrance intended for a Mass of some color other than white, blue, or pink.

An epileptic fit is never a small matter. Especially from atop a perron. The poor devil tumbled down the steps headfirst and began to plow, with his entire gesticulating body, the impeccable sand. It cost him a heel, two of the fingernails on his right hand, the seat of his pants, and a patch of skin torn off along with the cloth covering it.

In spite of their phlegmatic nature, the Percherons reared up, each of them trying to flee in the opposite direction, so that, unable to turn both ways at once, the cart that had gotten them into this mess wrenched apart, with no more remaining of it and the furniture it was carrying than a tangle of boards, shards of old bottles and porcelain, shreds of silk, on which the Percherons ended up falling after catching their hooves in them, tearing to pieces their panic-stricken breasts.

When calm returned and they had cleared the scene of the tragedy, the young newlyweds, in order to reduce to a minimum or to eliminate entirely the chance of further mishaps, decided that they would never go beyond the walls surrounding the castle grounds where, faithful to their word, they contemplated their fate for thirty years before procreating the same fellow who, now recognized as the Prince of Journalists, is presently recalling, full of gratitude, the two rare creatures whose existence, all wisdom and meditation, willingly became the sedentary prologue to an active life that would lead him, their son, to the highest honors.

From the funeral of a woman sodomized in spite of herself to the funeral of a French president might be the title of the memoirs of this very French family, whose lives turned out successively abominable, peaceful, glorious.

Aren't funeral ceremonies, more than any others, indicative of our civilization? It would thus be natural for the story to describe first some church where, after an appropriate but modest service, devoted relatives and an orphan keep a painful secret. As an epilogue, the distressing but heroic apotheosis of Notre-Dame. A naveful of kings, princes, ministers, archbishops, even loudspeakers that will broadcast the liturgical chants. But on this road taken, from the national as well as the familial point of view, through the changes in regime, as in the slightest intimate details which are faithfully transmitted by the folklore of every decent family, what a wonderful line of continuity! The Prince of Journalists has carefully continued to follow it. That is why, in an era swarming with "defeatists of capitalism" (the expression is his own and he finds it indispensable), he exhorts his readers, at least once a week, in the exercise of bourgeois virtues, which have never ceased being practiced throughout previous centuries, in spite of adversity and its many twists.

As for him, even though he doesn't like to boast, he can't help but admit that his life serves as an ending to the story of such a symbolically French family. The woman sodomized in spite of herself is none other than the France of 1870, invaded, wounded, the same France that would attempt to commit suicide but would not, thanks to God, succeed, at the time of the separation of Church and State. A wisdom sometimes painful but destined for eventual triumph, parallel to that shown by the epileptic and the hunchback, proved able to repair the damage and bring about the reign of the Prince of Journalists, whose glorious era, at least chronologically, coincides with the epic of 1914-1918.

Today, if he feels a string of ideas develop in his mind with the happy swiftness which, as paradoxical as it may seem, was only revealed in all its rhythm and jubilation at the funeral Mass for the

French president, it is, he observes, because the structure of this country attests to the sense of grandeur with order that made the funeral service in Notre-Dame "a celebration of intelligence despite the mourning of the heart," as he stated in quotes, in one of his articles, with so much success that he was defrauded of this find, which was borrowed from him and its birth attributed to the poetess Synovie.

. . . The Prince of Journalists sees the nave of Notre-Dame again in his mind's eye. The great organ is playing. The cardinal-archbishop officiates with an instinct for the train of robes which will earn him the compliments of the grand national coquette.

What can one of the mighty of this earth, one of the opinion makers, do about the distress that overcomes him when the altar boy's little bell bends so many heads, some of which are crowned, in a common meditation?

Thus, the hat which had been carefully set on a safe-looking prie-dieu falls, rolls, subject despite the braking effect of the protruding brim to a movement accelerated by its cylindrical form and very smooth material. And it would have gone all the way to the parvis if, miraculously, the man sitting next to him, as young as he was blond and as blond as he was obliging, hadn't, in the nick of time, caught the fugitive. But since the Prince of Journalists himself had already bent over, two foreheads bang into each other, two heads catch fire, and two arterial systems turn into streams of phosphorous. From these images the reader must not get the idea, however, that appearances were in danger for one second. No, nobody even suspected what sudden and reciprocal conflagration had broken out in the secrecy of the composed faces and the double-breasted vests, the ceremonious cutaways, and especially the black trousers with white stripes. Capable of increasing the intoxication of any heat, the incense, with its mystical breath, fanned these two proper blazes. Now the huge cathedral of Paris was but the tightly fitting container for this enclosed throng, whose sweat was fuel on the flames. Be that as it may, wasn't this a well-mannered, well-groomed crowd? The male element was composed of those men who are always dressed to the teeth and never forget to spray their underarms with cologne before going to official ceremonies.

The staunchest guardians of tradition, professors, superior officers, and dignitaries of the high clergy who couldn't be suspected of hydro-therapeutic extravagance, all of them, either the night before, or that very morning, had, without exception, taken baths, to such an extent were they unanimous and absolute in their desire to honor the representative of France, of every layer of France: the France of liberals, colonizers, administrators, conservatives, mortgagors, Freemasons, religious devotion, and family values.

His excellency the rector of the Catholic University of Paris had carried his scrupulousness to the point of sanding his navel in honor of the man he called a lay saint and who was as holy as a religious saint, since he had paid for his place in the Elysian palace with four sons killed in the war. Yes, four times the man for whom the cathedral had been draped and lighted up granted to his country the sacrifice that Abraham contented himself with undertaking only once for the glory of his jealous God. And to think that they had assassinated the admirable father, the Father. Among all of those who were assembled there behind his catafalque and who, on account of the national eloquence cult, were not easily impressed by speeches, not one of them failed to repeat with emotion the now historic syllables into which the modern patriarch put his entire soul, his great soul, when he collapsed, fatally wounded. "Oh hang it all, this is a bit much," sighed the hero. It was simple but it came straight from the heart and went straight to the hearts of the most virile officials.

As for the women, the most elegant decorations adorning the spheres of the aristocracy, politics, industry, art, literature, even those whose reputations as undaunted coquettes seemed the most unshakable, in the sparkling of the candles their eyes burned like mournful stars. They couldn't hold back tears that worked their way down cheeks whose powder they carried off in torrents leading to the corners of their mouths. Little lipsticks came out of handbags. Hands that could no longer keep from shaking drew, in the form of dikes, a circumflex right side up, a circumflex upside down, and thus, each mouth defended by unctuous and impermeable makeup, underneath the streams that gathered into little pockets of water, created an entire bouquet of geraniums, sweeter-smelling than a garden after a storm. The melted, diluted perfumes complemented one another in penetrating scales of odor which occasionally exploded (for, alas! you can't count on the olfactory discretion of some upstarts found in high society or low society) amid the howling of a handkerchief dipped into one of these essences created to exasperate the nostrils during carnal encounters rather than to pay final tribute to the chief of state.

When the ladies of the family cried, their tears loosened the mourning veils, flags of austere grief, whose starch became the flour thickening this sauce of bitter pleasures instead of smelling, as usual, like the rags used to rub down wet dogs. Add the fact that fate made the Prince of Journalists brush, with the back of his hand, the obliging young man's pants. And because of fate, the obliging young man showed that he wasn't displeased. Ting-a-ling, ting-a-ling. The cardinal-archbishop descends from the altar to the catafalque. He manages the stairs of Notre-Dame better than the plumaged star of a spectacular revue coming down a staircase.

Grand Cross Chevalier of the Legion of Honor, member of the Academy of Moral and Political Science, president of the Society for the Reform of Depraved Youth, the Prince of Journalists wouldn't dream of compromising his career with the scandal that could result from some furtive groping. Glory advises prudence.

But today, at Notre-Dame, the crowd is handpicked. It would be sheer madness to suspect a professional blackmailer in the person of this adolescent, as distinguished as he is well-built, with his aura of innocence, lemon tea, lavender, and English tobacco.

> Ting-a-ling, ting-a-ling,
> Nothing ventured,
> Nothing gained.

Notice how desire makes one a poet. And since this young man with the manners of an embassy attaché is only too happy to let himself be explored, five fingers skilled at handling a pen and quill will soon find out what gives. What a big fat pen and how nice its ink must be. . . .

The master of ceremonies has ordered everyone to rise, to vacate their chairs. The procession begins. People jerk into action, with no wordplay intended, but with plenty of handplay.

"Hands that bluff, soon get rough," was one of the epileptic's favorite sayings. May his soul rest in peace. May all souls rest in peace. Holy water is sprinkled on the catafalque. The Prince of Journalists goes with the flow. He feels someone's breath on the nape of his neck. His right hand stirs and, whack, whack, the crowd is so compact that one can poke about quite comfortably, to the point of getting a cramp in the wrist. But, in spite of the warm moisture that he soon perceives through the cloth and the quivering flesh that cries for mercy even as it palpitates, he refuses to release his prey.

His fingers will let go only when it is their turn to shake the aspersing rod. But even then, the thumb and the index finger will indulge in a game of titillation that will catch the eye of the duchess of Monte Putina, a former beauty, indeed hardly timid at the outset of her career, but whose whorish faculties, in the course of a rather adventurous life, in an extraordinary case of transubstantiation, have become specifically social, political, and worldly. Nobody has Monte Putina's knack for saying the right thing. If she has earned her stripes, one by one, in the demimonde, it has only been by taking on, at the right moment, a distinguished little air, on occasion even resorting to evanescent manners and somewhat amphigoric language. Now that she is married to a genuine duke, she doesn't hesitate, in order to resemble a real aristocrat, to let loose if necessary words grosser than herself (who is not thin).

Thus, at the end of the funeral Mass, she made the Prince of Journalists shudder, simply by whispering these words to him: "So Voronoff pulled off our little operation so well that now we're tickling holy water sprinklers?"

Did this devil of a woman notice anything? With her you never know. Although, to put his mind at ease, the Prince of Journalists had merely to remind himself that she has a strong sense of solidarity. He knows from experience that her discretion can be counted on. Hasn't she acted as if she were his mistress for fifteen years, without ever revealing the mystery of their chaste relationship? Of course she had noticed right off that he was not a man to kid around with decorum. Besides, they have both played by the rules; he hasn't skimped on her salary but he has gotten his money's worth, and she has fulfilled her duties unflinchingly. She has never taken for granted the function of pseudolover earned by a tact rare in the small world of kept women.

Now that she has been adopted by the upper crust, she no longer needs to take precautions. She can breathe easy, revel in her triumph, cut up, explode, slap her thighs, say the first thing that pops into her head. Her awareness of propriety in all circumstances is nonetheless so keen that even the most prudish of the dowagers never fails to remark with a very indulgent smile: "Our dear Esperanza carries on like a silly goose, but she knows which end is up. . . ."

. . . "And my up is warmer than your down, you old hags," thinks Esperanza who, rather dissatisfied with her dysfunctional husband but full of respect for the name he has bestowed upon her, doesn't even entertain the possibility of adultery and has no other resource than that of feasting her eyes on the spectacle of other people's love affairs. They are also in the habit of saying, "Esperanza would bend over backwards for her friends." And in fact, a few days after the remark on the parvis of Notre-Dame, the Prince of Journalists meets at her house the obliging young man whose fairness was certainly more in harmony with dark, funereal Gothic than with the varied beige tones of the drawing room where Esperanza, to gain respite from the Roman palace where she has lived three-quarters of every year since she got married, has afforded herself the paradoxical pleasure of combining cubism (a tame cubism, to be sure, one whose angles offer their apologies with prudent velours) and Biedermeier style.

The obliging young man, if only by the way he failed to respond to those ever so discreetly fluttering eyelids with which the Prince of Journalists appealed to his memory, revealed his English nationality. And by this British phlegm the Prince of Journalists soon recognized the rescuer of his top hat as the son of a Londoner, formerly renowned for her beauty, the marquise of Sussex, Lady Primrose, the "divine lady," as they called her (because of her resemblance to Lady

Hamilton) in the cosmopolitan high society where her marriage to one of the noblest gentlemen had made it possible for her to reign, in spite of having been born into humble if not miserable circumstances.

She had, moreover, hastily left the capital cities for a Florentine, then a Provençal solitude. But when she found out from her son, who had come to stay with her on her hillside, that the Prince of Journalists was going to come to spend some time on the coast, she relished the thought of renewing her relationship with the man she remembered as a little Frenchman champing at the bit, whose hams were strung better than the rest. She hadn't forgotten a certain unfortunate experience thirty years ago, but in the meantime she had had other worries. From a striking little blonde child, hadn't she tried to metamorphose herself into a classic beauty? She had started with her nose, which she wanted so badly to become Greek. But the paraffin injected into it proved unable to keep its stability and came pouring down between the cutis and the cuticle, resting in that dimple on her right cheek that Edward VII, when he was yet but Prince of Wales, had called a well of love. And so, the well of love filled up to the brim and even overflowed, now showing up only as a lump whose removal no surgeon dared attempt.

After having long hidden her plundered beauty, the marquise of Sussex felt such joy at taking up again with high society that she allowed herself neither regrets nor rancor. What great pains she had taken in organizing the luncheon which the Prince of Journalists was urged to attend. She was, moreover, as happy to invite the opinion maker, the friend of old, as he was to be invited. Therefore, optimism, hope, confidence on both ends.

Since Monte Putina will be at the party, there's no reason not to send a postcard to Mussolini. And why not another one to the pope? For she comes and goes as she pleases at the Vatican, our Esperanza, ever since she became a sophisticated Roman lady. If in fact Il Duce counts on her, Saint Peter's successor, who admires her for having managed her affairs so well, scorns neither her advice nor her influence, and he personally asked her to use a charm consecrated by years of noble gallantry and a grand wedding in the service of the interests and the worldly possessions of the Church.

As for the Prince of Journalists, he never misses a chance to remind Europe that it was founded on the Roman Empire, its cult of work, public affairs, judicial affairs, military affairs. But what would have become of this Roman Empire itself if, right when the slaves were going to revolt, Christianity hadn't revealed the holy splendor of sacrifice to the meek?

It would have been the end of *jus romanum,* paternal power, roads running from one colony to the next, highway systems, terraces, aqueducts, this fountain on the square of the little town-village that you have to cross on your way to Lady Primrose's house. These two-thousand-year-old cobblestones are more probably used as a sidewalk than a forum by the grandnephews of the centurions' grand-nephews. But, two birds with one stone, and they should thank the Anglo-Saxon tourists instead of holding it against them if, here as wherever they go, they've taught the local youth to make eyes at everything that moves and blinks, from the roots of their hair to the soles of their feet.

From May to October the young boys walk around wearing only pants and skimpy T-shirts. Thus, the homeowners, male as well as female, realized the necessity of having teenage laborers work as artisans in their gardens or their houses. Young Lord Sussex, moreover, set the example and personally introduced neo-Greek architecture. The Prince of Journalists, as soon as he sees the masons busy on extravagant pergolas and pediments, suddenly realizes that, faithful to the great democratic tradition, he could help the most muscular of these young builders make their way in life. Once they were sanded, washed, and rinsed, finding jobs for them in conservative Parisian journalism would be mere child's play.

2

A Pair of Authentic Ladies
in the Grand Style

NO SOONER HAD HIS DRIVER negotiated a skillful turn, making it possible for him to catch sight of the divine lady whose loving looks and fingers are caressing the bottle of gin in front of her, than, recalling certain passes, unfortunately devoid of all magnetic power, performed by this hand, now yellow and wrinkled but white and plump back then, around something of his which was characterized by the same ridiculous smallness and the same indifference as the neck of this square decanter, the Prince of Journalists, without deigning to tell himself by way of an excuse, justifiable in this case, that a good deed is never wasted, realizes he has been given the opportunity to return the favor, and how! The son, knowing the joy which the mother had tried in vain to introduce him to, began, in spite of his confident nature, to blush so much that he took on the cardinalesque color of the material in which the drinking woman was clothed.

As for the boozer, the sight of this distinguished caller stepping out of his car was all that it took for her to turn back into the marquise of Sussex. Thus she stands up and moves forward with a stateliness accentuated even more by a pair of pants whose legs both end in a train.

For her, an innate sense of dignity is not incompatible with stylishness. She knows how to dress in a way that is both intimate and ostentatious. She uses an exquisite but not undignified gesture to hide the cheek where lay, formerly, the well of love. But then (ruse or chance?) the diamond on her ring catches a ray of sunlight which she beams straight into the eye of the Prince of Journalists. The latter is not about to be taken for a mere lark. He hasn't forgotten the song that the marquise of Sussex used to hum when, as young Primrose, she would try so hard to run his little red flag up the greased pole:

Lark, pretty lark,
I shall pluck your head.
Lark, lark in the sky,
I shall pluck your tail.

You must beware of pretty pluckers, you mustn't let yourself get fleeced, the hunchback told her son repeatedly when he became old enough to visit "whorizontals." So, stand up straight, especially if you're small. Besides, the powerful crimson monstress will feel inferior before long, since she must resign herself to uncovering the swelling on her face in order to extend her hand to be kissed. Her taffeta container nonetheless catches the eye in an apotheosis of light. She and the Prince of Journalists up on his high horse bring to mind an historic scene, something like the meeting that could take place between Frederick the Great and Catherine the Great, if they could resuscitate, at this instant, in this setting.

A solemn silence, the silence of noon, more distressing than at midnight, froze the footmen, planted here and there in front of the thickets.

The Prince of Journalists' chauffeur, a good little lad in our opinion, with quicksilver in his veins, holds his pose, leaning against the hood, and seems no less of a statue than these young pink and blond giants who, the divine lady is quick to explain, she and her noble lord of a son love to have around, for the sake of pomp (and can those boys pump!).

And here we must add a note on the linguistic ability of the first woman, after she got married, to be called marquise of Suck-sex and Lady Roseleaf. She speaks French with a deplorable accent and syntax, but in private she wouldn't use any other language to make puns, for which Monte Putina gave her a taste when they were, many years ago, dancer/singers in a Southampton nightclub.

Monte Putina, Esperanza Gobain at the time, exiled from her exuberant and native Phocaean city by the necessities of a whoring career off to an unpromising start, had no more intention, in the hazy mist, of hiding her Marseillaise birth than of disavowing her love of garlic, Pernod, and risqué stories.

Autochthonous on the other hand and having, due to the British humidity everywhere she had lived, a complexion as clear as liquid, Primrose lived with her abusive father. Esperanza sheltered her in her room where a parrot would repeat, mimicking the Englishwoman, the dirty words that her meridional friend had taught her. The *papagaio*'s jeering exasperated the chorus girl so badly that she began to monitor her accent on each word of classical smut that she spoke in their little household. As for other words or sentences, she didn't care about liaisons, differences between feminine and masculine, singular and plural. Thus, while she didn't know how to ask for salt without making ten mistakes in three words, she never ran the risk of getting lost in the arcana of the lewdest puns or double entendres. In order to encourage her pupil's progress Esperanza had even given her a *Selected Anthology of Bodyguard Talk* as a New Year's present, which remains to this day one of the two bedside books of the marquise of Sussex, the other being, as one might imagine, the Holy Bible.

After the Southampton nightclub went under, Esperanza and Primrose each went their separate ways to try their luck. At first they wrote to each other after parting company, but soon their epistolary activity became less frequent and then stopped completely.

Thus, their chance meeting a few years later in a Parisian dressmaker's shop made them cry out in surprise.

Esperanza was so delighted to see her Primrose transformed into a lady that, in spite of the fact that her manners had become refined and even a tad bit precious, she let out a resounding exclamation, giving the greatest fright (this took place before the war) to the ladies waiting their turn in the fitting room. Primrose married, and to a lord— Esperanza couldn't believe it. Primrose gave proof: her wedding band, this sapphire engraved with the coat of arms of the House of Sussex, and the love letters, right there in her purse, bearing witness to the joys of adultery, the very sanction of any legitimate union.

Some time later, as a result of her recent unhappy experience with the young man who was on his way to becoming the Prince of Journalists, and since it now became clear to her, from his excessive circumspection in public, as well as from his shortfalls in private, that in order to stifle any lurking malevolence, he had to have, or rather, display a mistress, Primrose clued Esperanza in—now Esperanza de Saint-Gobain for, while the luckier half of the little duo went off to the court of England, the other half moved in with the nobility of the demimonde.

Thus Esperanza simultaneously corrected her Marseillaise accent, learned how to use the imperfect subjunctive and the future perfect, and removed from her upper lip the peach fuzz which, although responsible for her success as a Mediterranean woman in Albion, would only expose her now that she had decided to pass for the illegitimate offspring of Catherine de Medici's love affair with a page from Tours.

So full steam ahead for the blonde Venetian. Esperanza keeps her head covered with little bonnets, wears princess dresses, and over a tight-fitting bottle green bodice with two pearl-laden braids beating against it, she lets floods of moonstones and amethysts stream down in such torrents that she's sued for impersonating Mélisande wherever she goes: at the races, at Maxim's, at dress rehearsals, as well as at the grand velocipede festivities.

Since she would only accept lovers who were artists, undernourishment had caused her to go rather quickly from a Valois stick figure to medieval evanescence. One must also add that, a good mother, she preferred to deprive herself of necessities and even luxuries rather than trim education expenses for the child fathered by an old friend of her family, a little Polish Jew who dealt in embroidered finery for brothels, and whom she surely would never have left (she always did have a taste for respectability) if the poor fellow hadn't been murdered by a pimp representing a tight-fisted customer to whom, in accordance with the law, he had sent a bill.

Esperanza was thus in a nearly hopeless situation when Primrose drove her to the Prince of Journalists' house. In business or love affairs, the latter was already, as he is today, a believer in precision. Esperanza, who was beginning to take her hennins seriously and enjoyed the lunar moods which, despite a basically positive nature, anemia, with giant steps, had brought about in her, at first rankled at the cynicism with which the conditions of the contract were revealed to her, accompanied by an ardor that resembled preventive anger rather than budding love. The more Primrose urged her to accept, the less she dared to cross the Rubicon of chaste, organized, high-class gallantry. Besides, all the gold in the world wouldn't have paid for the resentment she felt at the thought that the sparkle in her big black eyes would never have a chance of turning the little fellow on, even though he seemed to be made of tinder. Such was the extent of her troubles that she poured them onto the sole surviving member of her entire family, her older sister, a poor girl who, after a succession of avatars, had finally wound up in a brothel on Rue Blondel where, in spite of an elegiac nature, she earned her living by picking up pennies with her lips—though not with those of the mouth.

This tender creature was just starting to get annoyed at the straits to which her naturally pure heart had driven her. She coveted, moreover, her younger sister's medieval frock. Decked out in this finery, she would have had no trouble, it seemed to her, getting seated in one of those Latin Quarter restaurants faithfully frequented by Maurice Barrès in his sensual, anarchist youth and where he had pinched her right buttock one day. And now, in the enumeration of the pros and cons, Esperanza mentioned the old friendship which linked up her probable pseudolover-to-be with the man who was then basking in the glory incumbent upon a nationalist writer and member of parliament from the Les Halles district. The penny collector was beside herself with joy at the thought that Esperanza would surely meet him and could let him know that the beautiful girl whose rump had tempted the student would give herself entirely and free of charge to the vociferous partisan for the return of Alsace and Lorraine. So Esperanza finally gave up her dreams and quit trying to look like a damsel of yore. Between her and the Prince of Journalists it had been stipulated that she would pattern her clothes and hairstyle after Helleu, whose drypoint etchings had succeeded in creating the standard for elegant, proper womanhood. Very little makeup, simple furs, never any jewelry except for pearls, and above all she must remember to present her son as the child of a very rich, very noble, and very enigmatic Polish lord. Theoretically meals and evenings out belonged to her protector, too busy to spend time with his so-called mistress anywhere but in public. Esperanza got so much per month and had the right to sleep with whomever she wished, provided that nobody knew about it, for the Prince of Journalists was supposed to pass for the jealous lover by making, once every two weeks, a scene at the opera, in her loge, on the pretext that she had, with her white arm, brushed against a friend's sleeve when he stopped to greet her.

At first this verbal agreement was only valid on a trial basis, but as Esperanza's behavior left nothing to be desired, before long it became permanent. She was the first one, moreover, to talk about canceling it when the duke of Monte Putina asked for her hand. Even though her relations with the Prince of Journalists never amounted to anything but a show during their fifteen-year pseudo-affair, they had nonetheless been fortunate enough to manage a few private meetings, which Esperanza ably took advantage of to develop a subtle, innate sense of legality. Thus, she accorded a preference to her pseudolover for any union, legitimate or otherwise, that bound her. So she went to see him in order to explain the duke's offer and give him priority in case he wanted to tie the knot.

In this excessive thoughtfulness, unfortunately, the Prince of Journalists saw only blackmail and, wild with rage, he cried: "What do you take me for, madam, one of those men who marry their mistresses?"

To which, suddenly forgetful of her efforts to play the Valois, the damsel, or the very proper lady one after the other, Esperanza answered with this verse:

> "Supposing you were one of my aunts
> To you I would have extended
> The sausage suspended
> In my pants."

She was screaming at the top of her lungs. The hint was so obvious, the Marseillaise accent so sonorously revived, that a decade and a half of efforts seemed clearly wasted. The Prince of Journalists found just the right words to calm down the incongruous singer, thanked her for her cooperation, and let her become a duchess. They parted good, very good friends and, as he figured it would be more economical and less risky not to replace her, he played the inconsolable lover, never missing a chance to let a lock, supposedly of the duchess of Monte Putina's hair, fall out of his wallet. He even told a few close friends the moving story of the meeting when, torn between two loves, Esperanza made the decision by flipping a coin right in his office. As luck would have it, she followed the Roman noble, but before leaving, she picked up the scissors on the managerial table, where they served to clip and trim the prose of overly prolific contributors paid by the line and, instead of stabbing herself in the heart, as she was tempted to do for a minute, snipped off her prettiest curl. The Prince of Journalists made a point of rolling his eyes each time he happened to meet *his* Esperanza in public while, moved by such loyal devotion, she returned the favor, arranging dates for him with handsome young men, only sorry that her son, having failed to live up to his promises, didn't fill the bill, for she successfully combined family spirit with a taste for procuring inherited from her mother and her many great-aunts and grandmother, all madams on Rue Bouterie.

In her isolation, Primrose never stopped seeing Esperanza. She liked to hear about the world that she had left behind, for which gin was only a partial consolation, from the very lips of the woman who, wishing to return a favor, urged her to go back to it. Monte Putina was counting on the miracle of her lustrous eyes. The puffiness, the blue complexion ("now I've become lady Couperose" [Blotchy Face] joked the marquise of Sussex), the bulging waistline: what were these drawbacks compared to that lovely look in her eyes, that stately bearing?

How majestic she is! noted the Prince of Journalists upon seeing how high she was in stature and in tone, in the courtyard of the little farmhouse, whose façade was discolored by a light which shone too brightly.

All he could do was murmur: "Marquise. . . ."

As for her, with a head buzzing from sun and gin, she pleaded: "Do call me, as you used to, Primrose, Roseleaf, Couperose, or rather, no, I'm too old, call me Elizabeth, Betsy, Pète sec."

Hypnotized by the wonderful eyes, the Prince of Journalists returns upstream: Beat sick, Betsy, Elizabeth, Cut-rose, Roseleaf, Primrose. The lovely name is more precious than mountain air, rock crystal, edelweiss. Merely by uttering it, you're elevated to a considerable altitude! But before taking off, we ought to make sure the marquise is safe. Why did Paul Valéry insist that he would never write: "The marquise went out at five o'clock. . ."? Now that he has, in his welcoming speech for the admission of Marshal Pétain to the Academy, given proof of simple but all the more undeniable common sense by congratulating the brilliant tactician for not having forgotten to use cannons in the course of the European war, how could anyone think this great mind would persist in his prejudices concerning the coming and going of grand ladies and remain unjustly, scornfully silent—he, the very poet of "The Young Fate," if he could see that English marquise return to her arbor hand in hand with the opinion maker, while the footmen, imperceptibly, began to spring back to life, each one standing before his thicket. The chauffeur of the Prince of Journalists himself, this tough little lad who has his feet on the ground and carries a head on his shoulders with the face of a Marcel, thinks his boss is dancing a minuet with a large begonia. This flower doesn't usually play a very distinguished role in common expressions. But in this case the exception proves the rule and the young mechanic puts all the respect he is capable of into this comparison suggested, moreover, by the glorious memory of the paintings done by his former boss, a decorated artist, member of the Institute specializing in portraits of cardinals and begonias.

Primrose, however, who ordinarily drinks in order to forget about the lumps of paraffin in her right cheek, pours herself a double. Ah, yes! In addition, today she's trying not to remember a pitiful attempt, not even daring to suspect that he who perpetrated it long ago would be only too happy to try it again, this time for good. Yes, the Prince of Journalists, after having drunk her in with his eyes, raises them and is delighted to find, through the vine leaves covering the arbor, a patch of sky which he contemplates until he swoons, thinking he is Ganymede being carried off to ethereal heights by an eagle. All it takes is for his eyes to fall back to earth and the Prince of Journalists imagines himself seated in the freshest spheres of Olympus, to the right of Jupiter who has taken on the appearance of a swan, a bull, a shower of gold, the cardinalesque form of a marquise drinking gin.

He whispers: "Primrose."

She answers: "Darling."

Then he begs her: "Primrose, tell me about your life during those years that I had the misfortune to spend far from you. . . ."

He has adopted the sweetest voice, an almost cajoling tone, yet one not lacking in dignity.

But nothing, whether it be the need to confide that can suddenly come over even the most standoffish of people when some witness of their past glory appears before them, or the false memories invariably conjured up by the pride stemming from regret for what once was and hasn't continued to be—no, nothing could make her give up that discretion which, since time immemorial, hasn't failed to contribute to the grandeur of every English lady, even if she did begin her career as a singer in a Southampton dive. With her right cheek casually placed in the palm of the corresponding hand to hide the debacle of the well of love, she overwhelms the Prince of Journalists' little eyes with all the splendor she can muster. As for him, despite the protective shag of his eyelashes and eyebrows, his gaze can no longer keep afloat, his thoughts can no longer touch bottom. His strength is ebbing to such an extent that he is barely able to remark in a defensive outburst, "The woman is trying to hypnotize me." Hurry, hurry, a life preserver for a half-drowned conscience. Pinch the left arm with the right thumb and index finger, and vice versa. In a wink, his teeth bite the upper, then the lower lip, and again the lower and the upper. His knees knock together as hard as they can to hurt themselves, but what's the use of this violence? The Prince of Journalists can hardly keep from drifting into a deep, trancelike sleep. He gets up and he feels as though he is going to fall asleep on his feet. He turns around the impassable marquise, but regardless of his position on the circumference of the circle, the center of this circle, at any given moment, remains this gaze whose projection beams between his shoulder blades, goes around his neck and blends in with this tie that would choke him if he didn't pull it off at once. So now he can tell himself he will never be a dog in the lap of his future mistress. Heartened, he sits down again, determined to live up to his reputation as a man of reason.

First resolution, then: go on the offensive. You have to be ready to deliver an ultimatum. Besides, who could accuse him in good faith of having acted discourteously on the occasion of this summation?

"Answer, Primrose. You really ought to confide in me. I only arrived this early in the hope of a private interview."

Primrose says nothing in response. He insists. Primrose doesn't flinch.

Ah! how to touch this divine lady, how to get across to a deaf heart behind the majestic breast to which the paraffin has undoubtedly slipped its cuirass all the way down from the nose? It makes you want to be suddenly metamorphosed into a corkscrew in order to draw out secrets buried too deeply. But to what avail is the greatest strength in trying to pry open a hermetically sealed soul? No use grinding your teeth. Better to insinuate.

". . . And if you told me about your joys?"

Will the marquise answer? She has already opened her mouth. Disappointment. She merely gulps down her seventh shot of gin and simultaneously shrugs her shoulders to indicate that she and joy . . .

"And if you told me of your sorrows?"

Her shoulders sag under the weight of sorrows which it would be sadistic to insist that she bring up.

"And if you told about your life *at home?*"

Disdainful scowl on the lips that surely won't condescend to praise the intimate joys of pumped-up pomp, literally and figuratively, nor recall that unfortunate incident that caused the suicide of the most handsome of footmen after the same fellow's murder of a young lady with whom he was in love and couldn't marry, considering the meagerness of his wages which nonetheless wouldn't be increased, since he had not only failed to satisfy but even pretended not to see the desires that the mother and the son had made very clear to him.

". . . And if you told me of your travels?"

The wave of a disenchanted hand toward the sea reveals scorn for all the different kinds of illusions that can induce the dissatisfied to go see what's happening behind the horizon.

". . . And if you told me about the delights of motherhood?"

The index finger in front of the mouth says "Hush." The Prince of Journalists blushes. What's the use of playing with fire? His head is burning hot. He is nonetheless determined not to come out empty-handed.

". . . And if you told me about your husband's death?"

This time he has hit the mark. The death of the divine lady's husband! That's right up her alley. Every detail of this somber adventure belongs to the history of the English nobility. So she can talk. First she will have to explain that the old marquis of Sussex had always been a tiger-hunting enthusiast. He didn't feel quite right if, at least once a year, he hadn't gone stalking wild animals deep in some equatorial forest. It was there and not elsewhere that he had taken his young bride for their honeymoon. She had, we might note incidentally, sworn never to set foot there again, after seeing her charm devastated by the green veils in which the new husband had wrapped her in order to protect her from the sun and the mosquitoes, as they used to do, come summer, in the paternal hovel of hellish memory, in an attempt to shield the clock and the ceiling lamp from flyspecks. It was therefore agreed that the marquis would go big-game hunting all by himself while she would stay in latitudes better suited to set off her beauty. Their life followed this pattern up to the day when the indefatigable cynegetic hero became paralyzed in both legs.

In spite of the attentive care with which he was treated, old Lord Sussex was soon as grouchy as a bear. His disposition soured day by day, and when the anniversary of his usual departure date arrived, he made such a fuss that they had to send him off. In spite of his promise to her, wearing a lovely colonial helmet complete with carefully chosen veils ranging from turquoise blue to jade green with emerald in between, with eyes deeper than ever among these marine colors whose transparency revealed nothing of the face underneath, beautiful as an Amphitrite, and wearing an unbelievably convincing melancholy, pitiful expression, Primrose went with the marquis, that dear creature who so loved shooting big guns.

No sooner was he in Africa than they tried to take advantage of the invalid. They took him to the leafiest spot in the park surrounding the governor's house, but not about to mistake a grove for a jungle, nor for the odor of big game the stink of the garbage that the servants hadn't taken the trouble to throw farther away, he tore up Primrose's veils, then broke the Eureka carbine that she had given him by way of a rifle over the colonial helmet by which, fortunately, her skull was protected. Seeing that one of the Negroes placed at the disposal of the noble couple made as if to defend the martyred spouse, the marquis didn't hesitate to strangle him with his still vigorous hands. Once he had thus stipulated that he didn't intend to be fooled, they explained to him very, very gently that they were going to go hunting for real—and, in fact, they did.

The divine lady likes to describe the little troop on the march, first the porters, then the old English servants wearing wigs, short pants, and white stockings (liveried in the colors of the House of Sussex), then herself, tucked comfortably into her palanquin, with her veils patched up and, whenever the trail was wide enough, her husband by her side, otherwise right behind her, but always pushed by the particular Negro that the chief porter wished to reward, for, in spite of his somewhat lively show of temper in the governor's park, he was much loved and they fought over the honor of driving his little cart.

". . . His little cart," repeats the Prince of Journalists, dazzled, and he evokes a certain folding chair at the side of a little lake. The old lord's excursion is in fact not without resemblance to his father's fishing trips. As far as the animal hierarchy is concerned, there is undoubtedly the same difference between a tiger and a bleak-fish as there is, socially, between a marquis and a bourgeois and, medically, between an Olympian paralysis and the misery of congenital epilepsy. On the other hand, for the cosmopolitan beauty that a surgical blunder forced to retire under an arbor with the Mediterranean coastline at her feet, as comparable as her life may seem at first glance with that once led by a hunchback in Seine-et-Oise, hiding her hump behind the walls of a park whose entire liquid element was limited to the dimensions of a tiny and perhaps enchanting but in any case artificial pond, it does not follow that one of these creatures should or can be confused with the other.

There is resemblance and not identity.

The son of the epileptic and the hunchback is thus at liberty to enjoy remorselessly the atmosphere conducive to the blossoming of memories grafted with hopes, since nothing incestuous sullies his feelings for the divine lady.

Having established this fact and because his love, just like Caesar's wife, must be above suspicion, the Prince of Journalists dreams that he is Primrose's son, the teenage marquis. The hunchback certainly possessed a number of qualities, but her hump, which she hooked, cut, scraped on every obstacle, had given her a taste for self-effacement. Primrose, on the contrary, half supine in her armchair, hardly minds displaying the splendors that are revealed rather than hidden by the folds of her ample garment. She goes on talking, evoking the baobabs, the panthers, the Negroes who took her for a goddess, and her listener, captivated by the incantatory charm of the voice, doesn't need to catch every word to know that there's nothing she says that isn't perfect, wonderful.

The hunchback—since the memory revolves around the hunchback—the hunchback wasn't a real woman, with her chest going inward only to stick out, and how, on her back. So he didn't have a mother. He could have killed her without being matricidal. And he would have killed her and he would kill her in retroactive intention if the divine lady demanded it. For Primrose, he would kill anyone and even that handsome young man who, over yonder, with an imposing lady in black on one of his arms, the other laden with roses, is coming forward dressed in swimming trunks that match the color of the day. From the distance, he can recognize (owing to his age he is in fact farsighted, but evil be to him who evil thinks) the man who was sitting next to him in Notre-Dame. Despite the latter's complaisance and discretion, he knows that he will hardly be able to forgive him for having a mother by whom, in a mere twenty minutes, he has come to feel possessed. This countryside worthy of Attic demigods, these pergolas, this landscape, both grandiose and familiar, the light at this warm time of day, what more is needed to create the mood, the atmosphere of a Greek tragedy? Did he suspect yesterday, when his gymnastics teacher was teaching him to throw the discus, did he suspect that his soul as well as his body would make him deserve to appear on urns where skillfully draped women pull along in their wake a man with an orator's mask, that is, a man who would have been a journalist had he lived two thousand years later. . . .

The flowered adolescent tows, from one end to the other of the huge doormat that serves as a meadow, his godmother, the majestic Augusta. Beloved of fate, all he can think of is gathering bouquets and putting on airs for old ladies, even though his fortune and his birth allowed him to attend, at the earliest age and without a peep out of anyone, a national funeral; who could blame us for thinking that, in his place, we would take greater advantage of various possibilities to prevail over the *Times*, Northcliffe Press, and to cut the ground from under the feet of the *Manchester Guardian*.

Well, no use getting all worked up.

Instead, listen to Primrose, who seems to have become a female Ulysses narrating adventures in which, a male Penelope, the opinion maker delights in dreaming that he wasn't deprived of a role.

So, when she gets to the death of her husband (whom, the scandal-mongers dared to claim, though without being able to prove it, she had murdered in complicity with her lover at the time, an absinthe-sodden French warrant officer), when the divine lady tells how the noble old man, the dear creature who so loved tiger-hunting, sitting in his little cart, was lacerated by the claws of the prince of animals, the Prince of Journalists—that is to say, the most rational of rational animals, whose nostril swells at the memory of all the bloodshed—agrees: "Yes, Primrose, I did claw the marquis of Sussex, and for you I'm ready to do it again."

She who has already risen to greet her son and Augusta can now only murmur: "Oh! darling!"

3

An Imperial Highness
with Liberal Ideas

WHEN SPEAKING OF HER SON in private, as soon as she tries to explain some trait of his whimsical character, Primrose never fails to conclude: "Well, what do you expect, he's a Crapulet de Mountscrewyou."

This is intended not as a condemnation of her son's morals and the company he keeps, but as a reminder that the bride brought back from Italy in the sixteenth century by a marquis of Sussex was the daughter of Romeo and Juliet, whose custody the Capulets and the Montagues, despite their pact of reconciliation on their children's grave, had begun to fight over, soon deciding that neither of them wanted her. The poor little thing whom the Capulets offered to the Montagues, while the Montagues claimed to entrust her to the Capulets, would have starved to death if she hadn't been taken in by Juliet's nurse who, in turn, was only too happy to marry her off to an English gentleman passing through Verona. According to legend, it was from this ancestress, herself the fruit of the love of those most passionate of lovers, that the Sussex lords inherited their sensual, chivalrous, melancholic nature. Of course, it would have been rash to claim that the Italian woman was reincarnated in each one of her descendants, but her blood, though mixed with others, nonetheless continued to flow in the veins of the naked young man towing Augusta, his godmother, toward the arbor.

If Augusta, a genuine archduchess and distant cousin of the late marquis, had overlooked the difference in Primrose's religious persuasion and her shady background when the time came to stand godmother, it was because not only did the antiquity of the family speak for her godson, but above all, sentimental and not afraid to admit it, Augusta felt strongly attached to the child who had received and would be destined to pass on the good qualities of Romeo and Juliet's daughter with whom she, through a great-grandmother born of the marquis of Sussex, shared certain intellectual if not physical characteristics.

Hungarian by birth, Hapsburg by marriage, and widowed by the heart of a Czech national hero, Augusta has never lived for more than three months in a town that didn't number several of Beethoven's houses, one of Mozart's apartments, and a room rented by Schubert. She recalls with a touch of shame the weeks spent in Salzburg where only Mozart holds a place of honor. But, very musical, Augusta doesn't limit herself to the classics: despite the repulsion that Gypsies inspire in her, she is crazy about czardas and she has judiciously chosen the most excitable ones, producing a striking contrast with the funeral marches that she plays every morning in remembrance of General Štefánik, the great patriot, founder, along with Masaryk and Beneš, of the valiant Czechoslovakian Republic, for, though a member of the imperial family by marriage and having remained faithful to Austria when that great nation was partitioned, Augusta followed the example of her late cousin Empress Elizabeth in refusing to let herself be contaminated by the tyrannical spirit of the Hapsburgs.

During the war, Augusta didn't hesitate to conspire for the independence of Hungary and the reconstitution of the kingdom of Bohemia.

Until the tragedy of Sarajevo, she had scorned Countess Sophie Chotek, the morganatic wife of Archduke Franz Ferdinand. Like everyone else, she called her "the servant" because she had been a lady-in-waiting, and in order to regain her esteem, the Czech countess had to wait for the opportunity to use her body as a rampart for her murdered husband.

Shortly before his death, the archduke had met Kaiser Wilhelm II in Bohemia in order to discuss the further partitioning of Europe for his children, momentarily removed from the throne. Franz Ferdinand loved the Czechs and the southern Slavs, moreover, and he used all of his influence to prove it to them. When he died, Augusta decided to continue this policy, and she therefore pinned all of her hopes on the Czechs.

She was already a dignified person who, in spite of her liberal ideas and her refined tastes, wasn't the least bit eccentric and never kidded around with etiquette. Even when she was behind the wheel of her old jalopy, she could be seen with a feathered hat atop her most serene, aristocratic hairdo, and a dustcoat that in fact kept but very little dust off of the majestic gown streaming with the pearls of twenty estates in hock. In turning down the chauffeurs that were provided to her, she invoked her Christian sentiments and the universal need for penance in order to win the war.

In reality, her distribution of holy cards in the barracks, her hospital visits, her grand expeditions to inspect the abandoned countryside, and even her trips to the frontlines were mere pretexts: if Augusta didn't want anyone to be aware of her comings and goings, it was because she was conspiring. Always on the move, her action radiated from two centers: Prague and Budapest. Although born in Budapest, she preferred Prague, whose castle overlooking a host of baroque palaces would surely fit her like a glove when, as she enjoyed imagining, she and her husband entered triumphantly, as queen and king. Of course, they would start out as vassals of the senior branch, but, with the help of the so-called gymnastic organization of the Sokols which, her political instincts told her, would develop in the future, in ten or fifteen years, twenty at the most, the time would be ripe, overripe even, for a new expedition that would allow them to shake off the yoke of Austria forever. Among the nobility and the masses an awakening of national consciousness was taking place. The memory of the Czechoslovakian people, leaping over centuries of exasperating humiliation, suddenly recalled how the emperor used to tremble before his greatest captain: Wallenstein, the son of Hussites, whose wealth, power, and army were such that in a single wing of his palace in Prague he could quarter enough soldiers to defeat the Turks and the Venetians, rout Mansfeld's army at Dessau, drive the king of Denmark from Jutland, and receive, after the purchase of Mecklenburg from Ferdinand II, the title of Admiral of the Baltic.

But, as Schiller showed in his trilogy, every iambic pentameter of which Augusta knew by heart, Wallenstein, not content with his great fortune, aspired to the crown of Bohemia, but never wore it.

As for the kingdom that the great captain hadn't succeeded in carving out with his sword, Augusta planned to use her influence and her talent for stirring up public opinion to treat herself to it threefold, since she threw in Slovakia and Moravia along with Bohemia.

Her hopes knew no bounds and sometimes, in the middle of the countryside, she would stop her car just to rub her hands and say in French, a diplomatic language well-suited to her little projects: "We'll let it simmer, then throw oil on the fire at just the right time." Thus, squatting, depending on the season, in the dust or in the mud, she would crank up a motor that nobody would have dreamed of starting automatically. If the weather was cold, she had to turn the handle around and around before hearing the symptomatic rumbling under the hood, but what did she care?

She already knew what kind of party she would give for her coronation and, being a gourmet, she had begun immediately to compose the menus for the banquets with which she would interlard the official ceremonies. She had written to Cosima Wagner and to her son

Siegfried, whom she begged to leave Bayreuth to follow her into an Eden which, however, she didn't name. Cosima, right off the bat, thought it was Tahiti, and being a good-hearted girl and remembering the unhappy peregrinations of her poor mother, the baroness of Agoult, who had suffered considerably on account of her lover's vagabond romanticism, Cosima, vestal virgin in the temple of memory having no desire to abandon her place of worship yet nonetheless wanting to practice the art of accommodating crowned heads in her best interests, a trade whose tricks had been codified by the great Richard in order to improve his relations with Ludwig II of Bavaria, Cosima who was thinking of resting on her laurels rather than lugging around the souvenirs of her genius among which, in petticoats and lace alone—his composing attire—he had left enough to fill a freight train, Cosima said neither yes nor no. And with that, Augusta, by return mail, implied that the new Eden wasn't as far from Germany as everyone seemed to think. Furthermore, always ready to play a patriotic tune, Augusta let Liszt's daughter imagine that it might be Poland. In any event, the artists wouldn't be responsible for the moving costs and as for Siegfried, they would make it worth his while. . . .

The correspondence with the Wagners, moreover, gave a very incomplete account of Augusta's organizational activity. Thus she looked in Prague and vicinity for some local Goethe to set up in her palace or in one of the nearby outbuildings of that palace. For the glory of a reign which unfortunately never was, she encouraged the arts with such enthusiasm that the initial stimulus continued to animate minds, hearts, and talents. The present renaissance of historical painting in Czechoslovakia is, for example, the result of her efforts.

In the middle of the war, she had fearlessly set up exhibitions and shows, and organized a contest whose subject was and could only be the famous Defenestration. She was willing, moreover, to pay her dues and went so far as to remove her usual attire to pose in a national costume for an old painter who was all the more flattered to be representing an archduchess as a local peasant woman since, in his portraits, all consisting of scenes meant to inspire the patriotism of an oppressed people, he was used to placing on the shoulders of his subjects the heads of his wife, his friends and acquaintances, even his maid if she had cleaned and cooked well.

Since she had to reckon with Israel, Augusta curried favor with anyone who could boast of being closely or distantly related to the Rothschilds. She spread the word that if it had been up to her, she would have arranged long ago for the disappearance of the inscription in Hebrew that adorns the Christ on Charles Bridge and recognizes him as the true son of the true God. For centuries, the Jews have had to regild this inscription each year, as a punishment for the spittle with which one of their number, in the fifteenth century, gratified the second person of the Holy Trinity.

The latter promise, as one may well imagine, was a pious lie on the part of the very pious Augusta who, despite the hope she had given to the sons of Judas, had, in her heart of hearts, decided to collect a tithe substantial enough to encrust the Christ on Charles Bridge with precious stones.

The old emperor Franz Josef didn't like to hear about Augusta's excursions, not that he suspected her of playing the rebel, but simply because he who had sworn (and kept his oath until death) never to touch an electric switch and never to get into a car couldn't tolerate an archduchess of such a perfect kind who drove all by herself. So he called Augusta a little anarchist. There was, naturally, a touch of ironic indulgence in this accusation, which he grumbled more and more often. In order to forestall such reproaches, she was obliged—a real feat—without ever breaking the rules of etiquette, to invent new pranks every day. But whenever she got out of line, on the occasion of each outburst, under the pretense of paradox, she managed to expose, on the subject of foreign or domestic affairs of the Empire, views that were original enough for her occasionally to be compared with her great-aunt by marriage, Empress Maria Theresa.

Thus all was going well. Augusta envisioned herself with a crown on her head. She was already dreaming of suites with hot and cold running water, main drainage and central heating, a whole series of conveniences that would avenge her for the waiting-room armchairs, armoires, and beds which had ruined the white and gold of the imperial palaces, when the archduke, her husband, died of indigestion on the Romanian front. Now that she was a widow, the throne was beyond her grasp. She gave some serious thought to finding a new husband with whom she could make a triumphant entry into Prague, but everyone was busy fighting and, the height of disgrace, the emperor advised her, in a tone that disallowed any refusal, to spend her mourning period in Hungary on the lands that she had inherited upon her parents' death.

For her, this meant exile.

On a dark November morning, Augusta left Vienna.

She was abandoning her best friend, the old asthmatic car, and, just as a sentimental amazon places a kiss on her horse's breast, she brushed her lips against the hood whose heart had beat only for her. Thus, at the height of emotion, she couldn't bear to remain a minute longer in the presence of this companion of her dearest hopes, now destroyed. In spite of the snow that had begun to fall, she went outside and waited for her baggage to be loaded. While she paced up and down, she noticed that even though the Venetian blinds and double windows were hermetically closed, the porter's daughter had already taken possession of the piano at which she, Augusta, had dreamt of seating one of the Wagners by her side. And the stupid girl, all the better to flout her, was banging out "The Beautiful Blue Danube" with all her might. Augusta, on her sidewalk, brought to mind Mary Stuart, whose portrait had fortunately inspired her arrangement of her widow's veils. Like Mary Stuart, she was going to address a few well-chosen words to the riverbank before boarding, for, again like Mary Stuart, she was destined to travel by water. The beautiful blue Danube was no longer the waltz known to make chairs dance, now the beautiful blue Danube wasn't even the refrain massacred at the hands of old housekeepers, the beautiful blue Danube had let itself turn into a gendarme, a hangman by whom the sentence of exile would be carried out.

Augusta had already been on the embarcadero for quite awhile when a little lieutenant, a small-fry baron of a species no rarer in Austria than the herring in the North Sea, came up and handed her, on behalf of the emperor, a bouquet of violets, nearly black violets, for, in high circles, there was less concern for offering her flowers than for reminding her of her mourning. So she wasn't going to take the trouble to thank him. Besides, the young Turk, as though he wanted to duck a well-deserved slap, broke himself in half in a bow that was more servile than respectful. When he stood up again, he took from his pocket a little round cardboard box which he gave to Augusta. Exasperated, she asked him if the ridiculous carton contained goat droppings or a pearl necklace. The young officer, frightened by the lorgnette that she had trained on him with the tenderness of a machine gun, stammered out that it was caviar. He made the mistake of adding a few words in praise of sturgeon eggs.

Augusta slapped him with one hand while, with the other, she threw his presents into the river. Then she gathered up her robe and, without so much as a glance at this town and its inhabitants whom she cursed, stepped on board.

To add to the melancholy of the naturally greenish waters which, with the first snows, seemed black, the ship that would take her from Vienna to Budapest was called *The Empress Elizabeth*. From stem to stern, including the first-class cabins, there were nothing but busts and effigies of the unfortunate sovereign. Augusta began to miss the violets for, as a good lesson to the vulgar, rowdy crowd congesting the stairways, the walkways, and even, despite the inclement season, the deck, she would have gladly laid flowers before one of these statues whose plaster reproduced the majestic features and bearing of her cousin and friend with a crying resemblance.

And, in fact, Augusta began to cry out loud.

The lady-in-waiting who always followed her at a respectful distance had a hard time keeping away the circle of onlookers that formed around the archduchess who, moreover, soon fell silent, collapsing against the feet of the imperial effigy in a fainting fit so well simulated that a couple of robust stewards picked her up and carried her to a cabin from which she didn't emerge until lunchtime.

Anger and strong emotions had worn her down. So, noticing the meagerness of the menu during a period of rationing, she upbraided herself for having drowned the caviar, just as she had been angry with herself on account of the bouquet.

When she finished her short meal, night was already falling.

In spite of the entreaties of her lady-in-waiting, who feared another attack, seeing that the cold travelers had all gone inside even though it had stopped snowing, Augusta decided to go meditate near the bow. On her knees, with clasped hands, she prayed for the eternal repose of the empress's soul and for the damnation of the emperor. And peace came to her. A thousand familiar memories warmed up this cold night. For example, one morning at the Hoffburg: the empress in an acrobat's costume, just as Maurice Barrès depicted her in *Amori et Dolori Sacrum,* hanging on to her trapeze swing. Sad thoughts had interrupted her acrobatics and, on a forehead wreathed with heavy braids, one could read anxiety and an anxiety all the more poignant since, the ground being twenty feet below her, thus in danger of breaking her bones if she lost her balance, the empress was biting her nails. Through the shredded silk stockings the blood had already started to flow when Augusta, always touched by the suffering of the great and the small, threw herself on the floor in a burst of pleading commiseration spontaneous enough to make her corset split. From that moment dated the intimacy between her and the empress, and since in Hungary Elizabeth had been loved as much as the emperor was hated, Augusta wouldn't fail to evoke the affection devoted to her by the former in an attempt to play tricks on the latter.

And already, impervious to the fog which, penetrating inanimate objects and living beings, had eaten up every last reed on the riverbank, our exile began to decide, organize, scheme once again.

The future?

Her schoolteacher (a Frenchwoman whom Augusta never failed to qualify as a Jacobin and a real Jacobin), on any pretext and even in the absence of a pretext, had, all throughout her childhood, drummed into her this versified thought of Victo Hugo:

> The future, sire, the future belongs to no one,
> The future belongs to God.

Today, leaning over the handrail, with her lorgnette probing the darkness, the Mary Stuart of the Danube repeats fearlessly: "The future . . . the future" and, though a very good Christian, she dares to say in a very loud voice:

"The future, Augusta, the future doesn't belong to God,
The future belongs to Augusta,"

but does God, who hears her, want to punish her for her pride? Later, she will tell her confessor that she saw the devil and her confessor won't contradict her.

Even if she lived for a thousand years, she would never forget how the dark haze that enveloped her, little by little, thickened until it became wadding, and not the kind of wadding that gives the impression of deafness or blindness, but the kind that obliterates the very memory that sounds ever existed. And the other senses, thin bristles, wilting magicians, captivating balloons which became captive, then died of captivity, didn't take long to crumble into dust. Thus, the dome which, under each orbit, three minutes earlier, was still filling up with air, was now nothing but ashes. As many holes as there had been spheres. The convex collapses into the concave. An archduchess who held her position in the oldest and noblest court in Europe, one of the few women with whom the chancelleries must reckon, will soon have left no other trace of her existence than a void in the atmosphere.

And yet, the drop of conscience, all that remains of the lady who was such a dignified person, refuses to let itself be swallowed up by the overly voracious fog. Resignation: this puddle wouldn't even be gray but rather called Isabella, named after that other archduchess who, faithful to her vow, didn't change shirts during her husband's three-year siege of Ostend. No, Augusta wouldn't allow such filth to erase the venous purple and the arterial indigo of an unsubjugated blood. The porous hour insisted on absorbing every trace of color. A drop of conscience can still murmur:

"The future?"

And shreds of shreds, which had nonetheless seemed incapable of making an echo, repeat:

"The future?"

—Future, future, are you here? Explain yourself. Tell who you are, where you come from, where you're going. . . .

—The future, present, does no more than sputter invisibly.

Two resuscitated nostrils perceive a strange smell of broiled pig.

—Whose odor is that?

—Mine, of course, for I am the future already transformed into the present, just long enough to greet you. You have met your match, Augusta. But don't get impatient. Your senses of speech, hearing, and smell were miraculously restored. Now you will regain your eyesight. Open your eyes, look at me. There. Hello, hello. I am tiny and you are grandiose. And yet, in me, in me alone and at your expense, is concentrated all the force of a couple. So please, don't make fun of the little piece of wire, the twisted vibrion with no means of transportation other than an amazingly springy tail. The head which has the honor of greeting you is, moreover, not so ugly. I chose that of a horse so that the sea horse, without risking all plausibility, would represent the question mark shooting straight up from the depths in response to your call for help.

Augusta would naturally have preferred some other companion to this holy hell of a crankshaft kid whose sharply pointed virility, in spite of the humidity and the cold, had succeeded in drilling through the darkness.

She who, awhile ago, hadn't hesitated to slap a lieutenant, wasn't about to let an obscene, insolent little monster push her around.

—Sure, you have thermocauteric blood, little fellow, but do you know to whom you are speaking?

—I'm talking to the archduchess Augusta.

—So?

—So, may her highness note that I do not lack resemblance to Gypsies whose bows refuse all strings other than the nerves of those princesses who thought they were invulnerable underneath the rib-boned breastplates from which, however, they soon spring to follow naked, heavy, and shamelessly the irresistible little roosters. You want to reign, Augusta, you who aren't even capable of reigning over yourself. You must be punished for your pride. But as punishment, I won't metamorphose you into a meditation tree as I had originally planned. With your widow's veils, you would have made a great weeping willow, but I'm making a point of refusing you that satisfaction.

—If you were defoliated of all present to such an extent that you didn't dare dream of future buds, gnomess in the woods of regret, curled up in bark that neither memories nor hopes would proffer, having fallen from animal to plant life, in order to console yourself, you would knock back little sips of nursery and forest, that is to say, flattering comparisons. You would give the name liana to the arms, the legs that immobility had already demuscled, and that of bindweed to the hands which, before wilting forever, had joined on your breast in order to gratify the most symbolic of organs and its rib-roofed tabernacle with a delectation similar to that with which you enchant your widow's dawns.

—Your limbs, if I turned them into strings, well, they could still tie packages of gnarled resentment. Reduced to fiber, you would remain superior, in voracity, to elephants' trunks. And you wouldn't spare the least palpitating twig and you wouldn't leave until you had *taken away everything,*

> Taken all away,
> The beds in which we lay,

as they sing at charity concerts, in France, on the other side of the front. And you, in spite of your name, traitress to your country, you didn't hesitate to bring back from Paris, smuggling it through Swiss customs, this piece, supposedly because you're mad about Debussy who put these pretty words to music. But don't you know you could be shot for trading with the enemy? Well, let's leave it at that! For those of your ilk, all bitterness is delightful as long as you're the one secreting it. In your Hungarian solitudes, you're going to piss vinegar at first, but you'll remember, quite appropriately, the little saying used by your uncle the great waltzer, seducer, racer, gambler, etc., who, in his old age, went into a monastery with, he used to say, the firm hope of being as happy there as a little onion in a jar of brine, for, "from acetic acid, an ascetic becomes asceticized." Yes, Augusta, you won't forget to drink, as an apéritif, nice little sips of bile, and the best, the only, the unrivaled, your own.

—But wait! I wanted to punish you for your pride and suddenly, I notice that I haven't said anything that you can be proud of. The elements preferred to vaporize rather than, forever and ever, serving you. Too grand a lady to deal with these traitors, you didn't deign to take us in Asian style, by becoming disincarnated. You preferred to let your life fizzle out like a fishtail, without even affording yourself, on the occasion of this image, the luxury of effortless poetic revenge, despite the fact that coldness is a characteristic of fish. Augusta, my sturdy one, they won't get you with vapor. As for the intermediate state, that of liquid, you make it your business, for you are an artist, Augusta, and artists like to frequent oceans, just as, moreover, oceans are happy in the company of artists. Too easily in fact, according to your wishes, salt water gives in to the caprices of decorative aquariums. If the liquid plain were to let itself be caged up, along with its treasures, behind plates of glass, there would be no further mention of the Pacific. But you, you don't like colossi gentle enough to let themselves be put into bottles, scooped up in spoons, rolled in hair-curlers around atolls. You dream of an ocean that would be the opposite of the Pacific, that would be called the Bellicose, and would invent such typhoons that navigators would pretend to know nothing about it and its fits of anger. And you, with no hope, today, of ever reigning in Prague, you would be the sovereign of the Bellicose, its whale. Even the most sharply pointed of fish wouldn't dare call you an amphibian. In return, full of indulgence, you would make little signals to hearts lost in the fog, letting everyone hope that the next minute will ripen if not the eternal, at least the most precious part of themselves. And how you would exhort those hunting for treasure, *the* treasure! You ask what treasure? You really disappoint me. What could we be talking about if not the soul? Beings deprived of creatures to caress, objects to put away, money to count, why they must be convinced to fall back on the imponderable. Experience has, moreover, taught you that each person wants to build, with his own bad odor, a most elegantly ornate little niche, with encrusted rot no less rutilant than the rainbow that hangs from turkeys' necks. So, advise everyone to wear on their tiepin or, depending on their sex, lukewarm and dripping over the arm, their sweat and their blood.

—From the Bellicose, your empire would quickly expand to others, to all of the seas. Yes, Empress of the Arctic and the Antarctic (just as the rose is queen of the flowers, the leek asparagus of the poor), this sea horse, your obedient servant, has no other ambition but that of becoming your majesty's prince consort. Too smart to look for difficulties where there are none, you managed to spare yourself the least temptation, even if only that of tulips. So, free from fits of conscience, you fattened up more and better than a Batavian queen.

—Augusta, your destiny is for show.

—A question of vocation: he who works at aping you is wasting his time, but amazon of the highest seas, grand mademoiselle, why couldn't a sea horse be your Lauzun? Louis XIV's cousin who turned down the best prospects, a king of England, an emperor, yes, my dear, regardless of what everyone thought, took for a spouse a simple gentleman who came up to her shoulder.

—Remember your grandmothers as well. They were hardly rotgut! Those beautiful individuals who all had big breasts, big hearts, and, saving your reverence, big bottoms; Augusta, my little whale, they bore a certain resemblance to you.

—Your lovely bust brings to mind those breasts so heavy that they made Directory tulle burst and 1830s corsets bend under their weight. Such creatures' contemporaries could think of nothing but love. They lived in a softly upholstered half-darkness, preferred opaline to crystal and, take a sea horse's word for it, we'll show you what opaline makes you think of. You're fidgeting, Augusta, you're licking, smacking, sucking, porking your chops. But don't get so excited, honey, for, my word, what will become of us if whales start jumping like carp? And you jump rope, pole-vault, yes, go ahead and fondle it, your sea horsey's spout. You blow up in a dynamite explosion. By the way, if your sex has its flirts who, merely by brushing against them, send he-men head over heels, why wouldn't it too have its teases? You're catching fire, my fat friend. Don't count on me to blow you out.

Give us some flame,
Spark and candle,
Your soul's within my aim,
You can take my handle. . . .

Augusta let out a tremendous scream: "Hellfire!" and the fire that was preying on her wasn't going to be put out by the black snow which had nonetheless begun to fall quite heavily. The universe was a huge catafalque upon which the sea horse, the highest dignitary of the new apocalypse, celebrated the office with, for altar boys, squirrels with monkeys' hands whose ritual costumes with fur trains didn't exempt their faces from a distressing resemblance to rats, for the time had come for the glory of rodents. The black pope of question marks, the sea horse passed the collection plate and Augusta gave him all she had and gave herself as a plank worthy of the hell that she could no longer bear to see merely paved with good intentions. . . .

Already, the lights of Budapest were sparkling. The lady-in-waiting, after having looked everywhere for her and finally finding Augusta on a coil of line, picked her up, straightened her Mary Stuart hairdo, but wasn't able to rid her mind of certain thoughts. On the landing wharf, everyone stepped aside as is proper to clear the way for the archduchess whose eyes were still so full of the frightful vision that they didn't notice the arrival of the pickpocket who, with one hand, snipped off, and with the other, gathered up the pearls of her most beautiful rank.

A holy clergyman, informed of her visit, was waiting to bless her on the threshold of the Hungaria Palace. But she whom he called the wisest of highnesses could only throw herself at his feet and plead: "Father, father, I gave an entire necklace to the devil for the repaving of hell!" Despite the holy man's assurances that God would grant her his forgiveness if she gave the clergy of the Hungarian capital a hundredfold of what she believed to have been extorted from her by the Evil One, Augusta gesticulated, screamed with such violence that travelers in civilian, religious, and military dress, porters and head-waiters, even though their curiosity would have preferred not to lose a mouthful of the sight, moved away from the possessed woman.

Her hair had come undone, pulling down in its wake the headband that made her hairdo a cushion for crowns and very dignified hats. One of her large breasts had popped out of her tattered bodice. She was finally able to pick herself up and walk toward the elevator. But the elevator man, frightened to be in such a small compartment with such an imposing demoness, began to tremble and shiver, and his teeth began to chatter; in short he showed the first signs of the brain fever that would carry him to the grave a month later.

Then there was talk of having Augusta exorcised. She, however, always in search of novelty, thought best to entrust herself to the care of a German professor who had come to gather firsthand evidence for a thesis dealing with *Gypsy Psychology and the Diverse Reactions Brought about by the Residence of Nomads among Stable Populations.* He diagnosed a gypsiphobia that appeared quite likely to be chronic.

Augusta rather liked the idea of being afflicted with such a subtle disease.

Beneath her windows, a violin was squeaking and, hearing the *musicanti* of the Corso, she reveled in her pain. She didn't have the least desire to leave the Hungaria Palace and go bury herself alive in her castle on the unfriendly banks of Lake Balaton. Everyone was fussing over her and when lilac season arrived, she felt such a renewal in her heart that in spite of her well-known respect for etiquette, she shed her widow's veils one by one and began, well in advance of the official end of mourning, to dress in a violet that quickly turned, moreover, to mauve, then to pink. The only fly in the ointment was the presence of Turks at the hotel. The war had necessitated an alliance with this ancestral enemy, and now the descendants of the hideous little men who had been so hard to expel from Hungary, under the pretext of military collaboration, diplomatic work, etc., were running the place.

Whenever she thought about Turks or met one, Augusta suffocated. She would hurry back up to her suite to ask her chambermaid to loosen her corset and apply ice-cold vinegar compresses to her temples. If her gypsiphobia was a complex, romantic disease, her loathing for Turks was unmitigated. It so happened that a fat Ottoman who lived on the same floor would lie in wait for her in the corridors, entranced by a rump that he couldn't look at without whinnying. To get away from the Turk, Augusta climbed from the third to the fourth floor, then went back down to the mezzanine and back up to the sixth floor, but the Turk, more and more love-crazy, followed her to each landing. Every morning he would send her candy, flowers. Since the Corso was between the Danube and her windows, Augusta didn't take the trouble to throw them in the water, but neither did she take the trouble to thank the sender, who kept sending. Well, one fine day he accompanied his bouquet not with sweets but with a proposal. She dressed up in her widow's weeds, donned the little Mary Stuart hat, took down the old painting of her spouse the late archduke, from which she had never, in any of her peregrinations, separated herself, pressed it against her breast, and left her apartment.

For the first time, the Turk, even though he was most certainly waiting for her answer, failed to open his door, after she had gone to to the trouble of slamming hers as hard as she could. Thus she went downstairs and sat in the lobby where she remained for two hours without showing the least bit of impatience. She hadn't forgotten that vengeance is a dish best served cold, so she carefully prevented herself from coming to a boil while receiving this fellow's homage, that fellow's compliments, and everyone's congratulations on how nice the archduke looked in festive attire.

Finally, the Turk arrived. She gave up her armchair, took the portrait, and with all her might, for its frame was heavy, holding it at arm's length, she lifted it up as high as she could and struck the Turk with it so hard that the poor man, whose skull had punctured the canvas, appeared to everyone's delight with his head caught in an iron collar like a Chinese torture victim. The lesson was well worth a masterpiece, but Augusta, being too much of a lady to take advantage of her triumph, let the boor extricate himself and left, carrying her head higher than ever as she went to church, where she was in the habit of hearing daily Mass. After having prayed many times that he who, even dead, was still able to avenge her for Moslem insults, might rest in peace, she returned to the Hungaria Palace where she had the double satisfaction of receiving the manager's apologies and learning of the beys' and pashas' departures. The satisfaction was short-lived, for not only did the emperor fail to stand up for her but, on the contrary, more servile than a hotel clerk, as soon as he got wind of the incident, he wrote to the Turk, and in his own hand, that he disapproved of Augusta's conduct, while in the driest, typewritten letter which he had sent to his cousin's widow, he advised her, if there was still time, to apologize, patch up relations, and earn imperial forgiveness by accepting the marriage. Augusta became dizzy upon reading this missive. Europe was decidedly crumbling and the situation had to be really desperate for them to propose selling her in this way. But even if the fate of the Hapsburgs depended on it, she join a harem! she belly dance! never.

From that day on, Augusta expected the worst and followed, without a flicker of surprise, the events leading up to the collapse and removal of Franz Josef's successor from the throne. She was able, moreover, to leave Budapest at an opportune time, sparing herself the pain of being run out of Hungary, of seeing her dear palace become the home of the Soviets, and seeing Béla Kun, whom she hated more than all of the Turks combined, sleep in the bed which had been the proud nest of archduchesses' dreams. She settled in Prague, and even though the city wasn't what it would have been had she reigned there, she couldn't complain. First of all, the young Czech Republic was not lacking in consideration for the White Russians, each of whom received from it the sum of one thousand crowns per month, which, of course, was not a great deal, but gave evidence of goodwill that was all the more impressive considering the fact that the new government wasn't free with its money and, for example, steadfastly refused to let itself be swindled by the unemployed workers to whom it didn't give a penny in benefits.

In Prague, the epic air was quite worthy of her highness's nostrils which it intoxicated with every breath she took. General Pellé, representing Clemenceau, and his staff were accorded the rare honor and privilege of enjoying this atmosphere. Augusta began to hate the French less, almost to love those whom, with all her scorn, all her hatred, she used to call Jacobins.

The Commission of Four, namely, Lloyd George, Wilson, Clemenceau, and Foch, at the instance of its president, Clemenceau, had decided to back Czechoslovakia and Romania in the war against Béla Kun, whose army currently occupied all of southern Czechoslovakia. Augusta could only approve of her former enemy, now collaborating beyond her wildest dreams, the Entente whose leaders had decided that it was best to attack the Soviets from both ends, kill a revolution which neither the bourgeoisie of the old republics nor the nobility of the crumbled and crumbling kingdoms wanted to let live. The triumph of Béla Kun would have grouped together the peoples of the Danube in a communist peace in which none of the advantages of the wealthy class would have been respected, none of the time-honored privileges of an aristocracy that, aware of its interests, intended, from the remains of the great empire among the hodgepodge of races, to create out of nothing and at any cost little nations whose factitious national unity would generate antagonisms which were both irreducible and well-balanced enough that the European concert would not be lacking in instruments and would be able to continue its traditional music so dear to all grand ladies' music-loving ears.

Since the task at hand was the patching up of the old continent, there was no time to lose: before the treaties were signed, suggestions had to be made and schemes had to be devised. This was a period of stifling activity, one of the most beautiful times of Augusta's life. Everyone was sending her coded telegrams, and she was sending back others. She would receive at least five per day and would send off twice as many. She lavished advice, by the fastest of all postal routes, on her compatriot Count Bethlen who, in southern Hungary, with the help of General Franchet d'Esperey, was organizing the struggle against the triumphant Soviets. Heroes seemed to spring from the ground, but from the countless number of them, Augusta had wisely chosen her god, General Štefánik.

June, July 1919.

On June 8th, Clemenceau, president of the Commission of Four, wired Béla Kun:

The allied and mutually friendly governments are on the verge of inviting the Hungarian government to the Peace Conference. The Allies have already proclaimed their firm intention to bring to a halt all unnecessary hostilities in view of the fact that you have stopped the Romanian and the French armies at the Hungarian border. Under these circumstances, if the government in Budapest does not put an immediate stop to all attacks against Czechoslovakia, the allied governments have decided to take the most vigorous measures.

A few days later, Béla Kun wired Foch's representative in Prague:

What guarantees can you give concerning the retreat of the Royal Romanian Army from the territory designated by Clemenceau?

General Pellé answered:

I will pass on to the president of the Peace Conference your question concerning the territories occupied by the Romanian army whose evacuation is guaranteed by the decision of the Peace Conference.

Thus, according to the commitment made on June 13th by Clemenceau, in the name of the Commission of Four, the Romanian army was to evacuate the Hungarian territories that it was occupying, at the very moment when Béla Kun's army withdrew from Czechoslovakia.

On July 11th, Béla Kun would vainly remind Clemenceau of his word. The Red Army had in fact suspended hostilities on June 24th. The Royal Romanian troops, instead of withdrawing, invaded all of Hungary in complicity with the Hungarian nobility and clergy who had succeeded in leaving Budapest. And Augusta was pleased to see Horthy deliver her country into the hands of royal, purifying armies, even if they were the enemy. But if she was all eyes and ears for every deed accomplished by a man who would organize the white terror so well and so durably, she didn't forget the president of the Commission of Four who had saved civilization, honor, tradition, and, last but not least, her property on the shores of Lake Balaton.

She therefore sent a message of thanks to the old Tiger and, since she was in no mood to skimp on heroes' recompense, she bought General Štefánik a little gold cannon set with diamonds. For such a present she had to mortgage her land, but it wasn't a bad investment. Indeed, if she couldn't reign in Prague, she was nonetheless thinking of settling there permanently as sovereign in the third degree, that is, as the spouse of the soldier who had been one of the three founders of the very reasonable (if very young) republic.

She was in no hurry to question the particular party on that precise subject. In advance, she was sure of his answer, for he surely couldn't be indifferent to her beauty, presently in all the magnificence of a sumptuous summer that gave no hint of approaching autumn, apart from the red foliage of a head of hair whose blondeness, prematurely whitened by the European upheaval and personal grief, had been touched up with judicious applications of henna.

Such was the situation, and one might say that things weren't going too badly, when Štefánik's airplane crashed into one of the Little Carpathians. The entire nation went into mourning. Prostrated with grief, Augusta didn't even have the strength to go cry on the cadaver of the man by whom she legitimately considered herself to have been widowed, at least spiritually. She attributed the accident to the designs of Providence (Thy will be done!) which, in order to punish her for her conversation with the Gypsy devil, the devil Gypsy, the devil of a Gypsy, would never allow her to be happy again.

The official version was engine failure. It was rumored that the general had been shot down in combat by his own army, intentionally according to some, by a stroke of bad luck according to others, who explained that the Czechoslovakian soldiers had mistaken the (enemy) Hungarian flag for the (friendly) Italian flag with which his wings were decorated, the colors of these two flags differing only by their arrangement. Still other claimed that he had committed suicide.

Augusta, as one can imagine, didn't listen to these slanderous rumors. The entire Czechoslovakian nation, moreover, was preparing to glorify the hero. At the top of the mountain where he had met his death, a commemorative stonework worthy of his accomplishments was being completed. In order to keep an eye on the architects, on the contractors and the laborers who were working on this monument, and then, when the last stone had been laid, to wait around for the inauguration, our Augusta had taken up residence in this place. She had chosen a Czechoslovakian spa where she had, each morning, by way of a pastime and a distraction, the resource of the mud baths. On afternoons when she wasn't being chauffeured to the cenotaph, she would take walks along a little river that she thought a perfect symbol of her destiny. Indeed, this river flowed calmly, majestically, making no claim to needless depths or complications. From the bottom of its bed, the water would have only come up to the navel of a man of medium height, supposing he had been able to remain standing. But even the best swimmers who ventured two feet from the edge were carried away by a deadly current and, when it was possible to pull them out, they were already lifeless. At the hotel, the old ladies whose rheumatism prevented them from going anywhere would spend their time making wagers: "How many drownings will there be today? More or fewer than yesterday?" Augusta went down and checked the daily score, placed bets. One day when she was on her seventh drowning, by effective use of her elbows she was able to slip into the front row. The professional rescuers (in this country the most lucrative of professions, though already a bit overcrowded), under the pretext of artificial respiration from which they were the last to expect any results, were massaging a young lady's corpse.

The trunks of one of the lascivious lifeguards gave evidence of an excitement that even the most liberal of archduchesses couldn't tolerate to see publicly displayed, especially since, the height of outrage, the man performing the spectacle was very dark-skinned, very dark-haired, thus a Gypsy. A Gypsy profaning a virgin whom God, via the waters of a tributary of the Danube, had summoned back to heaven! This was more than she could stand.

With the handle of her parasol, which bore the sculptured ivory head of Franz Josef on its end, Augusta restored justice by striking a blow in the right place. She used all the might of an arm strong enough to hold the scepter of the heaviest of thrones. The skimpiness of a poor little cotton jersey was unable, all by itself, to absorb the shock. And yet the Gypsy didn't budge, while her uncle the emperor's head broke into two pieces that rolled on the ground. Thus, years later, the great politician was finally getting back at her persecutor, for what could be more ignominious to a Hapsburg than breaking his nose on the lower parts of a man belonging to the accursed race?

Augusta accorded the person standing next to her the honor of being asked to retrieve the broken pieces. This man, a lieutenant in the Czechoslovakian army, as if he had guessed that he would be the drowning victim on the following day, handed her the fragments of ivory with a respect which was not only of another era, but already of another world. To pay him back for such gracious deference, Augusta asked the lieutenant to keep, in remembrance of her, the remains of her parasol and, armed only with her lorgnette, she elbowed her way through the crowd of onlookers who couldn't understand why anyone would give up such a good seat at the very minute when the panting Gypsy was staining his swimsuit with stains that weren't from sweat.

Augusta promised herself that she would learn a lesson from the incident. Already she was hurrying toward the large wooded area whose silent heart is conducive to meditation. But no sooner had she entered the forest than she met a little five- or six-year-old boy who was dancing naked in the middle of a clearing. He accompanied his entrechats with a song whose words were summed up in the refrain commonly used even in the mystery of the Czechoslovakian woods, where the penetration of Esperanto has nonetheless remained out of the question. This child's features and complexion recalled those of the sacrilegious young man of awhile ago. But how could she take umbrage at a cherub who awakened in her heart the sweetest of sentiments, a maternal love that a too eventful life had not yet accorded her the leisure of knowing? In three seconds, she had thought of turning this singing baby first into a general, then a philosopher, and finally an industrial giant. But, her reason told her, there has never been, but there will never be, a Gypsy general, philosopher, or industrial giant. "So I will make an artist of him," she decided. And with that she begins to caress the little savage, wrapping her scarf around his loins for, although this swarthy little angel was not yet of an age to shock his majestic benefactress, the latter, who couldn't tolerate indecency, was obliged to dress him in order to take him to her hotel where she stuffed him with pastries and café au lait, and gave him a few coins which convinced the lad to return on the following day.

The sea horse in her hallucination (Augusta was unable to forget it) engaged in mischief to a far lesser degree than any son of the accursed race which imposes its soilers of pretty drowning victims on a young, brand-new nation. But since she was one of those saintly women who want to pull out of hell, if not Lucifer himself, at least the demons whose youth is so touching, she persisted in her resolution to civilize the singing baby. It would be impossible to eradicate the essential differences between an archduchess, the most representative, most perfect incarnation of European culture, and the descendant, even if reformed, of horse thieves. But she was going to attempt the impossible and she knew that the transformation of this young plantigrade animal into a little gentleman would in itself represent a significant achievement.

Though very musical, she decided—because she put art, like everything, in a proper perspective—that neither ear training nor dance would suffice for the singing baby's education. Since he was an artist, it was important for him to arrive, via finishing-school activities, at the threshold of a wise future.

In a sewing shop, they bought him a needlepoint print portraying General Štefánik, whose profile, a real medallion profile, was crowned with a kepi made of oak leaves.

Once the tapestry was completed, Augusta planned to use it as upholstery for a piano bench reserved exclusively for her personal use. She alone would be allowed to sit there, and she would sit down each morning to quench the warrior's soul with funeral marches; for he was still present in the little drawing room where, during his glorious lifetime, he had come to visit her one day. But she would never allow any profane buttock to defile her god's features. She was particularly anxious not to share the aquiline nose which, right in the middle, in intimate communion with the part of herself that she would offer him with shameless, passionate love, would make one of those cup-and-ball toys!

A benefactress could scarcely help but feel legitimate pride when, sitting in the ladies' circle at her hotel, she forces them to acknowledge her protégé's progress. But in Czechoslovakian lobbies, among native or foreign invalids, there like elsewhere, jealousy goes its merry way. To avoid being wounded, they criticize, they discourage. Augusta recalls a perfectly appropriate saying dear to her Jacobin of a schoolteacher: "Paris wasn't built in a day." But these small-minded plebians have no worries aside from their rheumatism. They are women without any ideals who have never had the least intention of collaborating, in any way, with Augusta in her fight against a gypsiphobic epidemic so widespread that it has made the entire region forget its anti-Semitism. One of these defeatists (who, incidentally, plays a very strange game, for she doesn't mind acknowledging the Jews with curlpapers in their hair who greet her in the park), what if one of these defeatists doesn't just start accusing the singing baby of brazenly poking her with her embroidery needle whenever Augusta turns her head? The complainant, of course, comes from Sarajevo where the population is Moslem and the women are veiled. The archduchess doesn't go to the trouble of speaking with Turks. Only a Polish theosophist has some feelings for the singing baby. Augusta, who in spite of the results obtained can't keep from experiencing more than a little fear about her protégé's future, asks this sympathizer if she will be so kind as to make a table turn so that they will know what to expect. And, although turning tables perform their feats sparingly, the latter hammers out: "Tapestry for a Gypsy is peach melba for a tiger, vegetable bouillon for a shark." Hardly satisfied with this statement, the inquisitive ladies call on the pedestal table to explain itself, but at that moment its fragile wood begins to tremble so badly that it collapses with a terrible crash.

All of this keeps Augusta awake at night and, in the morning, she decides to entrust her tiger-shark to a real leader of men.

Ever since she had read in the newspapers that the queen of Romania had visited Ford during a trip to America, Augusta had in fact become passionately interested in the rise of Bat'a's factories which, if they were as yet to Ford's what a shoe is to an automobile, looked promising nonetheless. She served as an example, and her motto—"Let's put our boots on, Czechoslovakia"—had prevailed over the resistance of a snobbery always ready, out of small-minded vanity, to turn its nose up at mass-produced goods. Well it so happened that the singing baby couldn't stand to wear shoes. Each day she had to buy him a pair that he unfailingly metamorphosed into little boats.

Insomnia having made her susceptible to the seeping virus of gypsiphobia, that morning, when Augusta finds her protégé in the park, she loses no time in announcing to him that they are going for a drive, adding for her own benefit, mentally: "So, my little tiger-shark, you can't stand any kind of shoes; just wait until we have a pair of army boots made for you." And that very afternoon she handed the singing baby over to the man who, twenty years earlier a mere village shoemaker, could presently delight in the idea that soon, through his efforts, there wouldn't be a bare foot anywhere in the world. With the generous heart that she is known for, one can well imagine that impunity did not characterize Augusta's meeting of this man of ideals, quite the opposite of a dreamer, so energetic that he would never get sidetracked by considerations of the eight-hour workday or the bad odors in the tanneries that the leather must pass through.

"I don't change, I don't get old, I still need a great man like before," she had noted while she was enjoying an ice cream. The bowl in which it had been served was decorated with Bat'a's signature as were, moreover, the walls on the houses, the dishes in all the cupboards, the cyclists' caps, and even, or so they said, what the workers usually only took out of their flies in order to satisfy the most urgent needs, but whose very legible tattoos—the one day per week when they didn't have to get up at five o'clock to go to the factory—their wives could leisurely admire before making love, at the very moment when it was important to remember that, all forces having been recruited to serve Bat'a, it was now time to make a baby, male or female, destined for Bat'a's factories.

On the factory's visitors' book, she had written—in French, because, according to her, this language, more and better than any other, lent itself to the music of free verse—

> In Zlin,*
> Dressed in muslin,
> Augusta
> Admired Bat'a,
> Then hastened to bring
> The baby who loves to sing,
> And had for dinner
> A zmrlina. †

This constituted, unquestionably, a kind of declaration, but Augusta wasn't the least bit afraid of compromising herself. She had the courage of her feelings and her ideas and, if she hadn't sworn total fidelity to the memory of Štefánik, if she hadn't, in the course of the week following the accident, come into possession of a uniform specially ordered to the hero's size in order to fill the gap left in her museum of relics by the destruction of the archduke's portrait, the

---

*Bat'a's hometown.
† In Czech: ice cream. [All footnotes are Crevel's—Trans.]

shoe king would have certainly found a place worthy of him in her heart. Wasn't she in step with the times, didn't she know from experience that a trust is well worth an empire? Industrial giant, hero of peace, field marshal of the assembly line, wasn't Bat'a destined to die, moreover, that same violent death which never failed to befall all of those whom Augusta honored or could have honored with her love? A few kilometers from the place where the generalissimo of the Czechoslovakian army had met his glorious death, Bat'a similarly perished in a plane crash. But let's not get ahead of ourselves, although actually, without pretending to be a prophetess, Augusta can say that, during the unveiling of the cenotaph in honor of Štefánik, she had a presentiment of the second tragedy. Perfectly legitimate chagrin added to her grief, making her view the entire future with a sense of dread.

Why, for example, hadn't they put up, plunged in sorrow, a statue of a veiled woman that she would have willingly agreed to pose for with the Mary Stuart hat and the cascade of crepe which she had just taken out of her closet again on the occasion of the present funeral ceremony? And why did she, the godmother of Czechoslovakia, have to keep silent, refrain from holding forth at the Sokols, drink her tears without saying a word? It seemed to Augusta that the entire universe, the earthly and divine powers were thumbing their noses at her.

She could feel herself living her own Mount of Olives, without suspecting, however, that her Golgotha had to be so near. As it turned out, upon her return to the hotel, as soon as she reached the porter's lodge, she learned that the singing baby had run away from Bat'a's house and had succeeded in slipping into his benefactress' bedroom to steal the general's pants, jacket, and kepi.

Unable to tolerate the idea of these relics polluted by a member of that accursed race, Augusta promised a decisive reward to whomever would bring back to her, in any condition whatsoever, the perpetrator and the objects of the theft. But it would take three more days to find them at the bottom of the river.

The singing baby, having all but decomposed in such a short time, barefoot as if, while dead, he were thumbing his nose at his benefactress, still alive, was dressed in the keepsake-uniform which could have held at least four people his size. Upon hearing this and in spite of so many horrible details, Augusta couldn't keep from letting out a victory cry: "I drowned the devil, I drowned the devil," she repeated with a rhythm that was both lyric and epic. The next day, after having thrown the profaned uniform on the fire, she left for Vienna to order a new one from the best military tailor, formerly supplier to the late archduke.

Since she didn't want to entrust her treasure to the railroad, she decided to wait for it to be delivered to her before returning to her headquarters, Prague. Day after dreary day went by in the Austrian capital where her peers had refused to forgive her conduct before and after the war, until one day, when she was passing by the Hoffburg's ticket office, she read the word *Paneuropa* on a door. In this palace, years ago, she had heard too much about Pan-Slavism, Pan-Germanism, and even pantheism for her to be surprised at seeing a new pan established there now.

So she pushed open the door of Paneuropa, and the meeting between Augusta and Paneuropa was as simple yet as decisive as that between Newton and the apple.

Before buying the brochures, she began by asking for a little clarification. She thus learned, not without pleasure, that England was destined to be part of Europe no longer and to form a confederation, British, of course, with an insular metropolis and dominions. Despite her family relationship with the marquis of Sussex, or rather because of her relationship and in spite of the fact that since 1914 she had met neither the deceased lord who so loved tiger-hunting, nor Primrose, nor their son to whom she was godmother, Augusta—to whom neither London eccentricity nor Irish madness nor Scottish melancholy held any appeal—was quite pleased to see the wisest, most centrally located, most Catholic continent cast off forever this islet of pride and Protestantism. This highly pertinent initiative had won her over immediately. She applauded: "Very good, very good," and she emptied her purse for the privilege of taking home the books and journals in which the doctrine was expounded.

And she got her money's worth, for, upon returning home, what a delight to read an article penned by a French general who told, with all the impartiality one could wish for, how he had, during the occupation of the Ruhr, understood that the Germans weren't meant to be exterminated by their western neighbors after all. The general was therefore joining Paneuropa in the hope of an alliance with those whom he had previously scorned, fought, killed, and even called Krauts. This alliance would prepare the way for subsequent just wars of which the first, he didn't mind suggesting, would be undertaken against the Soviets. Augusta was moved to tears when she thought about how much Štefánik would have liked this general. And her amazement grew with every page she turned. Africa, Asia, and Oceania were only too happy to offer their best to Europe's blotches of color, for there was no question but that the new confederation would keep its former colonies and even manage to make new ones. This lace doily of uncivilized countries could only please an archduchess who, for all her keen sense of politics, didn't sacrifice anything in femininity. The British Empire, on the one hand, America, on the other, and above all Europe: that was certainly enough to respond to the so-called awakening of the black and yellow races, not to mention the communists.

She who had dared, in the heat of enthusiasm, to write to the old Tiger to congratulate him for having, by his clever triumph over Béla Kun, erased the very memory of his former Jacobinism, how could she have hesitated to enter the Paneuropean movement which, all flattery aside, would be able to put to good use the perspicacity resulting from her experience—for example, in shedding light on the Jewish, Turkish, and Gypsy questions that (this was the only fly in the ointment) nobody had thought to ask.

Augusta's Paneuropean activity would soon take her to France. She had insisted on making a pilgrimage to Cocherel, where the best advised of Paneuropeans, Aristide Briand, sleeps his last sleep. She hadn't had the good fortune of knowing him, for, at the time of her conversion, he was already in the grave, for which she had been the first to congratulate him. Indeed, after all the good things she had heard about him, his charm, and his deep, cellolike voice, she was bound to fall in love with him. And so, the poor guy, instead of dying in his bed, had, just like Štefánik, just like Bat'a, gone down in a plane crash, just as may very well have happened to Count Coudenhove Kalergi, the man to whom, in spite of his half-Japanese, half-Austrian descent, befell the task of founding Paneuropa.

How proudly he speaks, this dear Coudenhove, and what a joy, too, when one is on the banks of the Seine, to read, in a French newspaper, a translation of an article recently published by the *Neues Wiener Journal,* in which he deals precisely, in his usual brilliant manner, with "World Revolution through Technology": "The aim of technology," he writes, "is the universalization of wealth, freedom, power, beauty, civilization, and happiness; not the proletarianization but the aristocratization of humanity."

Not the proletarianization, but the aristocratization of humanity. Augusta could repeat these charming words for hours upon end. This profession of faith is music to her ears. Just let them try talking to her about the proletariat and they'll see what happens.

In France Augusta received at least as warm a welcome as that reserved for film stars. Her arrival at the Gare de l'Est train station provoked an immediate flood of interviews and a burst of flashes. She could be seen and heard in newsreels in movie theaters everywhere. The Prince of Journalists himself, despite his systematic mistrust in any movement calling itself internationalist for one reason or another, would have felt that he was failing in his sworn duty as an opinion maker if he hadn't sent her his top interviewer on the very afternoon of her arrival. The president of the Association for the Literary and Artistic Development of the Feminine Crème de la Crème organized a tea in honor of Augusta, who had the distinct pleasure of meeting there the populist novelist Marie Torchon and the poetess of *The Effusions,* the famous Synovie. She was invited to the presidential palace, to police headquarters, and to academic receptions.

On the day of the national funeral at Notre-Dame which gave the Prince of Journalists the opportunity to bump into the heir to the House of Sussex, she played, more and better than ever, her role of Paneuropean ambassadress and, in spite of the master of ceremonies who wanted her to sit with the ladies, she sat down right in the middle of the diplomatic corps, whence she refused to be evicted, defended as she was by the papal nuncio. On her way out, the distraught look on her godson's face seemed quite auspicious to her and, although the young lord, as a British subject, had no claim to be a part of the world's brain, his godmother, touched by his emotion, didn't hesitate to set him clear on a few aspects of international politics to help him become the smallest cell in the great Paneuropean body. She recognized very quickly, however, that this handsome adolescent had a greater gift for choosing ties than for penetrating the arcana of the temple of aristocratization where she reigned as the great priestess.

La Monte Putina had been one of the first and most eager to invite, cajole, flatter Augusta. She is the one who convinced the divine lady to give today's historic luncheon. Marie Torchon, Synovie, a young American couple, and even a singer will be among the guests. Everyone is late. And yet Esperanza had promised to arrive very early in order to greet the archduchess and set the tone. Primrose is afraid of committing a faux pas. The Prince of Journalists doesn't seem too self-possessed. Fortunately, Augusta takes it upon herself to steady her cousin who has become entangled in the complicated pantlegs of her pajama bottoms and has run the risk, in the deepest phase of her bow, of simply falling on her behind.

For someone who has to take the bus (Augusta isn't rich) and walk two kilometers in the sun (which is no fun for a person of her volume), Augusta seems all sweetness and light. The Prince of Journalists defers to her with all the courtly manners he can muster, but she, with the exquisite condescension of those too well-born to worry about exaggerating simplicity, tells him: "Do call me Augusta. If I am a Hapsburg by marriage, I am also Hungarian by birth, Czechoslovakian at heart, and Paneuropean in intelligence—yes, Paneuropean and almost a vegetarian."

4

A Respectable Pastime

THE YOUNG LORD WENT AND put on a pair of trousers and a shirt, for even though his trunks are perfectly matched with the daylight, he felt ashamed at being so scantily clothed in the presence of his archduchess of a godmother who, most definitely, has not yet evolved to the nudist stage of her development.

The Prince of Journalists, offering his right arm to Augusta and his left to Primrose, leads them under the bower where the threesome sits down. Esperanza's ex-pseudolover is endowed with a patriotic conscience that is equalled only by his sense of dignity, of grandeur, one might say; if for seventy years he has, as far as relations with women are concerned, made a point of putting himself on display just enough to silence the gossip columnists, it is because, from one fashion to the next, his female contemporaries had neglected the secret of this nobility, this imperious little something that the Roman Empire, among so many other treasures, bequeathed to the world, and it eventually died out. Of all the finery he has seen, both great and small, he can remember no other dress but the one whose ruches, flounces, bonnets, bows, puffs, bustles, plaid bias bindings, cloaks, and fluttering hat ribbons gave his late mother, in spite of the hump which provided only meager decorative help, a stateliness such that, even now, he feels capable of resentment at his beloved father, the epileptic, for having shared the hollow lady's parasol-halo, on those walks, as tender as they were matrimonial, inside the never-crossed walls of that park where love had managed to remain intact for half a century.

Today, not only has Primrose succeeded in concocting a pair of pajamas that command respect, but it can also and most importantly be said that Augusta, with the help of the heat, is bursting with nobility under her black silk armor. If Esperanza were here, they would form a veritable trinity of magnificence.

As a child, the Prince of Journalists used to sing:

> Hey little sleighbell,
> Is my wooden shoe full of coins, pray tell?

Later, when his parents, in order to fill up the long winter evenings, had taught him not baccarat but blackjack—a game which the hunchback and the epileptic considered to be, by virtue of the very fact that it dated from Molière's time, free from the hazardous, low-minded trickery usually inherent in cards—the rhythm of "Hey Little Sleighbell" served as a skeleton for these new lyrics, fitting encouragement for a nascent puberty:

> Knick knack, paddy whack,
> How many loves for my little bone?

Ah! Old French songs! The women who sing them really do deserve the Legion of Honor.

For some fellows, when they were young,

> There were ten girls on a prairie,
> Ten girls old enough to marry.
> There was China, there was Lina,
> There were Martine and sweet Colleen.

For the hummer of "Knick Knack, Paddy Whack," the song had quickly turned into the anxious query immortalized by Villon in the famous ballad "Oh where are the snows of yesteryear?"

> Oh where are those she-cocks
> Who traveled by threes, in flocks?
> Oh where are those she-fowls
> With triple bowels?
> Knick knack, paddy whack,
> There's no more love for my little bone.

Despite the classical bent of an imagination which shunned the monstrous even at the height of its furthest leaps and giddiest masturbatory tangents, for years and years, neither she-cocks nor she-fowls managed to take on human features. Absent fairies, their sweet names in real life remained elusive. Today, however, as it turns out, if Primrose resembles a she-cock, Augusta looks more like a she-fowl. And vice versa. That much is clear, luminous, blinding even. And the third time's a charm. If on either side of him are seated these two creatures always invoked but never seen, then yet another, in the person of Esperanza, can't fail to make her entrance soon.

And with that, the Prince of Journalists begins to rub his hands together, recapitulating:

Augusta: symbol of political intelligence despite a bold internationalism.

Primrose: symbol of beauty despite the lump of paraffin under the skin of one of her cheeks.

Esperanza: symbol of French clarity leavened with Gallic wit and, thanks to her marriage, the scent of Roman legal wisdom, despite the vaporous airs she occasionally affects.

The sum of this she-cocky, she-fowlish trio must be at least equal to that of those historic ladies, they too numbering three, whom the Prince of Journalists has always particularly admired: Madame de Maintenon, Madame Roland, and George Sand.

Now precisely because Beauty is using abundant quantities of gin to soak up the compliments which Intelligence heaped on her at the sight of the footmen lined up in front of these laurels that are dying an oh so poetic death in the excessive sun, because Intelligence herself hushes up, all the better to use the livery worn by the footmen of the House of Sussex for inspiration in choosing a uniform for the future Paneuropean army that will eventually have to be raised and sent all the way to Moscow to show what stuff an Augusta is made of, because only the buzzing of the heat wave qualifies somewhat the absolute silence of these hieratic souls, Madame de Maintenon, Madame Roland, and George Sand double as Primrose, busy with her alcohol, Augusta, busy with her world reorganization projects, and Esperanza busy with her absence.

> Knick knack, paddy whack,
> When you've got a she-cock
> Caress her on the buttock.
> When you've got a she-fowl
> Tickle her under a towel.

Knick knack, paddy whack. Throbbing beat. And what handplay! Madame de Maintenon, queen of clubs (she's the most serious one), Madame Roland, queen of hearts (oh those beautiful Girondins!), George Sand, queen of spades (the jokers make fun of her daring choice of clothes).

Wait a minute! Madame de Maintenon is already talking about retiring. Her spouse, the Sun King, doesn't like to go to bed before the evening prayer which they usually say together, at twilight.

GEORGE SAND

Praying together! I know all about that. My dear Alfred de Musset, oh yes, madam, the author of *Hope in God,* in Venice, belted out his little (oh! very little, and the male of a lady of letters is not necessarily a man of letters) but I'm getting lost in my parentheses, it's Alfred's fault, Alfred who . . . who . . . ah yes! now I remember, Alfred, who in Venice, belted out his little devotions, at the back of a chapel, I

daresay, just like those found in Le Berry, to which I had shown him
the way:

> Hometown chapel in the trees
> Where we enter on our knees.

as they sing it in Nohant.

Mme. DE MAINTENON

I beg your pardon?

GEORGE SAND

I was saying, my smooth-chinned morganatic friend, that women of
genius are never cleanshaven. Sappho wore sideburns, Joan of Arc
long black whiskers, and Mona Lisa a little goatee, as you would
know if you hadn't been holed up in the provinces.

Mme. DE MAINTENON

As provinces go, Nohant is well worth Versailles.

GEORGE SAND

Even so, the court and the town know that you tended the turkeys [*les
dindons*] at Fouillis-les-Oies and the geese [*les oies*] at Fouillis-les-
Dindons. For a pious king, wolfing down Scarron's leftovers, a sure
way to do penance!

Mme. ROLAND

A pious king who does penance. When it comes right down to it, with
the Girondins, we didn't ask for more. Fouillis-les-Oies! Fouillis-les-
Dindons! Such bucolic names. Eat cream cheese, drink milk, pick
cornflowers, daisies, red poppies, tie their tricolored bouquet with a
ribbon and come home in the twilight singing some arietta, oh Caius!
oh Gracchus! oh Brutus! oh Mucius! oh Crocus! oh Anus! my dear
Romans, a citizen yearns for the sweetness of country evenings. I was
born at Le Pont-Neuf, but I love raspberries and the angelus. My
marriage was a brilliant success. I ignored the difference in age and
rightly so, for Roland is worthy of the ancients. Why don't they call
him Rolandus?

In the heyday of the Revolution, I gave very nice little dinner
parties. Roland was a government minister. We could entertain, save
money, and stay honest all at the same time. I thought about the little
house where I would have watched my virtuous companion die

honorably, at a ripe old age, before getting married again, to some handsome Girondin. Jealous people picked a quarrel with us. Roland committed suicide because I had been guillotined, but wait a minute, now that I mention it, that bothers me. We are among famous women, so, if you don't mind, ladies . . . (*And at that moment, with both hands Madame Roland takes off her head which hadn't even been reattached, but merely placed on the pillar of her neck. She casually sets it somewhere, anywhere.*)

Mme. DE MAINTENON and GEORGE SAND

Oh!

Mme. ROLAND'S HEAD

You haven't forgotten my historic saying: "Liberty! how many crimes are committed in your name!" It might not sound like much, but it's like Christopher Columbus's egg, just try thinking up something that original. Moreover, it cost me a great deal of effort, countless migraines, that little sentence, and on top of that, at the foot of the scaffold, it almost slipped my mind. Lord! I was beginning to lose my head after all I had suffered since the day old man Duchêne had dared to write about my hair—my wonderful hair, pride of the Girondists, coveted by the members of the Montagne—that it was false hair!

Mme. DE MAINTENON

Butcher's daughter, fie on you! Manners and Madame Roland are as different as night and day. One could hardly imagine greater tactlessness than mentioning wigs in the presence of Louis XIV's wife. A little stint at Saint-Cyr would do these Republican women a world of good. I won't waste my scorn on them. Let's go get our royal spouse. How pleased we are when he calls us his security,
his se se
his cu cu
his ri ri
his ty ty
his security. . . .

Madame de Maintenon goes off humming. All alone now, George Sand, who as a conscientious novelist insists on using her own powers of observation to find out what's going on, stealthily approaches the table where Madame Roland has placed her curly head. She pulls on the hair to see if it's real. The head falls down and breaks. A gust of wind and the pieces are strewn about. Then the good lady from

Nohant remembers that she used to enjoy wearing disguises, so decides to dress up like a tree and leave.

No sooner thought than done, and the Prince of Journalists, full of respect for the drowsiness which Primrose and Augusta have gradually slipped into, ends up waiting for the other guests, free of all company. Now he might as well just bite his nails, as he used to do during his teenage years, after having read Balzac's works from which he loved to draw lessons in ambition. Since human corneous matter is a narcotic for man, his intoxication revealed that Rastignac and Rubempré had never been other than one and the same character, self-nourished, and perpetually resuscitated by his self-digestion, forever and ever capable of feeding on himself.

So if Rastignac is but the devouring part and Rubempré the devoured of a single individual, one can deduce from this fact that a master (be he master of the universe or—it amounts to the same thing—master of opinion), by collecting taxes from his subjects or fair profits from publicity and classified ads, is merely recovering the rarest piece of his moral being, his authority. Authority, that's what gives its decisive tone, its national virtue to the editorials with which a Prince of Journalists, following the dictates of his conscience, daily feeds the voracious masses. Aware of his duty, he has never forgotten that people expect everything of a superman. That is why, until August 2, 1914, for his part he had been 100 percent Nietzschean. Then his patriotism commanded him to break with everything German. He was in fact so busy exhorting civilians and soldiers that he didn't have, in the course of four years of hostilities, one minute to dream of the dear she-cocks and she-fowls in whom, today, he enjoys all the more looking for himself—especially since they have the tact to evaporate or fall asleep whenever they run the risk of becoming so real that they could swallow him up, or he swallow them up, in a single bite.

Who would have been the lamb, who would have been the wolf? Nobody could say, for although his enemies accuse him of being voracious, he has never devoured anyone. Rather than taking a bite out of Primrose's thigh or Augusta's breast—pieces fit, if not for kings, at least for marquesses or archdukes—he would prefer to eat his shadow. And he tells himself that he ate this shadow because the sun over his head doesn't allow the least projection of it on the ground. With his own silhouette, moreover, he has already had relations that were not without complexity or violence. He is certainly not one of those who can be accused of taking stabs in the dark. As a matter of fact, during one of his reserve officer training sessions, on a day when he had given in to the temptation to follow downstream, in the Oise, a rather well-built second lieutenant who was walking doing occasional handstands on the river bottom, suddenly realizing that, despite the constant concern for protecting his reputation, he was dishonoring the uniform, in order not to repeat the myth of Narcissus, in order not to give in to that mouth, that body cut to the same size as his body, his mouth, he put his hand to the saber, drew it, and, with large strokes, sabered (there are no other words) the temptation.

The first time in the course of his affair with Esperanza he had to drop by her house unannounced, he felt such rage upon finding her naked in front of her mirror that he almost broke it off, in spite of the outstanding services that she had already rendered him. He can still remember the words he flung at her: "You, playing the dressing-table nymph, you whom I call my goddess Reason." Esperanza was in a tight spot, but one must concede that, subsequently, she did her best to deserve his forgiveness. The Prince of Journalists was moved to tears when he thought of the little godsend she had become, thanks to him, but unfortunately had stopped being when, at the pinnacle of ducal grandeur, she decided to give free rein to an impulsive temperament.

Esperanza. He likes to think of her in her heyday with all the qualities of a young kept woman, certainly fit to hobnob with the wives of industrialists or engineers who spend the winter within the confines of Passy or the Trocadero, the summer in the suburbs, in simple but charming villas, in half-vegetable, half-flower gardens.

The Esperanza of that period of moderation was the perfect example of the person who is thirtyish, neat as a pin, poised but not in the least a poseur, a chic little writer, a deadpan conversationalist, and possessing a rare talent for the arts. Her specialty: the embossed silver spoonerism. Her son, as far back as he can remember, liked to squash his nose against the bookcovers and blotting pads produced in industrial quantities for her pleasure and perhaps also with a view toward increasing her respectability, as if she had not simply an only sister shut up in a brothel near La Porte Saint-Denis, but an entire family constituting a perpetual source of worry as to what gifts to choose for weddings, baptisms, first communions, etc. Delightful memories of an era when she devoted all of her time and energy to forging a respectable background for herself. Esperanza loves to dwell on it. Why not accompany her on a stroll down Memory Lane? She is there. Now we are, too. Come outdoor watercolor season, she sets up her folding chair, places the box with a selection of fresh colors on her knees, pours water into a nickel-plated goblet. At the end of an extended arm, a sovereign right hand establishes the perspective. The thumbnail goes back and forth, drops down, moves up again, careful to measure, to the closest thousandth, the temperature on this day of warmth and light with, by way of a thermometer, this pencil whose lead, all of a sudden, dips irremediably, making dots through which, if it so decided, the contours of the universe would have to pass.

Thus, on the nearly blank page of a Wattmann sketchpad, a few barely perceptible dots are forever pointing out their contours, their borders to these houses, these forests, these fields, these shadows, and this sky-rending horizon as well as these rank tufts of weeds whose job it is to represent the foreground.

"Everything in its place in a landscape just as in a cupboard. With a little order, a little method, it's no harder to do a successful painting from nature than it is to pack a trunk."

Ever since her days on tour as a chanteuse, she has always stuffed her suitcase with three or four times her volume in linen. She was thus in good enough shape not to be pushed around by the capricious elements. The first time a big silly cloud came up and taunted her, she knocked it flat. "Chance of rain? No, not a chance." Once you know how to handle her, you can get Mother Nature to jump through hoops and eat out of your hand.

Before she ever dreamt of becoming a duchess, how many streams Esperanza tamed! The strongest currents had no other choice than to go down fighting; the leaves gave up without a struggle and the wind, following their example, got by with only those whims that she allowed them. As for her, from the bottom of her so-called Charlotte Corday hat, whose lawn she had embroidered herself, to the very tip of her ankle boots, she felt a legitimate intoxication spreading through her caparisoned waist a drop at a time, like the contents of an hourglass, one grain at a time, for just as long as it takes to cook a soft-boiled egg. Once the watercolor was ready, she moved on to other exercises. Although a photographic plate sensitive to backlighting effects leaves nothing out from a landscape which has in fact been chosen for its inherently magical qualities and which the twilight has transformed into a real stage set, a woman of refinement won't register her satisfaction with a photograph album, even one embellished with a wealth of masks.

Therefore, instead of wasting her time idealizing, from variations on sky blue paper, picturesque sites and monuments, instead of tiring herself out framing them in the delicately denticulated contours of oak leaves, she entrusts to the cake plates, screens, fireguards, and cushion silk the poeticized memories of her outings and honeymoon trips, which she and her pseudolover took time and again so that their love would become not merely a Parisian, but a national, even an international, phenomenon. Hence the spread of painting on porcelain and poker work, the mammary glands of distinguished interiors just as grazing and ploughing had been in Sully's France.

Upon signing the contract specifying her relations with the Prince of Journalists, Esperanza had burned her hennins and princess gowns. But since the contract wasn't unilateral, after this sacrificial act, she solemnly deemed herself free to apply the clause acknowledging her right to whims of any sexual, vestimentary, or capillary nature whatever, provided that they remain unknown to those Parisian socialites who thrive on gossip and opening nights. She had thus lost no time in unearthing a hairdresser who, until her marriage to the duke of Monte Putina, came by each day to arrange a real (albeit ephemeral) fireworks display of buns, waves, puffs, curls, and cauls.

Esperanza never tired of devising, just for herself, artistic hairstyles in harmony with her dear little interior, but by the ostentation, the studied fullness as well as the intimacy of the portraits, this hair opera, whose stage was her scalp, recalled the heroic, royal era of Wagner's works, when Ludwig II of Bavaria deemed no one worthy of sharing with him the honor of hearing the tetralogy.

In order to amplify the monuments with which she crowned her head, Esperanza didn't hesitate to supplement her abundant, inherited pilosity with the considerable help of wigs, around which snaked a ribbon of the same salmon-colored hue as the silk favors on the branches of the dwarf palm trees, asparagus ferns, araucarias shooting straight out of a shag whose effervescence revitalized their anemia, which was indeed unworthy of the Chinese flower-pot cases at the mercy of the lady of the house's paintbrush. With her proud face in the shadow of these machicolated marcel waves, Esperanza, naked or wearing a transparent blouse, then poured a finger of Frontignan from a gilded silver and crystal ewer for the imaginary visitors straddling chairs, each of which was paired with some nest of tables, under the protection of plump, fat-bellied, fat-bottomed, fat-cheeked, well-fed, well-to-do, well-plastered lovers spread over walls and ceilings of her neo-Louis XVI drawing room.

Since no one actually came to drink the Frontignan, Esperanza would put it back into the decanter after having levied just the tithe of two glasses, one of which was for herself and the other for the hairdresser, Monsieur Gustave, with his black cutaway coat, waxen face of a very distressing symmetry, and three parts dividing his hair right down the middle, wherever it was to be found: the first one between two tufts on his head, another part to separate his mustache, and the third part by way of a spinal column for his beard. With a diaphanous hand, Monsieur Gustave brandishes his curling scepter and spreads, with the good smell of hot hair, the secret of undulating waves. Although it didn't take him very long to realize that he would never have a better customer than Esperanza, he began by scorning her. The primary source of his resentment was the imagination that she made him exert in order to invent something new, something beautiful, day in and day out. Besides, you can always judge a woman by her hairstyle.

So how can one tolerate the somersaulting flip-flops of a mechanical wig capable of giving vertigo to the most daring hairstylist? How can one possibly avoid suffocating from the lyre of surprises which only a demoness, madly playing scales on it, would dare to offer, the whole lyre of her unruly mane multiplied by thousands and thousands of artificial finds? She receives her guest with bare tits and powdered navel. From the tips of her toes to the roots of her hair, she's plastered with paint and makeup. No one surpasses Monsieur Gustave, either quantitatively or qualitatively, in the major principles of commercial etiquette. He has never been disrespectful to any of his customers, but this one is definitely being too provocative and, one day, in spite of himself, he can't help but poke the points of Esperanza's breasts with the two tips of his red-hot iron. And she, instead of recoiling to avoid getting burned, offers her tits to the instrument of torture. Monsieur Gustave closes his eyes. He hears a body fall at his feet. With eyelids still closed, he gropes around on the rug. The metal is no longer hot enough to dig into this scorched chest. Then, while with his right hand he twirls the tool of his trade, like a court jester his bauble, with his left he takes out a more intimate but no less inexorable object, with which he penetrates the lifeless beauty ever so carefully, using all of his hairdressing skills to impart soft, undulating waves. Scratching against the low-grade cloth of off-the-rack trousers, her thighs resuscitate and, in their intoxicating pain, the bloody breasts take delight in putting gigantic Legions of Honor on each of his lapels, only one of which, until now, displayed the honorary academic insignia, a highly deserved and long overdue decoration, but received only recently by Monsieur Gustave who, for twenty years, has shorn and shaved office managers from the Ministry of Justice.

From this memorable morning onward, Esperanza never failed to add to the daily pleasures of hairdressing those of love. When she married the duke of Monte Putina, she gave Monsieur Gustave a tidy little nest egg. He settled in Nice where his business thrived until the Crash. Now he is on the verge of bankruptcy. Thus he is taking advantage of Esperanza's stay on the French Riviera to pester her. If she has not yet arrived at Primrose's house, it is because last night she received an urgent, almost threatening message. She wanted to send over a third party with some cash for him. She asked the Prince of Journalists' advice. He urged her to run her own errand, alleging the necessity of a permanent etc., etc. Sly as a fox, so that her husband and son wouldn't tire of waiting for her, she sent them both to pick up the singer Krim, whose presence was also requested at the marquise's house, for her unwaveringly Wagnerolatrous family had once met Augusta in Bayreuth.

Esperanza will never forgive herself for having extended a favor to Krim whom she hates and takes every opportunity to accuse of having destroyed her son's future.

A mother through and through, Esperanza wasn't about to entrust anyone else with responsibility for an upbringing that she had both the right and the duty to supervise.

He who paraded her around as his lover had made her worship Madame de Maintenon. Paid to know that distinction alone makes success possible, she began by forbidding the blood of her blood to go out with no socks on, even during the summer at the seaside.

She invoked the Age of Reason, the theological virtues, slapped him more than once because he persisted in believing that the symbol of the apostles was a consecrated cup, yes, the holy bowl from which Jesus Christ's boyfriends drank without letting their lips touch it.

She made him drink Evian water and eat stewed fruit and braised lettuce. She also expended a great deal of energy teaching him to hate the sun, which makes curtains fade. She took herself to task for having once let him, when her friends were all bohemians, run naked, and for having called him "seductive child," a name which, at the time, fit him well, too well. Her feelings of remorse gradually faded away, moreover, and she had the joy of seeing the formerly seductive child follow her on her way up. First he lost his bad habits of boisterousness, and was able, at all times, to assume a quite reasonable and even, on solemn occasions, sufficiently oldish appearance to give his mother reason to hope, together with the Prince of Journalists, that they might be able to make a diplomat of him. If it weren't sheer lunacy to believe that the little fellow would get from her the qualities that make it possible to succeed, what would have prevented him from receiving a talent for languages as a legacy from his father the secondhand clothes-dealer, who spoke Polish, Russian, French, German, Italian, Spanish, and even Yiddish.

So they gave the child an English schoolmistress and he became "Rub-dub-dub," because the first line (and massacred at that) of the song

Rub-a-dub-dub
Three men in a tub
The butcher, the baker, the candlestick maker
They all set out to sea . . .

summed up everything that the Anglo-Saxon miss had succeeded in teaching him after a whole year of verb forms, fables, vocabulary drills, and Salvation Army hymns, never omitting a rousing "God Save the King" before his porridge every morning.

Finally throwing in the towel, the little miss had left France for a Russia that was still the home of the great polyglot dukes. From Moscow, she would send postcards on which, in the square reserved for correspondence, she described the prodigious feats performed by the aristocratic babies whose gift for languages rivaled that for the natatory arts of those little black boys who plunge from their mothers' wombs into the middle of the ocean.

Resembling neither the former nor the latter, Rub-dub-dub was ridding himself so completely of his instincts, in accordance with Esperanza's method, that he risked drowning in his bathtub. He felt more and more uncomfortable with the elements. At night, he dreamt that his ears were floating, like water-lily leaves against the drift, on the current of English words. Water and hearing, water, hearing. With all those liquid syllables, how could one avoid being swallowed up in the end? Water, hearing. Was it out of vengeance that each morning, during garden season, he went down at dawn, on the pretext of picking flowers, to crush the dew? Paltry revenge. He felt guilty for the rest of the day.

Three kingdoms, four cardinal points, five senses. You can't find your way simply by sniffing. At the end of every stroll the world turns into an escape, a lie. Who or what can be trusted besides snails? They are continually being told

> One-eyed slug,
> Show your mug,

and they get caught. In all fairness, one should also thank earthworms who, without being killed (finally a pleasure that doesn't result in feelings of guilt), can be cut into several pieces, like the ideal mouse in the song:

> A green mouse
> Running through the grass.
> I catch it by the tail,
> I show it to some men.
> These men tell me:
> Dip it in the oil,
> Cut off its tail,
> That'll make two of them.

Water, English, they're the opposite of snails, earthworms, green mice. Rub-dub-dub, nobody can do anything about it.

And the little miss who insists on trying to shame him from the midst of all the Russias is wasting her time. He is determined to remember only the colored illustrations of her postcards, the rainbow splash of a palace standing out against a background of too blue sky and too white earth. It's the Kremlin. Seated on a stool, they repeat: Kremlin, Kremlin, Kremlin, and so forth for a quarter of an hour until they don't know where they are any longer, or what they're doing. What does it matter now whether or not some Russian babies read Dickens in the original? Nothing counts but the Kremlin, the Kremlin—far more beautiful than the garden kiosk in Louveciennes. Louveciennes, what a beautiful place nonetheless, with a name as sweet as a wolf's wife [*louve* = she-wolf] who would deserve to be called Lucienne.

When he was still but a seductive child, Rub-dub-dub could play music on his belly, his thighs. Now that they no longer let him walk on the lawns, much less roll on them, he consoles himself with the portico. With his hands gripping the pole which his legs grasp and squeeze with all their might, he hoists himself up. No sooner is he at the top than he lets himself slide down in one fell swoop. And he repeats this trick two, three, four, five, six times, until a smarting sensation emanates from something between his legs which must be bleeding, something he doesn't dare name, much less look at, for, if he were to unbutton his shorts, lift up his shirt, the soft little skin that likes to be rubbed would come with them. One can be in pain and enjoy it, and what's more, be in just the right state of mind to appreciate the chromolithograph that the cook nailed on the pantry wall and never fails to describe in these terms: "As a matter of fact, the Municipal Charity Bazaar gave me a lovely gift. And with the caption that explains the whole story, it's as clear as a clarinet. It's about a scoundrel of an Italian, Fra Diavolo, a name that means the Devil or something like that, in the guinea language. The rascal lived more than a century ago under Poleon, up in mountains that send a shiver all up and down your spine. But the joker didn't give a damn about gendarmes, God, the Devil, anybody, or anything. He earned his keep by holding up stagecoaches. Rest stop, but no snack. So there he is, when he comes upon a bunch of flashy tarts. In our day and age they would be treated like rabble. Back then, they couldn't have been more popular. The Diavolo is putty in their hands. The good-for-nothing lets them get back in the coach. The dumb sluts make a curtsy. And home, James, and don't spare the horses! And every Jill went back to her Jack."

Rub-dub-dub is already dreaming that he is Fra Diavolo. A Fra Diavolo who wouldn't let his beautiful captives get away like that. But before you can think about keeping them, you have to find them, and in Seine-et-Oise there are only button boots, dustcoats, and pointy umbrellas, instead of those cothurnuses, dresses with trains, generously lowcut blouses and high, ribbon-trimmed canes that added such a pretty touch to the mountains of Calabria.

The Napoleonic ladies in the chromolithograph were not alone, moreover, at least not for long, in getting back at real-life women for him. A chimerical friend on a poster plastered on all train-station walls soon nourishes his dreams with a mauve smile. She was receiving from the hands of a young man in a light frock coat and a dove-bellied four-in-hand tie fruit picked in a nebulous, faraway land; but the fruits themselves were as nebulous as their faraway source; how else could they have made their way into her body just at the point where the ribbed points of lace beneath her hoop skirt yielded to the oscillations of a rocking chair which presented an amazing spectacle to those who saw the lathe-shaped wood force its whims on such a whimsical frame.

Then it was Krim. Esperanza had known Krim's father and mother in the days when she went around with rhymesters and daubers; they were hunger married to thirst, as she put it. Thus she threw a perfect fit when she found out that they were going to move into a shack right near the comfortable villa given to her by the Prince of Journalists.

Krim's father, what a sucker! A so-called poet who thought he was a poet, better than Déroulède, when in fact he didn't even know how to count to twelve and dared to use the term *free* to describe verse that was merely lame. He had infant's eyes but mailman's feet, the braggart who managed to go *pedibus cum jambis* to Germany, where he made a fuss over Wagner, as if in Paris, the greatest city in the world, the Opéra and the Opéra Comique didn't amount to anything. His parents (whom he had succeeded in killing by breaking their hearts after having ruined them) had christened him Jules, but he insisted on being called Lohengrin. His other mania: precious stones. He had founded a school based on them: gemism. No more difficult to write "sapphire" than horse's ass. So long as it's just literature, no problem; but the real world is a horse of a different color. Too poor to buy his wife and daughter the real thing, Lohengrin covers them with fakes. Even these trinkets are too expensive, if you're flat broke. By the grace of God Mrs. Lohengrin was able to pick up a first-place prize in a piano competition. To keep the pot boiling, she gives private lessons, climbs stairs four at a time, runs around in ankle boots turning on her heels and wearing out her soles. At noon she pretends to visit museums. In one of the Egyptian rooms in the Louvre she hides behind a sarcophagus and devours a slice of cold veal. After she has finished drinking her tears, if she is still thirsty she knocks back a goblet of Wallace spring water and, after she has finished running, shivering, tickling the ivories, she has to go back home to the boondocks where Lohengrin, lazy oaf, has sat daydreaming from morning till night, not even going to the trouble to make his bed or shine his shoes. But the same woman who hits everyone up for money is such a dummy that, once home, she forgets all fatigue as soon as her good-for-nothing opens his mouth—he knows her by heart and never fails to tell her some rubbish like: "Listen to the flight of the Valkyries, my Opal."

The flight of the Valkyries is the wind doing its tricks in the tar paper, by way of a roof, over their heads.

Lohengrin and Opal had three children. First a son, Parsifal, who was never able to stand on his wobbly legs. At home, in his armchair, with a blanket on his knees, he is very handsome, worthy of the name that on the outside, because of his crutches, becomes Alfred. But if the poor kid has trouble keeping his balance, fortunately, the eldest daughter, Brunnhilde, has trouble keeping her wits. She works at the rental agency and, since one reaps what one has sown, Esperanza just sent her a repoussé tin frame on the occasion of her engagement to her boss's son. But alas! the last-born, Kriemhilde, shortened to Krim, nobody trusts her any further than they can throw her. This Krim couldn't be called beautiful, not even pretty. Esperanza, who is an expert when it comes to human proportions and knows how many times the head should be contained in the body, wouldn't hesitate to call her hydrocephalic. Seeing men purr like pussycats over a creature with an enlarged noggin when you have taken it upon yourself to sacrifice everything for distinction is quite enough to drive a woman mad. Esperanza will nonetheless continue to fight the good fight for respectability. In order to console herself, she will show no indulgence for an era in which bizarreness reigns supreme, for Krim is a hit, a bigger and bigger hit who eventually becomes a triumphant success the day she appears on the scene in her new invention, a black velvet dress, open to the waist in back, but with long sleeves and a bodice high enough in front to guillotine her neck at its base, as if the fabric wanted to punish her for a criminal homonymy.

Krim was soon basking in glory thanks to her realistic creations, of which the most famous remains "Gaslight Is My Sunshine."

As a rule, she must always take the last train home; but actually, at least three times a week, she claims to have missed it.

One day when Lohengrin was taking a walk, a passerby who had bent over to pick up a board struck him three times on the head with it. If the Wagnerolator, consistent with his own logic, had been wearing a tinplate helmet, Nibelungen-style, he wouldn't have felt a thing. As it was, his occiput being protected only by a poor old felt hat, he dropped dead, overjoying the gentleman with the board, who was even crazier than he and who didn't know him from Adam.

Inconsolable, Opal gave her necklaces, rings, and bracelets to her daughters and went on being a professional sponge. Esperanza, who had taught the Prince of Journalists what role charity should play in the life of a proper lady, decided that, each morning, after the voluptuous session with the hairstylist and the Frontignan ceremony, Opal would come play and even, since she had the remains of a beautiful voice, sing something for her.

For this little recital that took place in the middle of the day, Esperanza had the shutters and curtains closed. She would settle comfortably in her wing chair and, with a nod, give Opal permission to begin. The sumptuousness of the damask that served as a background for the musician's face exaggerated even more the wretchedness of the skin, which was deathly pale, loose, and so worn that the sobs accompanying her romantic ballads, instead of rising in vocalization exercise bubbles, broke, in their harsh, painful ascent, the hypotenuse of the triangle of shadow inscribed between the prow of the jaws and a wrinkle, once a Venus necklace. And with that, the listener would applaud and demand: "The sad song one more time, Opal."

Such insistence takes Opal quite by surprise. She is out of breath. So what. To give herself a boost, all she has to do is think of her loved ones. Her own nearest and dearest. But Lohengrin is in a box, Parsifal won't be around for long, and Brunnhilde, armed with scorn, sits enthroned at the cash register in her rental agency. And Krim, who, in spite of her ear, refused to like Wagner for her family's sake, lives and breathes for her lovers and her realistic creations. Opal closes her eyes. She would like to have cement poured under her eyelids, down her throat, into her nostrils. But Esperanza, a paying customer who wants to get her money's worth, becomes impatient: "Come on, come on." The show must go on. Opal's voice quavers. Will she have the strength to make it to the end of a song that ends in hope [*espérance*]? She resists the last chords, the last phrase, one, two, three, four, five, ten, fifteen, twenty, thirty, forty seconds, almost a minute. She is going to decide to resist forever, eternally, when, with an imperious little cough, Esperanza calls her to order. Finally, she resumes. Esperanza decides that she has no further business in this drawing room and takes French leave. In five minutes, a tray-bearing servant will appear to present Opal with a glass of water and a five-franc piece.

When Parsifal dies, the magnanimous Esperanza will adopt Opal who, too proud to accept being a burden, will perform hundreds of exhausting chores to earn the bread, meat, vegetables, water, gas, electricity, and weekly baths that are being so generously dispensed.

5

A Well-bred Young Man

ON THURSDAYS, OPAL takes Rub-dub-dub for a walk. They pretend to head for the botanical garden or the museums, but they dash over to the music hall to admire Krim's singing act. A gentleman emerges from the mahogany box office and, all smiles, gives two orchestra tickets to the mother of the young lady known for realistic creations. And in the first row, no less, which promises, as soon as the curtain is drawn, the nice smell of face powder, Russian eau de cologne (oddly enough), warm fatigue, and other intoxicating things to breathe, with, by way of flour to thicken the sauce, the dust kicked up on the stage floor by unseen drafts.

The limelight deifies eccentrics, guitarists, acrobats, monologuists, and illusionists, but jokes, tricks, pizzicati, feats of strength and of skill, impeccable tails, baggy checkered pants, tights, spangled tunics opened right down to incredibly green petticoats, and whether they be stars with solitary disdain or large families whose members are climbing on each other's shoulders, with the father and the older sons at the base of the pyramid and, at the top, the last little girl, not a bit stingy with her kisses—everything and everyone only amount to preludes, very unworthy preludes to Krim's appearance.

Krim's figure is so delicate it looks as though it would flop over if removed from its black velvet sheath; she has a large head but such a small face one is amazed not to see her pulled backwards head over heels by the weight of her long chignon. In her green eyes—but of a green that is closer to yellow than to blue (alcoholic clown eyes, says Esperanza)—the budding flames of absinthe are dancing, and if these flames don't fly away, uprooted by the storms that make them quiver, it is because tiny golden paving stones protect their tear-fed roots. And Krim, she hardly wears any makeup on her little papier-mâché girl cheeks. She doesn't need the least bit of kohl for her eyelids, charred by the fatigue of working-class love affairs. Her nails are stained with the blood of the handkerchief that her hands knead over and over before deciding to tie it around the neck for her final song.

The applause forces Krim to reprise each one of her songs. She nonetheless leaves the stage too quickly. And impossible to follow her behind the incredible rose-covered flats. Opal would never dare to bother her daughter in the dressing room, which is probably full of pushing, shoving admirers. So it's right out to the street, with the icy slap and all of the fingers that the cold is able to slip through the loose-knit mufflers to grip an exposed neck. And yet, throughout the night, one can still hear the fluttering words that Krim used to free the countless swarm. Invisible at first, it didn't take them long to reassume their original shape and come land in the glass cages that the gas lamps put at their disposal. They are strange hummingbirds, streetlamp flowers, birds not even humming to the dancing down of molten metal. Krim's eyes and Krim's eyes alone light up the Paris night: "Gaslight Is My Sunshine." Through purely theoretical lessons as well as, in practice, through her own example, Esperanza has already succeeded in turning a seductive little wild child into a Rub-dub-dub who makes it clear to the Prince of Journalists that he would like an umbrella as a New Year's gift.

Incapable of stopping when she is so far along, Esperanza plans, following the advice of her sagacious protector, to continue metamorphosing an unbroken colt into a good little horse and why not even a fiacre horse, for she wishes her son an intellectual's muscles, a paleographer's thorax, and Scarron's legs, so that he would be if not a legless cripple, at least sufficiently knock-kneed to serve as the first husband for some reincarnation of Madame de Maintenon. Esperanza likes to struggle: "You've got to pull yourself up," she tells her son, "by your bootstraps." So what a treat for her to have succeeded in changing a purely animal animal into a human animal and to see him, today, ready to be transformed from a human animal into a social animal. But a future social animal doesn't reveal the secret ecstasies of his afternoons.

Thanks to the indiscretion that goes along with the function, the formerly seductive child is not unaware that his mother was a singer, and "not a singer like Miss Krim," insists the cook, "but a poor little wailer who belted it out off-key in a dive full of drunks and jerks." He has forbidden himself, in spite of his curiosity, to ask her about her youth, just as caution prevents him from ever mentioning Krim's name in her presence, for he has realized that she who must earn the stripes of distinction one at a time couldn't fail to hate her, the woman who reminds her of a loathsome past, all the more loathsome since in the present light of star-studded success, her miserable tunes of earlier days can only appear more miserable. But when he is alone, instead of repeating: "Kremlin, Kremlin, Kremlin," as he did in Louveciennes, reveling in the name of the world's most beautiful monument, now he says over and over: "Krim, Krim, Krim, Krim."

And then, since a portrait of his mother is hanging on the wall there before his eyes, he notices, in the ecstasy of the monosyllabic incantation, that the impeccable Madame Esperanza de Saint-Gobain is as inferior to Krim as the Louveciennes kiosk, in its day, was to the Kremlin.

But the mother's room is right next to her son's, and one morning when he is repeating the abhorred name too loud, despite her strong reluctance to interrupt the ritual hairdressing session, she suddenly tears herself from Monsieur Gustave's grasp so abruptly that the poor scalper's celluloid oversleeves fall off. The slapping of her mules forces Rub-dub-dub to turn around, but he immediately closes his eyes to avoid seeing this naked demoness whose head bears still uncompleted monuments that are already in ruins, as if this morning the castle of hair had been erected only as a refuge for the most dreadful phantoms.

Esperanza yells: "Krim is a witch and that stupid tune of hers is nothing but a fake. She's putting on that sophisticated act, but she's as much of a rube as that cornball excuse for a piano teacher whose daughter she is. And in that black dress, really, she looks like a pig in a poke. But don't forget, little sucker, that there are three types of women: the sexy type, the artistic type, and the distinguished type. You must respect your mother for achieving success as all three. And now you're taunting me with this bitch? I'm too kind. I should have left that old hag Opal to die on the street; now she's tickled pink because her monster of a daughter gets five hundred francs for just twenty minutes of yelping at the queen of Portugal's sister-in-law's lover's cousin's brother's whore's house. Well, I don't give a damn; I swear on your poor father's ashes that I'll pay a visit to the queen of Portugal herself, and without playing the fool, and I'll go to the court of England, and I'll have lunch with the pope. Besides, I've already gone drinking with cabinet members. I'm not a pretentious bitch, but a serious-minded woman, and I intend for my son to become a gentleman—hey, answer me, if you don't want to get slapped, hey, are you listening to me, you son of a ragpicker? . . ."

Rub-dub-dub sobs.

Esperanza strikes the iron while it is hot and her child while he is crying. She punctuates her statements with resounding blows: "Yes, I repeat, son of a ragpicker, and I shall add, son of a dirty Polack, of a pimp, of an ugly duck, son of a whore, son of a cow, son of a bitch. . . ." And she continues on in the same vein, forgetting that she herself is the mother of this son of a bitch, cow, whore.

With Rub-dub-dub crushed by a good two hundred pounds of abuse, she goes back to her room when, all of a sudden, a mirror reminds her that she has a Greek profile. As a result, the triumph, the mere success of any nose the least bit turned up becomes a personal insult to her. So she is not going to leave without pointing out that Krim has a mushroom nose right in the middle of her face:

"A mushroom nose (for one thing), eyes of a color that is impossible to determine (for another), the mop of a demoness (for a third), barely six notes in her voice (for a fourth). And to think that there are poor fools who let themselves be taken in by her. What's really so special about this Krim? You prefer Krim, you little squirt, but I prefer reality. Only yesterday I had you recite your Roman history lesson. You remember how Caesar hesitated between pleasure and virtue? Now it's time for you to choose: Krim or reality. Krim is falsehood in female form. I am reality."

And suddenly calming down, possessing enough strength to avoid taking advantage of her triumph, Esperanza goes away just as she had come.

To explain her absence and the cries he heard through the wall, she tells Monsieur Gustave that she has been discussing the most serious matters with her own flesh and blood. An ounce of prevention is better than a pound of cure. She has no intention of playing the hen that hatched a duck. Krim as reality! Krim *or* reality, is more like it. She, Esperanza, is all for English upbringing. Let children assume their responsibilities. Krim as reality. Krim or reality? One or the other. She is reality. Esperanza. Spread the word. And may Rub-dub-dub cross the Rubicon.

Monsieur Gustave agrees, repeats everything he hears. Rubicon, Rubicon or ruby cunt, he suddenly begins to sing softly and then, realist or krimist, he kneels down and lets his well-raked beard mingle with the foliage of a pubic forest that he dreams of civilizing with the iron and the comb . . . but that's another story.

Krim as reality.
Krim or reality?
Rub-dub-dub has chosen Krim.
Alas, Krim hasn't chosen him.

She is on tour abroad and he must let his memory of her fade into a pale gray image beneath the shadow of secondary school, Latin and Greek declensions, exam worries.

Esperanza, more and more determined to see him succeed, learns the dead languages for the sheer pleasure of hearing him recite his lessons. But she herself gets caught up in the game and now she murmurs one of Anacreon's pieces of poetic filth to Monsieur Gustave every morning. To see her swoon, you would think her navel was getting tickled to death.

She translates: "Eros, long ago, in the roses. . . ." Ronsard, du Bellay, the Pléiade, and all of the others tried their hand at rendering this famous piece in French. Esperanza notes her agreement with these gentlemen. As regards poetry, for her there's nothing like a baby who takes refuge in his mother's arms because a bee has stung him. Jealous of the demigod, the hairstylist silently curses the plump little fellow. A bee has stung him on the ass. But his ass will have to go through far worse. All lovesick asses go through far worse. Starting with Esperanza's. And he'd love to put his curling iron somewhere. He doesn't dare. Now Esperanza will only make love while reciting the "Prayer on the Acropolis," and she spit in his face one morning when he hadn't succeeded in building a little Pantheon atop her head: Ah, if Renan were still living! She could seduce him, make a hairdresser of him. And in the capillary realm, as in others, what couldn't have been accomplished by the man who, rejecting Gothic superstition, had hoisted his clear French intelligence and his no less French potbelly to the summit of the most brilliant eminence. How he would have loved Esperanza with her forehead of marble, Esperanza and her hair whose scent is sweeter than the honey of Hymettus! Yes, long live Esperanza and her hair, Hymettus and its honey, Olympus and its gods, Aristotle and his rhetoric, Plato and his cave, Renan and his prayer on the Acropolis. And she doesn't stop there. Rub-dub-dub must follow her and be polite with the animal spirits, the categorical imperative, the monads, algebra, trigonometry, sine and cosine. Enough nonsense. Esperanza agrees with Plato: Poets must be driven from the republic. She only asks him to spare Virgil, considering the importance of family and patriotism in his work. Although she is well aware that, until the end of her days, she is guaranteed fast, comfortable means of transportation, she likes to tell her son the story of how Aeneas carried his father Anchises on his shoulders. From the peregrinations of "pius Aeneas" she draws the conclusion "Latium to the Latins." At night, she dreams that Potassium is a country inhabited by the Potassians, and each evening sees her more and better prepared than the previous day to demand the return of Alsace-Lorraine. Late in the afternoon, before going home, she never fails to make a detour in the direction of Place de la Concorde in order to lay, at the feet of the statue from Strasbourg, the bouquet of Parma violets with which, after lunch, she always decorates the lapel of her astrakhan jacket. Maurice Barrès and Déroulède instructed her protector to let her know how much this gesture touched both of them. She simply answered: "What do you expect? I have an epic sense."

Yes, she has an epic sense, Esperanza does, and it is so well developed that, at the end of July 1914, when the war begins, she claps her hands. She trembles, she fumes with impatience upon reading the famous poster: "Mobilization is not war." The Prince of Journalists cheers her up. This time it's for real. Isvolsky promised.

Then, she is heroically overjoyed to learn of the first French soldier's death and she understands why her parents christened her Esperanza. So this time, since hope [*espérance*] there is, she is not going to let herself lose her composure. She will follow the government to Bordeaux. She will arrange for Monsieur Gustave to be excused from military service so that he can accompany her and plant a halo of little flags all around her head, while the Prince of Journalists calls for cannons, munitions. Too bad Rub-dub-dub isn't old enough to be a Saint-Cyr cadet with a plume and white gloves!

Krim is in some remote spot, halfway around the world. She wouldn't dream of crossing the blockaded borders, the torpedo-infested oceans. "One of the unforeseen advantages of this war is that it will rid us of a piece of nightclub scum," rejoices Esperanza, and to give an epic turn to her son's dreams at the most ungrateful age, she hangs above his bed, next to the crucifix, a reproduction of Rude's *Marseillaise.*

During puberty, a woman of stone just won't do. But Opal is dead. So who wants to hear about the departed one and why even hope that a memory nourished by nothing, by no one, will have the strength to expel a mineral intruder?

Krim, the Krim who used to live in him and whose survival is inversely proportional to the growth of his body and, a fortiori, his genitals—he can feel her disintegrating bit by bit. Besides, Rude's *Marseillaise* has the mouth of a scavenger fish. She devours first the voice, then the gestures; next the perfume which used to waft its way across the stage, and finally the absinthe eyes. And she could never be replaced, though they might try, by one or another of these so-called imaginary creatures, goddesses made entirely of mist, except around the loins, wishful refuge for dreams, when the real machinery of meat and hair have scared off the days, when too many nights and too many dawns have reared up in hot pursuit of an illusion which, perhaps, would like nothing more than to emerge like new, resuscitated, from the gullet of the monstress with a national anthem mug.

Krim.

In order to make Krim disappear forever and entirely from his memory, he has strictly forbidden himself the temptation of writing to her. If she had bestowed an answer upon him, its charm would have been slashed, murdered by censors' scissors and police fingers. The slightest contact would have soiled the envelope, the page tattooed with her delicate sentiments.

Over there, far away, who knows where, may the nightclub smoke protect from the snares of memory Krim's fluttering hands, diaphanous, palpitating birds on the black velvet background of her realistic creations!

Just as she had already succeeded in metamorphosing the seductive child into Rub-dub-dub, Esperanza has in turn made a pipsqueak of Rub-dub-dub. The pipsqueak is ashamed of his miserable anatomy. His phantasm is worth no more than his carcass. For example, a crummy professional woman will crouch down, rotate, squeeze a nipple against the ticklish spatula on the end of this rod which should be beautiful and proud of itself, since it is the cock, yes, the rock, the great cock of small stock, what the alchemist's great edifice (erected in his search for the philosopher's stone) is to a small stonework. But wait! There is no north star (or any other star, for that matter) in the skies of his fifteen years. He is no longer pointing north and his mother rightly blames him, she who is complimented for knowing which end is up.

Adolescence: a head vaporizes and, itself a cloud, mingles with the other clouds. If the scattered possibilities gather themselves together in a single point, death will come too quickly, in the form of a useless geyser, to the thunderbolt of the testicular storm.

Since he personally abolished the woman who had, in her time, abolished this, that, those within hand's reach, what or who else does he have in the world? The minutes are working away at a mosaic without a uniform plan. Proximity in time could hardly suffice to legitimize, much less deify a jumble made of anything but lead. Specks of cork.

Is an individual's physical weight a function of the density of his mental world? Esperanza observes that one can be called Wenceslas de Saint-Gobain and be a mere pebble-headed pipsqueak, a pebble, a pip, a pebble of a pip, a pip of a pebble, a wretched mixture of mineral and vegetable. She had decided, in the person of her son, to sacrifice the body for the mind. A real swindle. Must she live to see the flesh of her flesh, the blood of her blood, turn into nothing more than the other side of the coin bearing her effigy? This goofy kid's dirty looks and capricious temperament surely can, must be the beauty spots on the complexion, on the joyous lucidity that characterizes her. But try as one might to make a slight impression, one is nonetheless a mother capable of fearing the worst for a puny child as sickly yellow as the cover on the book *Onanism for One or More Players,* which he keeps hidden in his armoire, behind a stack of briefs.

Sometimes Esperanza thinks of encouraging her son's solitary vice, in the hope of some nerve injury that reminds the Prince of Journalists of his father. One day when she was in a philosophizing mood, it in fact occurred to her what she stood to gain from possible epileptoid coincidences, suggesting a miraculous soul heredity between two beings never united by any real kinship but linked together by a spiritual bridge, in this case the Prince of Journalists who must be moved, and convinced, by the resurrection of a well-respected infirmity, to adopt the boy in whom she is reincarnated.

But if there are pros, there are also cons, and Esperanza feels a traditional repugnance at encouraging masturbatory practices, the worst enemies of professional, itinerant lovers. And by masturbatory practices, here she means solitary ones, because she has a weakness for homosexuality and homosexuals, since her own experience has shown her that some men compensate for their aversion to women by providing one of them with an unhoped-for position.

Things are not as simple as they were made out to be by her mother and grandmothers who, specializing in primitive whoring, hated pederasty the way a bartender hates water and those who drink it. But as for Esperanza, she has improved with success: "Now that my goose is cooked, the ideal can bloom," she happily declared to her sister on Rue Blondel.

Henceforth the question is, can the ideal, at least for her son, take the form of the solitary vice which up until now she found unworthy of any indulgence whatsoever?

Questioned on this particular point, the sister on Rue Blondel failed to answer. As a matter of fact, the apartment where she was received had left her dumbstruck, overwhelmed at the sight of an interior of such distinction, such opulence, whose riches intimidated her so much that she couldn't even guess what purpose they might serve. All gratitude for the one who had lavished silk and velvet upon her younger sister, surrounded her with gilded, lacquered, carved woods, scalloped ivory, large and small bronzes, which a numerous domestic staff cared for, as if the least among these knick-knacks had deserved its nurse, the girl from Rue Blondel found herself dreaming out loud: "And to think that our mother wanted to castrate them that don't stick it in where nature intended!"

Along the same lines, Esperanza wonders: "Castrate someone who doesn't put it anywhere?" But she is revolted by all unnecessary violence. She isn't going to mutilate her son, she is simply going to have him circumcised, to teach him. Teach him what? About life, of course.

She therefore takes him to a surgeon who, firmly reprimanded, discovers that he has appendicitis and is able to persuade him to undergo an operation.

Upon waking, frightened at a pain not located where he expected it and incapable of thinking that the part had been sacrificed for the whole, he lets out such a bloodcurdling yell that his mother, sitting at his bedside and writing a few postcards to pass the time, spills on her immaculate opéra comique nurse's blouse the contents of a pen which she had, at dawn on this surgical day, quite appropriately filled with red ink. Subsequently, she will take an uncommon interest in the dressing of the wound, insisting on personally applying the compresses around the scar. As a result of seeing his mother's hands always stained with his most intimate blood, the son feels a need for vengeance spring up inside. He would like all members of the fair sex to expiate the crime of one of them. He imagines very clever injuries. But once he has a body at his disposal, his cowardice prevents him from cutting into the flesh. He flees, goes to a brothel, requests a resident having her period or, if unfortunately none of these ladies happens to be unwell, sprays the one he has had to settle for with the contents of a bottle of catsup.

But substitution for want of something better has never satisfied anyone. Not having eaten his fill, the pipsqueak soon begins to feel ravenous. In a restaurant he orders a symbolic fried whiting. What criminal joy one can feel extracting from their sockets two little globes whose whiteness makes them stand out against the golden brown crust covering the entire fish, head and body. Since [in French] whiting also means hairdresser, Esperanza's favorite is thus replacing her as the object of vengeance. Vengeance it is, or rather that's what it appeared to be, for these little opaque spheres, having no memory to light them up, are as powerless as the buttons on the ankle boots of a little girl at her first communion.

And yet, since the organizer of secret buns and maternal pleasures has, in his punitive obsessions, usurped the father's place, the next time he goes to sleep the pipsqueak will dream that he was misinformed about the status of the fish. It wasn't a whiting, but a "mackerel" [pimp]. These colorless spheres, these pills of insensitivity that he swallowed without daring to bite into them, they were two hardened drops of the sperm from which he happens to have been born, through Esperanza's intervention. As for him, the puny child that her dream places high in the hierarchy of a viscous humanity with pupils of pearly felt, he has probably only revised the Oedipal myth this way for a marine adaptation. But since, instead of killing the father, he merely ate his eyes, he is not going to poke out his own. The order of murders and bruises has been reversed. He must therefore kill himself, poor Oedipus at Colonus. But not even in a dream could Colonus be the name of a town. In the desert, man is going to die of his blind dream. He has already emptied himself of all his bones. He uses them to prop up his gibbet, the organ of his desire, this column on which, poor wilting bloated skin, he must hang himself. He resuscitates in the morning, floating on the leaden waters of memory which, to the reflections of times past add the face of the present, the face of one who is looking at the present. Will he endure, for his whole life, this suspicious mirror? He shoots himself in the chest with a revolver. Of course, he misses. He is taken to the hospital. He is put to sleep and he wakes up at the summit of a pyramid of pointed hats, whence he commands such a vast horizon that his tongue spontaneously finds the words that will make him understood by all, even the pebbles. The words make sentences, the sentences a book. The book will be called *Bones, Hair, Blood.* It will be the book par excellence. The author of this new bible would undoubtedly hear the facetious critics call him a Barrès for dogs. But what does that matter? What matters is knowing the thoughts, the opinions of the cormorants wandering in a line around a dying body. Instead of answering this question, one of the cormorants proclaims herself a nurse, point-blank. The blank is understandable since all of the color is washed, rinsed out of the caps, smocks, walls, sheets. But the point, where is the point?

"Enjoy your ether while it lasts" recommends the nurse-cormorant. Utilitarianism now. This is not the stuff that pointed hats are made of. Indignant, they start fitting into another, forming a pyramid which soon falls down flat. A man's dead weight remains, lying on his mattress, without even the possibility of slipping, since the slope of days isn't greased with the least bit of hope. Time becomes a shapeless mass that its container, place, is unable to mold. Thus, little or nothing to say about a convalescence in Switzerland where the day's lifespan is a mere ten seconds, when the dawn thumbs its nose at an alarm clock:

"Petunie, petunia in an orchid's dream, failed poison, oh you whose minuscule maliciousness skipped out on a previous life far too lacking in vast porticos. Throb abandoned in a jar of flesh, quicksilver erected into a useless column at the crossroads of the thighs, on a pitiful lawn of curly hairs

> "It's a dog's life
> When you're dog-tired.
> Dogs soon tire
> Of a lonely life
> And the sound of gunfire. . . ."

On the day he is allowed to go down to the lobby where the less moribund patients get together each Thursday for the movie, he discovers the same desire to leave his sanatorium bed that a fish has to leave its riverbed. And to be moved all of a sudden by the memory of the seductive, that is, untamed child he once was, before seeing himself changed into Rub-dub-dub who would end up as a pipsqueak whose only talent was self-torture. Esperanza, under the pretext of teaching him good manners, has used his person solely as a human receptacle for the hatred which she has certainly never ceased nourishing vis-à-vis the universe since the day she signed an agreement to become a distinguished lady. She hadn't fallen short of, but has exceeded the promises made to her protector. Now she will be able to rest on her laurels, i.e., cut, whittle the raw flesh of a society that she dominates from the considerable height of her well-invested fortune and her new name which is old, legitimate, and unassailable. But you can't make an omelette without breaking an egg, and the broken egg of the tasty, frothy, unctuous, heady, amorous omelette whose name is henceforth duchess of Monte Putina, is her son. And this egg is none too fresh, but who would dream of pitying him, who would dream of complaining about him, since nobody has let himself be splashed by his poison yet? Without being real stone, morover, the pipsqueak's malice is not the least bit liquid. It is fibrous, rather, well suited to follow all of the contours, to choke, with its devious strength, real wood its support, like ivy its oak.

This poor disposition gets annoyed with the life that is going to begin again, simply because it must give up the complaisance of pajamas, imprisoning its limbs instead in the stovepipes of a pair of trousers, the cylinders of a jacket and its sleeves. It resuscitates. But to resuscitate to one thing is to die to another. What possible reason for ending up dying in the elevator, for the sole purpose of being reborn in the lobby, under the protection of a hunter whose head is so lacking in thickness that we must hope to find, in his heavy hands, brain and cerebellum. The smiles that will flash across the screen are too photogenic. So what? The femme fatale, sticky with the gelatin in which her charms have become trapped, will not leave the crackling canvas of her adventures to follow a wretched Orpheus in need of a Eurydice. . . .

In the afternoon, the male nurse came and exhorted his patient, promising him miracles from the film showing: "Very well, sir! I will reserve a seat for you next to the lady in room 95. She's French like you, sir. And very well connected in Poitiers. Her father's a general. She collects tin soldiers. But please, don't try to confuse her, that would be a dirty trick. After the movie, you can have a *midnight snack* served. I promise to keep you company during the *midnight snack*. It'll bring back memories of my youth, yes, sir, because my godmother, a noblewoman who had martlets on her coat of arms, was so fond of *midnight snacks. . . .*"

"*Midnight snack* yourself," thinks the pipsqueak.

The lady in room 95, with her great connections in Poitiers, her general father and her tin soldiers, what a program! Nevertheless, if he ends up deciding to go along at the last minute, he'll have to get dressed up. Thus, he rings for Moysette Crotas, the manicurist.

From the very first finger, she confides in him completely: "I'm a native of Vaud province," she declares, "but I'm in love with a German. We got engaged. So my daddy said to me: 'Moysette, I'm only a Crotas, but a Crotas can die of shame.' So I told my daddy that he couldn't prevent me from marrying my German, because, even if he was a Vaud native, and even if Mommy was a Vaud native, they had nonetheless gotten into an argument. So my daddy said that I was right, and we cried all night. My mommy died after a cesarean; that's why my little brother's name is Caesar. She would have helped me marry my German. And I would have been happy. Besides, he's a virgin. Me too. I think about his virginity all the time. What a beautiful wedding night we would have had, both of us being virgins!"

"Not necessarily, Miss Moysette Crotas."

"Why 'not necessarily'?"

"You wouldn't have known how to go about it."

"The day before our wedding we would have bought *The Helvetic Guide to Conjugal Rights, Duties, and Pleasures.*"

"Books teach theory, not practice."

"So you think we did it wrong? I'll have to ask one of my clients."

"The lady in room 95?"

"No, not her. When it comes to love, the lady in room 95 is not so *vigousse.*"

"*Vigousse?* What do you mean by that, Miss Moysette Crotas?"

"You're a funny one! We say *vigousse* in Vaud dialect, like vigorous in French. The more of a virgin you are, the more 'vigousse' you are. The lady in room 95, she had twelve children and she's an idget. The Englishwoman in room 72, who is called Canary because she dyes her hair yellow, she is so thin that she must scare men. Ah! My fiancé and I, we're virgins and we're vigousse. With the good Lord's help, everything will turn out fine."

"And if there is no good Lord, Moysette?"

"You're right: the pastor can talk all he wants, but you cain't be so sure. I think I'll ask a client, a singer. You can bet she's had lovers as fat as she is, fatter than she is, because she doesn't have too much meat on her bones, poor Madame Krim, just plain Krim as they call her."

"Krim, Krim, you have Krim here?"

"Yes, Krim. And not fresh. No more vigousse than she is a virgin."

With Moysette gone, the pipsqueak hurries out to the balcony, leans to the right, to the left, to see if, in one of the baths, he might find the woman whom, for years, he tried to expel from his memory. To him the big sanatorium all rigged up with venetian blinds, at the top of the highest geological wave, appears, from the caravel to the ocean liner, to incarnate the general idea of a ship. Embarkation for Cythera. He is so happy that, for twenty minutes, he forgets to laugh in his own face. But suddenly, with no rage, he is afraid. Afraid of Krim, his dream, afraid of his dream of Krim, of his Krim of a dream, of the dream that is going to become reality. Dream reality. Reality dream. The dream loses its reality, the reality its dream.

Krim as reality?

Krim or reality?

Reality?

Krim reality?

Does he want Krim in reality, does he want Krim's reality, he whose spite swears not to try to compensate, through bookish cuttings and mnemotechnic grafts, for his physical and mental possibilities, his erectile chances spoiled by years of waiting and permanently unraveled by months in a sanatorium. His desire, a sour plant, writhing, thirsting for acidulous caresses. He is too aware of the deficiency of his sap to expect flattering blossoms. Esperanza and the tortuous tortures of this tough-minded tutor have deformed it forever. His social qualities should have nonetheless allowed him to represent a conforming palm tree in the shade of the official wainscotings, or else, in ultramodern settings, he could have appeared as a cactus taken with erotomania, aestheticism, or sports. If, to imagine the worst possible case, he had developed a taste for debauchery and slipped into the gutter, he at least deserved to end up as a reseda on the counter of a bar. . . .

Palm tree, cactus, reseda. There is no mention of them, there is nothing, there is no one, there is still no sign of Krim.

"Krim, Krim," someone's calling you. A hollow voice in an empty landscape. Echoless slopes descend all the way to the Rhône River valley. This valley is the way back to life, or so they say. A train whistles, hurrying toward Italy. As a matter of fact, Esperanza is in Rome. In the neighborhood of the Vatican, she never fails to be eternally in the mood to forge souls. A Monte Putina of a mother would like to have her pipsqueak under her thumb all the time so that he would be twisted, melted by the flame of her will, with a spinal column softer than pith cut from the elder. Yes, reduce him to such a pitiful state that he will agree to receive holy orders. There is nothing she wants more. And then, she would have him wearing the tiara before long. Pope: now there's a career with a future. Mother of a pope, that's not bad either, especially if you can manage to add European or even, at the very least, extra-European possessions to the derisory Papal States. In no time at all, Augusta could find us some cozy little colonies. There's no such thing as a free lunch. Once the pipsqueak is seated on Saint Peter's throne, if Augusta takes care of him, Esperanza swears on the holy cross that she will furnish the Paneuropean army with portable altars for soldier-priests. The model has already been designed. By a graduate of the Ecole Polytechnique, no less. It will be light, pretty, portable, and collapsible. The tabernacle will also serve as an arsenal, with just enough room for the holy ciborium, the hosts, and a precious little machine gun that the chaplains will be able to use while saying Mass. . . .

But Esperanza can dream in Rome.

Here in Switzerland, there's Krim.

He whose childhood had sworn to itself that it would love her for the rest of his life suddenly wonders if he didn't lie to himself. What will he have to say to her, inside these walls? White paint. Color is born from color alone. Space categorically refuses the least temptation of infinity. Try betting on time? You have to go see first.

Go see Krim to exasperate his Monte Putina of a mother.

He is received by an emaciated woman.

Against the attack which emptied the body of its flesh, the face of its charm, only the gaze held out.

But how to accept the transformation of the most touching of faces into what it is now: this jewel-case of wilted skin wherein are set, still what they always were, the eyes that bewitched a distant childhood.

Krim has plans. She is going to travel to the south of France and write her memoirs. As long as she has any voice left at all, even a thin, weak voice, she'll always be able to peddle her act. Besides, she is not yet voiceless. She's going to sing, she's going to sing her prewar hits. She leaves her chaise longue, leans against the wall so as not to waste her energy holding herself up. She must conserve every ounce of strength, for without all of her might, she would surely not be able to climb back up from those hoarse, low notes that give her songs their killer effect. But her will alone cannot consolidate tissues too fragile to hold up against the passion of the words, the violence of the tone. She has to stop at the second verse. Her handkerchief first goes to her mouth, then comes away bloodstained, and the pipsqueak who, for years and years, thought he was a vampire fails to drink from her lips the blood for which he thirsted. He leaves, runs off in search of the nurse. They give Krim a shot. The pipsqueak returns to his room, goes to bed. Through a window opened out onto the night enters a song that rises from another window opening out onto the same night: "Gaslight Is My Sunshine."

Krim asked them to play on the gramophone the refrain that she no longer has strength enough to sing. Words without lips, lips without words. The pipsqueak closes his eyes. One by one and forever, behind his eyelids, out go the last of those little glimmers that flicker on the most desperate street corners for the ultimate consolation of fagged out creatures. No more sun than there are gas lamps. It's as cold as can be on this planet. The stars? A figment of the imagination. The moon? A cruel invention. He shivers. One more darkness shouldn't make any difference to a disillusioned fellow like him. Everything has been switched off. And then? Everything must be switched off. Krim's voice along with the rest. There's really no reason to get all worked up. She was not the one that he loved, but the one who prevented him from loving others. Henceforth, what body can be expected to furnish his pleasure along the way? Persons, sexes? No use scrutinizing their mess in the hope of recognizing yourself. Others are welcome to make do with resemblances, stopping at each more or less, wishing for oases everywhere. He's not one to persist in the search for the violent perfection for which Krim, before the age of love, had made his daily mediocrity nostalgic.

Krim: head too heavy for her body and, in an alcoholic clown's face, absinthe eyes in which all the weeds of crazy gardens wave about. No fence protects those tufts. Thus before long, not a single one will remain, all of them uprooted by death. And he who has lost even the right to forget, will tomorrow open his door to find a desolate universe. From the threshold, he will let himself slip into life, losing body and possessions, body and soul, for want of Krim, for want of a life preserver, the arms that she alone could have thrown him.

6

Poetess, Novelist, and Transatlantic Couple

ALTHOUGH HE HADN'T WRITTEN a word to her about it, Esperanza was not in the dark about her son's visit to Krim, at least not for long. Thus, before her son had joined her in the south of France, where she knew the execrable singer was going to settle and eventually die, and since there are many other fish in the sea, she came up with the idea of marrying off the pipsqueak to Synovie, the Catholic poetess.

In the course of the demoralizing summer of 1932, Esperanza wasn't disappointed to read poems that are a refreshing break from all the fashionable eccentricities she has had to put up with for the last twenty years. One can be unpretentious and still hold very sensible literary opinions. The duchess of Monte Putina knows how to laugh, but with a laugh that doesn't exclude the seriousness of thought. And a more or less decadent youth had better not try to soften her up. She agrees with Mauriac: "In all eras there have been beginners who are rebellious and enemies of the law; these young madmen, however, were they not flattered and lavishly praised like those of the postwar period, but advised, guided, overcome by the prestige of talent and glory, would recover quickly from the sickness from which all puppies suffer."

Esperanza, who, when she married, went from neo-Louis XVI to cubism which she flatters herself, moreover, for having tamed, adapted to the noble uses of a ducal salon, deserves, by the same token, if not to be congratulated as a pioneer, at least never to be called backward. She has a feeling for modernity just as, without ever losing her taste for classicism, she had been taken first with irresistible, vulgar southern French jokes, then with the medieval style, and finally with distinguished manners. This has given her all the more right to condemn puppies and their sickness. She is one of those who, in writing, painting, music, no longer accepts the destructive innovations of a world where Southampton singer/dancers, in a respectable, noble mood, have had so much trouble finding their place in the sun and keeping it.

Primrose, although she has become a Lady with almost no resistance, is nonetheless of the same opinion as Esperanza. Thus, when the duchess of Monte Putina had spoken to her about Mauriac's article and quoted from memory the sentence in question, she exclaimed—more than ever determined not to waste her gift for scatological more or lesses—"Puppies to the pooper."

Esperanza has, moreover, not failed to trot out this witticism again, which she attributes, depending on how the listeners react, either to herself, or to Léon Daudet.

Synovie, whose *Effusions* constitutes the synthesis, believed to be impossible, of classicism and romanticism, Synovie could therefore only by protected by one or the other of these ladies. Unstudiedly exquisite, with the modesty natural to great talents and admirable intelligences, the poetess thanks heaven and notes: "I worked at it for a good while." Synovie is in fashion: the regionalist fashion, a fashion that gives her both her moral climate and her clothing style. Laureate of the Academy of Floral Games, crowned with the olive branch which, indeed, doesn't go too badly with her dress cut from the checkered cloth used to make inn tablecloths, Synovie dashes from Toulouse to Maillane where the Provençal poets are only too proud to receive her. She belts out her little sonnet to Mistral, makes a sensational entry into the town of Arles, then, since she is a woman of her time, presses on to Juan-les-Pins.

Mauriac devoted an article on the *Effusions* as decisive as Barrès once did to her first book, *Hands Clasped in Prayer.* If, moreover, he admires the poetess, he reveres a compatriot in the person of Synovie, born in Bordeaux, and not Bordelaise mushroom-garlic style, but a very strict type, that is, cultured, expert at morose delectation, and incapable of going out without gloves or stockings, even in the middle of the summer on the Côte d'Azur, for which she has not failed to receive additional affection from Esperanza, Augusta, and Primrose. A common and undivided fear of congestion forbids these three grand ladies from lying in the sun naked in a crowd whose permissiveness and immodesty—which they condemn loudly—nonetheless continue to haunt their dreams with Byzantine fantasies, with lavish display of tanned bodies.

Ten minutes of conversation with Synovie were enough for Esperanza to proclaim: "This poetess is just the thing for my pip-squeak. If he doesn't want to be ordained, he could at least marry a woman both serious about religion and capable of teaching him to write rhyming verse. A collection of alexandrines of Catholic inspiration signed Wenceslas de Saint-Gobain is not bad for starters. And even if my husband the duke refuses to adopt him, he will have a name and major literary works that will make it possible for him to get into the Académie Française. I'll take care of it personally. . . ."

And, always mindful of Mauriac's lessons, Esperanza recalls that in his authoritative article entitled "The Masterless Generation," the author writes: "At no other time in history have we seen, as today, the cult of the go-getter, the sure thing. Ten years beforehand, they kiss up to the future member of the Académie and they count on his vote for 1950." She doesn't need to be told twice. She goes from shop to shop, chooses a tie for the novelist, candied fruit for his wife, and scooters for the babies.

Synovie is not the least bit frail. One might even say that she looks just right. The face is noble, with a regularity that could eventually risk becoming tiresome, if a convenient stabismus didn't add its romantic little touch.

Synovie's family was sufficiently infused with evangelical principles to remember that the right hand mustn't know what the left hand is doing. Thus her kin saw a delicate intention of Providence in the irregularity of her gaze. The convent schoolgirls, her companions, unfortunately did not share this opinion and wouldn't stop persecuting the little cross-eyed girl, who was clever enough to take advantage of her handicap by spying on her classmates and telling the sisters what she had been able to see from the side, without any of the children with normal vision suspecting that she could see them.

Later, when she had reached marrying age, the future poetess would lower her eyelids, raise her little finger, stand on her dignity—in other words, never let herself go to the point of touching the backs of chairs and playing the piano without looking at the music—but all to no avail. She found herself alone, without so much as a well-groomed poodle to whisper her sweet nothings of puppy love to. Her mother, an accomplished woman, was growing tired of seeing her remain a wall-flower. So one day when a young man was introduced to them, the old lady got an idea. They were staying with friends in the country, having come from Bordeaux to meet Synovie's would-be husband. When she got off the train, the young lady was instructed to complain about the cinder in her eye. She pulled it off without a hitch. The fiancé, an engineer, but a baby when it came to anything other than numbers or inventions, swallows it hook, line, and sinker. The accomplished woman is honored to grant him her daughter's hand. He has reason to be proud, happy as a king. Besides, Louis XIV loved a child. Thus the wedding takes place. The couple gets along fine. Alas! there are always malicious tongues who will take out their frustrations on others' happiness. There comes a day when someone lets the engineer know that his wife is cross-eyed. He has his dignity, this man does. He hates to admit that he's been had. So, once he returns home, he acts like a maniac. He breaks all the dishes, relieves himself in the conjugal piano, announces that he is going to leave for Kamchatka, and after a roaring "Good-bye, Mrs. Cinder-in-the-Eye," locks himself in his room where he packs his suitcase, while the poor Cinder-in-the-Eye decides to put an end to her days, so goes down to the garden and picks a magnolia flower whose fragrance she hopes is fatal.

At dawn, going downstairs with his bags never to return, the husband finds her lying on the lawn. Since the magnolia flower is no longer on the branch where he used to admire it, he calls himself an assassin, and goes back up to his room and, determined to inflict on himself a retaliatory punishment, unscrews a light bulb, not to sniff it but in order to swallow it, no less.

One can be cross-eyed and have a solid frame. The young woman, merely unconscious, overcomes the magnolia flower's supposedly murderous emanations, while the crushed glass in the engineer's bowels isn't as nice. Widowed, Cinder-in-the-Eye explores some poetic consolations under an elegiac pseudonym. After her very first efforts, a Catholic poet and an academic priest, both in love with the Béarn region, beg her to come settle in the department of Basses-Pyrénées. She gives in to their wishes and moves to Pau, where her life would have gone by most peacefully if, one day at the races when she had climbed onto a chair to see better, her dress hadn't been lifted up by such an unexpected and indiscreet wind that the poor thing, with a heartbreaking voice, asked: "Was my swallow showing, by any chance?"

Strangely reminiscent of Paul Claudel, with the blackbird in the rising sun. But neither the hour nor the place justified this evocation. It was the west, at twilight. Scandal had come in the form of a feathered thing which, from black, had turned white.

In the most beautiful gardens of Béarn, Synovie would indeed meet, the next day, a swan. Virginal and vivacious, according to Mallarmé's definition, which was very much to the liking of our great lyric poetess, corseted like a cavalry officer of General Boulanger's time, wearing old ankle boots with plastic sides, in the best style of those oh so poetic symbolists, this swan, very literary, liked to leave his waters for little walks along Maurice-Barrès Memorial Lane. One day, Synovie notices him perched on the running board of a car with an inside steering wheel. "Interior steering, interior life, it's all the same," thinks the poetess and, delighted with the symbol, she smiles at the bird, calls him. He won't wait for the invitation to be repeated twice. He is only too happy to take this inspired woman for Leda, slips his head in among her skirts and, with his long neck sticking straight up underneath her slip, begins to peck at her swallow. Synovie runs away screaming, chased by the indiscreet creature, every bit as vivacious as he is virginal. Fortunately, the academic priest happens to be passing by. He takes her in his arms, defends her, beats back the filthy beast with his umbrella. Synovie then returns home on the arm of her rescuer who, after a few preliminary considerations about Racine in Uzès, fervently reminds her that pure poetry should end in prayer. He therefore exhorts her to disincarnate an inspiration that the lyricism of the *Effusions* would risk leading along paths full of danger for a Christian soul.

Synovie protests, insisting on her good intentions. She is Catholic, apostolic and Roman. The priest agrees, but, precisely because she is anything but frivolous, he expects a great deal of the pacifying, purifying, long-suffering, redeeming influence this rhymestress with a chaste matrix can have on an era in which anxiety takes on the ferocious, indeed diabolical form of humor. He could quote a thousand novels, essays. . . . Synovie wants titles. The priest simply says *Bubu* and our good Christian, feeling that he has spoken enough to die of thirst and ask for a drink by onomatopoeia, invites him in for some liquid refreshment. The saintly man laughs at the mistake and corrects her*:

"*Bubu roi,* by Charles Jarry, or *Ubu de Montparnasse,* by Alfred-Louis Philippe, seem to me, my dear girl, the very type of works that one shouldn't look at. As far as I know, from hearsay, of course, because I don't take chances with such reading material, the first is an indecent mockery of the institutions deserving our greatest respect, while the second was written for the glory of a sinful woman who, instead of converting, like our sainty Mary Magdalene, offers God a mere wisp of a prayer, between two strolls, whose destination we'd best not mention. . . ."

These words and the musings that followed them determined Synovie to compensate with a masterly poem on Mary of Egypt. And just as the saint, for Christian purposes, was willing to endure a young man's embrace, when she learned that Esperanza was counting on her prestige as a poetess laureate of the floral games to confer a redeeming love, she proclaimed herself ready to fornicate with the pipsqueak. But the poor duchess of Monte Putina's troubles were not over, for her son, more and more determined to defy her, scorned the poetess whom she had chosen for him, rushing into the arms of a prose writer, Marie Torchon, a novelist for the masses, as her name indicates.

Marie Torchon is playing the Paneuropean. No one has forgotten that she gave a tea in honor of Augusta. "Let us beware of this

---

*Author's Note: Truthfully, with my own ears, I heard Father Bremond, the inventor of pure poetry, make this confusion between *Ubu* and *Bubu.*

Jacobin," insinuates little Miss Monte Putina, who, a duchess, has not only adopted an archduchess's views on Jacobinism, but—in order that the product of titles according to Monteputinesque principles will be equal to the product of titles according to Hapsburg principles—has arch-adopted them.

In the meantime, rather than seeing her son subjugated by Marie Torchon—who is fit as a fiddle—Esperanza would have preferred that he remain in love with Krim. At least that moribund thing wouldn't have bothered her for long. But this Krim, what a jerk! In spite of Esperanza's flattering, cajoling, she is dead set against doing anything whatsoever to rekindle in the pipsqueak the flame that was alive in the seductive child, then in Rub-dub-dub. Krim has eyes (and her eyes are huge) only for very young, very handsome, very vigorous teenagers. Esperanza doesn't intend to feign all this kindness for nothing. In the past she humiliated Opal quite efficiently, through charity. She is going to arrange to have Krim die while singing for her. And it won't be hard at all. Krim has nothing but debts; she is harried by process servers. Thus, although her voice and strength betray her, she must accept the chance being offered her to earn a few pennies. Esperanza rubs her hands together, smiles, hasn't stopped rubbing her hands together, smiling, in the car in which she is seated between the peaceful duke and her victim, Krim, with her son on the folding seat, small enough, in other words, to appear to be on his knees before her. She made superhuman efforts to keep from abandoning this smug expression when she noticed, at Lady Primrose's door, Marie Torchon's little car and, at the same time, Synovie, who, very thrifty, took the bus and walked over from the station in a sun so hot one fears that one of the torrents of sweat running down both sides of her nose might carry away her drifting eye. Marie Torchon, on the contrary, looks as clean as a dried bean (the image is her own), quite chic in pajamas whose cut and material, of populist inspiration, cause Esperanza to grumble: "Bitch in britches."

The last of the Sussexes, whose forehead is obstructed by a lock of blond hair, and wearing an emerald green silk jersey and mauve leather sandals, is fixing cocktails. Synovie, who is dying of thirst, dashes for the heady beverage. She lets out a cry, drops everything: "A spider!" Marie Torchon warns her: "Spider early in the day, trouble's surely on the way," then, since she never misses an opportunity to curry favor with the mighty of the earth, this condemned woman turns toward the Prince of Journalists, whose paper comes out in the middle of the afternoon, and, with a curtsy, whispers to him: "Yes, but evening journal, hope springs eternal." The compliment hits the mark, and Esperanza fumes when she hears the master of opinion respond with praise for the novelist's last book, *Tootsie of the Batignolles.*

"At last, some French art, some of the good stuff, some of the best. Our dear little soldiers will not have shed their blood in vain. Those foreigners can still try to intrude with their insane fashions. Thanks to Marie Torchon, from now on they'll leave us alone. Her heroine, that dear Tootsie, a real tricolored bouquet. What a good mother she would have made, one of those who name their daughters Joffrette or Fochette. 'Joffrette, fetch my locket. Fochette, turn off the faucet!' How charming it would have been! Alas, Tootsie's fiancé died heroically in the factory where he manufactured poison gas, for not only war but peace too has its share of glorious deaths for the nation. The funeral of Tootsie's fiancé, what a panorama! And the cemetery, what an anthology piece! Tootsie, after having declared that rebellion is a characteristic of the weak, Tootsie, in an admirable tirade, warns Europe, from the height of Père-Lachaise, of the dangers of communism and pacifism. Some critics have said, and our dear Marie Torchon hasn't spoken a word to the contrary, that her Tootsie is a Paneuropean. In any event, if Tootsie is addressing herself to all of Europe, it certainly does not follow that she wants to cancel Germany's debts.

"No, valiant Tootsie is not in favor of revoking the Treaty of Versailles. On the contrary, she calls each and every person to their duty and, before the still-open grave, she adjures her younger brother to enlist since we won't have, she can feel it, enough forces to set against the dangers home and abroad if we want to save capitalism."

During the Prince of Journalists' peroration, there arrived a very "mass-produced"-looking young American couple, with nothing unusual about their double freshness apart from a voluminous Ace bandage extending from the wife's wrist to her right elbow. For weeks, the husband had been promising a gratuitous act. Last night, he decided that the time had come. He offered the casino barman a thousand francs if he would spend the whole night with them. The barman accepts and, a deal's a deal, the three of them drive away, stop on the edge of a forest where the Americans ask their companion to undress. The latter, once naked, is tied to a tree. The American takes a saw out of his car and announces to the bound man that he is going to cut him into pieces. And, to prove to him that it's for real, he rips into a tree, saws off a few branches, then approaches, gnashing his teeth. The barman, usually a rather brazen little Italian, in spite of his aptitude for the skin trade, feels that things are getting out of hand and, to avoid seeing the rest of the work of which he will be the object, the material, prefers to faint. Regaining consciousness, the fellow is amazed to notice that none of his limbs are missing. He is alone, but in one piece, with a one-thousand franc note between the toes of his left foot.

As for the American couple, once they have returned home, they break the news to their friends and acquaintances over the telephone.

"A thousand francs, very expensive for a gratuitous act," the last of the Sussex lords can't help but object, moreover, in a voice roaring with all the anger of one startled out of his sleep, despite natural sweetness and a good upbringing.

This objection makes the young American lose his haughtiness. He scratches his head and, very quickly, his distress proves contagious to his wife. Soon it is total, undivided despair. To console themselves, now all they can do is knock back little morale-boosting drinks so that, in an attempt, at dawn, to fix toast for breakfast, she, with a determined knife, cuts into her sun-baked arm and yells: "Jimmy, Jimmy, the bread is bleeding." Hence this swatch of cloth constituting the most opaque part of an outfit otherwise composed of veils and transparencies.

Jim feels guilty for all these misfortunes and accuses himself above all for their arriving late at Lady Primrose's all-important luncheon. Both because he is obsessed by the memory of his night and in order to impress those listening, since the conversation revolves around moral questions, he asks:

"Is the gratuitous act a form of perversion?"

"Remember," answers the Prince of Journalists, "remember, young man, that the word *gratuitous* is as un-French as the word *impossible*."

Jim opens his eyes so wide that it seems he is going to cry.

"In France," it is explained to him, "there has never been, there will never be anything gratuitous. I say and repeat that Germany is dead wrong to believe that its debts will eventually vanish into thin air. I am amazed, even hurt, to hear an ex-ally, a young American brother, talk about a gratuitous act. Explain yourself."

Terrified by the summons, Jim doesn't dare disobey. He tells about his feat of the night before, attributing it to another couple, of course.

"But that couple was also from America?" asks the Prince of Journalists.

"Yes."

"Then, you can tell your compatriots that I can hardly congratulate them. Behaving thus, they appear to me quite unworthy of their great country, the land of Washington, Franklin, Lindbergh. . . ."

". . . and also quite unworthy of Paneuropa," adds Marie Torchon, just in case, with a smile directed at Augusta.

But the duchess of Monte Putina is bent on cutting the ground from under the schemer's feet. She hammers out a sentence which condemns the hysteria of the new America and the unscrupulous ambition of certain prose writers. She is becoming a real Juvenal, our Esperanza. Of course, she makes use of satire only for edifying purposes, and, just as hogs snatched by certain machines come out transformed into ham and canned meat, so does the divine lady observe that the seminal fluids lapped up by her former colleague in whoring and present colleague in aristocracy take wing in the form of austere conclusions. Herself, the marquise of Sussex, she feels intransigent maxims ready to fly out of all her orifices. The Prince of Journalists would be only too happy to pluck them from the edges of all her sphincters.

Yes, while to the well-contoured lips of contemporary women he long preferred so many other rough ones smelling of garlic and table wine, why is it that today he hungers only for the mouth (and not only the mouth) of the noble Englishwoman, that mouth of his dreams, unctuous beneath the thick layer of rouge and scented with a mixture of gin, Cointreau, and orange juice?

He would like to have this desire, whose sudden birth and such rapid ascent are incomprehensible, explained to him by this fashionable psychiatrist, chairman of the Department of Mental Health at the University of Paris, another one among the distinguished guests, currently bowing to Augusta, who is thrilled to be introduced to him since he is the author of that authoritative work *Libido and Paneuropa*.

One of the too-too cute valets finally announces that "Your ladyship is served."

The troop of guests starts walking toward the table set up in the garden, shaded from the sun by a large section of wall.

A cloudless sky serves as a ceiling for this outdoor dining room. The majesty of the hour is worthy of Esperanza, Augusta, and Primrose—the dear she-cocks and she-fowls—and of their predecessors Madame de Maintenon, Madame Roland, and George Sand.

7

The Fourteenth Guest

IT TOOK ESPERANZA A MERE three seconds to dispatch a slice of melon. She is going to speak, and searches for the first word of a sentence that will allow her to bend the conversation in the same direction as her interests. A glance around the assembled luncheon guests permits her to observe that, as usual, she dominates the situation. It sometimes happens, however, and as a matter of fact does so now, that from the summit of her optimism, a duchess famous for her control and her vivacious temperament drops, as a result of a sudden emotion, the fork and the knife that she was going to place on her empty plate. But by the simple act of having brushed against its edge, the sterling silver cutlery succeeds in pulling down with it the platter which ends up, with a great racket, rolling on the floor tiles, although the squash rind that followed the movement of the fall failed to act as a buffer between the metal and the stone which covers the floor with an inexorable resonance.

And to mask all the noise, this cry:

"Thirteen, there are thirteen of us at table."

Faithful to the habits of order and precision with which the Prince of Journalists has inculcated her, Esperanza offers proof of what she affirms and counts out loud: "Lord Sussex, one; Archduchess Augusta, two; the psychiatrist, three; Synovie, four; Wenceslas, five; Marie Torchon, six; the duke of Monte Putina, seven; the marquise of Sussex, eight; the Prince of Journalists, nine; Krim, ten; Kate [that's the young American woman's name], eleven; Jim, twelve; myself, thirteen. Our last hope is the unoccupied chair between Krim and Kate. But who will come, will anyone even come and sit in this chair? Who will be, who *is,* the fourteenth guest?"

The mistress of the house is too saturated with gin not to burst into flames at that last word. It's a real flair, her taste for indecent puns. She lights up, just as, from the slightest spark, the rum in an omelette ignites. Esperanza is frightened to see sordid flames dancing in the eyes of her Southampton companion in debauchery. By way of oil on the fire, the divine lady pours herself large doses of white wine and empties her glass several times before raising it to the health of the man who didn't participate in the previous toast and, moreover, doesn't participate in this one either, which is quite unfortunate since the thirteen others want nothing more than to be happy, provided that the fourteenth . . .

And Esperanza must, here, put up with the sectioning of the word *convive* [guest], finding its seven letters sufficient to supply both a subject and a verb. . . [*con*=cunt; *vive*=lives].

Should the incongruity be overlooked? The duchess would go so far as to make a scene, if she weren't convinced that the majority of the guests would make neither head nor tail of the anger resulting from her offended dignity, since, among the thirteen, there are, first and foremost, foreigners too unfamiliar with French to grasp the play on words, and among the French themselves, at least one soul (Esperanza is thinking of Synovie) whose purity forbids her from suspecting a foreign mouth of such a perverse knowledge of the language, and finally, in the person of Krim, one whose indifference prevents her from taking the trouble to speak or even listen.

Thus Esperanza doesn't flinch, but, despite memories of a thirty-year-old friendship and mutual favors, her silence won't forgive Primrose for not only allowing her luncheon to assemble a fatal number of guests around a table (served, one must concede, with great pomp), but even letting each person choose his place, so that this weasel of a populist has, in order to flout the duchess of Monte Putina, succeeded in slipping in between her pipsqueak son and her senile husband. No one is sitting where they should be. Whence a disarray multiplied by the cry of alarm: "There are thirteen of us at table." Even Augusta, although no one would question her vigorous qualities, is tormented by remorse, crosses herself, and thinks that she would prefer a Jew, a Turk, a Gypsy, a Bolshevik in this empty seat between Kate and Krim. Hearing the latter cough, each of the twelve other guests tells himself that if there must be a death within the year it will be hers. But Krim, who guesses the thoughts of her inexorable lunch companions, even though she knows that the presence, by her side, of an extra guest would do nothing to change her fate (conceded, moreover, once and for all) as an imminent corpse, is all the more delighted to note that her name is that of a murderous act, not of a victim. She thus feels protected from a death which everyone's numerical superstition would like to see swoop down upon her. With a stiffened body, clenched fists, her fingernails digging into her palms, her lips tight as if to hold in, with her last bit of strength, the breath of life which the others would like to see suddenly taken away from her, she puffs out her nostrils so as not to lose any of the good smell of human semen wending its way through the scents of a bouquet on the table in front of her. Ravaged but still famished, hungry for warm flesh even at the most feverish hours of her afternoons, she will never accept the risk of appearing to be the expiatory victim whose immolation would ensure the salvation of these twelve among whom only Kate's defenseless youth seems possible to her. So, like a huge butterfly nourished on poisonous herbs, her absinthe gaze flits from one to the other, and in the winged double orb of her eyelids, among the dancing tufts, there are such intentions that twenty-four eyes close. But they will open again, and then it will be a nearly universal coalition.

Even the pipsqueak, who scarcely wants to give his mother the impression that she is victorious on this point as on others, can't help but pass judgment out loud on people who always manage to show up in places where they have no business being. And as far as he's concerned, he adds, his mind is made up: no more confusing sunshine with gaslight. Thus he is not content with playing the pretty boy between the populist novelist and the poetess laureate of the floral games. He claims victory mercilessly. He takes revenge on the woman who once charmed the little animal whose senses were so fresh, so spontaneous that Esperanza had to ignore his suffering in order to toughen his desires and their shadows, his thoughts.

He and the others still feel that they have many reasons to hate Krim. Hasn't she, for example, lived by no rule other than her own freedom and her love affairs? What Esperanza is waiting for most of all, in order to justify her sordid whoring in the past and the gloomy cautiousness that followed it, is the coughing of blood whose torrent will eventually take away, with the ruins of an overly moving voice, the last warmth of a life. Esperanza knows that there isn't a she-cock nor a she-fowl who doesn't agree with her. Primrose, frozen in her monstrous aristocracy, tries, but in vain, to empty enough glasses to drown the nostalgia for the carnal festivities which, through the fault of her ambition, she missed. All of these women are unsatiated, starting with Augusta who, each morning, after having rubbed her nipples with the cloth of the souvenir trousers that Štefánik never wore, prays that her Paneuropean god will forgive her and, having been won over to the Monteputinesque cause, swears, with all her contrition, to give colonies to the pope.

No less unsated than Augusta, Synovie promises an ode to Saint Anthony of Padua if she is able to seduce the man next to her, the psychiatrist (the chances are good: he is on the side of her good eye), since this pipsqueak Wenceslas has decidedly gone over with bag and baggage to the service of Marie Torchon who, a toady as usual and in spite of the fact that she actually isn't feeling too comfortable, claims that the danger of thirteen people around a table doesn't exist for her. Indeed, Augusta and the Prince of Journalists, considering their situation, each count for two, making four to a pair and thus bringing to fifteen the perilous number.

Despite the populist's oratorical talent and skill, confidence is not revived.

It seems to take forever to get to the lobster. So, as if by a miracle speech had been given back to him, the old duke of Monte Putina, who hasn't spoken a word yet, suddenly hurls at the archduchess a resounding: *"Ad Augusta per lobstera."*

Augusta rather likes this kitchen Latin. During the summers of her distant childhood, she built with this Roman nobleman sandcastles on Adriatic beaches. She holds no grudge against him either, for his noisy familiarity or for the spice of barbarism added to the already tangy sauce which serves as a swimming hole for this shellfish, whose pedigree an Old World gentleman certainly won't split hairs over. But the civil status of a piece of seafood which happens to have been prepared American-style must be more worrisome for a Jim quite unfamiliar with ancient languages. The poor fellow, who hasn't forgotten the Prince of Journalists' scolding when, awhile ago, he came up with the idea of talking about gratuitous acts, can't help, despite all the dreadful things he suspects such a question capable of bringing about, asking his companions to translate—since it sounds so nice— the old duke's sentence. All he gets for an answer is a scowl from Augusta, a pout from Primrose, and a disdainful look from Esperanza. The Prince of Journalists, revolted by so much ignorance, pretends not to have heard him. So, despite the innocence of the roses which he personally arranged in front of each place setting, in bouquets matching the guests' presumed states of mind, the last of the House of Sussex begins to think that he is presiding over a diabolic feast. Upon his face he fastens an impeccable smile, meant to cover up the double shame of not having prevented the perilous words and not being able to stop them. Thus, the perpetual adolescent, the pride of Oxford where he took his degrees, and tennis champion, both an aesthete and an athlete, lover of red meat and Lake poets, worthy great-nephew of the gentleman whom the seventeenth century thrived on, with an appearance nice enough and a complexion delicate enough to deserve, just like his insular curio of a country, to be put under glass, even though he has never, and today no more than other days, failed to abide by customs, suddenly, among the flowers where he has been living magnificently for years, finds himself tortured by the presence of those he invited. And he who had something to ask his godmother! he who would have liked to see her promise to reward, during the reorganization of Europe, Lord Rothermere whose efforts on behalf of the country where Augusta was born are certainly capable of touching an archducal heart in which the hot blood of the Magyars mingles so successfully with the more peaceful variety common to the children of Albion.

The young lord, with this end in view, even asked his secretary to collect all of the pro-Hungarian articles that Lord Rothermere has, since 1927, published in the *Daily Mail,* for such has been the burst of enthusiasm aroused by the king of the English press with his generous campaign that he was able to announce to his readers that he had, on the occasion of his very recent birthday, received 72,000 letters and postcards. Which was not bad for starters. But above all one must not forget the "memorandum signed by more than a million Hungarians, transmitted by a delegation made up of leading Hungarian political figures, headed by former government ministers.

"All over Hungary," concluded the king of the English press, "streets and squares were named after me. I learned that my portraits decorated all the peasants' houses; my name was etched in huge letters on Hungarian mountainsides. The country's universities awarded me the greatest honorary degrees. This national enthusiasm is what gave rise to the plan for me to declare myself a candidate for the throne of Hungary. . . . I was deeply moved by the honor that my Hungarian friends bestowed upon me when they designated me for one of the most ancient thrones of Europe. But I didn't feel that it would be in the interest of Hungary to choose a king not belonging to her dynasty or her race."

Wasn't the final sentence proof, however, of an excessive scruple on the part of a man as modest as he was superior? Shouldn't they hand him the scepter, in spite of what he said? On questions of such gravity, the first person to consult was incontestably Augusta. But how can you question her, how can you recite to her Lord Rothermere's prose, learned by heart, when you are not in full possession of your faculties?

Sweet, so *sweet* that there is no one *sweeter* to be found in the *sweet* style, this pretty Amphitryon would nonetheless like to drive from his land, indeed from the very face of the earth, the guests who have complicated his life to the point of a headache. In spite of his desire to boot them out one kick at a time, he must assume a harmonious pose, dream up some photogenic gestures, for the photographers have just arrived with their cameras. So, with that, each of the thirteen signs a truce with his apprehensions. Nice little chicken's-ass faces are only too happy to hatch charming smiles. Primrose can breathe easy. Exquisite images of this historic feast will be passed on to posterity. But, cheese time having passed, the sheepish invitees go back to the subject at hand. In their evolution, however, said sheep follow an opposite course from that of the biblical kine, that is, instead of going from fat to thin they go or pretended to go from anxiety to casualness. This is literally and figuratively the case, moreover, for they have just brought on a saddle of lamb so succulent that each person gets the urge to pull pieces of it from between the teeth of the person next to them, as well as taking the words out of their mouth.

Jim is the most frantic. He eats, drinks, speaks all at once and chokes, and everything comes out through his nose. The young marquis of Sussex is thinking seriously of leaving the table. He too feels like asking his godmother to wage war on America, for he hates Americans, those wild children who destroy everything in their path. First of all, he is less and less willing to accept that gratuitous act which costs a thousand francs. News of this madness has probably already reached the hills and their little towns. Thus, the young men who for a fair price provide a service for gentlemen of refined taste are certainly not going to forget to put the question of voluptuous salaries on the agenda.

They will undoubtedly decide to hike their rates. A Lord Sussex doesn't like to imagine the day, probably soon, when village kids will dare to demand *horse-guard* prices. But to them it will seem like average pay, since the most popular ones give themselves for free to Krim who, of course, doesn't need to be asked twice. Thus a consumption of stocky little dark-haired fellows on the sunny hillside where it's more pleasant to finish living than in the ice-cold air of the mountains. The stars of venal, tourist love affairs, even during the loveliest moments of their success, didn't dare hope to hold in their arms, squeeze with all the strength in the muscles in their legs, as they say, the creator of the songs which made their precocious childhood thirsty for violent drinks, short-step dances, and bittersweet flirtatiousness, as bitter, as sweet as a mixture of sweat and cheap violet perfume under the arms, after a wild, sensuous night in the month of August.

Krim is, all wrapped up in one, both the Circe who charms those little guys and the Homer who sings of their deeds. Seeing her so frail, now almost transparent, they feel ashamed of the thickness of the hands with which they caress her. They bring her flowers, give her scarves reminiscent, by their disturbing paleness, of anise aperitifs. But in order not to reproach themselves for a generosity contrary to the traditions of their skin trade, they make up for it at the expense of late-night strollers by lifting wallets, watches, and devising expert blackmail schemes. The marquis of Sussex, even though he knows his Riviera down to the tips of his fingers (pun both intended and unintended), hasn't managed, despite his prudence, to avoid two or three unfortunate incidents. He has a hard time accepting the pound's drop in value and an even harder time, he a lovely young Englishman, going broke in order to compensate for the free flow of sperm cooperatively allotted to the singer by the swarthy little fellows. And this moribund slut is so hungry for men that if there's an empty chair between her and Kate, it is probably because she ate the person destined to sit there, the fourteenth guest whose absence the others will begrudge the marquise of Sussex for their entire lives. The light of the Chambertin wine illuminates that hypothesis which cleanses the venerable, exquisite lady of the suspicion of thoughtlessness. So the young lord's lip and tongue are considerably appeased when they begin to suck on a long, cylindrical ear of corn. Esperanza, who doesn't miss a thing, recognizes that unbridled eating pleasure. She tells herself that Primrose has a very ill-mannered son. So she asks the psychiatrist what he thinks of perversions and what role they should play in the Paneuropean confederation.

The man of science condemns them because they risk depriving Augusta's army of a necessary contingent. On the other hand, he doesn't fail to recognize a certain elegance in the neuroses generated by perversions. Hence this question: Should neurosis be eradicated?

Although decadence is not his specialty, an uncle of his once knew Rollinat; thus he states his preference for the latter's *Nerves* over *The Flowers of Evil.* Marie Torchon interrupts him and asks Augusta if she thinks that populism will soon be recognized as a contribution to the commonweal. Esperanza loses interest in such a disorganized conversation. She dreams of neuroses, contemplating her son whose nervous twitches prove him capable of jumping right to neuroses without having to pass through perversions. The exceptional nature of filial psychology is comforting to maternal pride. In order to be promoted to general, the pipsqueak wouldn't have to be a lieutenant, a captain, a major, or a colonel. A pity he refuses to take holy orders. But there's no use repeating the same regret over and over. Good blood can't lie. And, imagining the most catastrophic scenario, namely, Marie Torchon getting someone to marry her—even that marriage, which Esperanza doesn't hesitate to call foolish, can have its bright side and allow for etc., etc., etc.

It would be tedious to follow the meandering path taken by all the remarks and vagaries of thirteen individuals during a meal, in the course of which Lawrence and his heroine Lady Chatterley were discussed: English ladies are so worthy that, even in the midst of the worst debauchery, they know how to choose, as if by chance, in the person of irresistible gamekeepers, highly respectable former officers of the royal army. From Lady Chatterley, moreover, they will move to considerations of sexuality which will lead Augusta to confess that, for her part, she deems herself to be at the anal stage. "Me, I'm going through the cannibalistic period," adds Krim.

Cannibalism.

The scion of Sussex could have guessed as much.

Krim the cannibal would have devoured the fourteenth guest. But what if he didn't mind? What if, in spite of the summer, he were shivering to the point of wanting to warm himself by her fever? What if he wanted his blood to turn to light in that fire? What if he has come away from it clothed in a mantle of invisibility, yes, invisible but a spectator? He is there, the fourteenth guest, a spectator whose intentions are in no way inferior to those of the Commandant as he appears at the conclusive end of the Don Juan myth.

But the Commandant determined to crush between his jaws of stone the man whom a perpetual dissatisfaction set on the trail of every passing woman, the old man bent on killing the young one in order to do away with the competition, intent on displaying a sort of avenging virtue, his senile jealousy, his very anger—all this pays homage to the seducer, like Saturn devouring his children because he is frightened of foreseeing gods in them, like all fathers determined never to forget the right over the life and death of their descendants granted by their Roman predecessors. In order not to be eliminated by his own flesh and blood, the man must take precautions without delay. He can deduce the ancestral appetite, the boundless, deadly willpower of those gums, still defenseless but already full of teeth which, destined for monstrous growth in a few years, will turn a little heap of soft meat into a nonetheless formidable carnivore, either because in the course of a religious feast he wants to assimilate what he respects in the person of his progenitor, or because he intends to get rid of a rival that he will not unrightfully hate with all the force of his unconscious, since the engenderer, if a preserving will doesn't arm him against the engendered, will nonetheless conceive an implacable hatred for this engendered one who, at the most innocent moment of his crying age, throws himself with all the violence of his hunger onto breasts that the adult, in his most daring caresses, touches only with infinite respect.

The Commandant is old. The Spectator is not much over thirty. The Commandant is standing, inexorable, on the edge of the abyss that he has dug as deep as his hatred in order to hurl Don Juan into it. As for the Spectator, he seats himself between Krim and Kate.

Among this entire great Paneuropean family, yes, the same kind of great family as the army was praised for being in the jingoistic days before 1914, they are the only clean ones, washed of all parental filth. There has never been room for a placenta's thickness in that dying flame, Krim. As for Kate, she is a child and the Spectator thinks that merely by intertwining his fingers with hers he could abolish a nauseating world on which his anger agrees to feed only in order to vomit it.

In spite of having fornicated quite a few times with both sexes of the species and even with a few dogs, the mere fact of brushing up against a certain freshness can retransform one into an adolescent ready to drown his memory in the eyes of a little girl out for a stroll.

. . . But, on the pretext of drowning your memory, won't you get tied up in the reminiscences of scarcely brilliant pre-puberty? The author of this book, who has not only "fornicated with both sexes of the species and even with a few dogs," in addition and above all, for thirty-two years, twenty-four hours a day, from January 1st to New Year's Eve, has had to put up with being confined with the Spectator under a single name in a single bag of skin, with no exit allowing one of them to escape from the other, even in the middle of the night, even in their dreams.

A resident of the Sologne area, in the *Journal* of September 19, 1932, after having declared himself determined never to give up the pleasures of hunting without a license, concludes: "Even if I became a music lover, I would remain a poacher." The author is ashamed to admit: "Even while in love, I remain a spectator." And the Spectator reciprocally: "Even while a spectator, I remain in love."

And now, dear reader, if you read this book during the rainy season, you will think that the water from above has swallowed the last patch of solid land; if it is during the dry season, you will believe that, in the sand, the last stream has been lost forever. But, patience, don't get upset if we serve you something shapeless when you ordered something carved in stone. You like precision. Everyone likes precision. But, by slicing ever thinner, you end up with hashed meat, mashed meat. After the fibers, the powder. A cyclone invents swirls of white dust at each reawakening. Mornings of shivers and plaster. Everything is mixed up. And as a matter of fact, mixing the plaster, isn't that one of the first, if not the first thing to do when building a house, the House? But beware of metaphysics. In three minutes, three words from now, if order is not restored, it will be the house in and of itself.

There is a lot of talk about phenomenology these days, and yet every moral science has pretensions to noumenology.* And that's

---

Phenomenology of angst, announces Heidegger, the most famous of present-day phenomenologists. Instead of studying the *how* of angst, he merely points out the why which expresses it, the *why springing from the mystery of the Being who oppresses us.*

But the philosopher of Freiburg doesn't mind being in the metaphysical cul-de-sac, since he himself answers his own question: "Each and every metaphysical question can be asked only if he who asks it is, as such, included in the question, in other words, is himself called into question."

It remains to be determined whether, for such an asker of questions, for an why we are not too advanced in psychology. In spite of the symbols which, along with movement, intoxicate a century that likes to pride itself on being the century of speed, we haven't, in some areas, progressed beyond the means of transportation of the Merovingian kings. What are you ruminating, ruminants? Ox of an ox. Long live peasant literature, regional novels, long live the horse, and the cart that has been put before the horse. But is it possible to turn over the surface of a hard sufficiency? Pretty music, that agricultural stroll on marble hearts, petrified skull bones. And if the plowshare can no longer bear the impenetrable, if it revolts, if it steps outside of itself? It will finally discover its furrow to plough, deepen the furrow already ploughed by a scar, itself resulting from the tearing off of the balls from between the hind legs of the emasculated animals, for the whole flock of priests intends to take the good Lord by the horns, since they won't take any more bull from those who want absolution without confession.

Ah! wisdom, wisdom of nations, centuries-old, I should say millenary, joint possession of Paneuropean stars, ornament of little caparisoned soirées and grand captivating receptions of capitalism, it would only be to condemn you that he would take a seat among the thirteen other guests, that fourteenth person, ambassador of the man who holds the pen, writes the word *pen*, the word *word*, the *the*.

Everything scatters, but in the center of the scattering there remains anger. The Spectator especially doesn't intend to assume a stone shape. The time has come for the Commandant to have recourse to the pompous, sclerotic, mineral symbolism of that supposedly capital, absolute justice whose rudiments the father forces on the child with punches, slaps, and other chastisements.

Today, it is no longer up to the father to punish the son, but up to the son to punish the father—punish him because he, the father, was unable to keep the son from appearing punishable in his eyes.

Periods of so-called decadence have the merit of illuminating with an exceptionally violent light the conflict between what is and what should be. Opposites, ice and flame burn with the same fire. The world is blazing with crystals and conflagrations. The world is blazing with antitheses. Then it seems as if the earth were suddenly opening, having been impregnated by the storms aimed at it for months, years, lusters, centuries. It will blossom with all the hot, fecund dangers, in the form of trees of sulfur, trees of suffering, trees of freedom, fountains of blood. The cowards, the lukewarm chickens did all they could to make us think its carapace had grown cold, incapable of such blooming.

---

asker of such questions, every metaphysical question is not the means to avoid other questions, concrete ones.

Detour via the abstract. Evasion.

The grand obscurantist societies, all of those having something to do with repugnant religiosity, will talk about the reign of the Antichrist. But it's not a question of reigns, Christ and Antichrist, you miserable snails. The world is disinfecting itself of your rubbish, priests. The clay of the engulfing trails rises up of its own accord as if, from within, it had kneaded, molded itself in a movement that will undo the ruts, give back to the traffic that which, made for it, didn't take the trouble to stir.

Then the sirocco, the animal with gigantic strides that doesn't come out every day, instead of blowing out a breath which frightened the unprotected nape of man's neck, the great sirocco lies down on public squares as vast as its original desert and, with its lips made of equator ribbons, gives assurances that what must be will not be prevented from being. And it didn't lie, since, from explosion to regenerative explosion, red terror will be carried out. So men no longer become all knotted up in metaphysical coils. They have already broken the shackles of hypocrisy. Transgressions no longer having anything to do with sin, thus nothing to do with the hodgepodge of abstract repercussions in the hereafter. It's simply a question of eliminating certain living conditions, and certain beings, as those living conditions made them, and as they allowed those living conditions to continue.

He who threw thirteen characters on top of a hill no longer disposes of them. He is not master of the reactions to which he will be pushed by those drowning victims brought back from the swamps of memory, the wells of nightmares. He is not sufficiently mithridatized to rediscover with impunity in the poisonous mirror of his writing the gestures, the faces of a world that hasn't ceased to be. His dreams that wanted to deny the world have resuscitated it. On all the street corners, on all the sleep corners, after thirty-three years of an existence which is not yet blasé with disgust, with hatred at nearly every step, at nearly every encounter, there is a new opportunity for detesting. An opportunity never to be fled. He who did not have his eyes and eardrums poked out the day he was born cannot set his face against the swarmings of influential rot, high-sounding names, princely or ducal marriages, liberal hypocrisies and various assorted demagogies. It swarms even in the silence, in the light of the rising sun, when the return to the waking state is hailed by a warmth which, when you listen to it rise, gives the same pleasure as that derived from sniffing, before going to sleep, the sheet fragrant with the sun that dried it.

The perpetual repetition of the same great crimes, sinister, idiotic little tricks, has stained the memory forever. One swallow doesn't make a summer, but a tiny black spot spoils the most beautiful of skies. One recollection poisons even the giddiness you feel when, lying on your back, you scrutinize the ether of the most flamboyantly empty summer.

One can laugh.

Laughter has never erased, never corrected anything.

Supposedly satirical, risque works are but one of the faces of edifying literature. A certain devilishness, merely by declaring itself an expert in bad sentiments, recognizes as good those which the opportuno-pen-pushing custom presented as such. Pride in badness, quite debatable, moreover, thus determines the so-called daring to be only, but to be with all their somber colors, the shadows projected on the wall, always the same, where all momentum shatters upon impact.

By opposing traditional morals, their rank stupidity and their no less rank dishonesty (one relying on the other), those who dared to push intelligence to the point of honesty (or, what amounts to the same thing, honesty to the point of intelligence) passed for immoralists.* We should be grateful to them for having brought about scandal's success. But scandal, having "arrived," must not remain, for remaining, it is no longer a scandal. Besides, a particular scandal is worthwhile only insofar as it denounces the most scandalous attributes, the scandalous monotony, the scandalous hypocrisy, the scandalous boorishness of a society that considers as a scandal everything that is not as scandalously monotonous, hypocritical, boorish as itself. Scandal that seeks to remain within the confines of itself, that freezes into an aesthetic posture, scandal elevated to the dignity of something in its own right, transformed into an object of metaphysical luxury, scandal for scandal's sake is no better than art for art's sake.

And above all, what a source of further confusion if scandal, in its author's conscious or unconscious thought, merely served as a magic tithe. A well-simmered scandal, that's the price (reasonable) to be paid for the transaction, fifty-fifty. He who is out of sorts makes advances to provoke public opinion, before satisfying it. The acknowledger has anticipated, contemplated his acknowledgment. And he has carefully

---

*Let us speak frankly here, dotting our *i*s on this word which contains two of them and serves as the title of a book that moved the Spectator so strongly when he was still a high school virgin but destined for a bisexual future. Along with that bisexuality (first point), let us mention the intermittent use of various alkaloids by the same (second point). That eclecticism in sexual relations and drugs has always seemed a bad mixture to the eclectic himself. A free-floating libido risks becoming a real aviary of frivolities. But the big carnivorous birds have entered the house of the little birds, the little songs. When you keep company with vultures, you eventually sprout sharp claws, a piercing beak. You learn to defend yourself, to attack, if you aren't masochistic enough to want to have your liver eaten, like Prometheus, who let himself be punished, who in turn gets punished for having invented what he is—man.

chosen his time, his words. Question of measure. Formal measure preventing any real measure. Yes, we begin by insinuating. We certainly don't have the ambition to weight what is imponderable, etc., etc.

The pose of a purely external originality: what does that signify, apart from the underlying bad faith of the poseur, a conformist more or less well disguised as an "enemy of laws," but in complicity with those laws, since he has just declared imponderable that which it is in his material or moral interest not to weigh.

Sentimental fog, what a refuge!

But, the other side of the coin, the mind in that warm, blind wadding on which it has fallen back becomes rigid, paralyzed, turns to entity like wine to vinegar.

Individualism, personality. In order to deify egoism, didn't some so-called philosophers carry complaisance to the point of slipping an insulating *t* in between two vowels that were rubbing together, all too obscenely, their dirty, miserly little ant noses. Now we have egotism. A lot of good that does us.

The bourgeois who wants a strongbox to protect his material values locks up what he believes to be moral, intellectual values in suits of armor, ivory towers.

Suits of armor

The little intellectual condemns himself to rot, caterpillar victim of his vanity, in the cocoon of indifference and tin that defends him from others. If he stepped outside of himself, he would feel far too deliquescent. He would then want to swallow his umbrella. But he has no umbrella, for true English stylishness is out of his league. He's done up like a two-bit dandy. He lays claim to a shrewd mind, although he has anything but a wasp waist. Besides, all the little analytical thistles with which he would like to nourish himself have crumbled to dust.

Ivory tower

Alfred de Vigny was a lucky stiff who, from his ivory tower, could dispatch, by registered mail no doubt, his sperm to Madame Dorval. So much masturbatory delirium, disdainful of other bodies, can only produce enervation,* sluggishness, neglect for a world appearing intolerable, even to its profiteers, but for which not even the profiteers are willing to lift a finger in order to make it a bit more tolerable. The individual is both the contour and the center of that vicious circle.

---

*In the criminal court of Versailles (December 1932, Wahl *vs.* Davin), it was stated that the accused had become a criminal by carrying self-love and its practices to the point of brutishness.

But now, the cracking up of the suits of armor,
                    the ivory tower,
                    the vicious circle,
                    and all containers.

No individual in good faith could continue to allow his individualism to protect him from the outside world and the problems that the outside world poses to all eyes not made of glass and drives into all brains not made of lead.

Not to denounce explicitly a regime fomenting unemployment and war is to remain its implicit accomplice. The decrepitude, the impending bankruptcy of that regime, of its millenary iniquities, don't make its intentions any better—on the contrary. There is still much to be done before a clean sweep can be made of the bourgeoisie, its culture, its institutions, before the proletariat can finally begin to build.

Capitalism doesn't commit suicide, you force suicide on it, and not simply by blowing hard. Its monuments are more firmly planted in the earth than the legendary wall of Jericho. The humanitarian song that so many dromomaniacs go around the world singing, the little canticles of religious-tainted pacifism, all of that will not only fail to loosen the official stones, but on the contrary helps to cement with opportunism, with resignation, the smallest quarry stones, the tiniest fragments of what must be torn down.

The liberal lie, a specifically French product, everyone knows what it is worth, what it costs us. We haven't forgotten what it cost us. We can foresee what it will cost us. France poses as the champion of individual freedom, meaning that it intends more than ever to defend the freedom of a few people, a minority of exploiters in whose goodwill and whims they are only too happy to go on indulging themselves at the expense of the exploited.

If the profiteers don't like to break into the nest egg, dip into the savings (do you know the country where avarice flourishes?), they are, on the other hand, lavish with beautiful words (do you know the country where eloquence flourishes?), words, always words, words that have lost all value. We are at the peak of verbal inflation. No sooner is that counterfeit money printed than its promising effigy becomes soiled. Its features fade. With what remains, it would be impossible to reconstitute a face. In bourgeois speech, nothing makes any sense now, means anything, or rather makes sense, means something only by grimacing, odious antiphrasis.

Since war rages endemically in the colonies, as soon as the colonizer engages in his butchery in a precise location, on a precise day, a little more ferociously than elsewhere, than usually, there is talk of pacification.

It is thus recognized by imperialism itself that its form of peace is not in opposition to war. Imperialist war and peace are indistinguishable. United front against their bloc. *United front to turn the imperialist war into a civil war.*

Thanks to the League of Nations, there is no longer anywhere in the world even the smallest patch of Switzerland that might, with the help of slyly Christian symbols (the white cross from a flag, the red cross from the organization of the same name), try to feign that evangelical, biblical impartiality under whose cloak the belligerent countries' spies, in the course of the world war, carried out their little tasks, gathering documents (preferably false) in order to bring the death sentence down upon those of their compatriots who didn't applaud the hecatomb.

Thanks to the League of Nations, now Geneva has officially become the police headquarters of the bourgeois world and the Prince of Journalists was able to headline his article "Notice to the Defeatists of Capitalism" in which he thanked, in his name and in that of civilization, the Swiss colonel who gave the order to fire on the crowd during the meeting for the report on the proceedings and resolutions of the Congress of Amsterdam against the war. But to insinuate that the bludgeoning in front of Bullier's was child's play compared to the shooting at Plainpalais surely wasn't meant to flatter the Paris chief of police. After the congratulations to the Helvetian commander, however, there followed thinly veiled reproaches directed at the nonetheless consecrated purger of the City of Light, as though he hadn't proved worthy of his job, his reputation. "When a star grows dim," concluded the opinion maker, "it's never long before a sun eclipses it totally."

Being a woman with a head on her shoulders, a broad chest, and protuberant buttocks, the police commissioner's wife, a sharp customer, smelled the threat beneath the metaphor. She threw a splendid fit of anger, or rather anger threw around her splendid frame, shook her to such an extent that the Juno of the Criminal Investigation Department (as she was called by a poet among her admirers) suddenly turned into a bacchante. In fact, it wasn't long before the Olympian creature, whose low-cut dress, on evenings at the theater, used to fill the opera glasses of all the other skirt-chasers, was no more than (and no less than) an earthquake, a fleshquake, one of whose tremors flung, far from the bodice where it was moored, a very expensive brooch, a gem of a little tricolored policeman with a ruby face, a sapphire kepi and tunic, and a diamond truncheon. Only a miracle prevented its edges from breaking off as it fell, this poor darling not accustomed to the soft pillow of doubt, but rather to the firmly stuffed sofa of certitudes, for the cupolas of a brassiere (reinforced model) can restore self-confidence in law-enforcing breasts. Thus, despite the Prince of Journalists' insinuations, the most tightly corseted of Third Republic-style grand dames was not about to be convinced that she had a millstone around her neck or a rhinestone dangling from the tips of her boobs, a jewel having nothing to do—on the contrary—with the embassy of her dreams.

Among the police commissioner's numerous enemies, none had ever been of sufficiently bad faith to dare accuse him of laxity in repression. Was the Prince of Journalists then carrying his double-dealing to the point of pretending to have forgotten about the unemployed worker quite simply killed by the police commissioner's men at a construction site six months earlier? They know how to set examples in the department of La Seine as well as in the canton of Geneva.

There is nothing frail about the commissioner's wife. She is even heftier than her anger. She has already picked up her little tricolored cop. She puts him in his place, rings her chambermaid: "Hurry, hurry, my hat, you know, my little police commissioner's heart-colored turban,* my fur, but there's no time to be lost, my girl, the future of the French Republic depends on it." A darling little hat is placed atop marcelled waves, a silver fox is wrapped around a sensuous body. The goddess of police heaven runs rather than goes, flies rather than runs to consult the files. It doesn't take her long to find what she is looking for. Perfect, perfect. Now, she is at liberty to weigh her entire weight (which is not featherweight) on the scales of justice. In order to restore a balance, the Prince of Journalists will have no other resource but a counterweight of five hundred thousand francs. Not a penny less. And woe to him if he's slow in forking over this nice little half million for works of police charity. The commissioner's wife, with one stone, will have thus killed not two, but at least three birds:

---

*It's the latest color; a very delicate color since, as Synovie wrote (to be sung to the well-known tune "A Gypsy Heart Is a Burning Volcano"):

> A police chief's heart
> is a paradise,
>   nice.
> A policeman's heart
> is the best part,
>   so smart.

The "police chief's heart" is thus a golden, radiant pink which translates into a fashionable tint the famous words: "Every human life is the color of daylight to me," spoken by the Sun King from the Pointed Tower in the middle of a city council meeting in order to shut up those who were asking for very indiscreet explanations concerning an arbitrary imprisonment.

—punished injustice;

—worked for the well-being of her dear protégés;

—and deserved, for having found such a sum, to be promoted from Chevalier to Officer of the Legion of Honor.

Ah! if it weren't for the economic crisis, all it would take are a few pretty agents provocateurs and some curvaceous little policewomen to catch a dozen American billionaires in the act of indecent exposure. They could be released, for a fee of course. And what a fee! From then on, Mommy's dear little coppers would wear nothing but gold lamé pajamas, suspend their virilia in lace pouches, and wash their feet in patchouli. As for their protectress, she would put the cutest little commanderess tie around her neck!

And yet, in these times of misery, you can't complain if you've got a Prince of Journalists where you want him—and they've got him by the balls. In his file, there's enough to make an entire city of six million tenors burst into song.

At police headquarters they had been looking the other way. Now they look back this way. A nice little check, they look the other way again and all the more intently since the hostage, a good loser, accompanies his ransom with a gift that goes straight to the heart of the beautiful ransomer.

It's a belt made of sapphires, diamonds, and rubies (imitation, unfortunately). But its frame is carefully finished, and considering the recipient's waist measurement, well worth its price. The stones are arranged in such a way that one can read: *Liberty, equality, fraternity*. The Prince of Journalists, who came up with the idea, obtained a patent. He figured that nobody could advertise his gimmick better and in a more lively fashion than the commissioner's wife. He wasn't going to miss the bus because of a grudge. It was quite interesting, moreover, to think that, thanks to his beautiful enemy, he would get his money back, recover the sum that she had demanded. The moral of the story would really be worthy of a fable by good old La Fontaine.

And in fact, it only took one policemen's ball with the hostess wearing her *Liberty, equality, fraternity* belt for the fad to catch on. Every one of those ladies wanted to have her own—Esperanza too, as well as Primrose, Augusta, Marie Torchon, and Synovie. For an entire winter, an entire spring, there wasn't one she-cock, not one she-fowl who didn't adorn herself with the proud inscription. Later, the item became rather commonplace, and by the time of Lady Sussex's luncheon, women of real elegance had already quit wearing them.

As a consolation, the Prince of Journalists need only remind himself that, all over France, the walls of barracks, churches, courthouses, prisons—of greater perseverance than the laps of even the most intelligently conservative women—have never stopped repeating: *Liberty, equality, fraternity.*

That triple promise, which no bigwig of the Third Republic ever dreamt of keeping, is repainted by the professionals of obscurantism, of repression, of war, as soon as it is worn away by the elements. As a real Frenchman, in love with paradox and irony, the Prince of Journalists is delighted by that. He's rubbing his hands. He is certainly not one of those who washes them. He's no Pontius Pilate asking himself whether the blood to be shed is that of an honest man. No. He knows how to assume his responsibilities. And merrily. Which, of course, doesn't prevent him from moving with the times and knowing that you catch more flies with honey than with vinegar. So long live religion which softens hearts and minds with its balm, pours holy oil on the wounds, the necessary wounds, for it is blood that flows through great empires' irrigation systems as they fertilize their wastelands, their uncultivated lands, their uncivilized, barren lands.

But the French Republic is also and most importantly a great colonial empire. A right-thinking opinion maker must remind the police commissioner that a keeper of the peace, i.e., of authority and, a fortiori, the chief of all the keepers of peace, would no more hesitate to kill than would a bishop to give his blessing. To each his own work. During the war, soldier-priests undoubtedly did several jobs at once. With the cross in one hand and a gun in the other, they didn't have a minute to lose. How badly overworked were the representatives of God on earth! But the faith that moves mountains spares the con-secrated arms of all stiffness. Thus, when it was a question of the world's salvation, the Prince of Journalists, in an epigraph to his "Appeal to French Clergymen," quoted the Holy Bible: "Without shedding of blood is no remission" (Hebrews 9:22).

He was sure of an effect that promptly came about, he who, brought up on Catholicism, had always patronized its rituals and its clergy. He is extremely grateful to them for it. The finest of his romantic memories, without a doubt the most touching and certainly not the least intriguing, he owes to a darling little priest who wore silk stockings and ladies' underwear. It was in the days of Grille d'Egout, the cancan, "The Lady from Maxim's," and all those swish café-cabaret entertainers. At that time, the lingerie of women in love, instead of paring down to unfeminine slips, proliferated in Valenciennes chemises, flouncy pants, and large- and small-pleated petticoats, all well-ironed, well-starched. The young priest had an appreciation of the undershirt and underskirt that was rare even in those blessed times. From the modesty of his bearing, the austerity of his skirt, the keenest psychologist couldn't have suspected the fireworks of English embroidery, point d'esprit tulle, and imponderable organdy that lighted up the secret night of the cassock.

Son of General and Mrs. Oldentide (née Mossyhole), he was christened Dumbo, like all the eldest sons of the family for centuries, in remembrance of an ancestor, a valiant knight who had particularly distinguished himself during the crusades. The Oldentides and the Mossyholes could no longer even count the quarters of a nobility dating back, for the former, to Pepin the Short, and for the latter, to Pepin of Herstal. Young Dumbo considered numerous excellent marriages, and was sufficiently well endowed to leave it entirely up to the grace of God. With his social and physical advantages, he combined intellectual and moral ones, not to be discounted. A doctor of theology before coming of age, he never risked wandering into the labyrinth of heresies, the maze of schisms. He was one of those lucid French thinkers who finds his way out of the thickest of evangelical contradictions and the thickets of civil proceedings. He descended from a long line of jurists and Church Fathers. He dominated the spiritual and the temporal. With lowered eyes, joined hands, but an enticing petticoat, he went through life, always patterning his conduct upon the great principle of his holy mother the Church: *There are pious lies.* It wasn't long before the pious lies turned a little priest into a great bishop *in partibus,* it goes without saying. And since, as far as parts were concerned, Monsignor Oldentide of Mossyhole preferred those of Negroes, he began crisscrossing Africa in all directions. After having flitted all over the dark continent gathering pollen, the noble prelate had settled in Dakar with his crosier, his miter, his violet skirts, and his underthings, always dainty, but singularly reduced because of the heat and the local fashion. He had, moreover, interrupted his equatorial odyssey only to remain under the charm of a male Calypso, a former boxer, now a brothel-keeper.

Her sister on Rue Blondel no longer doing any business in the mother country, Esperanza, on the advice of the Prince of Journalists, had sent her off to Dakar, promising Monsignor Oldentide the pope's blessing if he succeeded in finding a home for her.

Since a cat, according to the traditional saying, may look at a queen, why would Esperanza's sister deny herself the right to fall in love with Monsignor Oldentide? The latter, if he allows his episcopal self to seduce his flock, always does so with honorable intentions, namely, the salvation of said flock. The holy man resists the sinner's advances, but after a good bout with the boxer/brothel-keeper, his flesh is calm enough to talk about the marriage of souls in Our Lord Jesus Christ.

The duchess of Monte Putina will soon receive, in her Roman palace, an epistle from Monsignor Oldentide that, in tone, will not be unlike the one that Saint Paul wrote to the Corinthians. She will read that the last sheep has now been brought back to the fold and is determined to offer up to God her virginity, which religion has suddenly restored after so many years of whoring. Esperanza is delighted to have a new Mary Magdalene for a sister. The trick is knowing how to use her. There is no lack of work to be done. In fact, she has far too much to choose from. Those chosen by God must rush to the aid of threatened capital. It's a question of defending the spiritual and the temporal. No Catholic would dare to contradict the duchess of Monte Putina on that particular point; just yesterday she had the pleasure of reading an article by Mr. Delcourt-Haillot, Catholic boss, president of the French Confederation of Professions, who speaks out in favor of the forty-hour workweek* in order to save the temporal through spiritual means:

Since the masses [writes Mr. Delcourt-Haillot] are in the unfortunate habit of holding the Church responsible for all the errors of the bourgeoisie, we ask Catholics as a favor to abandon those antiquated ideas and above all not to make common cause with the profiteers of the present regime who fear the intellectual and moral improvement of the proletariat, imagining, quite wrongly, that the spiritual perfecting of the workers would lead to communism.

It took tens of centuries for humanity to acquire sufficient productive strength to make possible a reduction of the workday and to spread the culture of the mind and the heart.

Recent progress in technology and industrial organization is taking place at a time when Pope Pius XI is asking workers and bosses to be the apostles of workers and bosses; they appear as the instrument of deliverance and progress in a society thus far too absorbed by material concerns.

The reduction of the workweek alone can give workers sufficient leisure, so necessary for the development of their religious instruction, for their entry into Catholic charitable societies, and for their formation, in accordance with the request made by the sovereign pontiff, as apostles of the shop floor. . . .

When you are the wife of a Monte Putina—owner, in Piedmont, of factories for the manufacturing of artificial silk that are just barely staying afloat—you would much rather hear about shop-floor apostles than unemployed workers. And hurray for intellectual and moral improvement, especially if it spares you a salary increase! Charity begins at home. Esperanza is not about to go against a providential plan that intends (divine simplicity!) for bosses to be bosses and workers to be workers. Impossible not to agree with Mr. Delcourt-Haillot and the sovereign pontiff. As for the former, since he has one of those compound names that are characteristic of the nobility of the Third Republic, that French aristocracy of money which, although

---

*La Croix, 21 January 1933.

not worth the Monte Putina's more ancient one, nonetheless has its value, Mr. Delcourt-Haillot will have to be introduced to Augusta when they are back in Paris.

No surprise that he concludes, this great bourgeois, this great boss, this great Christian, that we shall find a way to make apostles of the shop floor "with the cooperation of the great industrialized countries."

The admirable concision of style! Mr. Delcourt-Haillot is not only a capable, good-hearted man. He is also a born writer. A real humanist, Esperanza* compares Mr. Delcourt-Haillot with Tacitus who used only ten words where anyone else would have needed twenty, thirty, forty, or fifty. A lapidary form gives even more vigor to the most vigorous thought. Here, no one would dare to question that, by "cooperation of the great industrialized countries," should be understood the "greatest industrialists of the great industrialized countries." And there we are. It's a question of opposing the Communist International to an international of magnates of prominent, large, heavy industry. They would order cannons, shells, and machine guns in Latin. The Krupps' and Schneiders' stationery would bear crosses, mottos such as *Dominus vobiscum* and *Pax cum spiritu tuo*. What does it matter if the war crushes bodies to a pulp as long as minds remain at peace? Didn't Mr. Nobel, the philanthropist, the founder of the peace prize, make a fortune from dynamite?

A duchess of Monte Putina, an Augusta, a Prince of Journalists, a Monsignor Oldentide, and all those who are still honest and right-thinking in these times of capitalist defeatists know that, rather than becoming the enemy of the strikers—who refuse to be dispersed by orders of the police and rifle shots—one is better advised to transform the workers into apostles of the shop floor. If the task is formidable, those who attempt it will be all the more meritorious. What a noble activity for a wealthy man: to teach the poor to love their poverty and to respect others' wealth! There's a truly evangelical ideal. For twenty centuries it hasn't ceased to be that of the Church, Catholic, apostolic, and Roman, and that is why the no less Catholic, apostolic, and Roman duchess of Monte Putina is going to pay a little visit to the Holy Father.

She is always well received at the Vatican, but this time better than ever. She is politely congratulated on being called Esperanza, in

---

*She agrees with Mr. Alain, the man of "remarks," who believes that "anyone who doesn't know Greek and Latin is a feeble-minded imbecile." One can imagine her enthusiasm in answering Mr. Benda who invited (*NRF*, Feb. 1932) his readers to "honor the Church, regardless of its motives, when, at the Council of Trent, it rejected the use of national languages for the Mass, maintaining Latin."

honor of the one theological virtue that must be preferred to the other two, faith and charity, in this century whose overabundance of quasi-apocalyptic visions predisposes to pessimism those who do not put all their confidence in divine mercy. Esperanza never doubted such mercy. The Holy Father thus prefers this rich woman who accepts her wealth with cheerful resignation to all the poor people who, throughout the world, are exasperated by their poverty, and, since the sister of the pious duchess of Monte Putina wants to take the veil, she might as well do so in the spirit of joy and thanksgiving, as founder and superior of the order of Little Sisters of the Rich.

Rome writes to Dakar.

Monsignor Oldentide answers in the name of his converted sinner that she accepts.

Then the groundwork is laid, with bulls and encyclicals, for what must be, will be, and will remain the greatest event of Christendom in modern times. In order to give the ceremony an official luster, the Minister of Colonies sends troops to form a chain around the cathedral. Monsignor Oldentide orders himself a robe with a train made of crepellozinolinazinettachina, shoes with Louis XV heels of the same fabric, a slip of triple-layered veils, and a gold lamé miter which the top tailor from Reboux's, sent expressly from Paris, will cut, sew, and set with big cabochons on the end, according to the principles of the most famous house of fashion in the entire world. The heroine of the celebration—she who, after a good half-century in a brothel, will offer up to the Almighty Father the virginity that the Holy Spirit miraculously restored to her because Monsignor Oldentide wasn't interested in her charms—God's fiancée will don the white gown, the crown of orange blossoms, and the veil worn by every bride.

The Church has dispatched a complete selection of its regular and secular ministers in order to give international importance to the event which the government, moreover, intends to use as colonial propaganda. Thus, the Minister of Foreign Affairs hasn't skimped on the secret funds covering the costs of the collective spectacle. Unfortunately there is not a single native, male or female, who doesn't want to be draped, like Monsignor Oldentide, in violet crepellozinolinazinettachina. They find the religious livery offered them lacking in color and beads. They will have to serve an entire people glass after glass of rotgut before convincing three hundred of its men to slip on cassocks and three hundred of its women to don coifs and wrap themselves in the robe of the Sisters of Saint Vincent de Paul. Even so, right in the middle of the Mass, the three hundred Negresses, wearing no underwear and exasperated by the rough woolen frock scratching their asses, lift up, in perfect unison, their petticoats all the way to their navels. It must be said that no one in the congregation will take advantage of the exhibition. It's so warm and there isn't anyone, from young Lord Sussex who arrived the night before as the representative of the Prince of Wales, to the Japanese cardinal, an agent of the Intelligence Service, who isn't drunk. They snore, belch, fart, sweat, pray, and above all cry for joy when the old staggering bride disappears behind a screen to take off her white satin, reappearing as Reverend Mother Saint Savings, founder of the order of Little Sisters of the Rich. And there's a *Te Deum* loud enough to wake the deaf in their graves; then they leave the cathedral, taking a walk, in a great procession, through the city. The troops present their arms to the Blessed Sacrament, to Monsignor Oldentide, then to Saint Savings. Cameras follow the procession. Saint Savings stops to make a heartfelt speech. She says the right words, in the right tone of voice, to thank her bishop and her God. In movie theaters throughout France can be seen, heard on the newsreels, the sister who is twice a sister, once in humanity and once in God, of the duchess of Monte Putina, that "star of international politics." Yes, it's glory for Saint Savings. Not only can she be admired on the screen surrounded by three hundred Negroes disguised as priests and three hundred Negresses who have been convinced, incidentally, but only with great difficulty, to lower their skirts, but all the illustrated magazines will also feature pictures of her, interviews, and so much coverage that the most glorious of priest-women, the directress of Saint-Lazare women's prison—the most highly honored lady cop of all the lady cops of the Third Republic and, indeed, more rather than less decorated with the Legion of Honor than the police commissioner's wife herself—dies of envy.

You can't put just anyone in charge of a women's jail.

It will therefore be suggested to Saint Savings that she replace the directress whose glory killed her. So much honor leaves her dumbfounded, but Oldentide urges her to accept and she gives in to her converter's reasons. Yes, of course, a prison has nothing to do with a pigeonhouse, and a dove couldn't possibly enforce the law there. The best soup is made in old pots. The worst rascals make excellent informers. When the Devil gets old and gray, it's easy for him to become a hermit. Oldentide blesses Saint Savings and promises her canonization in exchange for services she won't fail to render as a representative of spiritual and temporal powers. The Church has never hesitated to go fishing for its saints in the deepest cesspools of whoredom, provided, of course, that the whores who want to attain the highest, the most ethereal degree of saintliness do their part. A mystic who was consistent and ventriloquial when he felt like it, Monsignor Oldentide doesn't even have to open his mouth for the Lord to be praised. Deeper than the bottom of the heart, his gratitude requires a chant that comes from the navel. Thanks are given by the episcopal guts.

Good, truly Christian souls are only too happy to organize and systematize the decline of certain beings. Then, they let them know that they are no longer of any worth and, finally, place them in the hands of the priests who will buy them back for the reasonable price of a few words mumbled in Latin. Those who were once victims of a certain social order thus become its agents, defenders, and collaborators. And that the old victim's experience may help the executioner to make new ones, such is the favor that Monsignor Oldentide wishes on the Reverend Mother Saint Savings, superior of the order of Little Sisters of the Rich and directress of Saint-Lazare.

Let's leave Saint Savings drifting toward the shores of France and Monsignor Oldentide snuggling in the arms of his boxer. Their episodic selves have done their best. It's up to us to conclude. And even though our conclusion is not new, it nonetheless remains with us, forever and ever. Capitalism and its accomplice religion feed on, live off the evils that were born of them. Thus, in order that the ricochets of such a touching reciprocity may continue, the aim of their laws is not to ward off those evils but to provoke them. Codes and dogmas began by ratifying, sanctifying the spoliation of the majority for the benefit of a favored minority. Just as the shadow clings to the object, particular crimes with their innumerable little black flames will continue, but will only continue the initial, general crime, the massive iniquity, the monstrous corpus delecti that still encumbers five-sixths of the globe.

That huge mosaic of rot, of nonsense, of rage is cemented with blood-soaked mud. Here it's a bourgeois republic. They take us in with democracy, liberalism, the separation of powers, but those gentlemen of the executive, the legislative, and the judiciary are in agreement, in complicity on one point and a well-established point at that, a point which always turns to their advantage. To govern is to repress. And there isn't a country that doesn't aim to rule the world. In 1914 every average Frenchman thought he was Empress Eugénie. It was *his* war. The last war, the last one until the next one. The nationalist is always a self-righteous man, and the self-righteous man a nationalist. "Thou shalt not kill . . ." his catechism once taught him, when he was six years old. He has no tolerance for anyone who doubts or makes fun of religion, but he wants them—and how!—to defend, to kill in defense of his strongbox. "It takes all kinds to make a world," he says sententiously, and, as long as it is not on his little self, he enjoys thinking that the stabber perfects his act at night, on street corners, during peacetime. Any day now, we'll need trench-cleaners. We must be farsighted.

Priests have deified fear and the hatred of love. After all, the family must be safeguarded for the making and handing down of money.

The son must continue the father's work, namely, accumulate on top of what has already been accumulated. Thus, when the time comes

to procreate, the problem is to find a vagina with a substantial income—
and virginal, it goes without saying, for anyone with a sense of property
knows the value of being the original owner. And that is why a hymen
is worth its weight in gold, in platinum, is worth a solitaire, a wedding
band on the ring finger and the sacrament of marriage. But self-interest
is not enough to make a strong-limbed male monogamous. Never
mind that. Patience, patience. Wait a minute. In the dank shadows of
cathedrals, brothels begin to sprout. My word, regular mushrooms.
Are they poisonous? Not for everyone, at least. Some people live
on them, and comfortably, with no detriment or obsession, but with
enough gratitude to know that nothing makes them grow like raining
holy water. A whole body of literature devoted to brothels teaches us
that their keepers are good Christians who provide their children with
baptism and Holy Communion, not forgetting to obtain extreme unc-
tion for themselves before meeting their maker, the God of procurers.
Countries where piety reigns (look at Spain, for example) have
always been and haven't ceased being strongholds of prostitution.
Is a great wave of religiosity breaking over the rotten Old World,
as its City of Light erects brothels alongside churches?

The bordello customer who has read Tolstoy and Dostoyevski gets
all misty-eyed. He starts thinking about resurrection as he buttons his
fly. That prostitute, when she turns inedible with age, will have to pray
for him. Then he, the well-fed gentleman, will scorn a bit less the
woman forced by social iniquity to serve as a dump for his nauseating
underbelly. And with that, our man hums a tune as he ties his tie, for
he is dreaming of women cops, women priests. It's charming. Hasn't
the grateful country just finished decorating one of its daughters who
put her ass at the disposal of the Intelligence Service? And she had an
epic mind, if in fact she had a decisive ass, that beautiful lady. She
wormed secrets out of the German officer who bought her a beauty
salon, pearls. For her trouble, she has just been awarded the Legion of
Honor. That's right! Undercover women are the glory of a civilization
that goes mushy over police commissioners and their females. All the
national filth is on display. Now it's nothing but one huge sewage
plant whose stench recalls those suburbs into which the world's great
sewers flow. And who cares about asphyxiation or typhoid? Self-
sufficiency has been adopted as the definitive solution and the con-
ceited man is delighted to think that, in the form of a cauliflower on his
plate, he recovers his own turd. Routine, avaricious, sordidly narcissistic coprophagy is all it takes for some, for many to think they are
supermen.

The unemployed die of hunger and cold while the wealth accumulated at their expense is burned and drowned. That much is true,
indisputable, both literally and figuratively. No less true morally than

intellectually or physically speaking. The minority of exploiters continues to starve the masses all the better to poison them. The great greasy-spoon owners let the cultural stew simmer in a hermetic pressure cooker. The Third Republic boasts of having established compulsory education. Compulsorily elementary education. And secularists with their liberalism, their humanitarianism, those bourgeois who pin evangelical smiles on their shark jaws haven't finished oozing with Christianity. They are not content with their solid profits. They also want satisfaction in their souls. So, from everything out of which they have cheated the masses, they deduct paltry alms that will do as little harm to themselves as they'll do good for those to whom they'll throw them. And they accompany their insulting charity with a stream of sugarcoated words. But hunger is not fooled by a few scraps, anger refuses to be drowned in a flood of twaddle. Each day the proletariat acquires a clearer class consciousness. Those bourgeois, those priests who wanted to make an idiot or a hypocrite out of every poor man, have been rendered harmless on one-sixth of the globe. The bourgeois, the priest couldn't imagine "their" earth, "their" heaven, without the halfwits, without the stool pigeons that they needed so badly.

"Happy are the poor in spirit" . . . "there is more joy in heaven over one sinner who repents". . . . To repent, however, to get religion, to return to the straight and narrow, is first and always to betray companions in misery and degradation: it is to turn oneself in, to turn them over to the cops who are all the same, the real ones and the imaginary one, cops in flesh and blood, specialists in roughing up suspects, or the great fog-skinned cop, God, whose name is never invoked (always the same taste for miracles) except to neutralize the people's anger, to pulverize the people's fists of rock and quench their eyes of flame. The days of inventing another world in order to make up for this one are over. A revolution is needed to rebuild this old capitalist world which enlists the aid of reforms to make it last. Someone ought to shut the mouths that still dare to speak of revenge in the hereafter, that dare to promise death as revenge against life. Comrade, only time limits the misery of your life, but all kinds of misery limit the time you have to live. Black men are paid by the rich to talk about eternity, about that which never ends, and you and your own, in peace as in war, you are finished off prematurely by the merciless capitalist disorder.

Witness the thirteen men executed in Geneva (October 1932).

Early 1933: A fuel-gas tank explodes in the working-class town of Neunkirchen. The big shots of the Saar can't be bothered with safety precautions. There's a conglomerate of avarice and negligence in capitalist countries. The Renault factory blows up: nine dead. The boiler was old, rusted, and the walls insulating it built out of little bricks of lightweight particle board. In the South Seas, Malaysian sailors and Dutchmen, whose salary the toadstone billionaire Wilhelmina reduced by 17 percent, mutiny. The *Aldebaran,* a French boat policing the Pacific, joins the Dutch fleet. They give chase to those natives, so ill-mannered that they don't even thank the colonizer when a fifth of their means of avoiding starvation is eliminated. An airplane drops a fifty-kilo bomb: twenty-two dead. If the mutineers hadn't surrendered, they would have been presented with another one weighing two hundred kilos.*

Meanwhile, a Catholic boss takes bossery and Catholickishness to the point of proposing, the good apostle, to reduce his employees' workday by one hour so that they will have time to go listen to the priests. But the Swiss colonel, the great factory owners of Saarland, Mr. Renault, and Queen Wilhelmina, although of different denominations, are all good Christians. They agree on the necessity of religious instruction and practices, for resignation must be taught to those whom they are determined to reduce to pulp for the preservation of their wealth, their prerogatives. This globe, five-sixths of which still belongs to them, to their fellow oligarchs, they'd like to smother completely with God, that pillowcase, that huge dirty bedspread that they used to bundle up their loot. In the East, they have torn up God. God is in rags. They want to mend him, for otherwise there will remain nothing but shreds, not even enough to make a bandage for one of his pairs of eyes which are starting to see better and better, more and more clearly, mercilessly.

The she-cocks, the she-fowls, and the Prince of Journalists all agree with Oldentide: "There are pious lies." They don't want anyone to spoil their pious lies, and the Prince of Journalists has his Parisian place of residence on Thiers Square, purely out of veneration for that great, generous man who, in the midst of the commission on primary education of 1849, proclaimed: "I want to make the clergy's influence all-powerful, because I'm relying on them for the propagation of that admirable philosophy which teaches man that he is put on earth to suffer."

In 1933, Mr. Thiers's successors have not yet given up propagating the admirable philosophy of 1849.

Across the street from the square bearing the name of that raging rat, at 154 Avenue Victor-Hugo, a poster on the wall of the Sacred

---

*That masterstroke was, moreover, no trial run for imperialism because, in 1930, in Chile, the fleet having revolted following a salary reduction and the workers in Valparaiso, Santiago de Chile, Coquimbo, and Antofagasta having in solidarity called for a general strike, the Chilean bourgeoisie sent for the American fleet, whose airplanes dropped bombs and thus crushed the rebels.

Heart convent makes the case for pseudoreligious obscurantism, its ethics of enslavement, its torture mystique: "The toiling elite entrusts its children to parochial schools," is the suggestion.

Always the iron hand in a velvet glove, the same flattery, the same caress—all the better to strangle.

Be that as it may, whether education is parochial or municipal, religious or secular, private or public, primary, secondary, or college-level, those whom the bourgeoisie put in charge of it, with very few exceptions, only bother to step outside the limits of their specialties in order to force youth into intellectual masochism. Greco-Latin superstitions on the one hand, Christian on the other combine to make a suffocating night. Play on words, play on ideas, we go from humanism to humanitarianism, a very Catholic game, played by a class that excels at cheating and intends to win, while twiddling its thumbs at the expense of those whom it not only condemns to work, to suffering, but whom it wants to persuade of the moral excellence of work and suffering.

The poets of those evils, of resignation to those evils, are certainly the old poets that a plutocratic republic doesn't expel from its bowels. Lamartine, for example, remains on the official syllabus. Bowlfuls of his nauseating nonsense, barrelfuls of his pious manure, that's what children and adolescents are offered these days to poison their thirst for learning.

And since he personally is as worthless as his work, the man holds no less a place of honor than it does. Scarcely a hundred yards from Thiers Square, open, spread out, in full bloom on the same thorough-fare, he has his square, he too, Lamartine, the saboteur of 1848, the big goofy guy with cotton balls for brains. He lounges there in the bronze of the statue earned by the ignoble words on the red flag. Like-wise, a bas-relief perpetuates, in the place where it stands, the pretty face worn by the executor of reactionary justice in 1871, the lover of admirable philosophy who, when the people of Versailles entered Paris, announced that he was going to perform a violent bloodletting and actually performed one so violent that the historic days of May emptied Belleville. And the wealthy district rejoiced, hasn't stopped rejoicing more than sixty years later. The gentleman and the bourgeois are partners in glory for having managed to combine so well their two strains of ferocity: ferocity by tradition, ferocity by unscrupulous ambition. The twentieth century didn't denounce the treaty of alliance signed in the nineteenth century against the proletariat. Underneath the profiteers' hair held in place with *brilliantina argentina,* under-neath their jackets with padded shoulders, there is no more emotion than underneath the clerical frock coat, underneath the toupee which crowned the most self-righteous of foreheads and didn't lose a hair of its pitiless self-assurance, while the repression cut into raw flesh on the revolutionary hill.

An elegant avenue whose birthplace is the Place de l'Etoile, and whose cradle is the tomb of the Unknown Soldier under the Arc de Triomphe, ends with a tribute to the murderer of sixty thousand communards. And indeed, instead of beating around the bush, one mustn't forget or try to obscure the fact that if the existence of a rich minority implies the misery of the masses, that minority, when it's a question of preserving its privileges, won't hesitate to massacre those masses.

Meanwhile, again and again, the walls of churches, courthouses, barracks, and prisons keep repeating: *Liberty, equality, fraternity.* Three words, two dozen letters, it's not much, it's less and less to camouflage and consolidate the ramparts which the capitalist mess persists in trying to impose on the movement of history, on its most irresistible leap, the proletarian revolution. Three words, two dozen letters, a promise to be taken as antiphrasis, on official stones, a no less official lie: the exploiter is not content with exploiting, he taunts his victim. Here boorishness is stripped clean of its facade, there irony clings with all its claws to the flanks of misery, to the flanks of the hovels, to the flanks of the misery of the hovels, to the flanks of the hovels of misery.

Provocation is rife in the streets, the streets of Paris.

Paris.

Paris, capitalist capital, Paris, capital of capitalism, because the residential hotels and the brothels wink with an eye in the form of a sign or a big number: since the billboards shout with glaring electricity the merits of their fake products; since in the music halls the footlights grab bouquets of shivers with tiny atolls whose pasties jiggle on the waves of the breasts, the swell of the sexes, at the end of the spectacular revues, when the torrent of stage lights has inundated the beaches of skin, metamorphosed their sand into an ocean of pink tepidness alas enslaved by the grand finale of some old whore from the Intelligence Service; since, from twilight to dawn, reflectors are trained on the stone quadruped which didn't even have to go to the trouble of having a head to devour the profusion of cadavers that explain why it is still, always called Arc de Triomphe; since the old corpses, to rekindle their ferocity, come and piously caress that minotaur's turd, the dirty little flame of the memory that he shits out among the flowers, Paris, in their very encounters, your monuments confess. In a square, Notre-Dame and police headquarters, female representation of a whorish living portrait, hookers in love with the Gothic, priests, cops, and other conservative riffraff, exchange bows and smiles worthy of ladies in a drawing room and the expression *bordel de Dieu* [God's whorehouse] isn't a mere metaphor useful in poetic bursts of anger but designates quite accurately that place in the universe just as it was bequeathed to us by the submissive, religion-smothered nineteenth-century man whose eyes, wherever they turned, saw nothing but cathedrals of forests, forests of cathedrals, temples where living pillars, etc.

Paris, the old capitalist world calls you its City of Light, so who cares if the sun never shines at the bottom of those cesspools where the hovels are falling apart. The rich neighborhoods have just shot off their fireworks. Watch out for the sparks when, after a little visit to the god of landowners, the shower of vitriol stars falls to the ground. Sections of wall scream out, skinned alive, saltpeter eczemas catch fire, mildews sob over low heat while gilt-edged more and better than ever, the sumptuous, blossoming cancer gnaws on, eats away at, corrodes the great lean body, tears its muscles into leprosy lace. The city's real blood doesn't have room to circulate, the major arteries are compressed to the bursting point. All of the breathable air is drawn away by the monstrous, murderous growth whose every cell thinks it is the queen of the Bungarians.

And that's enough to delight the Prince of Journalists who loves queens and Bungaria, who is as happy as a king if he can get bungered like a queen.

But since queen of the Bungarians there is, let's swap the Bungarians for sheep, and return to our sheep, the queen's sheep, going all the way back to Marie Antoinette who played the shepherdess, without having ever realized, perhaps, that each one of her mollycoddled, perfumed, pink-ribboned little lambs was in defiance of the dire misery of the times. A queen who plays shepherdess most certainly places complete, unconscious hope in the magical power of pretense, as if merely aping the life and labor of the people would silence the anger felt by that people, *her* people whom the scandals of *her* court were causing to think that the only means, if not of eliminating, at least of attenuating misery, unhappiness, was to eliminate, to attenuate from the head down the woman who was the greatest profiteer of the kingdom.

The queen's pastoral snobbery before 1789 corresponds, today, to the bourgeoisie's soup-kitchen snobbery on the eve of communism.

There's a crisis. The rich minority strikes a poverty-stricken pose. Not because they are ashamed of that wealth which hints at the real poverty of the masses, but first of all in order to save money, next as an attempt to fool their enemies, and finally because old habits of religious hypocrisy make man simulate what he intends, for real, to impose on others.

The fact that some get caught at their own game, the game of simulation and pretense, that's another story, the (hi)story of bourgeois philosophy and culture, which metamorphoses work from a means to an end and tries to force the most repugnant practices of intellectual masochism on the thinking man.

The elegant avenue, the rich one strutting from the Arc de Triomphe to Thiers Square, glorifying, along the way, Lamartine and the merits of parochial schools, that real queen of the Bungarians, since the other queen played shepherdess, why shouldn't she play shopkeeper? She wants to play shopkeeper, so there! she does. Not to sell cigarette butts, scraps, rotgut, of course. Boutiques are decked out with shellfish. Behind shop windows, orchids grow all by themselves, on moss, denser than dandelions in the fields. Aristocratic fruit sleeps in cotton. The little dears, one hopes they won't hurt themselves dreaming. There is a fashion that changes, each month, for the marquise de Sévigné's chocolates. And here we find pastry shop after pastry shop where Augusta, Esperanza, and Synovie, when acting Parisian, never forget to come stuff their faces between two services at Saint-Honoré-d'Eylau, the wealthiest parish in Paris, inundated by the smell of the finest grub. Upon leaving the sanctuary, those beautiful souls really believe they have found heaven on earth, for it seems as if humanity might just as well live on caviar, lobster, truffled poultry, little pyramids of ice cream, and pears at twenty francs apiece. And for Augusta, the music lover, here are the latest records, the complete Wagner played on the accordion. Esperanza always bears in mind her merits—of which, in the present circumstances, she is delighted to make a lively business— Esperanza, I say, awards herself a degree in philosophy, because she chose the most sumptuous of pajamas from among a disconcerting variety offered to her by a luxury store. Rare editions of Synovie and important articles by Marie Torchon add a sentimental tremolo and a decisive arpeggio to this symphony of sumptuous taste, while a herd of trunks as high as a house awaits, at the leather shop across the street, either of those ladies' next Paneuropean tour.

From the bottom to the top of each apartment building snakes, rather than climbs, a lasciviously monumental stairway, hundreds upon hundreds of times longer, more corpulent, thus more voracious than the boa that devours an entire ox for breakfast. All by itself, a stairway in a wealthy neighborhood eats up cubic yard upon cubic yard, enough to house quite reasonably at least ten of those working-class families (father, mother, and two children) forced by the present state of iniquity, in order to recuperate from their hours of work on the assembly line, to sleep four hours in a room where a pair of lungs doesn't even find air to breathe.

Neither a Prince of Journalists nor any of the she-cockfowlish ladies ever runs the risk of awakening the gigantic, sacred reptile that nobody touches except for the concierge condemned to breaking her back when she polishes it and makes it shine.

What foot, loose with freedom of movement, would be foot enough to take the trouble to tread on the blue felt that clothes those marble scallops and stairs? Messrs. the renters (bankers, major industrialists, big shots in the army, the navy, the press, and various public and private administrations of the Third Republic, the old bags they call their wives, and Messrs. the silly jerks and the stuck-up Misses who would like nothing better than to serve as their heirs and heiresses, the sooner the better), Messrs., Mesdames, and Misses the renters can play more than one tune on the elevator cables. Oh, the little darlings! As for the servants, the delivery boys with their inelegant packages, they can just take the back stairs, perfectly steep and dark. One can't expect a dignified avenue, after all, to shed tears over the fate of those who slave away, those whom it has taught the saintliness of slaving away so that it can smile at the angels through each of its windows. And how cheerful and cute they are, those curtains which bring to mind cancan dancers' underthings, maidservants' aprons in comic operas, and Monsignor Oldentide's petticoats. But wait a minute! some of the shutters close like pursed lips. For a little hotel in full bloom, in the middle of a garden whose every grain of sand seems to have been polished with rottenstone, what a lot of banners spanning whole lengths of building fronts, trying, in vain, to drum up business. At the main entrances, look at all the signs announcing "*Apartments for rent.*"

Those empty houses, floors, what a lot of space consumed by vanity in each residence, how wide an area is taken up by the broad foundations of Saint-Honoré-d'Eylau Church: you can see how much room the proletariat can be deprived of merely by walking down a single street.

The capitalist capital is not content with robbing the homeless of shelter. It filches air, light, heat from the poor.

The unemployed worker with his paltry unemployment benefits doesn't have enough to buy coal, but large buildings, half or three-quarters empty, are heated night and day, from top to bottom, from wall to wall. And they're still bringing in marble for new construction. And in order that the admirable philosophy dear to Mr. Thiers will continue to be propagated, they keep building new churches. God may not pay rent, but the wealthy know that the money they spend for his lodging is a good investment. Thus in a particularly sensational article, the Prince of Journalists suggested that the French ship of state do what the queen of Holland did on her ships. Yes, save money by cutting salaries and devoting, like the frog of the northern swamps, part of its profits to the new houses of worship it's trying to erect in the mother country, and to the missions being sent to the South Seas.

To be a master of opinion means also, and most importantly, to be a master in one's own house. A Prince of Journalists's contributing editors might as well just tighten their belts a notch. From the director's office to the latrines, signs paraphrase the famous proverb to remind them that "small privations make great successes."

From the fruit of the small privations, a tidy little sum will be deducted, an offering to the cardinal-archbishop of Paris.

This holy man is beating his breast in front of a microphone. Yes, he is begging for money over the radio, on the pretext that two million Parisians have no church to attend. And they're going to build, they *are* building sixty sumptuous pigsties for God, sixty cowsheds for priests.

"Yet another miracle: the stones turn into bread," the Prince of Journalists will write, congratulating the prelate all the more heartily, since at least the workers employed on ecclesiastical construction sites aren't putting up those low-rent houses that he is afraid to see built eventually, creating unbearable competition with those old shacks inherited from his father the epileptic and his mother the hunchback. They aren't palaces, but they bring in lots of money. That's what counts. A man who has a twelve-room apartment just for himself in a posh neighborhood isn't going to lose any sleep because the shacks he owns near the Place d'Italie and the one he lives in near the Bois de Boulogne don't seem intended for the same species of creatures.

A long, poor street.

Two hundred and sixty-five dumps repeat the same mangy facade, the same courtyard, the same dark stairway, with steps so worn that you risk breaking your neck twenty times from one floor to the next. An appropriate setting for tragic, miserable lives, and their epilogue: disease, death. Indeed, this presents the opportunity for a little joke. An enameled plaque repeats it: Investors' Castle Street. We're on Investors' Castle Street. Around here you won't find even the shadow of an investors' castle until pigs begin to fly, and that's precisely what the Prince of Journalists, witty fellow that he is, finds so charming. Irony, that so very French quality. After all, they couldn't call this sinkhole of desolation Unemployed Slummers' Street. You have to know how to smile. For example, what a riot to see a big wall with gigantic letters full of soot from the smoke of neighboring factories advertising the tuberculosis clinic across the street. How amusing for those who cough up their lungs in the hovels on Investors' Castle Street. As for the tuberculosis clinic, you can always go see it just for laughs. The rain comes through the roof, trickles on the inside of the walls. No water, gas, electricity. Plenty of cockroaches, though. The toilet is in the courtyard, the same one for everybody. A Turkish toilet, with no seat, just a hole in the ground. Not much of an incentive to visit Constantinople. In the summer, the cesspool gives off a stink that the winter attenuates slightly. But then you freeze to death.

Bronchopneumonia or typhoid fever, depending on the season.

What they were renting for 300 francs before the war now costs 1400.

The private individual is not, moreover, the most rapacious of landlords. The Department of Welfare owns vast lots on Investors' Castle Street. Instead of rebuilding, it simply divided them up into small plots facing an alleyway with no sanitation system. Each one of its tenants built himself a little house. But for the few square feet that it rented in 1914 for 95 francs per year, the national administration of benevolence and mutual aid is now getting 600 francs.

And that same charming irony! Right next to this hamlet, which enjoys the same privileges as the most sinister neighborhoods, here is the Nicolas Flamel night shelter where they condescend to take in for a few hours those whom the regime has thrown into the street. At daybreak they are kicked the hell out. They are free to go wherever they want—to be soaked to the bone, burnt to a crisp.

There might be "*for rent*" signs on all the doors in the rich avenue, but in the poor street not a single rathole is vacant.

In the rich avenue, the apartment for 7,000 francs, the mansion for 10,000 francs before the war are going for 20,000 and 40,000 francs respectively. Thus, the cost of housing has only tripled or quadrupled for the bourgeois, while the proletarian must pay a rent five, six, or seven times more than that bourgeois who condemns him to live in slums. And the landlord, who certainly won't overspend on repairs, demands respect for the heap of old scrap iron, rubble, plaster, and rotten boards: his property. *It is forbidden for children to play in the courtyard.* But the furniture inside, even reduced to the strict minimum, fills the one or two tiny rooms. Outside, the meager stalls eat up the sidewalk in no time at all, not even leaving enough space to play hopscotch. Heavy trucks shake the whole block.

It is forbidden for children to play in the courtyard.

It is forbidden for children to play.

On Investors' Castle Street, last January, a little fourteen-year-old girl committed suicide. A tragic episode in the life of the poor, explained the newspapers. The view from the window out of which she jumped certainly offered nothing to dissuade you from wanting to smash your head on the cobblestone street below. A miserable gut of an alleyway ruptured like a hernia, strangulated between the surrounding walls. Dead End of the Future was the name of that cul-de-sac. After all, the future allotted by the exploiter to the children of those he exploits has nothing to do with the heavenly Champs Elysées.

Capitalist capital, Unemployed Slummers' Streets follow upon one another, concrete, panting shadows, quartered by a merciless abstraction, admirable philosophy. But people can't take it any longer, people have had their fill of it. They clench their fists. They know that the sinkhole of desolation won't open to the daylight through a simple little breach. Its belly must be slit wide open, and for that to happen we first have to dismantle and raze the civil and religious fortresses of the regime, yes all the fortresses, the religious ones that are in complicity with the civil ones, and the civil ones that pay them back in full, since there's nothing official in this France of 1933 that, with its secular hypocrisy, doesn't sweat, doesn't stink of Christianity.

After having cut, trimmed, undermined, we'll have to dig and dig if we want to extirpate every last root of the Christian weed: purge underground, ground, atmosphere, the stratosphere of the ivy that claims to be celestial, all the better to carry out its strictly earthbound double-dealing, all the better to crawl along, splitting hairs, wriggling at day's edge to lift itself up suddenly, whistling its threats, poisoning the air with all its branches of the tree of God, therefore the tree of ignorance, tree of evil, since, in the very opinion of the makers of God, man was driven from the earthly paradise simply for having touched the tree of the knowledge of good and evil, therefore the tree of learning, therefore the tree of good.

It is time to hear from the blasphemer, it is time to hear from Sade who, on July 2, 1789, grabbed a tube for a megaphone and shouted from his window that the prisoners in the Bastille were being massacred and that someone should come free him; it is time to hear from Sade whose appeals were one of the reasons for which the people, twelve days later, took the Bastille. Twenty-seven years in prison, under various regimes, didn't reduce his voice to silence. Let him be heard even today by true men, true revolutionaries who are working, struggling, living, dying against the iniquitous old world for a new one.

"O you," he said to the people of his time, the partisans of the revolution of his time, "o you who have axes ready to hand, deal the final blow to the tree of superstition; be not content to prune its branches: uproot entirely a plant whose effects are so contagious. Well understand that your system of liberty and equality too rudely affronts the ministers of Christ's altars for there ever to be one of them who will either adopt it in good faith or give over seeking to topple it, if he is able to recover any dominion over consciences. What priest, comparing the condition to which he has been reduced with the one he formerly enjoyed, will not do his utmost to win back both the confidence and the authority he has lost? And how many feeble and pusillanimous creatures will not speedily become again the thralls of this cunning shavepate! Why is it imagined that the nuisances which existed before cannot be revived to plague us anew? In the Christian church's infancy, were priests less ambitious than they are today? You observe how far they advanced; to what do you suppose they owed their success if not to the means religion furnished them? Well, if you do not absolutely prohibit this religion, those who preach it, having yet the same means, will soon achieve the same ends.

"Then annihilate forever what may one day destroy your work. Consider that the fruit of your labors being reserved for your grandchildren only, duty and probity command that you bequeath them none of those seeds of disaster which could mean for your descendants a renewal of the chaos whence we have with so much trouble just emerged. At the present moment our prejudices are weakening; the people have already abjured the Catholic absurdities; they have already suppressed the temples, sent the relics flying, and agreed that marriage is a mere civil undertaking; the smashed confessionals serve as public meeting places; the former faithful, deserting the apostolic banquet, leave the gods of flour dough to the mice. Frenchmen, an end to your waverings: all of Europe, one hand halfway raised to the blindfold over her eyes, expects that effort by which you must snatch it from her head. Make haste: *holy Rome* strains every nerve to repress your vigor; hurry, lest you give Rome time to secure her grip upon the few proselytes remaining to her. Unsparingly and recklessly smite off her proud and trembling head; and before two months the tree of liberty, overshadowing the wreckage of Peter's Chair, will soar victoriously above all the contemptible Christian vestiges and idols. . . ." Thus spoke Sade in 1795.

Around 1909, when the Russian revolutionaries were wandering about in search of God or working to erect the deity, Lenin wrote*:

---

*This letter was quoted, for the first time, by Jean Guéhenno in an article entitled "Mr. Gide" (*Europe,* February 15, 1933).

At the time it appeared, Gide, after having declared himself, in his *Journal* (*NRF,* Sept. 1932), ready to give up his life for the Soviets, wrote ("Letter to Ghéon," *NRF,* Oct. 1932) that he condemned all wars, both civil and imperialist. He explained his scruples. But he could be accused of at least some duplicity in the way he turned around and around the idea of honesty, while no mere ripple but a merciless tidal wave of reaction surged forward so quickly that, without the slightest shadow of pragmatism—under a capitalist regime, for a writer from the ranks of the bourgeoisie, there is no pragmatism worse than saying that one is exempt from it, since claiming, according to the pedantic and underhanded formula, that one doesn't write *ad probandum,* means that there is nothing to prove, nothing to be proved against the regime of which one becomes an accomplice—intellectual courage consisted in searching for the shortest route, and perspicacity, in finding it. Concerning fascism in Germany, while so many others lost no time in dodging the

"The search for God is no more distinguishable from the creation of God or the production of God and other such things, than a yellow devil is distinguishable from a blue devil.

"To be opposed to the search for God—not in order to speak out against all devils and gods, but to prefer the blue devil over the yellow one—is a hundred times worse than not mentioning it at all. The same applies to all kinds of gods: the purest, most completely immaterial ones, and those sought no less than those 'created.' . . . It is precisely with this idea of a pure, immaterial, yet-to-be invented God that the people and the workers are stupefied. . . . Any idea of any God, even the mere fact of flirting with an idea of this kind, constitutes inexpressible infamy, the most dangerous and the most despicable infection. Sins, foul and violent deeds, physical infections are more easily recognizable by the masses and consequently are much less dangerous than this idea of God, delicate, immaterial, perfectly decked out in ideological costumes. A Catholic priest who rapes girls (I happen to have just read a story of this sort in a German newspaper) is not as dangerous as a priest without a chasuble . . . one of those immaterial

---

question of nationalism, Gide went straight to the heart of the matter and stated:

"Germany is presently giving us an appalling example of the oppression which fatally engulfs a country that seeks its salvation in nationalistic pig-headedness. It immediately seizes any pretext or creates one and all means of domination become justifiable. Such a policy necessarily leads to war. Those who claim that they want to avoid it should finally admit that class struggle alone, I mean that which sets each country against its own imperialism, can stop the new conflict that is brewing and that, this time, would be fatal."

For a country to fight against its own imperialism, however, it must fight against its religion and the confusion engendered, even in an era that considers itself secular, by the vestiges of religions. All of the aftereffects of Christian masochism and Jewish masochism—from which it sprang—are, in Europe, the allies of imperialism. In Asia, it is well known that the English couldn't complain about Buddhist passiveness and nonviolence.

One mustn't forget, moreover, that reformism, to which capitalism has recourse in its desperate moments, manifested itself, for the first time, in the form of religion. It was no accident that the Reformation was called just that, since Marx was able to observe that the aforementioned Reformation, if in fact it drove the priests out of some countries, made those who carried it out into priests.

We are not talking about replacing one priest with another.

We must eliminate all priests.

For a revolutionary intellectual from a bourgeois family, there is no revolutionary activity without antireligious activity. He must denounce the religion of his birth, just as he denounces the class of his birth, the former being a mere mask, though the most formidable one, of the latter, that hydra.

priests who preach the invention of a new God. For it is easy to unmask the former, to convict him and get rid of him; but the latter is not so easily expelled and he is a thousand times harder to unmask. No 'fragile, versatile' bourgeois will be willing to condemn him. . . . Isn't inventing God the worst way to spit on yourself? He who becomes involved in the fabrication of a god or merely tolerates such a fabrication spits on himself in the worst manner. . . . Any attempt to invent God is but the complacent self-contemplation of the stupid bourgeoisie, the fragile Philistine, the petit-bourgeois dreamer, spitting on himself, 'desperate and weary.' "

Without disregarding the paradox that a nondialectical mind risks seeing in his work, we must again quote Sade. By truly brilliant intuition, surpassing the views of mechanical materialism with which the most daring and free of his immediate predecessors were content, with which his contemporaries were still content, he arrives within sight of dialectical materialism:

"As we gradually proceeded to our enlightenment," writes Sade, "we came more and more to feel that, motion being inherent in matter, the prime mover existed only as an illusion, and that all that exists essentially having to be in motion, the motor was useless; we sensed that this chimerical divinity, prudently invented by the earliest legislators, was, in their hands, simply one more means to enthrall us, and that, reserving unto themselves the right to make the phantom speak, they knew very well how to get him to say nothing but what would shore up the preposterous laws whereby they declared they served us. Lycurgus, Numa, Moses, Jesus Christ, Mohammed, all these great rogues, all these great thought-tyrants, knew how to associate the divinities they fabricated with their own boundless ambition. . . . Therefore, today let us equally despise both that empty god imposters have celebrated, and all the farce of religious subtleties surrounding a ridiculous belief: it is no longer with this bauble that free men are to be amused. Let the total extermination of cults and denominations therefore enter into the principles we broadcast throughout all Europe. Let us not be content with breaking scepters; we will pulverize the idols forever: there is never more than a single step from superstition to royalism."

For one hundred and forty years, history has undertaken—and how!—the illustration of that truth.

In 1795, reactionaries could think of no other position to adopt but that of royalism.

In 1933, reactionary opinion assumes many forms, but all are uniformly accompanied by superstition.

By means of conservative republics and more or less parliamentary royalties, priests, pastors & co. hover like a kiss of death over an earth that their official or tacit alliance with those gentlemen of the government and the army dooms to further carnage.

Male or female missionaries (always, regardless of their sex or their denominational persuasion, agents of European imperialism) are like rats. On the big ocean liners that go back and forth between mother countries and colonies, one never fails to find a few of those pious rodents who are sailing off to nibble at the beautiful, massive continents, to bite, in the hope of infecting their blood with their own rabid rage, the great runners of Africa, the sages of Asia, and the divers of Oceania. The Blue Trains carry loads of nuncios. Cardinalesque skirts sweep governmental floors. Digestion visits. The Church may have a tremendous appetite; it is satiated. The crooked chefs of capitalism always save it a tasty morsel. Doesn't it help them, moreover, to keep the pot boiling? "Pass me the butter plate, I'll pass you the holy oil cruet." It's the sacred union, the sacred union against the proletariat. The saber and the aspergillum, the throne and the altar. Mussolini convinces the king of Italy and the pope to overlook their disputes about the wall that separates them.

In France, in Paris, where the bourgeois style continues to be inspired both by Vespasian urinals (classic model) and lucky finds with which the mortuaries proved to be lavish in the art of pluming hearses, caparisoning, escutcheoning the horses that pull them and draping the facades of funeral homes and churches—in France, in Paris, many can't wait for some old government marionette to be reduced to pushing up urinals and pissing in daisies, in order to deploy all the military and religious forces of the regime. Always the sacred union. That recalls the good old days, when nuns walked alongside the armies of the Third Republic, following the generals in order to tickle their prostates and knock back nice little swigs of military schnapps as an aperitif. Then Clemenceau decorated Sister Julie. So they cried and prayed to their hearts' content, those gentlemen of the clergy, at the death of old man Victory. He had probably refused the aid of religion. But religion forgave him, because the dear old Tiger, after having satisfied the ferocity of his senile bulimia by dismembering Europe, had, in concert with the carrion-eating vultures of the general staff, stabbed the German and Hungarian revolutions in the back. And indeed, how could the crows and crowettes continue to caw, in the name of the Father, the Son, and the Holy Spirit, if the victorious bourgeoisie didn't come to the aid of the defeated bourgeoisie, when the people, criminal enough not to accept defeat and its evils with Christian resignation, intends to rid itself of those who perpetrate those evils and deify them.

Admirable philosophy dictates that Bismarck collaborate with Thiers against the communards and that Clemenceau and Foch return cannons and machine guns to the kaiser's fleeing generals so that they can crush the Spartacists.

Once the bloodletting is finished and the veins of the proletariat have been emptied, the professional slaughterers that every privileged class automatically produces for the defense of its privileges have no intention of relinquishing their power. Boulangism, chauvinism, anti-Semitism, colonialism, etc., through various incarnations, from 1871 to 1914, French imperialism aimed only to spread and maintain fear of revenge. A huge representation was needed for the spectacular hecatomb being prepared. It was of utmost importance that nothing interfere with the order for the holocaust of capitalist disorder. Thus, with the same mystical rage, old men kept talking about man's redemption through suffering. And their speeches became even longer and more eloquent when, toward their sky illuminated only by the stars of death, with the earsplitting music of the artillery and the incense of poison gas, rose the formless, laughable entreaty of those choirs who piously sang on either side of the front "Mon Dieu, mon Dieu, sauvez la France" and "Gott mit uns," finally blending their voices into a single *De profundis*.

And now when will the deciding game be played? each bank of the Rhine asks its opposite number.

A good sport, didn't the French government, very courteously indeed, return—to the bourgeois Berliner—the favor which the bourgeois Parisian had accepted from the Prussian general staff? All of this went along with the aims of a good, healthy war and a good, wise philosophy. For the sake of good wars and good philosophy in the future, two former and soon-to-be-again enemy nations were duty-bound to conspire in a cover-up for a repression which, this time, counts among its victims Karl Liebknecht and Rosa Luxemburg, shot in the back in the center of Berlin and thrown into the Spree just as on a previous occasion, forty-seven years earlier, an unarmed Flourens had his skull split in two by a gendarme, and Eugene Varlin, turned in by a priest, was beaten so badly that by the time they propped him up in front of the firing squad, he had lost consciousness. Then, since the old foxes of foreign policy, just like those in charge of domestic policy, are not unaware that it is sometimes useful to try fooling one's constituency with reformist ruses, there was the ridiculous Paneuropean interlude.

But now all the old, more or less official coquettes find that their affectation just doesn't work as they continue their desperate attempt to cover up a world's nauseating decrepitude. Everyone agrees that capitalism is on its last legs, but for its swan song, it will thicken its slop with national anthems and canticles. Yes, before dying, it intends to have its fill of murders, that lovely little moribund creature that never failed to conform, in its thoughts and actions, to the ideal whose principle was thus formulated by old man Ubu, King Ubu: "Kill everybody and take all the moola." Religion, that old lady Ubu, since she knows very well that, once a widow, she will automatically crumble into dust, be reduced to nothing, to nought, Religion certainly intends to be present at the last waltz, at all the police and military balls. Von Papen put himself and his country under God's protection before delivering them both to Hitler, who in turn plans to base his government, the government that is now widely known, upon the principles of Christianity. The bishop of Munich* congratulates him on fighting atheism and Bolshevism. A minister of worship states that youth must be inculcated with "the fundamental principles of national existence: respect for the army, patriotism, and faith in God."

And in order to inculcate those principles, Hitler, after having clamored for "the blood and flesh of the Jews," † switches from words

---

*In liberal France, whose victory, for fifteen years, imposed "living" conditions on Germany that were, in the case of many, many Germans, more truly dying conditions—if Hitlerism is the unwanted child of the Treaty of Versailles, which is certainly the case, it must also be noted that the son is the spitting image of his father—in our beautiful liberal France, I say, where the fiercest capitalist riffraff sheds crocodile tears over the victims of the Nazis, cassock-wearers speak the same language as their fellow chasuble-swingers in Germany, the worst germs of the brown plague.

The facts speak for themselves and it is rather striking that in the country where a penny saved is a penny earned, the Academy of Education and Mutual Aid presided over by Monsignor Baudrillart organizes throughout the world (lo and behold the priests' international, worthy associate of the cannon dealers' international) a "literary contest intended to show the disastrous consequences of bolshevist doctrine on family, religion, society" (*sic*).

First prize is 50,000 francs, second is 20,000, third is 10,000.

† In order to lay bare the basely jingoistic ulterior motives which France, England, the United States conceal behind their campaigns against the anti-Semitism, abominable as it is, of the no less abominable Hitler, one merely has to note the racism of those three nations, rampant, for the first two, in their colonies and, for the last one, at home.

In Africa, in Asia, everyone knows how the white man treats the man of color. The muzzle of a cannon is the loudspeaker of imperialist Europe.

The guillotine, more discreet, is not gathering dust. New victims are constantly being added to the list of Annamese who died for the liberation of their country. In Saigon, one hundred and eighty communists and fifty Trotskyites are indicted—for having failed to play into the hands of their kind colonizer. In the Indies, in Bombay, men rot, die in prison, guilty in the eyes of Albion of being "natives" and of having tried to found labor unions.

In the state of Alabama, rich American farmers treat blacks no better than

to actions and persecutes, boycotts. Militant communists, sympa-
thizers, all of those who don't applaud at the very sinister, very fascist
buffoonery are provoked, imprisoned, murdered.

In Central Europe, in Eastern Europe, it's no better than in
Germany. A negative ink stain, white terror spread like an oil stain,
since, in complicity with the Romanian royalty and the Czechoslovakian counterrevolutionaries, Clemenceau, in the most cynical
failure of a man to keep his word ever recorded by history, crushed
(for a period of time that certainly won't be eternal) the hopes that
Béla Kun had given to the oppressed heart of Europe.

The French bourgeois has every reason to be happy. He can rub his
stubby, dirty paws together with glee. The foul smell of priests, nuns,
and cops is overpowering on those plains, atop those summits per-
meated with the secret, harsh ambergris emanating from the wave of
Huns, the purifying flood gushing from who knows what new country
of anger to unfurl suddenly on the surface of Christian resignation.
Very Catholic hangmen condemn the sons of Attila, the scourge of the
gods, the bishop-eater to look after the foreign religious communities
which, rendered harmless in their countries of origin, have come to
seek refuge in the reactionary stronghold. In order to clothe ecclesiastical petticoat-wearers, in order to fill the bellies of ogresses
devoted to the Lord, men, women, and children starve to death a little
more quickly, freeze to death a little more surely. Convents have very
thick walls, beautiful mansarded roofs. Herds of hovels with bodies of
clay and coats of rotten thatch wade in the mud.

The races haven't fused, haven't mixed the least bit over the
centuries in those countries where the despot, whether he be Turkish
and a sultan, Russian and a czar, or Austrian and an emperor, understood that, there as elsewhere, one must divide in order to conquer.
But in that mosaic defined by the Carpathians and the Balkans, the
proletarian elements which may seem the most impervious to each
other share the same misery. As always the community of fate gives
rise to the community of interest in transforming that fate, and that
community of interest in transforming fate gives rise to the union of
proletarians.

That much is as simple as it is indisputable.

Hitlerites treat Jews. One of the Scottsboro blacks is condemned to die in the
electric chair, even though the so-called victim of those young proletarians
denied having been subjected to the rape of which they were accused. And
that white woman is threatened because she refused to play, by a false testi-
mony, the court's game, herself being in bondage to a class of exploiters who
want to make an example, in order to crush, through fear, the will to revolt
brewing in the hearts of several thousand black slaves.

From the half-starved, singing Gypsy, with his knife-filled eyes, to the Jew in the ghetto whose eternal mourning bows under the threat of pogroms, all the races which the champion of people's right to self-determination crammed inside absurd borders where, for the luckiest, for those not reduced to living off the results of begging and theft, the working and living conditions remain, in the century of mechanization, abominable paradoxes of feudality, all of those oppressed, repressed, compressed races—they accumulate, gather, agglomerate their hatred for this forward leap that never fails to carry so-called backward people far ahead of those bourgeois from the country of the happy medium who know how to sacrifice just enough to progress without really accepting it and organize, for their own profit and for their even greater glory, the slowing down of the economy, therefore misery in all of its physical, intellectual, and psychological forms in the territories henceforth at their mercy or merely subjected to the overpowering influence of their voracious trickery.

They've painted themselves into a corner, hams* crowned with gilded rage, freshly gloved with blood, those sinister, grand leading roles in a tragic operetta, those burlesque, cruel majesties whose kingdoms were only patched up by the profiteers in Sarajevo in order to serve as the backdrop for dreams of war waltzes, and to become once more the theater of imminent diplomatic and military feats.

Today, the peasant of the Danube—yes, the peasant of the Danube, a dirty mongrel hanging around the banks of the Seine, that blond colossus that you make fun of, doubter in a bowler hat; that halfwit, that poor man you scorn, you the keeper of traditional ratholes and clever little cerebral filth; that boor, that clod for whom you have only merciless disdain, twisted, determined to imagine yourself delicate because hereditary syphilis has taken on the fluttering appearance of a lorgnette, alighting on your nose—that peasant of the Danube and his brother the worker of the Danube are fed up with seeing a great boulevard of water run its empty course, its dead course among the distress of the countryside and the towns.

Now the time has come for the seas of hot anger to flow upstream in the icy rivers, running over, fecundating with great breaststrokes a sclerotic, petrified soil, tearing down the borders, sweeping away the churches, cleaning out the hills of bourgeois complacency, beheading the peaks of aristocratic insensitivity, drowning the obstacles that the minority of exploiters sets against the exploited masses, allowing humanity to develop again by liberating it from outdated institutions, religious fears, jingoistic mysticism, and everything else that creates

---

*Hungary has only a regent, but he is a worthy replacement for the inheritors of Hapsburg senility.

and deifies the ills of the majority for the benefit of the two-pawed sharks, their old bags, and the whole clique.

The third liberal, French republic still has a quasi-official press that can be used to congratulate the silly boy with a king's face who sits on the Romanian throne and those gentlemen of the Sigurantza, his associates in murder. But was the Okhrana of czarist Russia able to prevent October? Those crowds of 1905 clinging to the criminal skirts of the religion that would hang them, those unarmed men whom the provocateur and Orthodox priest Gapone led beneath the windows of the Winter Palace to be executed, in the name of the Father, the Son, and the Holy Spirit and old buddy Nicholas, those muzhiks whom President Raymond Poincaré and his worthy compatriots thought of in 1914 as the very copious but very simple contents of a huge reservoir of cannon fodder, those millions of men who were taught to pray but forbidden to learn how to read, write, count, those backward, subjugated proletarians of a while ago, don't they constitute today the first liberated, liberating proletariat?

The great intercapitalist connivers can collaborate with indigenous cops in the murder of some old official buffoon by a paralytic general, mastermind the burning down of a parliamentary palace, pull off some even more sensational attack for repressive purposes, all under the protection of the sovereign master of informers, torturers, and hangmen, all the valets of a society that intends to damn in another life those who are already damned, the wretched of the earth, all the actors in the great repressive parade—from the last broad-shouldered police carcass to God the pure spirit, they all look like cops.

And the policeman is the absolute enemy.*

An absolute enemy calls for absolute hatred, and, since the enemy lays down the law, makes it rain blood, ash, dust, superstition, distress, death, always rain and never sun,

since he reigns over all the old hypocrisies of institutions, precepts, that chameleon whose shiniest uniform willingly agrees to turn gray in order to fool people, nab them, put them through hell, beat into a pulp, by kicking with earthly and divine boots everything that stubbornly persists in remaining capable of enthusiasm, erection, love,

since he grinds down the spectrum to paint the world black, tries to compress all imagination in his vise, reduce all intelligence to the poisoned misery of Christian ideas,

since he more than anyone disguises himself as an open-minded person, a skeptic, etc., he remains at the beck and call of a mysticism

---

*This is Baudelaire's definition. He used it in reference to Javert in an article on *Les Misérables*.

that the crisis doesn't prevent, quite the contrary, from fattening up his apostles,

since he reduces liberty to the status of an unrealizable abstraction, relegates equality to the heart of utopia, and asks fraternity to perpetuate the myth of Romulus and Remus in a world that apes so exactly the Roman Empire that man becomes a wolf to his fellow man as soon as he agrees to taste the milk of the she-wolf who nurses fratricides mounted with the heads of emperors, kings, and important civilian and military figures,

since the policeman intends to leave his mark again and again on five-sixths of the globe,

let hatred, for its part, take over and not give an inch of ground,

may it remain general but take advantage of the least opportunity to prove itself, to declare itself particular,

for the particular is also the general,

and a general hatred failing to be particular as well would quickly become mere words, ineffective, anarchizing cerebralism, soon turning into vapor, nothing but a light mist added to all the darkness, a mask on that big soft head which resignation loses, melts in the fog banks of an idealist philosophy.

And the great generalities of idealist philosophy are perfectly capable, as far as they are concerned, of becoming incarnate and reincarnated on every street corner with the particular, concrete features of some valet or agent provocateur of capitalism.

Absolute hatred, both general and particular, reveals itself to those who feel it in bursts, suffocating at first, which fill the gullet without leaving any room there for the least word to get through. But soon that hatred will become oxygen, incomparably better, for sick lungs, than mountaintop air.

Already, you feel restored to life.

You forget that you have, cooped up in your thorax, one fluttering lung and the other completely plucked, you forget about the bacilli strolling through the ruins of your bronchi with the ease of a Prince of Journalists who is enough of a lout to go collect rents personally on Unemployed Slummers' Street, you forget about the disease and all the sinister, self-punitive temptations engendered by it and from which it was born (but of what consequence are questions of probable priority in the interdependence of evils), you forget about the tuberculosis that brought you there, when you arrive at that big sanatorium*

---

*In this sanatorium, where Jews are frowned upon by Christians and the company is such that I wouldn't have had the heart to stay for five minutes without the presence of Eluard, my past, my tubercular past and probable future having already lost six ribs in the scuffle caused me to fly into a rage where the bourgeois dress up, wear their most pious, most pretentious finery, because idleness makes them feel a bit more here than elsewhere bound for death.

There is a chaplain. A real weasel in a cassock. But a weasel with the brain of a rabbit. That sly fox, foolish enough to take his vow of celibacy seriously, must not have allowed his ecclesiastical flesh any other caress, in his most daringly voluptuous fancies, than that of sandpaper. And the one that bled was more likely the sandpaper than the priest. Since the Church, like the muses, prefers alternate chants, another one of God's representatives on earth parades his bitchy irritation in the lobby on a nice plump sailor's arm. He's wearing a skirt whose cloth and cut would produce fatal envy among ladies whose expertise in tailored suits is a bit excessive. He must shriek with his entire soul, with his entire member, that repose be granted to the souls of the members of the clergy who, in the council convened in order to put an end to simony, prohibited marriage for priests who, henceforth, shared their beds with their maids, their altar boys, or even the Widow Thumb and her four daughters at the ends of their arms, and devoted to their own wardrobe those sums that their predecessors used to steal for the upkeep of their wives during the early centuries of Christianity.

And that is why, as soon as you open the door of a self-righteous nursing home, you find a big, spruced-up, perfumed, powdered umbellifer whose talents and flair for dressing in drag would have destined him, had he not entered the seminary, to become the most beautiful ornament in one of those pre-crisis tourist nightclubs, the queen of one of those places of trick, tricky, and tricking debauchery where he would have hidden his carcass beneath crêpe veils and turn-of-the-century widow's flounces, unless he had preferred to take advantage of the length of his nose to play Cleopatra.

Since the cassock was preferred to the other furbelows, Monsignor Oldentide gives an archepiscopal echo in response to the presence of that provocateur who is taking in the provocative one. Impossible not to put one's foot in the mouth of religion and now Monsignor Oldentide has slipped in among the she-cocks and she-fowls, while his young model, with a little bell in his hand, struts around the big joint where, facing Mont Blanc, a bourgeoise, tickled pink at having the

---

upon reading the words that Panait Istrati had the nauseating stupidity to write at the beginning of his last book. "This work," he announces, "this work which I tore line by line from the claws of tuberculosis in its last stages I dedicate in homage to the poor human body struggling heroically with that merciless disease and to all the tubercular patients on earth, whether they be honest people or scoundrels."

tallest mountain in Europe at the service of her respiratory passages, dressed up in her best Sunday sickness. It's the Mass. The Mass in the dining room said first by the weasel with the head of a rabbit, then by the bitch. At mealtime, they drink like they fart—hard. And that means a lot of running around for the servants, patients, of course, poor patients serving rich patients. The poor have to work in order to earn the right to be at this high altitude, and since the rich know that if the poor lost their jobs they'd probably wind up croaking on the plains, most of these ladies and gentlemen, the boarding patients, let themselves be waited on hand and foot, without ever giving the smallest tip. They are worthy of imitation along with the music, the music of their mandibles, those simpletons, at least one of whom will have his or her statue one day with the inscription: *To albumin, the grateful father-land,* for she is edifying, that one who looks like a big sack of flour for whom the technocrat, her suitor, puts military records of bugle calls on the gramophone. . . .

And then there is the intellectual who at the drop of a hat will inform you that he is in possesion of a doctorate in medicine, a master's degree in theology, and a mother-in-law. The mother-in-law has a cook. The mother-in-law's cook has six brothers, one of whom is a pimp, while another is the very respectable owner of a house, a family, a car. If the intellectual had been his mother-in-law's brother's cook, he would not have chosen the pimp's fate, but that of the property owner. Ah yes, he would have willingly accepted being born a worker provided he die a bourgeois. He would have saved his money. Why don't the poor simply do as he would have done if he hadn't been rich? Why don't the poor just save their money and become rich, etc., etc., etc.

Satisfaction marks all of the gatherings that the residents of the sanatorium organize in honor of each other, whether they be lectures* or dinner-discussions on Shrove Tuesday.

---

*Here is a list of the lectures, which speaks for itself: Fascist Italy, the Ecole Polytechnique, Gothic Art, the Constitution of the Church, Aviation and War, the Italian Renaissance, Mountainclimbing, Women and Progress, André Gide, French Canada, Father Wetterlé, Oriental Churches, Aviation on Mont Blanc, the Inspiring Alp, the Automobile and War, the Saarland, Laënnec.

The lectures were given by priests, lawyers, or officers. When the subject was Gide, the doctor of theology took the floor. Political and sexual questions were taboo. All the better to feign ingenuousness, the shrewd doctor of bodies and souls asked himself, asked his audience, how it was possible that he, such a precise man, could be moved by the words: "Nathanaël, I will teach you fervor." That former student of the Jesuits, therefore surely not ignorant of the touch peepee game theory, switching from the interrogative to the affirmative,

Even a hole in a lung is a pretext for each one of them to admire himself more, to like himself a little better.

Isn't loogie the name commonly given, moreover, to the insignia of the orders to which the henchmen of capitalist disorder belong?

In the absence of loogies of the Legion of Honor, those of tuberculosis.

In its sanatorium even more than elsewhere, the spitting, spat out bourgeoisie spits on itself, contemplates itself, and invents God.

High priestess and profiteer of the cult of work, the privileged class not only sees a crime in leisure (idleness the mother of all vices), but in addition wants all intellectual activity (for which, in spite of itself, it has had to grant time to some people) to be limited to the defense and illustration of its privileges.

Thus the sordid pragmatism of its culture.

Conservatives and the religion which helps them to conserve have never taken a favorable view of progress in natural science and its applications. As for the research techniques of sciences specializing in the study of man, even the most innocuous have always been seen as outrages against morals, indecent assaults. The only ones authorized were feats of virtuosity, variations on known themes.

In order to maintain the status quo, all bourgeois, from fanatics to skeptics, proclaim that there is nothing new under the sun and never will be. With that beautiful pretext they intend to discourage every hypothesis. In reality, imagination is uprooted, condemned to nourish itself on chimerical hurricanes, quench its thirst on rains of anguish, rave in the abstract. Such a diet soon dries it up, kills it, especially since it lives on the concrete, the essence of the concrete, of the most objective objects, of the most human humus, in return metamorphosing beings and things with its most flamboyant finds.

The catechism, still drummed into schoolchildren's heads in France, where there continue to be illiterates (15 percent according to a recent

---

stated a few moments later that "Alcoholism being a proletarian phenomenon, in a society without women and alcohol, men would feel the need neither to make love nor to drink."

So much foolishness, so much hypocrisy caused the forbidden questions to be directed at him as well as at the audience who deserved some answers. Somebody, one of the disliked Jews, read the declaration quoted above. Needless to say, it roused the indignation of the meat-whacking priests, the paddy-whacking officers, the yacking intellectual, and the spineless listeners who had been delighted to think of Gide surrounded in his immoralism, in his individualism, and unable to escape in order to take a stand—against them— unreservedly.

Henceforth, lectures will only be given on absolutely safe subjects: fascism, war, the Church.

statistic), defines God as "infinitely perfect." The wisdom of nations adds that perfection is not of this world and that well enough should be left alone.* And these are, indeed, arguments worthy of those misers

---

*We are all familiar with the antiphon on the good old days and the lamentations of the rich at the thought of what the future holds for them. The exploiting minority moans and groans as soon as it is reminded that mechanization, which has changed working conditions, requires a change in the condition of workers as well.

Poor dear bosses, who so loved to boast that they didn't pay their workers to do nothing. They paid as little as possible and demanded as much work as possible. They thus deserve well of society. Nonetheless there's a crisis. They have no idea what is going on.

Overproduction: the rapacity of a few exploiters hasn't allowed the exploited masses to consume what they have been forced to produce. Capitalism entrusts its national, international, and religious police officers with suppressing, repressing the bursts of anger born of misery, of war, of which it is itself the instigator. But the more the oppressed are oppressed, the more they tend to liberate themselves. He who is most oppressed is always the first to liberate himself.

The inner world is subject to the same dynamic laws as the outer world of which it is the reflection and on which it is reflected. Thought thus rears up, takes off, at the moment when it is most implacably censored. Dada breaks out right in the middle of the war and makes a springboard of each one of the defenses traditionally opposed to the imagination since time immemorial. Sentences fall, jump, dance in cascades just when everywhere else it is forbidden to say one word louder than another.

After the individual bombs, after the initial terrorism in response to the murderous iniquities, after the nihilistic phase, revolutionaries organize, study to learn about the actual functioning of the universe and why its laws are no longer in accordance with necessity and how the revolution will rediscover, resplice the thread of evolution broken through the fault of a minority who would like the society they exploit to be immutable or would only agree to insignificant reforms when absolutely necessary. Concurrently, in a victorious France where self-satisfied boorishness constituted an obstacle to all intellectual activity, intellectuals in favor of that activity, revolutionary intellectuals, after Dada, grapple with the actual functioning of thought (surrealism). All questions are asked, for the problem is to determine what courses of action and reaction give rise to the flight of the mind and what courses of action and reaction that flight in turn gives rise to.

Then spring forth vines of mercury, morning glories of quicksilver palpitating from one pole to the other. The curve extends from the innermost secret to the outermost edge, from the unconscious to the conscious and vice versa. Through things, feelings, sentiments and ideas, how many sizzling comings and goings. Writing is no longer a mere means of expression, but the fault line of a mind constantly in motion, and, just as a shadow clings to a body, it extends man to the knowledge of a poetic necessity, interdependent with all

eager to keep what they already possess by every means at their disposal. They invent God, hoping for a shameful transfer, in order to offer him their despair and their weariness—"Thy will be done"— thus exempting themselves from any obligation to those whose misery is a necessary condition of their wealth.

Only those who have something to keep, and therefore to lose (even if nothing more than too high an opinion of themselves), can derive benefit from the silent perfection of someone up there against all of those who are harassed by the howling imperfections of what is designated, by the scorn of the well-fed and self-righteous, as the here below. Absolute, abstract, invisible perfection only tends to ruin every chance, to discover every attempt to make less imperfect, in its most general laws as well as in its most specific details, a world whose manifestation certainly doesn't credit the notion that it might ever cease to appear perfectible.

Eternal *Truth,* with a cold, dogmatic capital *T,* is likewise but a pretext for turning a deaf ear to earthly truths. Reality* becomes the screen serving as a hiding place for those who scorn, ignore, deny the shifting density of realities, their projections into all spheres—intellectual, moral, scientific, poetic, philosophical, etc.—which are by turns transmitters and reflectors, whether of unexpected starfire or of the usual planetary dirt.

Encouraged by his class to continue the analytico-metaphysical tradition, the least petit-bourgeois intellectual needs only matchstick arms to find himself in possession of a thousand pyrogenic virtues. He is self-sufficient, that young lunatic who thinks he is a sun because he winks at the anemia of his desires with a colorless albino eye. A bit later, nothing will sprout in the rainbow christening of his decomposition and it won't take long for him to drown in the ridiculous prism of his vanity.

---

other necessities, and which, by their example, is only illuminated to give glaring proof of all other necessities, deep inside the most secret recesses of "communicating vessels."

*That Reality plays the sordid and very catholic role of antithesis in the sordid, catholic synthesis of which the cop of cops, God the immovable, is the thesis. The cult of that Reality, Thomistic Realism, is but the profiteer's consecration or deification of that which is to his advantage, that which he wants to continue being to his advantage, at the expense of the evolution of humanity, as determined by the needs and realities they imply. Hence the popularity of Saint Thomas among bourgeois intellectuals, hence the conversions of little literary minuet dancing masters, sly enough, nervous enough to have suddenly, more or less consciously, had the presentiment, deep in the heart of the aesthetic gardens where they were romping, that a great red wind would blow them away, them and their slim volumes.

*Necessity is blind only insofar as it is not known.**

The necessity of enlightening one's own necessary by other necessities and others by one's own, the necessity of harmonizing, as much and as well as possible, all necessities—that is surely the first and last cause of all knowledge.

Progress is only conceivable as the improved and constantly improving harmony among necessities, whose antagonisms can now only be exaggerated, aggravated by present capitalist disorder.

Sexual necessity being the most urgent, it always has been (and remains) imperiously repressed in a capitalist country. And no less than elsewhere, in a France that continues to simper and make ribald gestures but has never ceased to adhere to the imbecilic, ferocious views of its traditional psychology, a dirty little heap of analytic dust, a veritable residue of broken lines, that miserable psychology, scrapings of a geometry that, not even descriptive, is callous, reduced to the three dimensions of Phocaean whore-mongery, Roman garrison mentality, and Christian masochism.

A pretty triangle, or rectangle if you prefer. Yes, with right angles. One must therefore walk straight, follow the relentless hypotenuse all the way to the end, the religious part of that narrow ethic which defines sexual pleasure as a sin. A sin like any other science, for attaining orgasm is a science: "the use of the five senses requires a particular initiation and one which is only achieved by goodwill and necessity." †

The use of the five senses, the particular initiation—everyone knows what they mean in this country of risqué jokes, bordellos, and crucifixes hanging above the connubial nightstand. Religion made a sacrament of marriage. The middle class, upper- or lower-, attaches great importance to the wedding ceremony. The man has received instruction on the theory of sexual pleasure from a half-starved female soldier or a fat, jolly non-com in the women's barracks. He is waiting for his wedding night so that he can take revenge on the woman for his various disappointments, with a brutality all the more inexorable because, just the night before, he buried his life as a bachelor and he's afraid he'll be too exhausted to undo the bride's virginity. Meanwhile, he dreams of the American movie star who, in the storehouse of compensations, has replaced the storybook princess and the stage queen. It's more democratic. It remains as foolish, as hopelessly foolish, as foolishly hopeless as ever.

---

*Hegel.

† This observation by Baudelaire (Salon of 1846) sheds a peculiarly pathetic light on a man, the works of a man who separated, in spite of himself, during his life, making love from feeling love, and turned out impotent with the woman who inspired his most ardent verse!

She hasn't ceased to crush the days beneath the avalanche of her aftereffects, threaten the nights with her filterable viruses, the old idolatry that dared to pronounce the separation of head and heart, flesh and spirit, honor chastity, consecrate virginity, celibacy, set the essential forces of man against the walls of obscurantism, lead desire astray in the swamp of religious aspirations and lose, in the black sand of resignation, love, the need which makes life and makes life accept having been made.

From the prison where he spent twenty-seven years because he had committed the double crime of loving his sister-in-law and being loved by her, Sade, with the inspiration of dreams made bloody, tragic by necessity, used carnal strength to demolish the walls exiling him from the world of bodies and, in the refound bodies, struck down the ideas which those walls symbolized only too well.

Quite rightly, then, at the conclusive end of *Philosophy in the Bedroom,* after the most overwhelming erotic discoveries and the definitive indictment of all religion, the very devout Madame de Mistival (who had come to get her daughter Eugénie for whose initiation that feast of the senses and of intelligence had been given) was fucked, fore and aft, by a lout as well-endowed as he was infected with syphilis, before being sewn up by the very hand of charming Eugénie, and once her contaminated orifices were stitched with red thread, sent back to her beloved devotions.

If inspiration finds its source in the overflowing anger of bodies, it certainly doesn't follow, as the little dilettantes of the external epithelium or the internal epithelium believe or pretend to believe, that all it takes is a timid little act of no-risk debauchery to give any value whatsoever to acts, gestures, words, or writings.

In fact the logical result is often the exact opposite, and they express all the odiousness of an era, a regime, those bourgeois in cahoots with the police to break the rules laid down by those same policemen, who are only good for blackmail or exploitation of the majority by the minority. How can one avoid seeing additional homage to the Church in that minor onanism practiced by men of the world, high government officials, and powerful churchmen at the most solemn moments of national funeral masses?

As deputy editor of the *Nouvelles littéraires* and attending Maurice Barrès's funeral in that capacity, I had the opportunity to observe *de visu* that masturbation was present there, albeit furtive, shamefaced masturbation through the cloth, in complicity with the darkest Gothic wriggling, a real filthy little trick! and the exact opposite of full-blown, unbridled desecration, although the reader may bridle at what is being suggested here.

I subsequently met a few big shots of the Parisian press.

When I learned this year that the same man had died in a male brothel from a slight overdose of heroin, the same defender of country, family, and religion whom the pretender to the French throne had congratulated so warmly for having facilitated the banning of the admirable *Golden Age,* I said to myself that my Prince of Journalists had simmered enough in my mind. He thus climbed beneath the sheets of white paper, among the she-cocks and the she-fowls.

But, parenthesis within a parenthesis, one more parenthesis won't do any harm. Since the Prince of Journalists has been accounted for, the Sussexes' guests and the Sussexes themselves would perhaps be a little miffed if the fourteenth guest didn't give their pedigree.

Patience

Here we go,

There we are,

Here's the explanation,

We'll explain!

The Prince of Journalists: Already explained on previous pages.

The Sussex heir: There are many such creatures who rain down all over England, whose climate is certainly not renowned for its dryness. Those exquisite adolescents are probably not all lords. They would be only too happy to become as much. Nothing can shake the good opinion they have of themselves and their faith in the destinies of England, their respect for the Intelligence Service, and their scorn for the colored races.

At the end of the meal, the young marquis will ask Augusta what she plans to do with Negroes in the Paneuropean army. She will answer that she has decided to incorporate them along with Turks, Jews, and Gypsies into regiments destined to remain on the front lines until the death of the last soldier. The godmother's statement will delight the godson who, in the course of his travels in Africa, nonetheless tasted natives (especially when Sister Saint Savings took the veil, thanks to the leads provided to her by Monsignor Oldentide. Before closing the parenthesis, let us add that he never, in the course of those revels, punishable by *hard labor,* questioned the laws of his dear country, always transgressed and revered with an identically serene soul).

From Negro to Negro, Krim finally remembered a little bar in Marseilles where she spent an entire evening with two West Indians, each of whom, determined to seduce her, nonetheless boasted about his companion, one saying that the other was vigorous and the vigorous fellow answering that his eulogist was vigilant. Krim breaks her silence to recall that subtle gallantry.

The American of the gratuitous act, who as far as he is concerned has spent fortunes on extravagant ties and disconcerting silk shirts, will ask: "Have you ever seen a thrifty Negro?"

"And an organizing Negro?" says Augusta, upping the ante.

Krim cites Toussaint L'Ouverture.

The divine lady thinks out loud about a rather repugnant series of puns on the name of the Napoleon of Santo Domingo.

Little Kate comes to the aid of Krim whom a coughing fit prevents from answering. Kate asks what benefit white men were able to derive from that so-called knack for administration and savings of which they are so proud. Esperanza, very clever, manages to change the subject of the conversation. She doesn't want the singer, once she gets her breath back, to continue on that topic, especially because not since Southampton has she treated herself to one of those big colored fellows whose sexual organs her hand hasn't forgotten because of their volume and density, just as her tongue hasn't forgotten that they taste like vanilla all over.

The divine lady: In the eyes of a child born in 1900, England had the silhouette of Jeanne Avril on Toulouse-Latrec's well-known poster. Her southern coast was the hem of the petticoat with which, after having dropped her undergarments like a bundle resembling Ireland, she swept the peninsulas of the continent as casually as a showgirl so skilled in the use of pallor, long skirts, and a Scotland-shaped hat, that one was amazed not to see tufts of curly hair on the bass scrolls in the orchestra pit in the foreground.

That is why the marquise of Sussex was indebted to herself for having spent her youth in bars. Add a few recollections of Lady Hamilton, the misadventures that befell a beauty patched up after a paraffin injection that was supposed to give more regularity to her face, the confidences of an old Englishwoman whose paralytic protector liked only tiger-hunting, and there's our Primrose.

Esperanza, duchess of Monte Putina: The noble Esperanza de Saint-Alphaud, nicknamed "the kedt woman" by the landlady, lived on the ground floor of the house situated in Paris at 15 Rue de la Pompe, whose fifth floor was inhabited by the author/spectator's family and himself from 1904 to 1910. Every day, the hairdresser would visit "the kept woman" and stay for hours, giving rise to gossip and making it possible, thanks to memories of postcards and obscene films, to imagine the fictional Esperanza's morning pastimes in the course of the rehabilitative pseudo-affair.

The actual Esperanza behaved quite well, according to her co-tenants, despite the fact that all of them were determined to pick a quarrel with her. Rather than fattening up gigolos or leaving a fortune on the gambling table at Monte Carlo, the old tart, keeping her wits about her, preferred to devote her savings toward restoring the fortunes of her house. She therefore married:

The duke of Monte Putina: Of whom there is no more to say than what he says himself.

Esperanza's son: Between the ages of four and ten, each time he was slapped by the skillful maternal hand, the author/spectator said to himself that if he were the son of the prostitute on the ground floor instead of the irreproachable lady on the fifth floor, everything would be wonderful. Hence the myth of the seductive child.

Actually, the real-life Esperanza had a daughter, whose father was unknown, but who was nonetheless learning English and piano, to the indignation of all. The lack of a gift for foreign languages and music made the little boy on the fifth floor and the little girl on the ground floor equal in punishment. Similarly, while the author/spectator wasted his time on the religious exercises assigned at the priests' den where his parents had decided to have him raised and educated, "the keeped woman" 's daughter would collect alms every Sunday at Saint-Honoré d'Eylau.

Thus the goddess on the ground floor constantly aped the other tenants, her only desire being, if not to surpass, at least to equal in respectability the mere mortals of the upper floors.

Consequently, after having held a grudge against "the keeped woman" 's daughter, envying her for her mother, after having delighted his imagination, by way of compensation for his sinister childhood, with the fantasy that the little girl was actually himself, the son of a bourgeois was condemned to lifelong pessimism. To be honest, that pessimism made him rather indifferent to his own fate. He was nonetheless bent on avenging himself for the initial disillusion. That son of Esperanza that he had first dreamt of being was turned into what he likes to think of as his opposite; he made him into his opposite, and in order to enjoy him even more, the fourteenth guest has (in other words I, myself, have) strewn his path with a few flowers that were on mine.

Hence the circumcision which the author/spectator himself underwent at the age of three. It left him with secret memories of such force and in such quantity that, despite a number of voluptuous revenges, his nightmares up until 1932 confused blood with sperm. But last April he (I) saw once more the beach at Saint-Jean-de-Luz where, during the summer of 1909, my mother, dressed in an impeccably white serge tailored suit, wrote letters while watching me play at the edge of the water. All of a sudden, an unexpectedly violent wave nearly swept me away. Mother dropped her pen. The cap of said pen fell, got lost in the sand, while the red ink inside it stained the white dress.

The symbolism of that incident was too clear for it not to be used as a gift for the pipsqueak. After having put him in possesion of that viaticum, I had merely to let him fly with his own wings.

Augusta: All you have to do is take three meals in the dining car between Innsbruck and Budapest and you can be sure of meeting at least a half dozen of those ladies who, in order to eliminate all doubts about their noble birth, arrange their hair, real or false, in voluminous hairstyles resembling cushions, upon which should be placed not haughtily outmoded hats but crowns.

They don't intend to miss a single detail of the landscape, and when they finally deign to put down their lorgnettes, they do so with judgmental looks, gestures saying a lot about what they have been able to observe concerning the instruments and methods of labor, distribution of wealth, and customs of the peoples to whom (while sipping little spoonfuls of café au lait containing islands of whipped cream) they regret being able to devote only a mere glance as they pass by.

Krim: I, the author/spectator, upon noticing around the age of seven that "the keeped woman" on the ground floor was no less odiously maternal than the lady on the fifth floor, replaced that first unworthy idol with a young woman whom, even before seeing her, I was sure that I could only be enamored of. She was criticized for wearing dresses as tight as leotards and, since the *Songs of Bilitis* and *Lysistrata* were selling out, it was said of her, with such a knowing air, that she surely didn't have to be asked twice to undo her belt. Thanks to those allusions to beautiful music-hall acrobats or petite showgirls in Neo-Greek operettas, thanks to the words *maillot* [leotard] and *ceinture* [belt], that unknown woman qualified as fin de siècle and filled my dreams—as beautiful, as big, as gay, as the whole city of Paris, the city whose dances and laughter in a rain of confetti during mid-Lent tried to take shape in the imagination of a little boy confined to Passy, in those days almost country.

Every Sunday in the summertime, we would take the train called *La Ceinture* from La Muette to La Porte Maillot.

From La Porte Maillot we went to Rueil on a steam-powered tramway. But that was another story. The most important thing to remember about Sunday outings were the all-powerful, universal belts and leotards. At the circus we would hope to see the acrobats' leotards split, in back or in front—we weren't too fussy.

Porte Leotard, porthole in the leotard of whoever sports a leotard, a little tiny opening in a very tight jumper, and you manage to slip through, you find little warm places.

A father who is a music printer specializing in ditties has merely to say that the unknown woman is a real "titi" (as they call cheeky Parisian street urchins) and that phrase immediately turns her into the queen of the cafés-concerts, whose king had been Fragson—just recently murdered by his own father—for the worst dive to appear worthy of Greek tragedy and its slayings, owing to their comparable degree of pathos.

Since, moreover, "titi" designated a breast for the little sister, a bust bursting with laughter sprang from the idol's bodice and, rounding her off, of its own accord the Porte Saint-Denis—by way of a comb— came and stuck itself in her hair, complete with all the nostalgic embellishments contained in the memory of a little boy who, exiled in Passy, was born on Rue de L'Echiquier, between said *porte* and the paternal printing shop, a former theater that was a stone's throw from the Mayol Concert Hall where, a few years earlier, one could hear "Gaslight Is My Sunshine." The actual creator of "Gaslight Is My Sunshine" being worthy neither of the tune nor of the lyrics, it was only right to bestow the song upon Krim.

All the data on the metaphorical unknown woman having their source in a bouquet of remarks finally took on a diurnal, concrete shape when, announced by her perfume, as other mortals are by the sound of their shoes, lo and behold the younger sister of the lady who gave the author/ spectator piano lessons. A perfect example of what was considered to be a beautiful woman at that time, that young thing was a thousand times more alluring, more provocative than the author's mother.

Extremely musical, or at least claiming to be such, the author/ spectator's mother made her husband ashamed of the ritornelli emanating, ready to be sung, from his presses. She would have died rather than play anything other than classical music. She turned up her nose at the waltzes and the czardas that were fashionable. She pitied, with the probable hope of turning the knife in the wound, the piano teacher who, although one of her daughters won first prize at the conservatory, had to admit that the other one played the violin like a Gypsy.

To play the violin like a Gypsy was to make a child-listener become a walking medium for sound, a fabric of ecstasy whose thread consisted of strings like those upon which the horsehair bow went back and forth without the least concern for rosin.

A small white handkerchief had been slipped in between the instrument and the head which was too big, according to the bourgeoise who, during her girlhood, used to go to a painting class twice a week to educate herself in the true, inexorable canons of beauty. But what did her son care about her unannounced pauses? The cloth which protected the delicate flesh from the wood unfurled at night in his dreams, draping itself around the warm, flexible column whose lines would mysteriously continue those of the perfectly dolichocephalic skull, beneath the hat of hair.

That unfurled handkerchief was dyed with the blood of the crimes sung by Krim.

Two hands, two flowers of fever tie all the purple in the world around a neck. The footlights make up a face. An echo brings back voice fragments. From the November fog emerges the face of a woman who died on a day whose springtime deceit had become too unbearable.

Kate: Will she be the summer?

Will she be the morning of the most beautiful, longest day? At dawn, her arm bled like a rising sun. Her freshness is disarming.

Jim: Standard bit part.

Goes back and forth between America and Europe.

In America, seems to be a product for export to Europe. After doing Europe, thinks he's become complex enough to dazzle the folks back home.

Marie Torchon, Synovie: Women of letters who are worth every bit as much as their males. Memories of *Nouvelles littéraires.* Remorse at not having placed that pretty saying by the poetess Anna de Noailles who, giving her reasons for not flying in an airplane, concluded: "The carpet is my fate."

The psychiatrist: History textbooks when I was in secondary school were profusely illustrated. For each great man they provided a solution to the problem posed by his face. Subtle way of putting the oldest clichés in new frames. The least wrinkle was interpreted according to the most reactionary biases. Thus, sheltered by experimental pretexts, hiding behind so-called experience and alleged expertise, specialists in science, mental health, and justice decide with impunity between freedom or imprisonment, life or death. And they are not going to complicate matters unnecessarily. When Junka Kurès, a Serbian against whom no decisive evidence had been provided, was condemned to capital punishment, wasn't the chief argument the thickness, the heaviness of her hands, truly the hands of a strangler, noted the prosecutor in his indictment?

There is not a capitalist court anywhere that doesn't manage to find a psychiatrist worthy of it to join in the proceedings, and to affirm the responsibility—if not entire, at least attenuated—of the poor guy for his humiliating heredity. When dealing with the least offense, it's always a matter of encouraging reactionary policies. One good turn deserving another, a reactionary attitude will reap a handsome reward. I thus knew a psychiatrist who was rewarded with a promotion in the Legion of Honor for having meritoriously stated that kleptomania was not unrelated to theft.

The court's punitive rage was able to base its authority on that statement. Thus, since our main concern is to protect private property, how could we not put a psychiatrist in the nice Paneuropean crowd? Mine couldn't be better situated than between Augusta and Synovie. He drinks milk. He is as happy, as much in his element, as a fish in a river. Like a fish who drinks milk in the river. A phenomenon that is less and less rare throughout this happy capitalist world where the wealthy dump into the river products whose prices they don't intend to see lowered.

In his sanatorium near Paris, our psychiatrist takes in French presidents who have fallen out of trains. A head of state who climbs the trees on the grounds of a medical establishment in the company of a Minister of Finance accustomed to bouncing bad checks is worth his weight in gold. The psychiatrist is thus as fat as a pig. He sports a potbelly, which doesn't prevent him from courting Synovie to beat the band, although as a professional observer he has carefully refrained from noticing that she is cross-eyed. The poetess, delighted to feel, ipso facto, that she has gotten even with Marie Torchon, will take great care, when she gets up from the table, to show only her profile, the side with the good eye. And the gallant doctor, in order to seduce the lyric paragon, will recount a few spicy anecdotes from his career.

8

Etc., Etc.

". . . YES," THE PSYCHIATRIST is saying, "bear in mind that I treat women of the theater. They are sometimes rather strange people, but despite my refusal to surrender to their charms, I must admit, in all fairness, that they are capable of intelligence and courage. Only recently I had the famous Madame de Perpignan in my sanatorium. We all know that her nobility is merely light opera, in fact not even light opera, more like music hall. The name she goes by is merely a pseudonym, a nom de guerre. But if *guerre* means war, this is voluptuous warfare. She chose it years ago. I had just received, if my memory serves me, my secondary-school diploma. She had an act—a pretty snappy one, too—with trained rabbits. She had decided to drop her family name—it was unsuitable for the theater—and pick something that sounded better. She examined a map of France in search of ideas and chanced upon Perpignan, departmental seat of Pyrénées-Orientales. . . ."

Like a storyteller bent on producing the desired effect, the psychiatrist pauses for a moment. Esperanza would like to grab this opportunity to get Augusta's attention. But Augusta is sipping her coffee with her eyes glued to the narrator's lips, begging him eloquently, albeit silently, to continue. That a grand lady with no less grand Paneuropean responsibilities seems to take such interest in the story of a performing rabbit-trainer is quite enough to shock, even exasperate Esperanza. Besides, Madame de Perpignan was already an accomplished tart, a high-class "whorizontal," at the time when the present duchess of Monte Putina was but a poor little flirt. In those days, whenever the career prostitute spoke to Esperanza, she adopted a protective tone which, even today, the insolent old bawd hasn't given up. Esperanza doesn't condescend to answer and berates her with a look that says: "Don't be so familiar. To hear you talk, you'd think we were like two peas in a pod, or maybe I should say two performing rabbits on a stage." Perpignan won't hear the lesson. Ever since Jean Lorrain gave her a critical thrashing in a review more than thirty-five years ago, she thinks she will remain deified until the end of time. Really, how could she let a luncheon with the most specific political aims turn into a backbiting siren's tail? This professional turn-of-the-century beauty, now that she has no more men to lead around by the nose, to drive up the wall, has become the Sappho of the demimonde. But has a duchess ever let herself be intimidated by a psychiatrist, even if he is a professor of medicine? Come now. A vulgar stethoscope swinger. Stethoscope, rifle scope. There are some people you would like to train a rifle on, preferably with a telescopic sight, and fill their head with buckshot.

"Ah! if I were a carbine," says Esperanza, dreaming out loud.

"I beg your pardon?"

"I was just saying that Madame de Perpignan is . . . well . . . is . . . I've never been one to mince words, but this time, I don't dare. . . . In a word, I'm saying that Madame de Perpignan is a priestess of Lesbos."

"You're saying, dear friend, that she is a lesbian," responds the psychiatrist with a smile. "And yet my story tends to prove the exact opposite. Madame de Perpignan, who . . ."

Then begins a hardly bearable defense of the above-named. All of the she-cocks and she-fowls, unanimously, less one ear, Esperanza's ear, listen and nod their heads to signify that they approve of what they are hearing. How can you fight against a coalition of beatitudes when you can't count on a single ally, not even the Prince of Journalists who, he too, has opted for optimism because, he suddenly thought, if Viscount Rothermere has been offered the throne of Hungary, why shouldn't he himself unearth a little kingdom, Albania, for example?

But la Monte Putina is not one to molder in the slough of despond.

They are all against her. And even her husband, the duke, looks as if he had been hung out to dry. Well, she will go and remove old Monte Putina from the clothesline. And then, vamoose! Come on, hurry it up. Let's go. And too bad, so much the better if that surprise departure sends a shiver through the Paneuropean circle, badly compromised since no one wants Esperanza to be the center of it.

And already, she has gotten up, she bows to Augusta whom she damns to hell. She good-heartedly kisses her dear Primrose whom she would like to bite, really bite, with her whole set of dentures, to add a pretty scar to the lump of paraffin, extends a scornful hand to be kissed, pulls the duke by his coattail, gets into her car, which loses no time at all in taking off, like Esperanza herself, who is singing softly:

> Bye, bye
> Good-bye.
> Pa, pa
> Paneuropa.

And the chauffeur receives the order to turn to the left and not to the right, to go toward Italy and not toward the Estérel Mountains, to Rome and not to Cannes.

And step on it, for there's not minute to spare. We'll never go as fast as whirling thoughts,

> Bye, bye
> Good-bye.
> Pa, pa
> Paneuropa.

There must be a settling of accounts with Augusta. Marriage made her a Hapsburg. But she is a mere Hungarian, the daughter of Huns. As Esperanza drives toward her Roman palace, of white marble no less, she is in no mood to tolerate the memory of those who burned and destroyed everything in their path. Augusta is only capable of demolition. She hides her cards to no avail; Esperanza the builder sees, knows what's going on. The Romans built a great deal. One must therefore fight Paneuropa with a good-sized Panroma. Of course Mussolini won't be opposed to the plan. So Augusta can keep her nose out of it. The Monte Putinas are right at home in Italy. Anarchists, even if they have an aristocratic name and features, might as well just stay in their own country. Let Augusta come to Rome and she'll see. Just trip him on the Vatican steps, and slam, bang, the hairdresser will go to hell and stay there and his owner will follow him. The lady has requested an audience with the pope, but Saint Peter tells the bloated pig who gave away Trieste and Trentino to shove it. Augusta offers colonies, she who wasn't capable of keeping what she had and is reduced to taking the bus. As for Esperanza, she has a superb Lancia. So long live Latinity. We'll let our hair grow out. While waiting for it to get long enough, we'll buy an artificial braid in the next large town and do our hair up like Empress Fausta. Let the pipsqueak stay with his Marie Torchon. The duchess of Monte Putina renounces him, along with his fellow barbarians among whom she is sorry, sad to include the Prince of Journalists. But still, one has to make the best of things. She has a husband. Once they've grafted a monkey's balls onto him, he'll look great. He will be assigned diplomatic missions. Esperanza will return triumphantly to Paris as an emissary of the Fascio, as wife of the ambassador charged with delivering an ultimatum that has been carefully written in such terms that it will be rejected, since war is necessary in order for Nice, Savoy, Tunisia (don't worry, Holy Father, you'll get your colonies) to be handed down to the duchess's new country. And thus will be resuscitated in modern times the ancient empire of which Esperanza will be the model citizen. . . .

An Esperanza never miscalculates, never makes a false move. She was not mistaken when she said that her departure would send a shiver through the circle of guests. The psychiatrist doesn't dare to continue the story of Madame de Perpignan, but Primrose, through the vapors of her drunkenness, suddenly notices the effects of Esperanza's Machiavellism and apologizes to the man she calls the author of *Bang Boom Rat-tat Rub-a-dub and Pigeon Lamp.* Upon hearing such a name given to his principal work, the man of science gives a start. Would madame la marquise be making fun of him to his face? She has, throughout the entire luncheon, remained so tactfully and restrainedly silent that he can't conceive of bad intentions on her part. He doesn't dare ask a question whose answer would perhaps allow him to interpret that lapse which he wouldn't mind making his colleagues in mental health aware of.

Reduced to his own, his only means, he is quite incapable of figuring out how the first syllable of the word *Paneuropa* suggested, by association and onomatopoeia, the sound of a war whose imminence appeared so undeniable in the prisms of drunkenness, to his amphitryonic eyes, in the course of a great luncheon with no other purpose, however, than world reconciliation. A little drumbeat, to give some rhythm to the big parade. There's rat-tat rub-a-dub. By "libido," she knows that something raunchy is meant.

It is therefore quite natural, at that moment, for her to recall an expression passed on by Esperanza when they were in Southampton. With a very accurate image, that formula sanctioned masturbatory use (before the generation of electric lighting came and deprived male humanity of it) of the lamp glass, an assuredly fragile, but worthy auxiliary to the pleasures that each fellow metes out to himself with his own hand. Besides, Madame de Perpignan, who was the subject of the conversation, readily designated as a "pigeon sucker" anyone, man or woman, who asked for physical collaboration from their own sex. *Libido* had therefore quite naturally become *pigeon lamp,* and *Bang Boom Rat-tat Rub-a-dub and Pigeon Lamp* the title of the book *Paneuropa and Libido,* which was the reason for the psychiatrist's being invited and having to tell a story that he eventually concluded in the following way:

"So, dear Madame de Perpignan was in a sanatorium, together with a young French actress who was causing me buckets of anxiety. The young actress couldn't stand the nurses, as devoted as they were discreet, attached to my establishment. I knew how good-hearted

Madame de Perpignan was and who went so far as to reveal that she adopted, every year, the prettiest of the little girls whose parents had abandoned them on the doorstep of the public orphanage. I explained the situation to her and asked her if she wanted to become my associate. It was a simple matter of unlocking the door which led from her room to that of our little patient. No sooner requested than granted. And thanks to Madame de Perpignan, our anxious little actress soon recovered her calm, her sleep. One of my colleagues, to whom I was boasting about this cure, asked me with a sarcastic smile what I thought was going on at night between my two patients. He had a dirty mind and suggested that it was lust. Since I was of the exact opposite opinion, we made a bet. And so on the specified night, we entered together, intentionally forgetting to knock on the little French actress's door. We found the ladies naked, in bed. A most striking scene indeed. They rise. My colleague strikes a triumphant pose. With my psychiatrist's gaze, I nonetheless inspect the unmade bed. I had won my bet: not a trace of a lesbian act, and so if those ladies were naked in the same bed, it was because one or the other of the two women, being thespians and thus in the habit of walking around unclothed, must have gotten cold and had simply come up to warm herself in her companion's bed."

Everyone applauds the psychiatrist.

The Prince of Journalists, always gallant, turns to Marie Torchon and comments on that edifying tale. Courageous Madame de Perpignan! The heart of a true Frenchwoman. What a sense of solidarity. It brings to mind that noble thought of good old La Fontaine: *People must help each other. It's the law of nature.*

May each person do what he can in his sphere of influence. We mustn't forget the touching lessons of populism. Our models should be Madame de Perpignan and Marie Torchon's Tootsie . . ., etc., etc., etc.

The joy is shared by all.

Augusta throws in a very unctuous "*schön.*" Synovie thanks the moving storyteller and assures him that, from now on, she will ask no one else for her elegiac subjects. The divine lady pulls out from between her breasts a little album that she asks her guests to sign.

Each one of them comes up with a polished remark, but none as ingenious as Synovie who, laureate of provincial poetry contests, is nonetheless capable of demonstrating, in her delicate allusions, very Parisian wit. Under the title "Paneuropean Haiku," she writes:

> If each man were a pederast,
> The races would find peace at last.

Everyone applauds except for Marie Torchon who, with a stuck-up little air, lets her sister in lunching know that she has made a faux pas.

Synovie refuses to let herself be demoralized. She is in a haikuesque vein and no sooner has someone mentioned sending a card to Coudenhove Kalergi in homage to the Japanese half of the blood circulating in the vessels of the man who invented Paneuropa, than she has calligraphed:

> Samurai in love
> With his glance
> Makes fun of
> Sick romance.

That a famous darling of the muses can be so offhand only intensifies the psychiatrist's infatuation. Meanwhile, Marie Torchon and the pipsqueak flirt in a corner. The divine lady puts the finishing touch on her conquest of the Prince of Journalists with an archiepiscopal translation of the charms which the son used on him. And young Lord Sussex is so charming that, unable to bear seeing the archduchess at the mercy of mass transit, he offers to drive her home. She accepts. Since kindness always pays off, from now on he will be privy to everything that concerns the House of Sussex, directly or indirectly.

Thus, a few months later, when the Prince of Journalists has married the divine lady, Augusta will move heaven and earth to put that charming couple on the throne of Albania. And already, Synovie fires away with her haiku:

> In Durazzi enthroned
> Our king will be hard-boned.

The aforementioned Synovie will be swimming, moreover, in bliss. By the time the Paneuropean luncheon is over, she will have married the psychiatrist, and likewise Marie Torchon the pipsqueak. And, literally speaking, what an evolution for both of them. Scandalmongers will surely go so far as to say that Marie Torchon has become a snob. But snob or no snob, she has deserted her party, that Marie Torchon. In all things, small and great; in matters of food and ideas. She who used to feast upon breaded pig's feet, fillet of veal, beef hash, saveloy, and a dessert of almonds, figs, hazelnuts, and raisins, now needs grapefruit, caviar, and foie gras. The slice of life is too tough now for her little teeth. Plus the fact that she is always on the move. In one of the capitals she recently passed through, a reporter who had come to interview her having asked if the brocade in which he saw her wrapped wasn't rather sumptuous garb for the author of *Tootsie,* "that masterpiece of humble, everyday observation" (*sic*), she answered with a retroactive anathema on the mediocre places where her life would have been confined, dull and lackluster, if she hadn't miraculously discovered luxury hotels and sleeping cars. Moreover, one day when she met Paul-Boncour on the banks of Lake Leman, didn't they agree that, if a former leftist now Minister of War must be every bit as much of a disciplinarian as the most authoritarian general, by the same token a successful populist novelist who has just recently pulled off a brilliant marriage is automatically metamorphosed into the female Homer of the Blue Trains and the high-class caravansarie. It's a sovereign law of evolution and Marie Torchon, who had just finished rereading her Darwin between Paris and Geneva, certainly wasn't planning to break it.

Yes, she is going to sing, she sings of the Ritzes, the swanky neighborhoods in the cities, all the cities where she has picked bouquets, and what bouquets, with such varied scents, for there are cities and cities, the cities which . . . the cities that . . ., the Gothic cities so flamboyantly Gothic that they will never forget her, with two fingers of their hands in ogival mittens raised toward the sky, under the pretext of cathedrals, those bourgeois ladies so proud of the apartment houses where families sit in a circle watching the mimosa mimosate, courtesans (to be polite) extravagantly dressed in excessive browns, scarlet scarves, stylish red lanterns, both feet painfully bound in bronzed shoes, with multicolored, serpentine appliqués. Marie Torchon is hardly keen on hanging around those whores, who look good wearing any residential hotel sign, which brings a blush to the cheeks of the austere cities corseted with fortresses, and the rococos, even more unbelievable, beneath their ringlets, than the queens on the decks of Swiss cards smuggled through customs.

Marie Torchon and the pipsqueak paid a visit to the he-towns which are nothing but tie and racket boutiques for the glory of well-to-do adolescents. They did favors for the she-towns nourished with ostrich feathers, drunk on eau de cologne cocktails. And then there are the old-maid-towns which, well before autumn, despite the veils of rain, saw their freshness fade and their lovely oat-grass complexion turn into a goat's-ass ejection.

Oxford asked Marie Torchon to give a lecture, and with her knowledge of the human heart Marie Torchon seduced the college town, even though it is always ready to swap all sciences of all centuries for a pair of oars and a bottle of full-bodied, spicy Old Port.

But when Marie Torchon goes somewhere, spirits rise and shine. Sensuousness adds, moreover, to the incandescence of that lady of letters. Thus, while a train carries her away one day, a day on which she burns with fire and flame, more fire, more flame than ever, a gossip columnist who notices her will publish, under the title "Burning Rag" [*Torchon qui brûle*], a few lines making fun of both the enamored woman's ardor and the contrast between that ardor and the impassivity characterizing her beloved, metamorphosed by the flamboyant lover's choice of pink and beige shoes, suit, and shirt, into an ice-cream parfait.

But what does that passionate creature care about the malevolent sauce used to flavor him? Burning with desire, consumed by inspiration, she juggles with the red-hot coals which, shooting out from the wheels, line up according to railroad rhythm in couplets. And now she becomes the Queen Hortense of the twentieth century, for if Napoleon's daughter-in-law-sister-in-law, by celebrating "young, handsome Dunois departing for Syria," succeeded in giving the era its perfect romance, without Marie Torchon, the twentieth century wouldn't have had any songs worth speaking of, wouldn't have had that "Song of the Young European," which Augusta hastens to have translated into fifteen languages and sent via capital cities, major ports, villages, and mere hamlets, from Gibraltar to Danzig, from Bergen to Capri, from the Tatra Mountains to Perros-Guirec.

Esperanza, following all of her son's and daughter-in-law's travels in the evening and morning papers, foams with rage upon reading of all those Paneuropean feats. She who only goes on living for Panroma, how could she bear to see the pipsqueak on his way to becoming a star of the pan that she is determined to do away with?

Of course she disinherits him, takes all the proper testamentary precautions, so that her fortune will go to the fascist militia, provided that the latter make Panroman use of it.

She is somewhat consoled, slightly avenged at the thought that her squirt of a son, not content with being the young European, intends to become and is becoming Mr. Europe himself. Indeed, Marie Torchon literally tore the pen from her fingers in order to pass it to her husband, so that he might be for Europe what Mr. France was for his original republic, at a time when the civilizing mission was the work of a single country and not a continent.

That really is the limit.

Esperanza subsidizes a Roman newspaper purely for the fun of denouncing on a daily basis in the front-page editorial the novelist of mediocrity and a pipsqueak who, his mother all but swears, would sleep soundly during the operation if his skull were opened and his brain replaced with a sponge, wondering only, at the very most, how one could have such a bad morning headache.

D'Annunzio, touched by the duchess of Monte Putina's heroic attitude, devotes a long poem to her in which he compares her, by turns, with the mother of the Greeks, the she-wolf who nursed Romulus and Remus, a laurel, an olive tree, Paros marble, the Tyrrhenian Sea, Antony, Cleopatra, Juvenal, and Marcus Aurelius. In her spacious drawing room, Esperanza hangs the framed autographed parchment, illuminated by the very hand of the soldier-poet. Thus encouraged, bursting with indignation at Mr. and Mrs. Europe, she no longer limits herself to insinuations. She yells and screams that they are in the pay of the Soviets, the intelligence service, the Chinese revolutionaries. She pastiches Léon Daudet rather successfully. She ridicules the yellowish, youngish little squirt who plays the sleeping-car Casanova, poor anemic scribbler whose only drink is a cocktail made from ink of all colors, and whose only nourishment is a sandwich composed of an infinite variety of dust particles.

Penetrated with the profound political sense which, quite a few years ago, caused Italy to join the Triple Alliance, signing a treaty of cooperation with a neighbor that it was determined to dismember at the first opportunity, Esperanza, worthy of her country of adoption, writes very affectionate letters to the Prince of Journalists. She is waiting for him to settle in Albania so she can wage a tariff war on him with no holds barred. Simple with the simpleminded, she stirs up, on the other hand, the double feminine professional jealousy which, for the laureate of the floral games, has become implacable hatred since, without warning, the populist began versifying.

Synovie swears to herself that she will chop up the Europes like sausage meat, without questioning Paneuropa in the least, however, for whom her husband is the sole authorized medical representative and, as such must preside over a mental health congress right in line with Coudenhove Kalergi's program, since the task at hand is to establish the bylaws of a Paneuropean Association for the Aristocratization of Neuroses.

Synovie carries the invective so far that Marie Torchon, passing through Paris, has her hauled into court. Synovie's lawyer, in order to keep his client from being convicted, and also because the plaintiff bribed her (or so they say), enters a plea of temporary insanity. Synovie flies into a rage. In alexandrines springing spontaneously from her bosom, she refuses such a defense. Altercation, commotion, brawl in the courtroom. The poetess is taken to the infirmary reserved exclusively for prisoners.

The scandal is just beginning. During an interview, Marie Torchon states that even she can't tell whether her enemy is a criminal malingerer or a raving lunatic. She insinuates that there could very well be something fishy about the death of her first husband, even though she was, at the time, a mere Cinder-in-the-Eye. The gossip columnists go searching through the back issues of *Le Petit Bordelais* and expose, arranged in their own way, the story of the light bulb and the magnolia flower. Wasn't that suicide a murder? But meanwhile, since the great lyric poetess has never been afraid to hurl metaphor comets into the very grayness of the most banal conversations, they don't have to look very far to find, among the honorable practitioners of forensic medicine, three experts who, arriving at the verdict of insanity, decide on internment. The least of her verse, in spite of its very correct prosody, is teeming, or so it seems, with evidence of her madness. Everything thus appears to turn against Synovie. When, from the porch of the insane asylum, she cries out: "Apollo is protecting me, woe to those who harry me," those simple little words earn her a fitting for a straitjacket. She is nonetheless right in invoking the golden-haired god, for the psychiatrist returns and releases her. But her enemies won't get off so lightly. Too elegiac to become a hair-splitter, if she gives up the idea of bringing legal action against the Europes, whose shenanigans were, moreover, quite underhanded, she nonetheless has the story published in a major newspaper.

The Prince of Journalists, who doesn't want to compromise himself, refuses to say a single word about the affair. But apart from him, all the editors of daily morning or evening newspapers are only too happy to put in the first column, on the first page, in lead position, that affair which allows them, if not to avoid, at least to minimize a few colonial revolts which those in high circles are hardly keen on publicizing.

It is therefore up to Synovie to choose. She marches right into the office of the widely circulating paper, climbs the stairs leading to the editor's bureau, and shakes up his tintinnabulating head with vengeful iambs. Verses fall out, put themselves in order on the white sheets. They are taken to the printer.

Multifarious are the vicissitudes of that Synovie affair, continually reborn of its ashes. Later, when she dies, there suddenly arises some fresh scandal to be hidden, and she is resuscitated. Yesterday it was a cardinal caught in the act of indecent exposure; today it's a minister dipping into a pretty little financial scandal. But since Synovie walks around on the psychiatrist's arm, the government papers laud the fairness of a country capable of freeing those who have been unjustly imprisoned. A pamphleteer is accused of contempt of court for having dared to write that an iniquitous internment, even temporary, hardly proves that the judicial system is in good shape. Esperanza, who hasn't forgotten the good old days of the Dreyfus affair, sends secret funds from Italy to fuel a fratricidal war among Frenchmen. The Europes respond to all people and all attacks. Their frank tone convinces no one, only sows trouble all around. At the opera, during the Wagner festival, Synovie slaps the pipsqueak and Marie Torchon counters with a well-planted slap on the psychiatrist's cheek. At that very minute Augusta leaves her box, tries to separate the brawlers and restore peace, her lifelong goal. She manages only to get her dress torn and the poetess upset. Paneuropa's days of glory are definitely over.

Synovie and her psychiatrist are determined to show Hitler that
France too is capable of nationalism. The psychiatrist publishes
Coitus and Sweet France, while Synovie brings out her "Marseillaise
for Frenchmen Who Want to Be French."

And that's how the song of the young European is forgotten.

Marie Torchon is defeated.

Now Synovie's only concerns are: resting on her laurels, retire-
ment, silence, love.

Right-minded literary colleagues congratulate her, in private letters
as well as in dithyrambic articles. But the most Christian among them
rightly remind her that happiness is not of this world. Providence will
agree with them.

The psychiatrist, far from the capital where his appointments, his
reports, and his doubly generous personal and medical activity served
as insurance against dangerous ideas, one day having taken off the
prescribed frock coat in order to explore more comfortably the attics
of "Ancestral Memory" (he had thus rechristened, quite appropriately, the paternal place of residence) began to suspect that his
ancestors hadn't built that house, now his, merely out of fear of the
cold and the heat. And with that he knocked against the beams and
rafters of a burning hot roof which he prefers to the fields where, at
that very instant, accompanied by his beloved Synovie, he could be
walking, holding his head straight up. He thanks those who put stone
upon stone, less against drafts than to protect the mind from all forms
of vertigo.

And with that he kisses his sister, the frame.

And puts his frock coat back on.

And thinks about the return to the maternal breast and from the
maternal breast to the paternal penis, and from the paternal penis . . .
but where to go from the paternal penis? . . . one thing leading to
another, where to go? Just as sewing thread enters a tailor's needle,
gossamer thread seeks the eye of the pine needle. Finding none, it
comes to the conclusion of virginity. But enough of this rubbish. Too
bad if the chain is broken. Too bad for a too bad which is the reverse,
the tails side of the coin, a coin that has no heads side since too good
doesn't exist. Mrs. Europe, née Marie Torchon, is an evolutionist. A
lot of good it does her. The psychiatrist doesn't want to go messing
around. He and his dear Synovie stay home. In the Christian forest.
An ingenious suggestion for the title of the poetess's next work: *In the
Christian Forest,* in other words *in the heart of the infinite,* and it's no
more difficult, for if you fall from the maternal breast into the definite,
returning to the maternal breast is a simple matter of going all the way
back up to the indefinite, and once you're there you stay there, but not
without carefully dropping, with a flick of the finger, a bothersome

syllable, metamorphosing the vague indefinite into a very comforting infinite.

And that's why, in the attic of Ancestral Memory, a psychiatrist is curled up in a fetal position.

His wife searches for hours before finally discovering him. When she does, he refuses to get up, to follow her, to go down to the dining room, even though lunch, served quite a while ago, is there waiting for them.

Knowing how much he likes to eat, the sly woman talks to him of leg of lamb with green beans, of good grub.

He sneers: "Your leg of lamb with green beans, I can see it from here, my dear. Time after time, a two-edged sword. You bet in favor of it, I bet against it. Each of us is right and wrong at the same time, for there are pros and cons. I thus discovered that kleptomania and theft were six of one and half-dozen of another. But just suppose that someone were to steal the Legion of Honor commander's tie which that discovery won me. My thief's lawyer will use my scholarly works to claim that if kleptomania is theft, theft is kleptomania. He will therefore plead temporary insanity, say that his client is a raving lunatic and, as such, deserving of indulgence. And the man with nerve enough to steal my medal will be acquitted. And then what will people think when I go out and about? Because I want to go out and about, so there! It's hereditary. My late father, also a psychiatrist, used to visit Princess Mathilde. He was especially fond of reminiscing about the night on Rue de Berri when Count Primoli, having brought back from Rome a gramophone recording of Leo XIII giving his blessing, the venerable Latin words, strongly accented by the sovereign pontiff's cavernous nasal organ, were heard by a circle of men in tails and women in evening gowns, with bowed heads, bare shoulders and exposed breasts, piously down on their knees before the magic box producing the acoustic phantom of the papal *Benedicat vos.** I'm just as good as Primoli. I'm a prime lay, as our dear Lady Sussex would say, she who is a prime rose. But Princess Mathilde is dead. So I'll visit the duchess of Guermantes, you know, Marcel Proust's Ariane. I'll go to her ball this evening. Indeed I will. You, Synovie, you are too beautiful, too dignified to go with me. The celebration is in honor of the Misses Swan Down as well as Mesdames Diamond Dust and Messrs. Mica Chips.

"You can imagine how tongues are wagging in the Faubourg Saint-Germain and the posh neighborhoods. The bloated fat women who

---

*The author thanks Henri de Régnier from whom he took the liberty of borrowing this description of the pope on the gramophone, in Princess Mathilde's drawing room, published in *Nouvelles littéraires,* 2/11/33.

pump themselves up on sandwiches, the old maids who soak up champagne, and the brilliant chatterers who have just founded the Association of Aristocrats against Radiators because central heating deprives them of the fireplaces they liked to lean against when relating some spicy anecdote, no, none of those beautiful people received an invitation. Indeed not one of them would have cause to take offense, since only noble knickknacks were invited, but all nonetheless indulge in unkind remarks which Oriane scornfully listens to on the wireless.

"Oriane. Siren of turn-of-the-century social events and, as such, always ready to fizzle out evanescently, Oriane, instead of dressing her feet, as she usually does, in gossamer shoes, has imprisoned them both in one and the same pearl corset with seaweed ribs and kelp lace. I can think of more practical walking attire. But Oriane has decided to greet her guests reclining on a sea green woolen rug decorated with motifs of marine plants and rare shells.

"Marcel Proust, too discriminating to spend his Jewish money on a papal count's title, has just swapped the name of his ancestors for a new one in which the definite article takes the place of the noble 'de.' He has people call him Mr. Le Snob.

"Well Mr. Le Snob, just so that the gossip columns won't be devoted exclusively to Oriane's party, Mr. Le Snob decided to give a gala dinner at the Ritz. As for myself, being a psychiatrist, I'm in fashion. I could have been invited to both the Guermantes' ball and Marcel Le Snob's big splash. Nonetheless, I'm not going to shorten my visit to the duchess. Marcel Le Snob will most certainly notice unforgivable last-minute defections. Haven't the infinitely small-minded, those whose hearts and souls are devoted to their benefactress, already covered the whole city with graffiti threatening Jews and anyone willing to sit at Jewish tables? Memories of the Dreyfus affair are being rekindled. Flags are being put out bearing Joan of Arc's colors, and there is so much anti-Semitism in the air that those who are on their way to the Ritz turn back. Only a field marshal in the French army will continue on his way, a sweet dreamer, wrapped up in his beloved poison gas and too absorbed by his epic thoughts to notice the capital's unusual appearance.

"Marcel Le Snob will naturally have his revenge on the field marshal for the others' pusillanimity. That's life, Synovie. Instead of having his guest served everything the menu promises him, the host sends the butler to fetch a good ration of oats. But all's fair in love and war. And so, with that, the field marshal wolfs down his feed in nothing flat. And Marcel Snob laughs sickly as he sips his chamomile tea with that mean glimmer in his big heavy eyes which says: You act as dumb as an ox to get a little hay; so now, eat it. . . .

"When there's not a wisp of straw left on his plate, the field marshal, having acquired a taste for that food, will crawl around the table on all fours, tearing the gilded cane bottoms from the little widowed chairs who've lost their asses. Then, still on all fours, and without even taking the time to say 'Good-bye and thank you,' that great captain, a regular centaur, dashes over to Oriane's house at full gallop.

"He will begin by fighting over grub with the draft and saddle horses. Then, from the stables he will go up to the parlor, whence his kicking and bucking will soon drive away all of those present, with the exception of your servant, the psychiatrist. Suddenly lying down alongside the woman whom a pedestrian corset with seaweed ribs and kelp lace prevented from fleeing, with an imperious hoof he will flip her over. And with that, the madder cloth serving as skin for his hind feet bulges out, splits, giving way to a blossoming organ of a type not to be found in most churches. Such a spectacle transforms Oriane's aristocratic coolness into a blaze. Thick smoke rises from her knees, her thighs, her navel, her armpits, her mouth, her nostrils. . . .

"Fate will cause that smoke, Synovie, to gather in front of your husband. It's succubine ectoplasm. But what face to wear in order not to compromise one's future? When you have already quarrelled with Augusta, to offend Oriane would be a disaster. A poetic future, a medical future, are hanging in the balance. What's called for is the typical go-getter, what's called for is Julien Sorel, since the smoke has already taken on the form of his mistress: Mathilde de la Môle. *The Red and the Black.* Saved! You are, we are saved, Synovie. Don't be jealous, Synovie, if I promise this statue a broadtail and jersey outfit in coral or oxblood or purple. . . .

"But wait a minute! Where am I? The fog is so thick that Mathilde de la Môle can't see ahead. Perhaps she got lost on the way to the cemetery, where she had sworn to bury her decapitated lover.

"Synovie was right, Synovie with her leg of lamb and green beans.

"So we should eat while the beans are hot.

"Let's say a few words about beans. The bean is in the shape of a kidney. But what's the use of comparing kidneys and beans if we are completely ignorant about kidneys and beans? And if you were to learn, Synovie, that leg of lamb is eaten with kidneys? What would you say? From this day on, God will probe, not hearts and kidneys, but hearts and beans, oh bean of my heart, bean heart, kidney bean, heart of all beans. But wait a minute, you seem dreamy-eyed, dear. What's wrong, my charming princess? You think we're beating around the bush. Well, for your birthday, we'll give you this proverb: 'It's better to beat around the bush than to be beaten by the bush.' "

At that point in his speech, the eloquent psychiatrist begins to crawl around the odd collection of shadows doubling the objects accumulated in that chaotic place, for the sun, slipping through the oculus, is sufficient to draw a floor diagram of the thirty-two positions, you know, the famous thirty-two, with their moving triangles, ellipses and parabolas, and also parallelepipeds, to be used by assholes, dirty old men, and little golden mugs. Imagine how angry we would be with ourselves if we neglected the opportunity to contemplate the elements, thus disposed, superimposed, enclosed, of a kind of geometry which timid

Euclid

(long live rhyme, poetess!) merely supposed. And now, hangnails, uncles of angles, strangle the strange, staunch the stanks, scrape the nape. Geometry, born of Greek sand, can you believe it, Synovie, you, as visual as you are effective. But no matter how sensitive you are, you are nonetheless poised. We therefore add you to the thirty-two positions:

$$32 + 1 = 33$$

Thirty-three, the two hunchbacks.

Here we are now. We've been here all along. Thirty-three, the two hunchbacks. Are the darlings foolish enough? We'll pay their way to a whorehouse. Alas! as hoary houses go, none is more so than Ancestral Memory. Madame Irma, madam, certainly gives them a warm, touching welcome. And that beautiful thing is wearing, embroidered on her black satin crepe gown, a strass palm tree extending from her feet all the way up to her breasts, which a Wagnerian breastplate maintains at a very respectable altitude. In the shadow of that imposingly tailored vegetation, the hunchbacks' hearts are in their boots. To cheer them up, Madame Irma is going to take them to a porn flick. The film is called *The Geography Lesson:*

A classroom with empty benches and tables. On the stage, a lady wearing veils and a very pompous mourning gown. We can only see her from behind. Suddenly, she extends her hand and begins to caress, lazily, with one finger, a map of Europe hanging on the wall. Then Italy, tired of being a mere boot in a blue sea, tells herself that she is going to show what use can be made of peninsulas. So she raises herself, penetrates with a sudden thrust, rips open the contours keeping her imprisoned on a plane. The lady in mourning detaches the voluminous thing and turns around. We then recognize Augusta. Augusta lifts her skirts and, to prove both that she is at the anal stage and that she doesn't have to feel inhibited by Esperanza's presence, she shoves Italy up her you know what. But, having a Monte Putina in your bowels is no small matter. Violent earth tremors all throughout the archduchess's body, subject to such internal agitation that suddenly the underwear and the dress are torn apart. Esperanza naked, bloated, misshapen, and with her hat still on her head, but her veil participating in the incredible organic revolution which, little by little, moves to the rhythm of its very amplification. Tremendous racket. Ravel's "Waltz" is being played on ten gramophones out of sync with each other. Close-up: Esperanza's navel, first represented by a crown, has become an oculus. "The eye of Europe," say the infuriated little African bulls with a sneer. This eye's pupil is Esperanza's face. The pupil will get the better of the schoolteacher. Esperanza succeeds in getting out through that little window, but with such effort that Augusta explodes. The shapeless pieces of Augusta are strewn over the floor, while Esperanza, straightening her clothes, climbs back up on the stage. She contemplates the map of Europe in which the plucking of her dear homeland has left a hole. The Mediterranean, the Adriatic are not very rough seas, especially on planispheres. And yet, waves now rise all around the hole marking the great Latin sister's position. Waves rise and remain suspended in the air. Behold a bush of curly blue hair whose heart can only be made of coral. "But it's the burning bush of Scriptures," cries the great Roman lady, only too happy to reconcile the Old Testament with mythology. And she wraps her mouth around it, for it is Amphitrite's sex organ, those genitals which neglect to have a body. The Prince of Journalists, now king of Albania, has observed the scene from his palace. He feels congested, calls for his wife. But well-connected, long-armed Primrose is busy masturbating the Dolomites. A voice, the voice of conscience, sings to the new king of Albania:

> *Remember the Sybarites.*
> *Your Queen*
> *Loves.*
> *The Dolomites.*
> *So become, once more, one of the Sodomites.*

He won't wait to be asked twice.

In the hope of simultaneous and reciprocal fellatio, he leaves for fellah country. . . .

"And the next episode?" asks Synovie.

"The next episode? Well the two hunchbacks, two 3s of 33 make 69."

"The two 3s of 33 make 69?" recapitulates the poetess. She lights up with bliss, and declares: "Since pleasure is capable of such miracles, and since, for years and years, I had lentils instead of breasts, may those lentils swell; yes, swell, swell up my breasts. I won't be taken in, moreover, nor will I fall victim to your bursts of exuberance. If you push things too far, I'll cut you off and use you as a cream cheese cover. To cover each of the 3s in 33, for we really can't let them do 69 all day long. . . ."

The following day, the newspapers would report that the psychiatrist had committed suicide after having murdered the poetess. The poor thing was found with her throat slashed. As for the psychiatrist, before killing himself, he had written on the floor, in his wife's blood: "We decided to make cheese covers out of her breasts. . . ."

Bearing in mind that a whole generation for whom General Boulanger had been a god called him frivolous for having killed himself on his mistress's grave, one can imagine the entire French nation's anger the day it learned, over breakfast, about the scandalous death of its national poetess.

Mrs. Europe, née Marie Torchon, indulged in a certain Don Quixotism and, despite having given up writing, put pen to paper in order to defend the memory of her former enemy.

Esperanza was touched by such an elegant gesture and forgave her for having married her son who, moreover, had just received the Prix Goncourt.

And that was not the only reconciliation.

To a Panroman heart, the burning of the Reichstag by *schön* Adolf could only bring to mind Nero's burning of Rome. To a Paneuropean heart, Hitler's idea—"acquire lands for Europe at Russia's expense. But then the Reich must retrace the route once laid out by the Teutonic knights, and with the help of the German sword, give land to the German plough and its daily bread to the German people"*—the idea of colonizing the USSR appeared simply brilliant. For the dazzled Augusta, it was the road to Damascus. She converted to National Socialism. She and the duchess of Monte Putina now owed it to each other, owed it to world salvation, to make peace.

For the moment they are working, one in Berlin, the other in Rome, each in her sphere of influence and according to her means, for the establishment of a Holy Alliance against Bolshevism. Now all they dream of is a Directoire of the four powers. The White Russian newspapers published in Paris, between incitements to murder and homage to Il Duce and Der Führer, devote enthusiastic articles to them.

Augusta, a real Valkyrie, wears the late archduke's cuirass over her dress, in town and country, and she adds spurs to her boots. Wagner's daughter-in-law can make goo-goo eyes at *schön* Adolf. Augusta is not afraid of the competition.

And besides..........., etc., etc.

---

*Excerpt from *Mein Kampf,* by Adolf Hitler, Munich, 1932.

(To be continued at the outbreak of the next war.)

Afterword and Notes

Thomas Buckley

Imagine, if you can, Freud and Proust sitting down for a chat with Zippy the Pinhead and the marquis de Sade. Then, just when things are starting to get a bit silly, in walks Karl Marx with a dead serious face to deliver a vitriolic diatribe. After he has finished his speech, Jacques Lacan enters and slips a couch under the narrator, who begins psychoanalyzing himself and his text. Zippy soon prevails, however, and the narrative has turned into a political allegory with characters out of Felix the Cat: a surrealist, graphic (historiographic, geographic, pornographic) version of *The Romance of the Rose*.

In order to translate a work of literature, one must come to terms with the question of what it means, not an easy one in the case of *Putting My Foot in It*. Pound explains why we should read the novel, but as Roditi notes, either his aesthetic blindness or his blind enthusiasm for Mussolini makes him confuse Crevel's militant left-wing attack on the bourgeoisie with an attack from the far right on the political left. Roditi, on the other hand, seems more concerned with Crevel's private life and the reasons for refusing to publish the controversial author than with the reasons for publishing him.

Crevel refuses to separate art and life, which is why he insists on linking aesthetics and politics in a controversial way. I had occasion to discuss this very question with Roditi, in whose opinion specifically political satire doesn't reduce the scope of a literary work. After all, few would fail to qualify *Candide* as a masterpiece of world literature, in spite—or because—of its clearly ideological stance.

Crevel's indictment of capitalism and his warnings about fascism are certainly not lacking in pertinence in our time: witness the reawakening of the extreme right wing, massive unemployment, and exuberant consumption among an increasingly privileged bourgeoisie. But even if we agree, should we consider the source of these remarks: an opium-smoking dandy whose views were perhaps shaped by the immense physical and mental problems from which he suffered? And how can we read, interpret, translate the straight-faced, polemical part of the text without negating or at least crimping the phantasmagoria of Crevelian surrealism, which blossoms unpredictably throughout the rest of the book?

Salvador Dalí, one of Crevel's closest friends, provides possible answers to these questions in his preface to the North Point translation of *Difficult Death*. The artist's appreciation of the lyricism in Hitler's gaze and his plump loins in no way prevents him from engaging in the struggle against fascism, says Dalí. (Nonetheless, he is not making the case for the innocence of aesthetics.) In the same piece, the Catalan surrealist develops a convincing interpretation of Crevel's life based on literal translation of the words *rené* (reborn) and *crever* (to die). Grotesque, consciously chosen aesthetic criteria are thus deprived of, liberated from the restraints of political associations, while arbitrarily assigned phonemes, with the help of a little word-juggling, are given a very pertinent meaning.

In their revolt against the dictatorship of reason, the French surrealists invented "automatic writing." Unfortunately, however, there is no such thing as automatic translating. To translate is to interpret and often to transpose. My rendition of *Les Pieds dans le plat* being no exception, I have tried to be as creative in English as Crevel is in French. Some of the author's puns are nonetheless explained in the text, while a few others are elucidated in the notes. I would like to express my sincere thanks to David Rattray and Dominic Di Bernardi for their invaluable help, and to acknowledge the generous advice of Edouard Roditi, who died in May of 1992 just before this book went to press.

A complete annotation of the historical and literary references in *Putting My Foot in It* is beyond the scope of this edition; the notes below are limited to some of the more obscure references in Crevel's text.

NOTES

5.28 the woman sodomized in spite of herself: "la sodomisée malgré elle" echoes the title of Molière's play *Le Médecin malgré lui* (The Doctor in Spite of Himself, 1666).

5.29 Cambronne: nineteenth-century French general; "le mot de Cambronne" is a French euphemism for *merde*.

12.20 handplay/"Hands that bluff, soon get rough": "Jeux de mains" (literally, hand games) are games in which two people hit each other for fun. "Jeux de mains, jeux de vilains" ("hand games, villains' games") is a French proverb suggesting that hitting games usually end badly.

21.35 Pète sec: pronounced *pet sec,* meaning "authoritarian."

52.2 Marie Torchon: "torchon"=tabloid, rag, scandal sheet, but also a slut or slattern.

52.2 *The Effusions,* the famous Synovie: "épanchement [effusion] de synovie"=synovial extravasation, or forced effusion of water on the knee.

60.41 grazing and ploughing . . . in Sully's France: the duc de Sully was a seventeenth-century minister of finance, remembered for his observation "Grazing and ploughing are the two mammary glands of France."

66.22 pedibus cum jambis: Latin, "with his iambic feet."

70.22 Scarron's legs: Paul Scarron (1610-60), an invalid, was the author of burlesque romances and, as Crevel notes, was married to Madame de Maintenon.

77.36 Colonus . . . column: in French, both are the same word: "Colonne."

85.20 Academy of Floral Games: a literary competition in Toulouse, thus named because the winners receive flowers of gold or silver as prizes.

90.6 Joffrette or Fochette: after Marshals Joffre and Foch, World War I generals.

110.36 the days of Grille d'Egout: i.e., turn-of-the-century Montmartre: Grille d'Egout was a dancer in the Quadrille Réaliste at Le Moulin Rouge, founded in 1889.

111.4 Dumbo: "Cucufa" in the French original, meaning something like "Silly Cowl" (*cuculle*=a monk's hood).

127.32 "O you . . . vestiges and idols": from Sade's well-known pamphlet "Yet Another Effort, Frenchmen, If You Would Become Republicans," inserted in the fifth dialogue of his *Philosophy in the Bedroom* (1795). The translation used here is by Richard Seaver and Austryn Wainhouse and is taken from *The Complete Justine, Philosophy in the Bedroom, and Other Writings* (New York: Grove, 1965), 297-98.

130.17 "As we gradually proceed . . . from superstition to royalism": ibid., p. 300.

131.10 Blue Trains: traditionally associated with tourism, the blue train goes from Paris, France, to Ventimiglia, Italy, via Nice.

139.31 dinner-discussions: in French, "dîners de têtes," literally "talking-head dinners," alluding to Jacques Prévert's poem "Tentative de description d'un dîner de têtes à Paris-France" (1931).

140.12 the defense and illustration of its privileges: echoes Du Bellay's *Défense et illustration de la langue française* (1549), a treatise on poetry illustrating the doctrine of the Pléiade group.

142.32 "communicating vessels": see André Breton's *Les Vases communicants* (1932).